TIDEWATER

"Antoinette Stockenberg is pure magic."
—Susan Elizabeth Phillips

"A spellbinding thriller that is both intense and riveting."
—*Romantic Times*

"*Tidewater* is a fast-paced, intriguing, seaside suspense novel of betrayal, deception, family and love. Stockenberg writes strong emotions, relationships and sharp dialogue."
—*WCRG Romance Review*

"A compulsively readable suspense story."
—*The Romance Reader*

"Sparks your imagination and keeps your interest . . . a very good book!"
—*Old Book Barn Gazette*

"[A] fabulous ability to steam up a small-town environment."
—*Painted Rock Reviews*

"Stockenberg [is destined to become] a major voice in women's fiction."
—*Publishers Weekly*

Turn the page for more acclaim . . .

suspense. I love everything she creates."

"Well-written . . . Every sentence builds the tension as the protagonists try to find their way back to each other and Maddie tries to protect her daughter. Ms. Stockenberg's passion for writing pulses through this superb story."

"Ms. Stockenberg has a very witty writing style and wonderfully drawn characters."

"A captivating mix of mystery and romance with characters that seem so real they jump off the pages. Stockenberg is adept at capturing family relationships and conveying a real sense of the characters' feelings and motivations. An intriguing and passionate tale that will have readers longing for the next Stockenberg novel."

"Antoinette Stockenberg has crafted an insightful novel of lost love, hidden secrets, and smoldering passions, one with intriguing plot twists and well-developed characters . . . Stockenberg has incorporated suspense, romance, and a touch of the paranormal to bring readers a satisfying story of true love conquering all."

also tender. I will be on the lookout for other Stockenberg works."
—*Regency World*

"Pure Stockenberg. The author captures the flavor of New England life along with great family dynamics. The love story between Dan and Maddie gives hope for anyone who dreams of their first love."
—*Interludes*

"Buy this book! A truly fantastic summer read!"
—*Gulf Coast Woman*

"*A Charmed Place* is a great read, filled with extraordinary characters, compelling subplots, long-buried secrets, and a hero who is strong, tender, and irresistible."
—*B. Dalton's Heart to Heart*

"With each book she writes, [Stockenberg's] style and writing become even more gripping, her characters more complex . . . *A Charmed Place* has easily earned a place on my keeper shelf. Do yourself a favor—read *A Charmed Place*."
—One Magical Kiss (Daphne's Dream) website

DREAM A LITTLE DREAM

"A delightful blend of goosebumps, passion and treachery that combine to make this novel a truly exhilarating read. Ms. Stockenberg delivers once again!"
—*Romantic Times*

"*Dream a Little Dream* is a wonderful modern fairy tale—complete with meddlesome ghosts, an enchanted castle, and a knight in shining armor. *Dream a Little Dream* casts a powerful romantic spell. If you like modern fairy tales, you'll love *Dream a Little Dream*. Run, don't walk, to your local bookstore to purchase a copy of this magical romance."   —Kristin Hannah

"This humorous, well-crafted and inventive novel is certain to establish Stockenberg as a major voice in women's fiction."   —*Publishers Weekly*

"Well-developed, likeable protagonists; appealing relatives; an intriguing villain; and a ghostly pair of ancient lovers propel the plot of this . . . well-written story with a definite Gothic touch."   —*Library Journal*

"Kudos to Antoinette Stockenberg, who offers her trademark large, solid cast (the cook is wonderful!) and places them in a magnificent setting, background to a satisfying, indelible love story. A highly recommended read that paranormal and medieval lovers will treasure."

—*Romance Forever*

"*Dream a Little Dream* is a work of art! With deft strokes of a brush Antoinette Stockenberg layers humor, wit, emotion, intrigue, trepidation and sexual tension in just the right amounts to fill a rich canvas . . . This is writing and story-telling at its best, and as eager as we are to find out 'what happens next!' we savor each sentence."

—*CompuServe Romance Reviews*

"A thoroughly satisfying book. It blends suspense with just the right amount of humor. The characters are finely drawn. I enjoyed reading it and recommend it highly."

—*Under the Covers Book Reviews*

"Stockenberg is able to fully develop the characters and wrap the audience in the spell of the story. It's one of those books that will keep you turning pages well into the night and into the next night as well." —*Middlesex News*

"Ms. Stockenberg writes with a lively and humorous wit that makes her characters three-dimensional and unforgettable, and had me smiling throughout. It didn't take long for me to become caught in the magic web of the castle and the undercurrent of the mystery." —*Old Book Barn Gazette*

BEYOND MIDNIGHT

"Stockenberg's special talent is blending the realistic details of contemporary women's fiction with the spooky elements of paranormal romance. So believable are her characters, so well-drawn her setting, so subtle her introduction of the paranormal twist, that you buy into the experience completely . . . *Beyond Midnight* has a terrific plot, a wicked villain and a sexy hero. But the novel ventures beyond sheer entertainment and it is easy to see why Stockenberg's work has won such acclaim."   —*Milwaukee, Journal-Sentinel*

"Full of charm and wit, Stockenberg's latest paranormal romance is truly enthralling."   —*Publishers Weekly*

"Antoinette Stockenberg creates another winner with this fast-paced and lively contemporary romance . . . a definite award-winner . . . contemporary romance at its best!"
        —*Affaire de Coeur*

"A gripping and chilling page-turner . . . outstanding reading!"   —*Romantic Times*

"Spectacular! A terrific story."   —*The Literary Times*

"Ms. Stockenberg does it again! She's written a story that keeps you so involved, you can't put it down."
        —*Bell, Book and Candle*

ST. MARTIN'S PAPERBACKS TITLES
BY ANTOINETTE STOCKENBERG

Tidewater

Safe Harbor

Keepsake

A Charmed Place

Dream a Little Dream

Beyond Midnight

SAND CASTLES

ANTOINETTE STOCKENBERG

St. Martin's Paperbacks

SAND CASTLES

Copyright © 2002 by Antoinette Stockenberg.

All rights reserved. No part of this book may be used or reproduced in any manner whatsoever without written permission except in the case of brief quotations embodied in critical articles or reviews. For information address St. Martin's Press, 175 Fifth Avenue, New York, NY 10010.

ISBN: 0-312-98154-6

Printed in the United States of America

St. Martin's Paperbacks edition / May 2002

St. Martin's Paperbacks are published by St. Martin's Press, 175 Fifth Avenue, New York, NY 10010.

10 9 8 7 6 5 4 3 2 1

This book is dedicated to those who
volunteer their love and kindness at animal shelters.
You make the world a better place.

PROLOGUE

He ripped the phone cord out of the wall, then grabbed her and swung her around, knocking over a floor lamp and sending shards of glass skittering over the worn oak floor.

"We're rich!" he whooped. "Rich! We're rich! God, we're rich!"

He set her down so abruptly that he had to hang on to her to keep her from stumbling backward. Holding her tightly, he let loose a howl of triumph. His look was wild, exultant, new.

Wendy was aghast. She was pinned to his chest, breathless. She said, "Jim, what's *wrong* with you?"

"First thing, phone off the hook, that's what they always tell you. Wendy, we are *rich*, rich, rich. Don't you get it? Rich! No more jobs . . . no more bills . . . Tyler will get his pick of schools and you can have the house of—"

"Jim, stop; you're scaring me!" She was afraid of the thought that was forming in her head, afraid that it might not be true. Trapped in his grip, caught in a downward drift of cheap white wine and garlic chicken, she said, "For God's sake, just *tell* me."

"Powerball. No kidding, the lottery." His voice had dropped to a whisper, a tiptoe along the edge of a canyon. She could see that suddenly he was afraid, too.

"The office pool. Seven of us—no, eight, eight. What

am I thinking? Jack makes eight. He'll shit feathers when he learns. He's in Munich all week."

She was blinking rapidly, as if she had a speck in her eye. She was trying to comprehend. *Jack makes eight.* Eight of what? Eight of Jacks? Eight of what?

"How much? Tell me," she wailed, in agony now.

Her husband's lips were dry. He wet them with his tongue quickly, as if he were trying to get away with something. "Eighty—" He cleared his throat in one harsh try. "Eighty-seven."

"Thousand?" No; that wasn't enough. Not for this. "Million?" No. That was too much. She was bewildered by the math, staggered by the possibilities of it. "*Tell* me, damn it," she said, because she was getting light-headed and was about to fall into the chasm.

He exploded in a single loud laugh. "Wendy, sweet dufus, concentrate! Eighty-seven million dollars. Eighty-seven million dollars divided by eight and then by income tax, but—*eighty-seven million dollars.*"

Her face felt scorched by the numbers spewing over her like volcanic ash; they blasted through her mind, obliterating thought. She began to shake. She whispered numbly, "I can't believe it. Not us. That doesn't happen." Inexplicably, she burst into sobs.

Jim howled again and hugged her and lifted her off her feet once more, rocking her left and right and then swinging her around in a circle as if she were a rag doll. Wendy laughed and cried and said, "Jim, put me down, put me down."

He was six feet two; she was half a foot shorter than he was. When they were old, he would be able to see the roots of her dark hair in that awful week before a touch-up trip to the hairdresser. But for now they were young, with over half their lifetimes yet to come. Wendy had always assumed that they would spend them in love.

How amazing to her that they would be spending them rich.

CHAPTER 1

The place smelled of cat pee, but Zina didn't mind. She had come to associate the piercing scent with abandoned creatures who needed her love.

The old house was drafty, the budget tight. It was cold in the shelter—clearly too cold for some of the cats in the cages.

"Poor babies. Hang on; I'm here. Everything's going to be all right now," Zina promised the demoralized cats. She turned up the heat, then began the day's routine of cleaning the cages and replenishing the food in them.

Each of the cats was to be let out in turn as she tidied up; but the one that Zina invariably let out first was the Siamese female with the earsplitting howl—the kind of wail that made homeowners hang out of their windows at midnight and lob hand grenades of shoes and clocks. The Siamese wanted out. Now.

All of the volunteers were hoping, against all odds, that the cat, nicknamed Banshee, would somehow be adopted and leave (she was not only loud but bulimic). But not Zina. She loved every cat in every cage without reserve. Whether the cats were fat or skinny, young or old, male or female, mute or loud, she loved them all. After four years of volunteer work, Zina had made hundreds of friends: almost every one of them had four legs and whiskers.

The door opened, and a woman entered on a sharp gust

of April air. "Good morning, Zina. You're here bright and early."

Sylvia Radisson, volunteer director of Flo's Cat House, was much more clear-eyed than Zina about what it took to run a successful shelter.

Money. "Zina, sweetie, you've got a really heavy hand on the thermostat. Oil prices are sky-high; every degree really does matter," she said, throttling back the heat. "It's the Sphynx, isn't it?" she ventured.

Zina glanced at the bizarre, hairless cat huddled in the back of his cage. "He always looks *so* cold."

"Yes, he does, doesn't he?"

"I know! I'll knit him a vest," she decided. "You think he'd wear it?"

"It can't hurt to try," said Sylvia. She paused at a cage and wiggled a finger through the bars; a young calico inside plopped on her back and began gnawing gently on it.

"One of these days, Zina," Sylvia said over her shoulder, "you're going to find yourself a husband. And then you'll be knitting baby sweaters, not cat vests."

After a silence, Zina said softly, "She likes it when you drag a pencil across the cage for her to attack."

Sylvia turned her wise, middle-aged smile from the cat to the keeper. "Later. After I've caught up with my paperwork." The look she saw on the younger woman's face made her shrug. "Some people—you—are better at parenting than others, Zina. I just happen to shine more behind a desk."

"You're good at everything," Zina said generously.

"Not everything. Some things. And one of them is making sure that this shelter doesn't go belly-up four years after opening. Flo would not approve."

Zina glanced up at the historic photograph that hung, improbably, between the rows of cat cages. Florence Benson, a young woman with a sober expression on her face and a cat on her lap, was seated in a carved chair on an oriental carpet in the very same room that now smelled of cat pee. Below the sepia-toned photograph was a framed excerpt of her will.

> *I give and devise residential real estate that I may own at the time of my death, located at 24 Wood Road, Hopeville, Massachusetts, together with all buildings and improvements thereon, to the Hopeville Animal Rescue League with the wish that said real estate shall be used for purposes of sheltering abandoned cats.*

How old had she been when she died, this only daughter of a farming couple? Ninety-seven, someone had said. Nearly a century of living without a husband, without a child. So, yes, it could be done.

"Zina?"

"Hmm?" She had to rouse herself from her revery, as she so often did, and re-enter the world of the here and now. "I'm sorry; I was off daydreaming."

"I said, could you do the calico next? A woman is supposed to come in this morning to look her over."

Look her over. As if the cat were a used car. It didn't seem right. It never seemed right. Who could pick up a cat, pet it, play with it, and then walk away? The thought that people did that not only with cats and dogs but with children at adoption fairs never failed to shock Zina. But then, she knew that she was easily shocked. Sensitized, her brother called her. Because of that day.

"Okay, but that means the Banshee goes back in her cage ahead of schedule. She's not going to like that. Hold your ears."

The predictable howl of protest drove Sylvia to close the door of her office.

Saying awful things in soothing ways to the newly

locked-up Siamese, Zina began tidying the calico's cage while its lucky inmate roamed free. "Shh, bitchy-bitchy-bitchy Banshee, shh, there, now, Banshee, it's okay." She folded the dirty newspaper at the bottom of the cage and dumped it in a plastic bag. "Someday you'll have a real home of your own to throw up in. Shh-h. Don't be upset."

She opened the regional news section of the *Worcester County Sentinel* and was fitting it to the bottom of the calico's cage when a photo on the front page caught her eye. It was a shot of a group of men with arms folded across their chests and broad grins on their faces, looking as if they'd just won the SuperBowl.

JACKPOT! read the headline. Obviously not athletes, the very ordinary men were wearing suits and ties and standing around a cluster of desks. Zina read the caption below the photograph:

> Winners of the $87,000,000 jackpot in their downtown Providence office. The winning ticket was purchased by Ed Baynard, third from left. All eight men plan to continue working at their jobs in the insurance brokerage.

Eighty-seven million dollars! Zina scrutinized the third man from the left, the one who had made them all millionaires. Ed Baynard was a middle-aged, ordinary-looking man with an appealing grin and a pot belly. He looked ecstatic. They all did.

All except the tallest among them, the one on the right, the one whose face was slightly averted. Who looked somehow distressed to be caught on camera, as if he were ashamed to have won so much money without earning it.

What an odd pose, she thought. Maybe he dropped something and was looking around for it.

She studied his face more closely, aware that her cheeks had begun to burn and her heart to beat faster. It was impossible to see his features clearly, and his hair was so much shorter and receding, and there was a kind of puffiness that was different, but . . .

She studied his face more closely.

It wasn't him, of course. It couldn't be him. But her breath was coming short and fast now, and she felt weak. She found herself holding the folded paper up over her head and trying to see his face from underneath, an exercise in futility.

She studied his face more closely: squinting, tilting her head to one side, all the time aware of the thundering of her heart. What if it were him? Why couldn't it be him? He had to live somewhere, be something, do something. Why couldn't he be working in Providence for an insurance brokerage and buying tickets in a lottery pool?

She ran into Sylvia's office and, in a voice that didn't sound anything like her own, said, "A magnifying glass— please, I need one!"

Sylvia looked up, startled. "I don't have one."

Zina looked around wildly, the way she would for a fire extinguisher if the next room were ablaze. "Oh, God. Oh, God, I have to go home."

The director jumped to her feet from behind her desk. "Are you all right? Are you feeling well?"

"Yes, I'm fine. But . . . I have to go home."

"Now?"

"Now!"

"Is it truly important, Zina? Because we talked about how I was leaving at ten and wouldn't be back until one. And the woman is coming about the calico."

Her look of dismay said so plainly that Zina was failing her, failing the calico, failing Florence. All for a magnifying glass.

Zina raked her hands through the sides of her long blond hair while she reconsidered her overwrought reaction. It was not him. It couldn't be him. All this time, just a few hours' drive away? Not in Hollywood, not in London, but living in Providence? Not an actor, not a playwright, but an insurance agent?

She was making a fool of herself. Again. She had done it twice before—once, when she had chased a stranger down a street in Boston, and another time, more recently, when she had tried to convince Zack that she'd seen Jimmy in a home-mortgage commercial on cable TV.

Wrong then. Wrong now.

With a wrenching effort, she forced a smile. "I forgot that you had to go somewhere," she confessed. "This can wait, Sylvia. I'll stay."

"Are you sure?"

"Absolutely." She felt a nipping through her sock and looked down to see the calico wrapping its front paws around her ankle. Her melancholy smile turned more cheery.

"Monster. You're hungry, aren't you—or is it that you just want to play?" Scooping the calico up with both hands, she nuzzled nose to nose and then carried the young cat out of the office.

CHAPTER 2

"Dad! It's for you!" Tyler slapped the phone down and tore up the stairs, taking them two at a time, tripping near the top and recovering with a thump.

"Tyler, *walk*!" Wendy yelled up after him. "How many times do I have to tell you? And pull up those pants!"

There was, of course, no response from her son other than the slamming of his bedroom door to drown out the sounds of the new video game that he wasn't supposed to be playing until his homework was done. Sighing, Wendy brought in the overlooked newspaper, its underside damp from lying on the wet coco mat, and scanned the headlines before laying it alongside her husband's supper plate.

She was relieved to see that they were no longer front-page news in the *Providence Journal*. A new mess at City Hall, another empty mill burned to the ground, a groundbreaking ceremony for a new hotel—these were the stories currently on people's minds.

"Thank God," she muttered. "Maybe they'll leave us alone from now on."

After a glance at the upturned phone on the hall table, she walked over to the door of the basement stairs and called down. "Jim, did you hear Tyler?"

Her husband answered from the musty bowels of their tiny house, "Yeah, get that, would you?"

Jim was good at ping-ponging the minor irritants of life

back to her to field. After all, he was the one who had to handle all the big stuff—like winning an eighty-seven-million-dollar lottery. Wendy shook her head, unable, still, to come to terms with their new wealth. It had come so suddenly on the heels of their old poverty.

She picked up the phone and said, "I'm sorry; Jim can't come to the phone right now. Can I take a message?"

There was a short pause, and then a cheerful voice answered, "Wendy, hi, it's me."

"Hey, Dave. What's up?"

Her brother was the reason that Wendy had met and married Jim in the first place. Dave and Jim had worked together in a motorcycle shop one summer, had hit it off, and had been pals ever since. Why not? They were two of a kind: fun-loving, optimistic, impulsive, and eerily flippant about money. Which was fine if, like Dave, you happened not to be the marrying kind and didn't need a certain amount of it to feed and clothe a family.

"So what's Jim up to? Has he spent all your winnings yet?"

Wendy let out a wary laugh. "He's trying. He's down in the basement with the contractor and the plumber, working on the estimate for the addition."

"It's gonna look great." There was another pause, and then Dave went on. "So. Here's the thing," he said sheepishly. "I've got a lee-tle problem with my cash flow this week. Just until my next paycheck."

No surprise there. Dave Ferro routinely had a leetle problem with his cash flow. That next paycheck was the elusive brass ring in the merry-go-round of his life.

"How much do you need?"

"Just the rent. Seven hundred."

"I'll have to ask Jim."

"You know he'll say yes."

Wendy did know. "Stop by after supper, then; I'll write you a check."

"I'm keeping track, Wendy; so help me God I am. I'll pay back every cent the minute one of my ships comes in."

He had a whole fleet of them wandering around out there: Lotto, BigBucks, Powerball, a screenplay that he hoped Bruce Willis would option, and at least one patent that was apparently actually pending. Wendy wanted desperately for one of her brother's ships to sail back fully loaded—not because they couldn't afford to help him out, but because she couldn't bear the guilt for helping to corrupt him.

"I sure hope that that doohickey you invented for the motorcycle catches someone's eye," she said. It was a warning shot across his bow, but he never even heard it.

"Don't worry; it will. I may even go straight to the top and shop it to Harley one of these days. I mean, c'mon. Who *wouldn't* want a clamp-on fire extinguisher for his bike?"

Someone who didn't expect his motorcycle to catch on fire, that's who; but her brother sounded so hopeful that Wendy couldn't point out the obvious to him. Besides, he'd managed to set his own bike on fire, so maybe it was a more common event than she realized.

They hung up and Wendy went down to see what there could be in a twenty-by-twenty-four-foot basement that could hypnotize three grown men for nearly two hours. She found them gathered in front of the furnace, looking like detectives at a homicide scene.

"The furnace should go. It's iffy whether it'll be able to heat the addition," the plumber was telling Jim. "Not to mention, today's burners are a lot more efficient." He checked the tag hanging from one of the galvanized pipes. "Although, actually, this one's not doing too bad."

"Yeah, but everything else will be new—copper pipes, baseboards, expansion tank," the contractor chimed in. "So why stop here?"

She saw her husband nod calmly and say, "I agree. By the time you're done with this project, what I want to see is basically a brand-new house."

From behind him she blurted, "Good grief, Jim, the furnace is only five years old. You're just throwing money down a hole!"

Jim turned and grinned as he threw his arm around her. "That's my girl; a tightfisted Yankee through and through." With a quick, soft kiss to her temple, he murmured, "Don't worry, honey. There'll still be money for your curtains and couches."

"But shouldn't we at least wait to see if this one's up to the—"

"Nope. We want new."

It wasn't true. Wendy had no great love for new. She liked old. Old and soft and worn, which was exactly what their little house on the edge of Providence's fashionable east side still was. It had been built by her great-grandfather, and her parents had somehow managed to squeeze themselves and five children into its two and a half tiny bedrooms, and they had all somehow managed to keep clean and presentable with the aid of only one bathroom. It was her family's house, her house, abrim with memories she had no desire either to demolish or to plaster over.

All she had asked for, all she had wanted, was one more room and a bath; but her husband was determined to give her a castle.

One with a brand-new furnace. He looked so happy to be able to afford it all that Wendy found herself saying, "Maybe we'll be able to trade this one in or something."

"Nah. Not worth it." He waved it out of his castle-to-be. "Pete, you take it," he told the contractor. "Give it to someone who could use one."

It was a gesture that was typically Jim: impulsive, generous, oddly unnerving. He was such a loose cannon. He'd done the same thing with their refrigerator a few years earlier, after she had made the mistake of wondering aloud whether it wasn't cycling on and off too often. The next day it was gone and a new one in its place, courtesy of their overburdened Discover Card.

Their neighbors still had the old Kenmore, and it ran fine.

"Uh-oh. You have that look," Jim said as he followed her up the stairs behind the two men. "That if-it-ain't-broke-don't-fix-it look."

"I just think we need to sit down another couple of times with our—you know," she whispered over her shoulder to him. "The financial planner."

"Why? So he can slap us on a budget and make us miserable? The hell with that. I say, spend it before everyone else does."

"Shh!" she warned. He was so indiscreet.

Ignoring her, he went on to say, "Which reminds me: remember that express cruiser I was slobbering over last January at the boat show? I stopped in to look at one at Nathan's Marine yesterday. Man, that is one sweet vessel. Cherry interior, leather seats, air . . . It'll do thirty knots and get us to Newport in no time flat, and the sound system will be good enough to drown out the noise on the way. Unless maybe we wanted to dock the boat in Newport. Yeah, maybe we should do that . . ."

Wendy wasn't listening as he rambled on, mostly because for the past few weeks he was always rambling on. He wanted too many things, too much stuff. It was like listening to a dog bark on and on; if it was your dog, pretty soon you hardly heard it anymore.

Pete and the plumber left, and Wendy was able, at last, to serve supper. She still cooked most nights, just as she still worked in the bookstore on Mondays, Wednesdays, and Fridays. She found that she had a desperate need to soldier on in her routine until she absorbed the enormity of what had happened to them. Quite simply, it hadn't sunk in yet.

"New recipe," she announced as she set a platter of sliced meat loaf in front of her husband. "It has portobello mushrooms in it just for you, rich man," she teased.

She had put out cloth place mats, too, today, instead of the laminated. And the larger-sized paper napkins instead of the lunch-sized. If Wendy had had her druthers, that's how she would have approached their new wealth: in tiptoe steps instead of a flying leap.

"Meat loaf?" Jim blinked at the platter. "This is the best we can do? Meat loaf?"

Tyler was also looking askance at the meat, but for different reasons. "It looks lumpier than regular. What are those dark things in it?"

"Those are the mushrooms. People say they taste like steak. Try a slice."

She may as well have been feeding her son deep-fried tarantulas.

"Why can't we just have hamburgers like everyone else?" the boy muttered as he slid the spatula under an end piece. He took a tentative bite. His nose scrunched up and the corners of his lips, like two thumbs, turned down in rejection. "It doesn't taste like steak; it tastes like soot," he said flatly. "If these mushrooms are so expensive, why didn't you just buy steak?"

Sighing, Wendy said, "To torture you, honey; why else?"

"You know, Wen, he has a point. Why *didn't* you just buy a steak? Why go to all the trouble with some fancy recipe? Beef is beef. We can get mad cow disease either way."

"Very funny, mister. Eat." But she was hurt, and she let it show.

Instantly remorseful, Jim said, "C'mon, hon; you know I was only kidding."

Her husband had an arsenal of half-smiles that were very effective in smoothing the raised prickles on her skin. He used one of those smiles on her now as he raised a huge forkful of meat loaf to his mouth, chewed, considered, swallowed, and said, "I'd rather have this than filet mignon any old day."

Tyler pretended to stick his finger down his throat.

Wendy wasn't sure if her son was reacting to Jim's lie, the meat loaf, or both; all she knew was that, as usual, she was outnumbered. Father and son routinely took sides against her. It could be an interesting challenge at times; but this wasn't one of them.

"Listen," she said, only half in irony, "I don't like being rich any more than the next guy. But you won that money, and we're stuck with it, and until I get used to it, you're going to have to humor me. Now shut up—both of you—and eat your supper."

Tyler laughed at her twisted logic, but her husband found little humor in it. For Jim, there was nothing complicated about the issue: if you won a lot of money, then you could spend a lot of money.

They ate more quietly than usual. The phone rang, and Wendy, newly annoyed, said, "Let the machine answer."

"I'd better get it," Jim said, demurring. "It might be George. You're the one who's so hell-bent on this financial-planning shit," he added as he crossed the kitchen.

She watched his face, trying to gauge the depth of his exasperation with her. He was unhappy, no doubt about it. She could see it in the way he leaned against the refrigerator as he lifted the phone to his ear, studiously ignoring her.

"Jim here. Go," he said as he stared over the dotted-swiss curtains into the yard.

The woman at the other end was loud enough for Wendy to realize that she didn't know the voice. The caller was cheerful, too, obviously falling all over herself with congratulations. It was a tone they'd all got used to in the past few weeks.

"Yeah, thanks; it was a shock, you bet." Jim had a bemused look on his face; plainly, he did not recognize the caller.

The woman spoke at some length, with Jim answering in confused monosyllables. Wendy stopped eating her portobello meat loaf and laid down her fork, more curious than confused. Taking advantage of her distraction, Tyler put down his fork as well and asked to be excused.

"Yeah, okay," Wendy said, not taking her eyes off her husband.

Well into the woman's monologue, Jim looked at Wendy and winked. Then he said, "You know—Caroline, is it?—I really do think you have the wrong guy."

The woman went on a little while longer, until Jim finally interrupted. "Caroline, look, I'm sorry, but I'm just not the one you're looking for. Try one of the other eight. Hey, you just might get lucky."

He winced, apparently because she'd slammed down the phone. With a shrug and one of his half-smiles, he took his place at the table again.

"What," asked Wendy, "was that all about?"

"Another long-lost lover," he said.

She saw merriment in his eyes and was immediately reassured. "Oh, great. When was this one from?"

"Seven, eight years ago. She was a little vague."

"Does she have your child?"

"She has my twins."

"Wow. Gutsier than the others."

"What has she got to lose? What have any of them got to lose?" He thought about it a minute, then shook his head, looking almost sympathetic. "You know, this meat loaf's not half bad," he said, squirting a blanket of ketchup over it.

CHAPTER 3

Zina set the cat carrier on the rag rug and crouched down for a better look at the ball of fur huddled in the back of the box.

She said softly, "It's okay, sweetie. You'll be safe here. You can stay as long as you like, and you can sleep wherever you want. Just make yourself at home. Hey, now?"

She opened the door to the carrier and then stepped back. It would have been a minor miracle if the abused animal had felt secure enough to come out without being dragged; but Zina had managed minor miracles before. She walked the half-dozen steps to the kitchen area of her duplex apartment, then popped open a can of liver-flavored cat food, the smelliest choice in her cupboard. She set down a dish of it in plain view and upwind of the frightened cat, who had purposely had her breakfast held back.

After adding a bowl of water and a litter box to the array, Zina curled up on the homemade slipcover of her sofa, and there she sat without moving for the next fifteen minutes, watching and waiting. She was good at that—watching and waiting. She had been doing it for a dozen years.

A whiskered muzzle appeared at the door of the carrier. The cat poked her pink-and-black-spotted nose a little farther out, caught a glimpse of Zina, and promptly backed up into the carrier.

Zina smiled sympathetically; it was going to be a long wait. "No hurry, sweetie. I can sit here all night."

As it turned out, she couldn't. A shave-and-a-haircut knock on the door told her that Zack had decided to stop by. Zina stepped lightly around the carrier and got the door for her brother, who was holding an old wood chair in his arms.

"One glued chair, returned to owner," he said, lifting it up for her inspection. "This thing's a piece of junk, by the way. If you put it on the curb, no one would bother to take it home, even in this neighborhood."

"I know; I really should replace them."

"Except that you're too busy spending every cent you make on cat food and adoption ads," Zack said on his way to the dining area. He slid the chair under the small round table, opposite its mate. "I saw your last ad; get any nibbles?"

"Three calls so far. But no one's actually made it to the shelter," Zina admitted.

Zack pulled out the other chair and sat down gingerly in it. "This one's wobbly, too," he said in disgust.

"Not when I sit on it."

"You weigh two pounds. Look, about those ads, here's a tip. 'This cat needs a loving home' isn't going to cut it with most people. You should be pitching it as 'Your home needs a loving cat.' Tell people that their lives will be twice as satisfying with your cat. Tell them that your cat will fill a need they didn't even know they had. Tell them—"

"But this shouldn't be about the *people*; it should be about the cat."

The pitying look she knew so well settled over the rugged lines of her brother's face. "God, you're naïve, Zina. All right," he conceded, "if you're determined to stick with your approach, then at least pour it on. Don't make people feel guilty for not adopting your cat; make 'em feel *damn* guilty."

Her laugh was indulgent and affectionate. "Oh, you're such an expert."

He nodded absently, but his focus was on her furniture. "Zee, I'll buy you a set of chairs for your birthday. Just go to Cabot's or Pennsylvania House—hell, go to Pier I!—and pick something out. Anything. I'm begging you."

Ignoring his offer, she said, "You should be in sales instead of in cabinetmaking. Why don't *you* write the ads for me? Please, please?"

"Nothing doing. I don't like cats," Zack said gruffly.

"Yes you do."

"No. I don't. If I were going to like anything, it'd be a dog," he said, getting up to check out the wobble.

"Then why not adopt a dog? The main shelter has lots of them, too many of them."

"Not gonna happen. Dogs don't live long enough." He rocked the chair seat gently back and forth and saw that both spindles had come unglued from their supports. "You get attached, and then all of a sudden they're—"

"Gone." She added with a sudden catch in her throat, "I know."

"Oh, Christ, I'm sorry, Zina," he said, looking up from the chair at her.

She saw real regret in his eyes; after all these years, he still had the capacity to sympathize.

She was so grateful for that. She smiled at her older brother, because he was so wrong: he did love cats and dogs and human beings; he just didn't know it. She said softly, "I can't stop thinking about him, Zack. It was the picture in the paper; it hit me out of the blue."

"Zee, Zee," he said, shaking his head. "We've been

through all this. It wasn't him. It didn't look anything like him."

He came over to her and gave her a reassuring squeeze and said, "Hey, how about a beer for all my hard work?"

He was right. Change the subject. Because they really *had* been through all that.

She reached inside the fridge door for a Coors and handed it to him. "But don't you think it's odd that their first names and initials are the same? I mean, really; don't you think that that's quite a coincidence?"

Zack's broad shoulders slumped a little; his expression turned rueful. He took his beer and crossed the imaginary divide that separated the eating area from the living area, and he dropped with a sigh onto her brightly slipcovered sofa. She watched him take a long, thirsty slug and thought how quaintly bizarre he looked, sitting there: two hundred pounds of well-honed workman surrounded by yardage of blue lilacs and dainty butterflies.

He perched the beer can on his thigh and said, "God, I'm sorry you ever learned how to use a computer. Why couldn't you just stick to your sewing machine?"

He didn't mean it the way it sounded; he truly did just want to change the subject.

"But it's such a *coincidence*," she persisted. "I saw it right away when I looked up the names of the lottery winners on the Web site. James Hodene: it's so much like *Jimmy* Hayward."

"You don't even know if the name James Hodene goes with the picture of the guy you think is Jimmy Hayward."

"Oh, come on."

He shrugged and said, "The last names are nothing alike."

"The initials are."

After a burp came wry agreement. "Yes. That's true. You're right. The initials are the one thing, the single thing, the only thing, that's alike between the two men. What the hell is that?"

The long-haired black-and-white cat had come creeping out of the carrier and was slinking with flattened ears toward the darkened bedroom.

"That's Cassie, my newest foster cat."

"Cat, my foot. It looks like a skunk."

"Shh. Don't tease. She was taken from a woman who was watching her for her daughter while the daughter toured Europe." Zina jammed her fists in the pockets of her denim coveralls, reluctant even to relate Cassie's sad history. "The woman didn't want her on the furniture or bringing in fleas from outside, so she kept her in a cage in the basement all day, all night. It was a small cage, the kind you use to trap animals with."

"Jesus. How long was the daughter gone?"

"Six months so far."

Zack looked utterly repulsed. "You're joking."

Zina shook her head. "One of the woman's friends called the shelter, and they were able to talk the woman into letting us foster-care Cassie. With any luck, we'll be able to put her up for adoption soon."

Zack got up and walked over to the door of the bedroom and stared into the darkness within. "I don't see how you can stand working there," he muttered over his shoulder to her. "I'd want to blow these people's brains out. Or mine."

Behind him Zina said simply, "If we don't help the animals, who will? Besides, *most* people aren't cruel."

"Just stupid."

"Thoughtless. They don't think, that's all."

"Give me a break, Zina!" her brother snapped. "When you leave a dog tied up too long to a parking meter while you have a few beers with your pals—that's thoughtless. Keeping a cat in a cage for half a year is cruel. Genuine, bona fide, undeniably cruel. Jesus, what a bitch!"

Anyone else might have quaked in her socks at the ferocity of his outburst, but not Zina. She understood her brother well: Zack Tompkins had no use for people who didn't follow through on their commitments.

In that, she and Zack were nothing alike.

He was standing in the doorway still, staring into the darkened room, trying to see she didn't know what.

"I don't think that she'll be coming out soon," Zina volunteered. "She's probably under the bed."

"I'm sure." Zack slugged the last of his beer and turned away from the room, his face the picture of misanthropy. "I suppose," he said as he rinsed out the can, "that you're going to sleep on the couch tonight so that the cat can have a space to itself?"

She smiled. "Actually, it's a very comfortable couch."

"You'll be springing for an apartment with a guest room next," her brother said wryly.

"Are you kidding?" Zina picked up the food and water dishes and moved them into the bedroom. "Where would I find a landlord as willing to put up with my animals? No, I like it here. It's in the country, quiet, cheap, and close to the shelter. Best of all, Margie's hard of hearing. Remember last month, when that Siamese was in heat? She never heard a thing."

"There you go; the landlady from heaven. Did you lose this?" he asked, picking up a silver bracelet from the floor.

Zina was surprised—shocked—that she hadn't noticed it wasn't on her wrist. "The lock must have opened again!" she said in genuine distress. "I'm going to lose it for sure."

Zack looked at it closely and said, "The loop needs crimping, that's all. Do you have a needle-nose around?"

"A what?"

"Never mind; I'll fix this and bring it back next time. I'll add a drop of solder to keep it from opening again."

"Let me see."

He handed her the ID bracelet. She looked at the loop, then ran her finger lightly over the inscription on the plate: *J and Z Forever*. Defiantly, because her brother was watching her with wry amusement, she lifted the bracelet to her lips before handing it back.

"My good luck amulet," she said, her chin still high. "Don't keep it too long."

"Zina—"

"Don't. Just . . . don't."

Every once in a while Jim and his office mates declared a boys' night out; Wendy had got the word earlier in the day that tonight was going to be one of them.

Jim was good about warning her, just as he was bad about holding his liquor. She appreciated both traits in him: they defined a man who kept her in the loop about his comings and goings, and who didn't drink enough to have developed a hollow leg.

At ten-thirty, Jim walked in with a weave in his step that Wendy pretty much expected to see. She was glad that they'd had a designated driver.

He gave her a loopy grin. "Betcha think I've had—guess how many I've had."

"One too many?" she said, taking his rain-spattered jacket from him before he threw it over something upholstered.

"Two too many," he answered, heading straight—more or less—for the oversized recliner that loomed large in their small living room.

"There was a lot to drink to, I can tell you," he informed her. "Plenty of stuff goin' on. Plenty." He dropped with a grunt into his easy chair.

"What kind of stuff?" Wendy asked. She was wary nowadays about the possibilities.

"You know—all kinds of stuff," he said, elaborating as

best as he could. He used his right foot to pry off the loafer on his left, then fumbled through the process in reverse to get the other shoe off. The effort seemed to exhaust him; he collapsed and dropped his head back on the recliner and stared at the ceiling. "Man, I'm wasted."

"What kind of stuff?"

"Oh . . . bullshit stuff. Like Phil's getting a divorce from Cindy."

"You're kidding!"

"But not because of the money. Eh, well . . . maybe because of the money. Before the lottery—I have to say— the two of 'em seemed shaky. But not *that* shaky."

He sighed, then frowned. "What was I saying?"

"Phil. Cindy."

"Right. Now, all of a sudden, there's another woman in the picture. Where she came from, I don't know," he said, rolling his head back and forth at the ceiling. "Phil never said squat about her before. I think Phil, being Phil, would've said."

"It's because of the money, you can bet on it," Wendy said in grim agreement. She got up to bring her husband a cup of black coffee because she didn't want him falling asleep in his chair, the usual aftermath of a boys' night out. "Phil's always been a jerk," she said from the kitchen, dismissing him.

"On the bright side, Todd finally got engaged."

"Because of the money, by any chance?" Wendy asked dryly as she set the mug down.

"Damn right because of the money. You know how Todd is. Zero confidence."

"His winnings should be able to buy him a good supply of that."

"You would think. But—I dunno, it's weird, but—no one seems to be handling the money that well. Except me. I'm doin' all right with it. As you know. And Ed. But a lot of the other guys, their heads are pretty messed up over this. They're having real problems."

Ignoring the mug on the coaster, Jim yawned sleepily and closed his eyes. He was one step away from kicking his recliner all the way back.

"Don't you dare," Wendy warned her husband, but it was too late; he threw the lever before she could stop him.

She was surprised at how unwilling she was to let him do his post-boys thing. "Stay up, Jim. I want to know who's having problems with the winnings. What kind of problems? Stay up," she said, pushing on his ankles to get him sitting straight again.

"Cut it out, Wen," he groused. But she persisted, and he levered himself into an upright position. "What do you want from me? You want me to tell you that we all decided to give our winnings back? That's not gonna happen. No one's interested in giving back a dime, sorry to disappoint you."

"I didn't expect that. I want to know what 'messed up over this' means."

Jim rolled his eyes and said, "Why did I open my mouth? This isn't something ... I don't know ... it's ... some of the guys are ... restless ... antsy ... I don't know."

"You mean, about keeping their jobs?"

His response to that was a snort. "Forget keeping their jobs; they'll all be out of there by the end of the month. And that includes me, by the way. I can do better than pushing paper around a desk all day." He added dryly, "Don't worry, though; we should be able to scrape by while I have a look around."

"We've already talked about that," she said, surprised at his tone. "You know that I agree with you. You know that I think you should be happy in what you're doing."

"Well . . . just so you know I'm not going to stay there forever."

Something in his voice, something in his green eyes, made him sound a little lost. Even him. Instantly sympathetic, Wendy came over and curled on his lap. she laid her head on the back of the recliner alongside his and said softly, "This is such a huge change in our lives. In all of our lives."

"You've got that right," he said, idly stroking her hair. He sounded a million miles away.

"The one who's handling it best of us is Tyler, I think. As long as he's got what he wants in video games, he's happy. He's clueless about all the possibilities."

"Oh yeah? He clued in on a new boat fast enough."

"Well, okay, a boat," she said, smiling at the thought of the two of them poring over brochures days earlier. "That goes without saying. Still, I can see why the guys at the office are restless. They've just been handed what amounts to a second chance at life. How many people get that?"

Jim angled his head to get a better look at her. "That's exactly their situation. Exactly. They don't want to blow it."

"No one does," she said. Certainly *she* didn't. She wanted the money to be put to the best possible use, whatever that was, because she wanted to be the best person she could, whatever that was.

Her husband murmured, "I don't think you realize that most of us have already blown it. That half of our lives have already been shot to hell behind a desk. That's why everyone's looking around, trying to get it right this time. Everyone's second-guessing . . . everything. Believe me."

Something hot and sharp needled its way through Wendy's insides. Before she could identify the sensation, she said, "I hope their wives are helping them try to figure it out?"

Jim shifted his weight, and Wendy found herself sinking into the void alongside him. "That's just it," he mused. "I think the guys have this . . . this feeling of, *I'm* the one who bought the ticket, and the money's *my* responsibility to figure out," he said. "Except Ed, of course. Dorothy runs that show."

She tried to laugh away the unease that both of them seemed to be feeling. "Uh-oh; does this mean that from now on I have to fill out a written request to buy something?"

He gave her hair a quick yank and said, "Goof. I'm talking about the other guys, not me. Hell, I'm the one who feels like he has to fill out a form to spend any money around here."

"Because you're impulsive," she couldn't help saying. "It's the Irish in you."

"What about the Irish in *you,* Wenda Hodene?" he said in a fake but rich Irish brogue. "Ye've repressed it of late."

She sat up and turned to face him squarely. "Meaning . . . ?"

"Meaning it's been a while. I know things have been crazy, but . . . it's been a couple of weeks now."

There was no mistaking the look in his eyes. Wendy had seen the same look the day she walked into the motorcycle shop twelve years earlier, in search of a bicycle bell. The only bells around were the ones he rang that night when he kissed her. Within the month they'd gone to bed; within three months they'd become engaged. It was the O'Byrne in her that had made her do it.

She smiled at the memory but said, "You're tight, James; it'll take all blessed night."

"We have all blessed night. Tyler, do not forget, is at a sleepover."

"His first in a month," she said, keying in on the fact. "You're right."

Jim grinned, showing straight white teeth, and Wendy thought, I keep forgetting how good-looking the man is.

And loyal; she loved that he was loyal. His desire for her, coming hard on the heels of the news about Phil and Cindy, was a spur to passion.

And, they would be alone. All blessed night.

Motive and opportunity; Wendy had it all. "You know what, mister? I think I'll take you up on that offer."

She turned and straddled him, wedging her knees between his thighs and the arms of the recliner. Her kiss was fierce and deep, as reassuring as it was hungry for reassurance. She felt him rise instantly beneath her and realized that he might not be so drunk, after all.

He broke off the kiss and said in a raspy growl, "Let's go fuck."

His crudeness jolted her out of any expectation of fuzzy, warm intercourse between a couple with more than a decade of lovemaking behind them. This would be raw; this would be basic.

This could be fun.

Zack Tompkins was in bed with the hottest date he'd had in months. He lay back and closed his eyes, perfectly willing to let her do most of the work. "Ah, darlin', where *did* you go to school?" he murmured. At this rate, he wouldn't last; he was going to have to think about doing his taxes or something.

No need. The new phone on the nightstand rang, a shrill, unfamiliar sound that brought a string of expletives from him. "Ignore it, ignore it," he said hoarsely. "It'll go away."

But it didn't. The machine kicked in after the second ring, and after that they heard a tremulous, "Zack? Zack, are you there?"

Ah, shit.

"It's about Jimmy."

Ah, shit.

At the other end of the line, he heard Zina's voice falter and then turn sniffly. "I know . . . I know what you said. But it's him. It *is* him," she insisted poignantly to the machine. "I know it is. So I'm going to Providence tomorrow–"

Shit! He rolled out of and away from his date and snatched up the phone. "Zee, what're you *talkin'* about? Are you nuts?"

"Oh, Zack–you're home," she said, sounding less offended than relieved. "I hope I'm not interrupting anything."

"No, no, nothing," he mumbled, but he grabbed a corner of the sheet and pulled it over his groin. This was Zina he was talking to: an emotional, naïve, hopelessly fragile human being. The least he could do was cover up in deference to her goodness.

He tried, as gently as he knew how, to crush her plan. "Zee, I don't think that that's a good idea. It would be too stressful for you."

"I'm stressed *now*," she said simply. "Ever since I saw the photo in the paper."

"You'd be depressed if–when–you found out it wasn't him."

"Zack, don't you understand? I'm depressed *now*."

"It could be embarrassing–"

"Not to me. Maybe to him."

"It could be dangerous, for chrissake!"

"How? If he's Jimmy or if he isn't, the worst he could do would be to brush me off. You know–the way these lottery winners have to brush off charities and relatives and con artists. Who knows? Maybe he has a security guard that I won't be able to get past."

"Ah, geez . . ." Zack glanced at his date, sitting where she'd landed at the edge of the bed when he'd dumped her to grab the phone. Brittany was wearing a polite smile—but that was all, and she knew that he was well aware of it.

He smiled back, also politely, while he focused on the crisis at hand. "Zee, I haven't asked you for much in life, but I'm asking you now: don't do this. For me. Don't do this."

He heard her shocked intake of breath. "Zack! How can you ask me not to?"

He turned away from Brittany now and hunched over the phone with one hand slapped over his free ear, feeling like a soldier in a foxhole during a firefight. "What will you gain, Zina?" he said, forcing himself not to scream at her. "What can you possibly gain? He's moved on, wherever and whoever he is. Let it *go*."

After a long pause she gave him an answer, spoken softly but resolutely, that wasn't a reply to his question. "I have to see him."

He'd lost. It was a novel sensation. He felt the way he would have if she'd beaten him at arm wrestling, and for a moment he wasn't quite sure what to say. Later he realized that his ego had been smarting: he'd been her brother for thirty-four years, and yet there he was, outranked by an asshole she'd known for little more than that many weeks.

But at that moment, all Zack cared about was keeping his sister from a self-inflicted wound that he was convinced could end up being fatal.

"All right," he told her. "I won't object to hunting him down—if you agree to a compromise."

"What kind of compromise?"

"It's too complicated to get into over the phone; I'd better come over. I'm on my way."

He hung up and turned around to face the music. Beautiful, blond, naked Brittany was scrutinizing him through narrowed blue eyes.

Brittany didn't like what she was seeing, he could tell. Brittany didn't like it at all.

CHAPTER 4

"You can't be serious."

Wendy stood at the stove, a strip of bacon hanging from between two fingers, and stared in disbelief at her husband. He was in boxers and a T-shirt, sitting at the kitchen table with his hands wrapped around a big blue plastic glass filled with orange juice and ice. Five seconds earlier he had looked rumpled, smug, and adorable. Now he merely looked unshaven.

"Maybe I shouldn't have said anything," he said, going defensive.

"Ten thousand *dollars*?"

"It's not like we don't have the money."

"For *lottery* tickets?"

"It's not a big deal, Wen. Don't make it into one."

Ignoring the unmistakable warning in his voice, Wendy slapped the bacon across the Teflon surface of the griddle. "You couldn't discuss this with me first?"

"Aren't you mistaking me," he asked, "for Ed?"

She gave him a sharp look. "What's that supposed to mean? That I'm Dorothy?"

"I didn't say that," he answered coolly, and he turned his attention to drinking down his juice.

She watched him, thinking, *Ten. Count to ten*.

Sometime during the first, sleepless night after the news that he had won that staggering sum, they had warned one another that moments like these were bound to arise. They had promised as they clung to one another, that they would consider both sides of any differences that might pop up between them. Wendy, for one, was determined to keep that promise.

She took her time separating the next greasy bacon strip from the slab, trying to understand what could motivate him to grab for more when he already had so much.

"What's so *damned* urgent about lottery tickets?" she blurted. "It's not as though the state is running out of them."

So much for seeing both sides. "I'm sorry; I didn't mean to be snotty," she said, throwing him a glance of pale regret. "But you've got to admit, ten thousand is a big step up from ten dollars when it comes to a lottery budget."

"As it happens, Powerball is up to eighty-five million," he said, pouring himself more juice from the carton. "It was worth jumping in, statistically speaking."

"I do *not* get that," Wendy said, annoyed that she did not get that. If there were many more gazillions of people buying tickets in a particularly hot week, and only the same handful or less were going to win, then how could everyone's chances possibly improve? "It makes absolutely no sense," she grumbled.

"I'm a math major," he reminded her in a weary tone. They'd been through this so many times before. "*You* . . . are not.*"

"No. I'm a home major," she said, turning up the burner, "and in my simple view of things, we have enough money. One-eighth of eighty-seven million, even after taxes and the cash-out penalty, is enough to live on. In my view."

And in my view you have a gambling problem, Jim; you've always had a gambling problem. Not enough for Gamblers Anonymous, maybe; but you like it too well, that thrill of the wait. Who else plays the Numbers game by

*calling out digits as the Ping-Pong balls pop up on TV—
and then is genuinely disappointed when the balls don't
match your shouts?*

She said, "How did you pay for them? I don't suppose
that they took Visa."

He looked almost sheepish as he said, "I borrowed most
of it from Sam; he carries a money clip nowadays. I gave
him a check, but naturally I'll split any pot with him fifty-
fifty," he added. "That's only fair."

There it was again, that gambler's cockiness. *I will
split*—not *I would split*. In his mind, winning was a done
deal.

Wendy fixed her attention not on her husband but on
the cobalt-blue plastic glass in his hand. She had been toy-
ing with the idea of ordering real glasses from Pottery Barn
in the same deep blue as the plastic ones. But then yesterday she tossed the catalogue in the recycle bin; she wasn't
a hundred percent sure that she would be going with the
same blue-and-yellow color scheme in the remodeled
kitchen, and the glasses might have ended up a waste of
money.

Ten thousand dollars.

She felt woozy at the thought of how long it once would
have taken them to save that much. And now it meant—
what? Pin money in Sam's pocket that Jim had felt free to
glom onto like change in a dish on a dresser.

"If you're going to pout," Jim said, cutting through the
fog of her dismay, "then at least flip the bacon. It's burning."

"Oh!" Wendy grabbed a fork and began stabbing at the
underside of the bacon that was sticking to the pan on the
too-hot flame. The bacon popped, and a spatter of grease
shot out at her, making her jump back and drop her fork.

"*Damn* it!" she cried, and she grabbed the pan to move
it off the burner. She forgot to use a potholder and cried

out again, then dropped the pan onto the Formica counter and turned on the cold water, letting it run over her battle-scarred forearm and fingers.

Jim was behind her, turning off the burner and then grabbing a potholder and moving the pan–too late to prevent a burn ring–from the counter.

"God, Wendy, what the hell's wrong with you?" he said, but then he saw the red mark on her arm, and he turned instantly sympathetic. "Ouch, that's gonna hurt, poor kid."

"I can't believe I did that," she murmured over the running water.

Jim tried to be helpful by saying, "You were upset, distracted."

"Of course I was upset," she said, taking the clean towel that he offered. "Except for the mortgage and the car loan, we've never paid ten thousand dollars for anything in our lives. And yet here you are, tossing around thousand-dollar bills like–like rose petals at a wedding. I can't deal with it, Jim," she said, wincing from the pain she so stupidly had inflicted on herself. "I can't deal with this much money."

A tear rolled out, she didn't know why. Frustration, pain, fear, resentment–it was a complicated tear.

"Hey, hey . . ." Jim said. He slipped his arm around her shoulder as she stood at the sink, patting her arm dry. "This is nothing to get worked up about. Tell you what. I won't buy that many tickets from now on without telling you first. How's that?"

If Wendy were his lawyer, she would have told him that there were truck-sized holes in his pledge. But she wasn't his lawyer. She was his wife, and she knew that he meant well, and she wanted to put the episode behind them. Compared to their night together, the morning so far had been a disaster.

She tried to seem reconciled, so she nodded in mute

acceptance of the peace offering. But she was still smarting—enough that she felt entitled to ask a question that
burned just as much as hot bacon grease.

"What do you want more money for, anyway?"

"For you," he said softly. "Only for you. C'mon; let's
go upstairs and get something on that arm."

Zack Tompkins drove down Providence's Wickenden
Street past ethnic café's and funky stores and admitted to
himself that he liked the area. It was night-and-day different
from the row of intimidating, upscale shops right around
the corner on South Main. Here, a medley of bookstores,
thrift shops, grocery stores, and an honest-to-God old-
fashioned bread bakery snugged up against one another in
a jagged line that defined the southern boundary of Fox
Point, an old Portuguese neighborhood of plain, two-story
houses squeezed between Brown University and the Providence River. The street was colorful, vibrant—at the moment, overflowing with mothers, babies, and college kids—
and the best-smelling few blocks that Zack had ever tra-
versed.

Too bad he was there on business.

He crisscrossed through the maze of short streets on the
Point, losing himself not once but twice, and reminded himself one more time that he was on a wild-goose chase. Anyone who'd walked off with a lottery purse as big as Jim
Hodene had would have packed up his family by now and
moved, at a minimum, a few blocks to the north, where
brick mansions, stuffy Victorians, and revered colonials
stood in easy camaraderie on College Hill. Money went
where money was, and Fox Point wasn't exactly the Gold
Coast.

Zack was expecting to pull up in front of some modest
gable-front house wrapped in vinyl and with a For Sale sign
hanging on it. He was correct on two of the three counts.

The house was modest, the house was vinyl; but the house was not for sale.

Far from it. Apparently the Hodenes—still the owners of record—were adding on: there were two contractors' trucks and a van crammed onto the narrow side drive and hanging over the sidewalk.

The house had had a small side yard, but that was now occupied by a brand-new foundation and a framed-up first floor. A couple of dead, uprooted rhododendrons, tossed on the rubble of a brick barbecue pit in a corner, suggested that the house had a history of being loved and cared for.

By Jim Hodene? Sure, why not? But Jimmy Hayward? Fat chance. Bastards like him didn't care about anything except themselves.

Zack continued slowly past the house, then circled the block one more time before parking down the street from the construction, where he was able to sip his coffee at a leisurely pace while he watched and waited to see what developed.

The coffee was long gone and his boredom threshold reached and crossed when Zack jerked to sudden attention. A brand-new monster Ford Excursion, gleaming with optional trim, had slowed to a halt in front of the mint-green house.

Rubbing the growth of new beard since his predawn shave, Zack squinted into the afternoon sun and saw a dark-haired woman jump from the driver's seat to the ground like a guerilla soldier from a low-limbed tree. She didn't look used to the high-slung SUV, which was consistent with the vehicle's temporary plates.

The contractors were making a four-thirty beeline for their trucks, but the woman managed to intercept the last one out, apparently the boss. She gestured toward the bare studs of the first floor. The contractor nodded and turned around while she climbed back into the truck and pulled off the street and into the half-empty drive, blocking the guy's exit—no doubt intentionally, Zack thought wryly. He had worked in construction himself before turning to creating replicas of antique furniture; he knew all the owners' tricks.

The woman wasn't young, wasn't old. Somewhere in her mid-thirties was Zack's guess. She was in good shape, whatever her age; there was something in the way she'd jumped down from the SUV. His guess was that she didn't come from wealth, though, despite her yuppie transport.

Again, there was just something in the way she walked, the way she gestured. Her hair bounced too much, for starters, and she lacked that quietly confident air that his own wealthy clients either had or faked. She was too . . . intense, that was the word. It was obvious, even from where Zack sat, that the addition to the humble house meant a lot to her. She was *into* it.

Zack continued to watch, curious about the woman and her story, as she scrambled up a short ladder and joined the contractor on the first floor of the addition. She knew what she wanted, no doubt about it. She was pointing to a roughed-out window frame and was gesturing to her left: she wanted it moved.

"You're right to do it now, lady," Zack found himself murmuring in agreement. "Later, it'd cost you twice as much."

Whatever her contractor said in response, it pleased her. Zack saw her clasp her hands together and thump them once against her chest while she grinned and nodded. It was a weirdly endearing gesture; he felt almost gratified that she looked so pleased. There were some customers who wouldn't be happy no matter what you did.

The contractor tried to make a break for it then, but she wasn't done with him yet.

Ah. Something about the fireplace. She was pointing to

the jut in the foundation where the chimney would eventually go. God, wasn't that always the way. The day was over, the tools were stowed, and that's when the owners wanted to groove. Never mind that you were tired, grimy, aching for a shower and a beer. They much preferred that you hang around and discuss mantel styles and hearth materials and give them your opinion on just the right shade of white paint, even though those decisions were months away. He knew the type so well. Once they plunked down their deposits, they figured they owned your soul.

"Lady, give the poor guy a break," Zack muttered. "Can't you see he wants to get out of there?"

She couldn't, and Zack was genuinely bothered by it. And then, right about the time he decided that she was just another self-absorbed client, the woman reversed herself and began shooing her contractor off the site, urging him to go home, go home.

All right. That was more like it. Zack wanted to believe that she wasn't a jerk, he didn't know why.

There was another round of musical cars, after which the contractor finally left. Two minutes later another car, this one a five-year-old Taurus, rolled down the street and pulled alongside the house, and this time Zack felt the hair on the back of his neck stand up.

Wendy was still standing in the middle of her family-room-to-be, marveling at how quickly the framework had gone up, thrilled by the realization that she'd finally have room for a three-cushion sofa.

"Thanks for picking up my car, Jim. You can take your Excursion back; I was getting a nosebleed up in that driver's seat. You just missed Pete, by the way," she added, still smiling as her husband walked around to the front of the site.

"I know; I saw his truck turn the corner. No big deal,"

Jim answered with a shrug. "I didn't have anything to go over with him, anyway." He ascended the four-rung ladder and looked around cursorily.

"How can you not have anything to go over with him? I had a list as long as my arm. I never did get through it; only the most important things. Pete hates to be bothered when he's working, and then he hates to be held up when he's done. It's maddening. I keep wanting to throw a net around him."

"You wanted to hire him as much as I did," Jim said quickly.

"I know. And he's good. He's great. But he drives me a little crazy. Oh, well; I'll get used to it," she said happily. "As long as they keep making progress. Just *look*, Jim," she said, throwing her arms out and whirling in place. "We have walls! We have a family room! Isn't it wonderful?"

Jim didn't seem to be nearly as impressed. "The framework always goes fast," he said knowingly, the way men do. "Once the studs are up, that's when it starts slowing down. And keeps slowing down."

Wendy shook her head. "Nope, you're wrong. Pete was just telling me that he has way more work than he can handle; he's trying to hire more help, in fact. With or without more help, he's going to have to work like a maniac to get our addition done, otherwise he won't be able to go on to the next job."

Jim threw his head back in a loud, good-natured laugh and then took her in his arms. "You really believe that? *Wendy*. Everyone's not like you, you know—keeping at something until it's done. Definitely not contractors; it's just not how they operate. They're jugglers, Wen, better at it than anyone out of a circus."

"We'll see," she said, but she felt a little less smug than before.

They stood in their embrace in the middle of their

family-room-to-be, each of them caught up in his own thoughts, savoring the last warm rays of the afternoon sun. Wendy decided—for the first time, really, since the night that Jim found out that he'd won the lottery—that she was truly, unreservedly happy.

She was more convinced than ever that she didn't need a mansion, she didn't need a boat. All she needed, all she wanted, was room for a three-cushion couch. They could take all of the money back, but if she had her husband and her son and the rest of her family—and that little bit of extra room—then Wendy could honestly say she had everything her heart desired.

"Honey?" Jim murmured in her hair.

"Hmm?"

In a soft, sober whisper he said, "Quitting that job was the best thing I ever did."

"You don't miss it," she murmured, stating the obvious.

"Miss it? In retrospect, I hated it. Now I can figure out what I really want out of life."

"Isn't that funny?" she asked in a dreamy voice. "I think I already have."

Twelve years. It could have been twelve days. He was sporting a few more pounds, a little less hair, but Jesus Christ, it was Jimmy Hayward. Jim Hodene was Jimmy Hayward. Zina was right, poor kid; as right as rain. After all those years and all those red herrings, she'd actually stumbled across the man of her dreams, the bum who'd left her eight months pregnant and disappeared in broad daylight.

Zack wanted to jump out of his truck, throw the guy in a bamboo cage, and parade him through the streets for everyone to see. And then he wanted to beat him bloody. If he thought he could obliterate him and get away with it, he'd damn well give it a shot. Fucking bigamist.

He forced himself to sit until the adrenaline fury subsided and until the couple climbed down from the addition and went around to the front door and entered their house.

Zack was so unprepared for the possibility that Jimmy and Jim were the same asshole that up until then he did not have a plan. And now suddenly a hundred different options had begun roaring through his brain—so many that they were canceling one another out.

And he still didn't have a plan.

One thing Zack knew. Hayward or Hodene or whoever the hell he was—that guy was going to pay. With blood or money or preferably both, but he was going to pay.

CHAPTER 5

"Good heavens, how can you stand the *noise*?"

"It's music to my ears, Mom," Wendy shouted. "As long as they're making progress."

Grace O'Byrne Ferro followed Wendy, who had a tray with two mugs of coffee and a greasy, sugared doughboy cut in halves, out of the kitchen and into the living room, as far from the din as they could get.

"Wendy, there is a table saw on the other side of your kitchen wall," her mother pointed out. "There are strange men wandering in and out of your house all day. There's no place to park a car anymore. And–I don't know if you've noticed it or not–there's a bottle of suspicious-looking yellow fluid sitting outside by the lilac bush."

"Is it corked?" Wendy asked lightly.

"I didn't go over to check," her mother answered in a deadly voice.

"Yeah . . . it's too bad they haven't installed the Porta Potti yet. I'll ask Pete about it. But, you know? Whatever works. Just as long as they're making progress," Wendy repeated serenely. It was her mantra.

Exasperated, her mother said, "Why don't you just move out until they're done with construction? For goodness' sake, you can afford it."

Wendy licked sugar from her fingers and shook her head. "No rush. It won't be bad here–at least, not until they saw through the kitchen wall and open the old house to the new. To be honest, I'm enjoying this. Of course, Tyler's not crazy about having a crew hammering outside his bedroom window, and Jim thinks it's beneath us to stay here, but—I like it. Call me an idiot."

"You're an idiot. You'll just be in their way."

"I don't care. Really, I'm fascinated by it. I'm in awe of people who work with their hands to make something out of nothing. Every day I learn something new. Oh! And wait'll you see."

Wendy jumped up and ran out to the kitchen; when she came back she was holding a rusted horseshoe that was completely encrusted with dark, mysterious matter. "Look what the men found in the cellar foundation when they cut through. Pete says that in these old houses they used to throw anything they could find into the concrete to reinforce it—rocks, bricks, obviously horseshoes. Isn't it cool?"

"It's junk," her mother said, staring at the thing with distaste. "Throw it out. And wash your hands."

"It's a horseshoe! It'll bring us good luck."

"It'll bring you tetanus. You've already had ridiculous luck. Throw it out."

"I will not. I'm going to nail it above the cellar door."

"Go ahead, then. Be greedy. See where it gets you."

"I don't want more *money,* Mom," Wendy said, embarrassed to be suspected of it. "That's not the kind of luck I meant."

"You are tempting fate, missy," her mother warned ominously. "I don't know why you can't see that."

Gracie Ferro had a way of perpetually cutting her kids down to size. It was an old habit, established during the raising of three boys and two girls, none of them particularly timid or shy. Everyone wanted his fair share of everything, and since that wasn't usually possible, Grace O'Byrne Ferro had to use what she had to keep her kids in line: the guilt trip. It was cheap, effective, and in endless supply.

Wendy had already figured out that sixty percent of the problem she was having with her sudden, unearned wealth came from feelings of guilt. What she couldn't figure out was why she couldn't crush feelings like that once and for all. For most of her life, fighting guilt had been a daily, ongoing war, won or lost one small skirmish at a time. It was no surprise that she found herself back in the trenches, ducking her mother's missiles.

"This gets nailed over the cellar door. For luck in *general*, okay?" Wendy said doggedly. She returned the horseshoe to the shelf at the top of the cellar steps—but then washed her hands extra long as a kind of penance before going back to her mother and her deep-fried treat.

Muttering something about heathenish superstitions, Grace O'Byrne waited until they'd finished their pastry before saying what was really on her mind.

"So where's your brother lately? He hasn't been to see us in weeks."

"Oh . . . you know Dave," Wendy said, automatically vague. "Always on the move."

"Your aunt Genevieve is constantly asking me what he's up to—which of course she would; she knows it's always no good—and I really don't know what to say anymore. I think she asks out of spite. *Her* David's turning down business, her David's bought a new BMW. Her David has such important cases, Alan Dershowitz would be green. Her David, her David," she ended up darkly.

"Yikes, Mom, you're in a mood."

"Why shouldn't I be? I had *my* David first."

The two Davids had been born less than a year apart, and to that day Wendy could not understand how first cousins born to close family in the same neighborhood could be given the same name. What could possibly have been the point? Someday she was going to work up the nerve to ask her aunt.

"I think Dave's got a couple of things going on," Wendy said with a carefully offhand shrug.

Her mother picked off her discomfort instantly. "Have you been giving him money?"

"Money . . . ? Uh-h . . . hardly at all," Wendy had to confess.

The look her mother gave her was more mournful than critical. Dave was the youngest, the most charming, and the most unemployable of all five siblings. He was his mother's last hope, the one she was praying would become a priest and use his connections to get her skipping past purgatory and coasting into heaven—but Dave couldn't decide on a job, much less a calling.

"He's always on the lookout for work, Mom; really, he is," Wendy said, rallying to her brother's defense. (That's the way it always had been: five against one, and still they were outnumbered.) "But it's hard to find an exact match to his abilities. When's the last time you saw a want ad for inventors?"

"There *is* a shortage, you know."

"Of inven—? Oh, priests. Yes. But Dave has a girlfriend, don't forget."

"He's had a hundred girlfriends. He can't support any of them. He can't support himself. A priest would have room and board."

"Hmm. True. But I don't think that's considered sufficient motive for going into the priesthood."

"It'd give him a place to take a deep breath and figure out what he wants out of life."

Her words eerily echoed Jim's about himself. Dave and Jim: two men a lot alike, a lot at sea. Suddenly uneasy although she didn't know why, Wendy lied and said, "Dave seems happy enough."

"Your brother is going to be thirty-three next month," her mother said crisply. "How happy can he be?"

If Dave was going to be thirty-three, then Grace O'Byrne was going to be sixty-five; they were born in the same month. Was that, perhaps, what her tense mood lately was all about? Becoming a bona fide senior citizen who was eligible for Medicare?

It was hard for Wendy to believe that her mother had reached that milestone. For someone who had raised five kids in a house the size of a shoe, on a budget the size of a shoestring, the woman looked fit and ready to take on half a dozen more of them. True, she was a little heavier, a little grayer, a little slower out of the gate; but to Wendy and her siblings, Grace O'Byrne Ferro was and always would be the Amazing Grace.

"*What?* What're you smiling about?" her mother asked, cocking her head and narrowing her look.

Wendy lifted her shoulders in a bemused shrug to go with the bemused smile. "You. I still don't know how you did it. Raising all of us and working part-time besides— how did you do it?"

Now it was her mother's turn to shrug. "I had help. Your grandparents pitched in, and my sister, too, I'll give her that. Of course, Genny didn't have kids until late, and then only the one—but she was always there for me in a pinch, always."

Filled with a rush of affection for her indomitable mother (and ignoring the reference to "only the one"), Wendy jumped up and impulsively crossed the room to give her a hug. "You're being too modest, Mom," she argued, squeezing cheek to cheek.

Her mother made a dismissive sound and said, "You do what you have to do. I don't understand what's so heroic about keeping a family together. Why get married if you're not going to stick with it?"

She was clearly thinking of Charlotte, Wendy's older sister, who divorced after a mere four years. Poor Charlotte, happily married now and pregnant again by her second husband, was always going to have to answer to that little black check on the report card of her life. It wasn't that Grace didn't love Charlotte as much as her other children; it was just that she worried more whether Charlotte would be able to attend what she liked to call the Grandest Reunion of All.

Yet another reason, no doubt, for Dave to get with the priest program.

Wendy smiled and said, "Okay, Doctor Laura, we all know where you stand on wedding vows, so we won't go there."

But her mother wasn't willing to drop the subject of the lifetime vow. "You seem to be sticking with your husband, at least—even before the money."

"Because Jim's a good guy," Wendy answered. She knew for a fact that Charlotte's first husband was anything but.

Grace nodded and said, "That was generous of him, paying off the mortgages and letting your brothers and Charlotte pay you back with half the interest. I just hope it doesn't cause hard feelings down the line between you and Jim—because sooner or later, someone's going to get squeezed and miss a payment, I hope you realize that."

In that one way, Wendy and her mother were very much alike: leery of found money. There was too much of an easy-come, easy-go aspect to it. Nonetheless, Wendy said, "I'm sure everything will be fine."

"Is Dave expecting you to buy *him* a house, too?"

"Not at all. He has no desire for that kind of debt—low interest or not. He knows he can't handle it, at least now."

Her mother lifted her chin a little and said, "Well. Give him that much credit, anyway. He has some pride."

"I wish you'd let us do something for you and Dad, though," Wendy threw out. "There must be something you need; something you want."

Grace didn't take offense, but she looked genuinely puzzled by the offer. "What do we need? Now that you've paid us off for this house, we're all set—at least, until we get ready to go into the home," she said wryly. "Then maybe we'll need to sit down and talk."

One of the crew turned on the air compressor just then, sending earsplitting reverberations through the house and driving Grace O'Byrne to her feet. "Good grief, I can't sit through that! Please, Wendy—don't be so stubborn. Do us all a favor: move out."

"I'll walk you to your car," Wendy said sweetly.

"If I know Jim, he won't want to live here after the construction's done, anyway. Why would he? He can have any house he wants."

"Well, you never know," Wendy said sweetly.

"Rent this out if you're so set on keeping it in the family. Rent it to Dave."

"That's one possibility," Wendy said sweetly.

"At least I'd know where to find him. And don't use that tone with me. I'm still your mother, even if you *are* a millionaire."

Wendy sighed and said, "Sorry," but then couldn't resist firing one last volley. "Anyway, think about what I said, Mom. If you and Dad get a yen to charter a yacht in Greece this summer and go skinny-dipping with the captain and crew—you let us know. We'll make it our anniversary gift to you."

Her mother slanted her eyes and said, "You're my most evil child, you know that?"

"Yes, I do," Wendy said sweetly.

* * *

Luckily for Zina, two of the volunteers at the shelter were out of commission with bad colds; Zina was more than willing to pinch-hit for them, just to have something to do. Her job at the quilting shop wasn't enough just then: it kept her hands busy and her mind occupied, but her emotions were free to roam. Far better, she thought, to bring a little happiness to neglected animals than to anguish over her brother's mission.

So she groomed each cat an extra long time, and spoke to each with all the affection she felt, and made sure that each had a little side dish of the food he liked best—and still her emotions roamed.

Zack had warned her that he wouldn't call until he had news, so presumably he hadn't had news. How was that possible? If Jim wasn't Jimmy, then that was it; case closed. But if Jim and Jimmy were the same man, then—what?

One scenario was that Zack might knock Jimmy down and end up in jail. She never should have let her brother take the reins from her. She should've gone to Providence and seen for herself whether Jimmy was Jim or not. At least she wouldn't land in jail. Would Zack use his single call to contact Zina, or a lawyer? That was her only question by the end of the first full day he was gone.

By the end of the second day, Zina had spun another scenario: Zack might not have been able to get anywhere near Jimmy. In that scenario, Jimmy was now living in a mansion, surrounded by a high brick wall like the ones around the estates in Newport. In that scenario, Jimmy had a security system, maybe even a security guard. It was so obvious, by the end of the second day, what the real problem was. *Naturally* Jimmy would have had to put precautions in place; otherwise, people would be beating paths to his door and asking him for money all day, all night.

Zina had no idea how her brother was going to breach the high brick wall, but if anyone could do it, Zack could.

She went home with her spirits a little higher, and after she checked her messages she made herself a cup of tea and sat on the braided rug sipping the hot brew while she dragged a feather on a stick for Cassie to chase.

Back and forth over her legs she dragged the feather, with the black-and-white cat, her pupils dilated in the hunt, hopping over Zina's shins like a horse in a steeplechase. The sweet creature had come a long way in her rehab, and Zina was convinced that it was because she herself was spending most of her time at home on the floor, at cat level, relating.

When the phone rang, Zina jumped so suddenly that the cat went skittering off to hide under the bed again. Zina snatched up the phone and said, "Yes?"

"Hey, Zee," Zack said by way of a hello.

"Is it him?" she asked. There was desperation in her voice that she didn't try to hide.

Zack hesitated, then said, "At the moment, I'm not sure."

"But you did see him?"

"From down the block."

"Because of the security guard, you mean."

"What guard? There's no guard," Zack said. "He has an ordinary house that's getting a makeover, which I don't get. He can afford better. Jim Hodene is not living anything like the multimillionaire he now is."

"Maybe you have the wrong Jim Hodene."

"There's only one in Providence."

"Tell me everything you saw. What was he like?"

"How do I know what was he like? That's an impossible question to answer, Zee."

"I mean, did he seem nice? Does he have a dog? A cat? Does he care about his house and his garden? Is he neat? There are things you can tell about someone, even from down the block."

"I'll send you a written report when I find out," Zack said.

He sounded more sarcastic than amused, so Zina added, "I realize that they'd only be first impressions, Zack. I know he could be a serial killer or worse. I'm not asking for a warranty from you or anything."

She had learned, during their lifetime together, that Zack actually liked it when she was sarcastic; it made him somehow less worried about her. This time was no exception. Sounding relieved, he laughed and then said, "I gotta go. Say hi to the cat."

Her heart felt as if it were lodged between her ears. She said, "Wait! Do you have a plan, Zack?"

"Absolutely. My plan is to see him tomorrow. More than that, I will not say. I'll call you at night with an update."

Zina was thrilled to hear confidence in his voice. They hung up, and the first thing she did was to coax poor Cassie back out from under the bed.

Zack hung up more amazed than exasperated. His sister's powers of denial were awesome: it apparently never even occurred to her to ask him whether Jim Hodene had a wife. Besides her, that is.

The fact was, Jim Hodene had not only a wife but a kid, a young boy who looked like him. There was no dog, there was no cat, as far as Zack could see. Just, gee, a human family. Zack, who'd been to City Hall to check the deed to the house, had already determined that there was a Mrs. Hodene to go with the mister. But even though he was prepared for the fact, it hadn't hit home until he saw the son of a bitch take the missus in his arms.

And later, when Zack drove past the house again, that's when he saw the kid. A ten-year-old son easily trumped a baby that Hodene had never known—even Zack, a dedicated bachelor, could understand that. Another no-brainer:

a decade-plus marriage to one woman trumped half a year of wedlock to another one. Jim Hodene, once Jimmy Hayward, was right where he wanted to be, financially *and* emotionally speaking.

That, however, was about to change.

CHAPTER 6

Zack hitched up his leather tool belt, surprised at how heavy it felt. In the last few years, he had become used to working with more refined tools than hammers and prybars and fifty-foot rules: chisels and spokeshaves were his instruments of choice nowadays. Still, it took him less than a minute to adjust to the weight of the belt and slip into his old role as housebuilder.

The three men standing around their trucks alongside the Hodenes' house were in no hurry, finishing their cigarettes and slugging down coffee from Dunkin' Donuts cups. Zack introduced himself and learned that Pete hadn't shown up yet, which explained the general lack of hustle.

The crew showed no surprise at Zack's appearance on the site; he learned that a steady stream of carpenters had come and gone during the last couple of years, evidence of an ongoing labor shortage. When a better offer came along, a carpenter generally took it.

Pete turned up fifteen minutes late—flat tire, he explained with disgust as he shook Zack's hand. There was a harried look in his eyes, testimony to the ridiculous workload he must have had. Given the current building boom, it hadn't taken a lot of ingenuity for Zack to check the want ads and match one of the phone numbers there to the one on Pete's truck. Zack had called the number, and after a brief telephone interview, had been given a job sight unseen.

Pete sent off the youngest and the oldest of the men to work on another site; Zack was plunked right where he wanted to be, in Jimmy Hayward's addition, paid for by Jim Hodene.

"Billy, I want you to finish up the subfloorin' on the second level," Pete told his remaining help as he strapped on his own tool belt. "Zack and I'll frame up the south wall."

"Okay," said Billy, but then he added, "I should've mentioned yesterday, but the leak on the compressor hose is worse; the compressor runs pretty near all the time now," Billy admitted. He lowered his voice and added, "Someone, I think her mother, come up to us yesterday and said can't we shut the thing up, something like that."

"Ah, shit. I'll have to go back to the shed for another hose. Why the hell didn't you tell me this yesterday? All right. Zack, you and Billy can start pulling off the siding on the old outside wall. I'll be back."

Off Pete went, muttering ominously. Zack sympathized. He'd been there himself, riding herd on a crew, which is why he'd gotten out of house building and into furniture making. He was a loner by nature, skeptical of the very concept of teamwork; and besides, he'd never yet tried to call himself in sick.

The fact was, he loved having complete control of a project. Sculpting wood was one of the most satisfying highs he'd ever known. The thought that right then he had a half-carved corner chair waiting in his workshop for him to finish was almost as painful as the thought of a woman waiting in his bed for him to return and bring her to climax.

Damn. He had to get through this and get back to his real life.

He climbed through a roughed-out window onto the first

floor of the addition and, while Billy went searching for a prybar, sized up the task at hand. Years ago the plastic siding had been attached over peeling clapboard, undoubtedly to save money. Big mistake. Whatever modest, New England charm the house had possessed was covered over in a mass of featureless vinyl strips that trapped moisture and encouraged rot. Hopefully the house was going to be returned to its original look.

Not that it mattered to Zack either way; he had more pressing issues at hand.

Billy came back with a prybar, and together he and Zack began pulling off the siding that surrounded the two original kitchen windows. They were standing in what was going to be the family room; Billy explained that the entire outside wall they were working on would eventually come down, creating an open floor plan between the old kitchen and the new family room.

The kitchen windows were fitted with miniblinds, but these were hauled all the way up. Apparently the Hodenes weren't too shy. Sure enough, as Zack worked, a sleepy-eyed kid came moping into the kitchen and headed for a cupboard, oblivious to the two men on the other side of the windows. Behind him came his mother, apparently fresh from a shower. Her hair hung in dark wet ringlets around her clean, shiny face, and although she'd thrown on a T-shirt over tattered jeans, her feet were still bare.

The windows were old and anything but soundproof; Zack heard every word of her motherly harangue.

"Tyler, if you think you're going to a sleepover tonight and leaving behind that sinkhole you call a room—"

"What's the difference?" the kid shot back as he took out a bowl. "The whole house is a pit."

"Maybe so, but in this pit, the laundry is clean and the dishes are done. So you just march right back up to your room and collect all the dirty plates in there, and then march right back down to the sink and wash them."

"I'll be late for school!"

"Tough. Move it."

Fists parked on shapely hips, she was focused on the confrontation, with her back to Zack and Billy. Zack had a flash of that same awareness he had when he saw her jump down from the SUV: of a woman with strength to spare and a will to match. It occurred to him that he wouldn't ever want to tangle with her. And then it occurred to him that he'd probably have no choice.

"Ma—"

"And bring your dirty clothes down, too. It smells like a beach at low tide in there. Good grief, Tyler. Shape up, will you?"

Head low, the boy slunk past her in a full-body pout. The woman turned to watch him go, and that's when she saw Zack with what had to be a fierce look of attention on his face, because she did a double take, and her cheeks flared up in a very flattering way. She marched right over to the windows and slid one of them up.

"Good morning," she said, a little tersely. It sounded exactly like, "What's it to *you*?"

Zack gave her a sheepish hint of a smile and said, "Mawnin'."

"You're new here. I'm Wendy Hodene."

"Zack," he said in minimal response.

It was a weird sensation, having her talk to him through the double glass of the thrown-up window while from the shoulders down they were open to the breeze. He had an impulse to drop low and do his talking through the opened part of the window, but he resisted it and instead walked away. He wanted no more to do with the possible second victim of the Hayward–Hodene fiasco than he did with young Tyler—arguably its third victim.

Seething all over again at the risk of the carnage to

come, Zack began pulling off some siding farther away from the windows as he waited for the man of the house to make an appearance downstairs. He was aware that his heart had begun pumping harder and his adrenaline to flow in anticipation of the imminent meeting, and it infuriated him. He wanted to be calm. Collected. Merciless. Above all, satisfied.

He worked, and he waited.

After a while, Pete returned with another compressor hose, and they replaced the leaky one and began work on the second-level floor. Zack knew, everyone knew, that the first priority was to get the shell enclosed and the addition watertight. It had been a wet spring so far, and there was no reason to assume that the pattern would change.

The three of them worked quickly and with little conversation, which was fine with Zack. The less said about himself, the better. In the meantime, he kept his eye on the big blue Excursion parked on the street. He'd figured out that the monster SUV belonged to her husband, the Taurus to the wife. Wendy, yeah. She looked like a Wendy, somehow. A nice, normal, unaffected mom who obviously hadn't let that mind-boggling jackpot go to her head. With any luck, Zack would be in and out of her life without her missing a beat.

And if it turned out differently than that . . . if it all blew up in their faces . . .

That's the breaks. If she dumped the bigamist, so be it. At least she'd still have half—after the adjustment for Zina—of the winnings. And she'd have her son. Which is more than Zina had the chance to have, goddamnit.

His thoughts plunged back to that horrifying day when he drove his sister, bleeding profusely, to the emergency room. It still amazed him, how something so normal as having a baby could go so agonizingly wrong. He beat back the memory for the thousandth time, but immediately another, even more horrific one rushed in to fill the void: blood everywhere, on the floor, against the windows, in his eyes, over her, blood. His parents, bloody and broken.

"Hey. Zack. You listenin'? I said *sixty*-five inches, not fifty-five."

Pete was holding up the too-short two-by-four that Zack had just cut, and the look on his face was no longer harried but pissed.

"Agh, sorry," Zack said.

"You okay?" Pete asked. "You look a little green around the gills."

"Not at all. Green's my natural color," said Zack, unwilling to take it to a personal level.

"Yeah, well, okay then. Let's get on the ball. Like I tell the boys, wood don't grow on trees."

"Measure twice, cut once. I know," Zack quipped, but the reprimand stung. He was used to working within millimeters of accuracy, and he'd just blown a cut by a full ten inches. *Jesus, man, focus. You lose this job, you lose your entrée.*

Of course, Zack could've just shown up at the Hodenes' door, but he wanted, if possible, to avoid destroying innocent lives. He turned to his work with a vengeance, and when he looked up again, it was lunch break. The Taurus was still there, parked on the street where it had been all morning—but, hell and damnation, the Excursion was gone.

Pete and Billy took off in different directions, leaving Zack on his own. He wasn't savvy about the best place to grab a quick meal, but he'd noticed a little café on Wickenden Street called Hurry Curry that might fit the bill. It was a warm day, despite the threat of rain, and he remembered that the eatery had a couple of outdoor tables. He'd been holed up in his workshop for months—except, of course, for the necessary foray out for casual sex—and sitting outside for a few minutes, watching the flow of humanity pass back and forth, would be just the lift he needed right now. He was feeling tense and down in the dumps.

Hurry Curry was no more than twelve feet wide, with a take-out counter in the back and three fake-marble-topped bistro tables by the windows, in addition to the two outside. A handful of people were waiting to have their orders filled, and Zack resigned himself to eating his curried chicken sitting on the front seat of his truck back at the house.

But the customers were all on the run, and Zack was rewarded for his pessimism with one of the two coveted outdoor tables. He sat down with his Sprite and his curry and dug in, savoring the dish, wishing there were more of it. He'd come back the next day and get two.

He was watching a bouncy young thing—several of them, in fact; probably Brown coeds—when he was addressed from behind.

"Hi, Zack!"

Feeling somehow caught in the act, he turned away quickly to face Wendy Hodene. She looked friendly and approachable and—was he mistaken?—maybe contrite for having been curt earlier.

"I see you've found one of my favorite places," she said with a winning smile.

He accepted her unspoken apology, if that's what it was, with a pleasantry of his own. "The curry's great. I was surprised. It's such a little place."

"You should try their tandoori combo next time," she said, still smiling. "You'd love it, even though it's not curried."

Immediately he began to back away from any chitchat situation. His answering smile was reserved. "I like curry."

"Oh." Looking abashed, she held on to her own smile long enough to say, "Well, I'm off to work. See you!" And then the smile went away, followed by her.

He watched her go and was struck again by the natural way in which she carried herself. Her walk—he didn't know how to describe her walk. It was without artifice, not even remotely for show. She didn't carry herself in any provocative way or anything; she walked, basically, to get there from here. For whatever reason, he liked her walk. He smiled to himself as he bussed his own table; he could tell that he'd been alone in his workshop for maybe just a little too long.

When he got back to the house he saw her Taurus still parked on the street, which made him do a double take until he figured out that she must have been walking to her job. On Wickenden Street, presumably? There were more than enough shops there. What had she been wearing?

Instantly a picture of her in a clingy, swingy floral-print dress popped up in his mind, a look that seemed downright retro after the all-American jeans and T-shirt outfit of the morning. Where would she be working that required such a dress? Clothing shop? Antique shop? Herbal shop? Pottery? Futon? Ceramics? Doctor's office? Lawyer's?

Now that he thought about it, why the hell was she going to work, anyway? Even though after penalties and taxes they were worth only a small fraction of the mind-boggling ten or so million that they seemed to have won at first blush, it was still plenty to live on without having to trek to a job in a shop on Wickenden Street. Unless, of course, she owned the shop and loved the work.

Would he abandon furniture making if he were a multimillionaire? Zack found himself going back and forth on that. His first impulse was to assume that he'd never give up something that brought him such profound pleasure. But money changed things. Money changed people. So he couldn't quite say that he'd keep on creating heirloom pieces that he hoped people and museums would bid on frantically in the centuries to come—but he liked to think that he would.

And in the meantime, here he was, slaving for a few bucks an hour at work that bored him just so that he could shimmy up to a man he despised and squeeze him until he howled. Pisser! The afternoon wore on, and Zack's mood turned more foul. What had he been thinking? His plan was beyond cockamamie; it was insane. If Zina knew . . . God. If she *knew*. By late afternoon, Zack had resolved to bail out and try some other way to get at Jimmy.

"Pete, my man," came the shout from the ground. "It's lookin' good, real good."

Zack, a box of nails on his shoulder, had been coming up the ladder on the north side of the house when he heard the yell from ground-level on the south side of the house. North, south, east, west, it made no difference to him. He'd know the voice if it came from the opposite end of a stadium during halftime at a Super Bowl.

Careful to keep himself under control, Zack crossed the plywood floor and dropped the box of nails with a thud at Pete's feet. With both hands on the roughed-out sill, he peered at the sidewalk below. He didn't say hi, didn't say boo. He just looked down, as if he were curious about the shouting, and then he straightened up and went back to work.

But not before letting his brother-in-law have a good, long view of the man who was going to be within spitting distance of his wife and son all day.

Jimmy recognized him; there was no mistaking the stunned look on his face. His brow lifted and his mouth actually went a little slack. He was the kind of opportunist who was always scanning the company around him anyway, on the hunt for someone it might be useful to know. And Jimmy never forgot a face—unlike Zack, who only remembered the ones of those he loved and those he hated.

Zack allowed himself a grim smile of satisfaction. He would remember *that* face, *that* look, for the rest of his life.

They were ready to raise the east-wall framework. It was heavy work, but Billy was built like a linebacker and Pete had strength out of proportion to his compact size. Compared to them, Zack was out of shape: carving wood was a lot less rugged work than building a house from it. Huffing from the effort, he supported his end of the wall while Pete braced it.

"No point in starting the next one this late; we'll knock off for the day," Pete announced after the wall was secure. Zack remembered how his own men used to love to hear those words when he had been the boss. Now that he was the help, he felt—irony of ironies—bitterly disappointed. All it had taken was that one exchange of stares. It had convinced Zack to stick with the job, stick with the plan.

Pete took off to check progress at the other site, leaving Billy and Zack to clean up for the day. The younger man swept while Zack coiled the air hose and the electric cords. They covered the table saw, then climbed down the ladder to store the portable gear in the basement. Pete had a thing about keeping a site clean, Billy explained, which earned him a nod of approval from Zack. It was demoralizing to work in chaos, whether the help understood that or not.

Laden with coils of air hose and cords, Billy led Zack across the torn-up yard, through a small mud shed, and into the basement, with Zack carrying the compressor behind him.

The new part of the basement had been commandeered as a storage area for the construction crew. New windows, still in their crates, were stacked against the wall six deep. The lady really liked windows, though Zack couldn't understand why: all the views were of neighbors' houses. She must have been after the sunshine.

Why not in the country? he wondered. *Or on the shore?*

He was struck all over again by the strangeness of the Ho-denes' decision to add on when they could so easily buy bigger. It was a puzzle that Zack considered important to solve.

"Hey. Later," said Billy when they were done. He was ready to fly.

Zack wasn't. Zack wanted to bump into the owner. Zack wanted to see phase two of the look of shock on the owner's face.

He tried to stall by saying pleasantly, "So how long you been workin' for Pete?"

"Coupla years," Billy said. He looked unhappy that Zack was detaining him by even so much as two words.

"What's he like?"

"Good," he said, glancing at the mudshed door. "Good guy."

"Overcommitted?"

Billy shrugged. "He can't seem to say no. Well—gotta go."

"Sure."

He bolted, and a few seconds later, Zack heard rubber peeling on the street in front of the house. He smiled: all young crews, all over the country, ran like hell at the end of the workday.

He had been young and in a hurry once, but that was a long time ago. He looked around the basement and decided that, by golly, the place probably hadn't had a thorough sweep in a good long time. Humming a languid tune, he took up a broom and got to work. All the while, he kept his ears cocked for the sound of footsteps on the basement stairs.

A few minutes later, he heard someone descending. The steps were too slow to be a kid's, too heavy to be a woman's. Zack sucked in a lungful of air and let it out as a whistled tune; it was one way of controlling the pound of his pulse.

"Still here?" came the voice behind him.

Ripped by contradictory emotions, Zack turned around slowly. "You bet," he said, returning the steady look with one of his own. "I want to make an impression."

"Oh, you're doing that, all right."

"That's the whole idea," Zack drawled. He stood there holding his broom, looking as benign as a farmer with a hoe in Kansas. Only his eyes, blazing with contempt, were at odds with his manner.

His brother-in-law blinked, then looked past him at the stacked-up windows, as if he were counting to make sure they were all still there. He snorted, God only knew why, and said to Zack, "Pete mentioned that he'd been looking for more help."

"He found it."

"So I see. He tells me you're new to the area. Where you from?"

"Up north," Zack said dryly.

"Canada?"

Very funny. "Worcester area. We moved there after Summerville."

"We?"

You son of a bitch. "Zina and I."

"I'm sorry? Zina is . . . ?"

"Ah, Jesus!" Despite his resolve and knowing he was being goaded, Zack still ended up lunging at him, catching a handful of shirt in his fist as he said with pent-up fury, "Zina: my *sister.* Innocent. Naïve. Trusting. Betrayed. And. Still. *Waiting.*" With a shudder of loathing, he shook the fabric out of his hand as if he'd grabbed someone's entrails by mistake, and said, "Get the picture, asshole?"

Jimmy let his shoulders slump back to normal, gave his neatly pressed shirt a little yank at belt level, and kept on looking baffled. Obviously choosing his words carefully, he said, "You seem to have a lot of concern for your sister. Maybe you shouldn't be working down here in Providence. I used to be in real estate. I know for a fact that there's a boom going on in your neck of Massachusetts. Maybe you should be looking for work closer to home. Maybe that would be the best thing for your sister."

"Yeah, right," Zack said, infuriated that Jimmy was continuing the pretense of being Jim. "You asshole," he repeated, kicking the broom over to the side and out of his way. He was aching to inflict some kind of physical punishment; the broom for now would have to do.

Instantly he realized that he shouldn't have kicked the broom. He could see that Jimmy was heartened by the act; that he understood that Zack wasn't going to beat him bloody if Zack could avoid it.

Hell! He shouldn't have kicked the broom.

He tried to recover. "Get this straight. I'm not going—"

A car door slammed and Jimmy jerked his head; it obviously was a car door he knew. He said hurriedly, "The best advice I can give you is to go back to your family, to your sister."

"Oh, I will. Eventually."

"The sooner the better. For her, I mean. Look, give me your number. Maybe I can give you some help, pull some strings, do something for you."

"I'm open to suggestions . . . Jimmy."

It was a body blow, and Jimmy buckled under it. "Sorry, you must have got that wrong," he insisted. "It's Jim."

"Sure . . . Jim. Whatever you say, Jim."

A woman's voice called out above them. "Jim? Wendy? Anybody home?"

Family or a close friend, without a doubt. Either way, the lady upstairs had Jimmy Hayward running scared. He said in a low hiss, "Christ, will you just get *out* of here?" He just about stamped his foot.

Aware that he'd regained the momentum, Zack smiled and said, "Sure, Jim. See you tomorrow. Jimmy."

CHAPTER 7

"You've talked to him, yes?"

Zack swallowed hard and lied. "No, Zee, I haven't. I'm going to need more time."

"More time! Zack, *why*?" She sounded as if she'd been trapped underwater; he could hear her gasping for air.

"Because he's gone," Zack explained, piling it on. "I saw him load a carry-on bag into his car. I assume he was on his way to the airport." In a lame attempt to keep it light, he added, "Who knows? Maybe he's off pricing villas in Europe."

His sister's voice came back little more than a heartbroken whisper. "This is so disappointing."

"It's frustrating, Zee, I know."

"It's beyond that. Zack . . . I think about Jimmy constantly. I can't eat, I can't sleep. It's worse now than it was that day I came home and saw that his clothes were gone. At least then I went straight into shock. At least then there was *that* blessing. And I had to eat, to sleep, for the baby's sake." She let out a single, sad sigh. "So there was that."

And now there wasn't.

As far as Zack could tell, he had two choices. One, he could tell his sister the truth, that the bastard who married but never bothered to divorce her was now rich, re-wed, and a father—and risk the consequences. Or, two, he could stall until he was able to squeeze Jimmy for enough money to enable Zina to move far away to a happier place.

Zack pictured his sister in sunny California, running her own program for abandoned critters. There was a kind of gentle poetry in the notion of the abandoned caring for the abandoned. He clung to that vision, because the image of a happy-at-last Zina was profoundly, incredibly moving to him.

So, yeah, damn right he was going to stall. He would tell tender lies at this end, and he'd slash and burn at the other end—whatever it took to make the world a better place for a fragile, utterly compassionate child-woman who deserved better than the stinking luck she'd been handed so far.

Zina seemed to misinterpret his thoughtful silence. "I'm sure it's him," she murmured. "You were sure, too, Zack."

"I only saw him from down the street, Zee," her brother said gently.

"No, you really did sound sure. You were trying *not* to—but I could tell. You were sure."

Helpless to undo the impression, Zack decided instead to change the subject. "Anyway, so what's the deal with your latest foster cat? The skunk—what was her name? Miss Petunia?"

"Don't be so mean," Zina said, laughing. "Her name is Cassie, and she's really coming along. I think in a couple of weeks we'll be able to see about getting her adopted. She likes potato chips and frosted doughnuts; isn't that wild?"

"There's your ad, then: 'Junk-Food Lover seeks Like-minded Companion.' "

And on that lighthearted note, they hung up.

Over the droning of her electric toothbrush, Wendy heard a truck pull up on the street.

"Oh, nutch," she garbled to her husband as she peeked

through the shutters. "I yunt mow da Taurush. Udja dowa hor me, hweesh?"

"What? Oh. The Taurus. Yeah, okay," Jim said. He was threading his belt through his pant loops, looking totally preoccupied.

She glanced at him curiously. "You all right?" she asked between rinsing spits. "You've been out of it since yesterday." Letting the toothbrush run under a stream of water, she added only half in jest, "You haven't bought another ten thousand dollars' worth of Powerball tickets, have you? Because I have more than enough now to decoupage Tyler's room, in case you're wondering."

He threw her a wry look and peered over the shutters at the street below. "Oh, Christ," he muttered.

"What's wrong?"

"Nothing. I'll go move the cars."

He sounded tense and disgusted, and Wendy could see why. Every day it was the same old thing: rushing to get the household up and running by seven-thirty, getting in each other's way in the process. Tyler hated the disruption, and Jim, though he was gone most of the day, wasn't any better. Wendy had long ago figured out that males disliked changes in their domestic routines simply because they disliked domesticity: changes made them have to focus too much on a subject that bored them.

She sighed as she ran a comb through her wet hair, then poked it haphazardly into shape. It was scary to imagine what life was going to be like once the crew knocked down the kitchen wall between the old and the new parts, and construction dust could travel freely. Where would they run? Where would they hide?

"Damn it, we *will* have to move out," she muttered on her way downstairs. She could see the writing on the wall.

It was another warm day, like the one before but without the clouds. Wendy threw the front room windows all the way up and breathed in deeply, happy simply to be inhaling June. It was far and away her favorite time of year; nothing else came close. By July it could get unbearable on the Point, despite the fact that they were only a block from the water. (October was another fine month, but it came on the wrong side of summer and it could be mean, ushering in the first cold blasts from Canada.)

Nope. Give her June. Anytime.

Lingering at the open window, she watched her husband park the Excursion on the street in front of her Taurus as Zack pulled into the vacated drive. The new Excursion's days were numbered; since she didn't want it, Jim had decided to trade it in for something smaller and sportier for himself. A BMW had caught his eye.

She continued to watch as Jim walked toward Zack's truck. Her husband looked annoyed. Maybe Zack hadn't pulled up far enough—in which case, one of the crew was going to end up hanging over the sidewalk, and Mrs. Almeida wasn't going to be able to get past it with her shopping cart, and the elderly widow would mention the fact to Wendy's mother, who immediately would pass it on to Wendy.

Men.

Vaguely unhappy with the lot of them, Wendy turned away from her bright spring day and, listening to make sure that Tyler was done with his shower, began to round up the dirty laundry for a wash.

She found her son rummaging through the chest of drawers in his room and looking exasperated.

"What'd you lose?"

"My book report on Harry Potter."

"Why would it be with your socks?" Wendy asked, dumping the laundry basket on his bed. She began to wade through the mound of papers, magazines, and CDs on the small student's desk that was jammed between his narrow bed and the wall, but she had little hope. It would've been easier to find a contact lens in the ocean.

"When did you see it last?"

"I dunno. Last week, I think. I was almost finished; all I needed was to quote three lines of good description, and I couldn't make up my mind," he said, as if that explained the disappearance.

"When is it due? Stupid question; never mind," Wendy said, lifting the dark blue bedskirt and looking under the bed. "God, you're going to be late for school again. Tyler, why do you always do this? You know? You did so well, writing the report while the book was fresh in your mind—and now you go and blow it." She reached back toward the wall and pulled out a dirty shirt covered in dust bunnies. "If you're not forgetting one thing, you're losing another. How many backpacks have I bought this year? Three? If you would just try to get a little organized—"

"*Ma!*" Her son slammed the drawer hard enough to topple the lamp on the dresser; the ceramic baseball batter ended up hanging over the side with his bat pointed at the floor, his red shade askew.

Wendy sat back on her calves and said, "What was *that* all about?"

Wide-set green eyes burned with startling fury at her. "If I didn't live in this crummy hole, maybe I could find my book reports once in a while. Maybe I'd even have someplace to put them!"

"*Excuse* me? You have a room all to yourself. You have a desk! When *I* was growing up here—"

"Yeah, yeah, I already know about the bunk beds and the cardboard drawers under them. So *what*? Just because you and everyone lived like jailbirds, why should I have to? All the kids are *laughing* at me," he said, his jaw trembling. "They think we're so uncool, staying here. We could afford to buy some neat place, with electronic gates and stuff! But no-o-o, we hafta stay here because you were born here. What a *stupid*, dumb reason! I hate living here!"

It was the most he'd said at one time in weeks. Wendy was flabbergasted at the depth of his emotion. He had seemed so easy with everything that was going on, floating above it like a cork on a stormy sea. He'd certainly been happy before the windfall; why shouldn't he be happy after it?

Because he wasn't living up to his classmates' expectations of him. In a blinding flash, Wendy understood. His friends wouldn't think it was cool that he was still living an ordinary life just like them; they would despise him for it.

"Oh, honey, I didn't realize it bothered you so much." She stood up and tossed the retrieved shirt into the basket. "If that's the case, we'll move out—"

"For good?" he asked stiffly.

"For now. Tyler, you were born here," she said in a coaxing tone. "All of your family and friends live on the street or around the corner. You have a good life, a happy life, here. Why do you want to change?"

"Because we *are* changed," he said, with not so much as a hint of a sneer. He simply looked amazed that she didn't get it. "We have over ten million dollars now," he explained, almost in a kindly tone.

"No we don't. Not even close. Stop exaggerating. And even a millionaire should like this place."

It was pointless to explain that the house was a block away from one of the most historic, beautiful streets in New England, or that by the time he was grown up, gentrification of their little corner, for better or for worse, would be complete and they'd be yet another pearl on the necklace of Providence's exquisite east side. Tyler didn't care about pearls or historic. He cared about his friends, and his friends valued new. Or at least big. Big and new, preferably.

Aware that her value system was swaying like a battered dock in a vicious storm, Wendy struggled to reach safer ground. "We'll talk about this later. Now you have to get going or you'll be late."

He moped his way down the stairs with Wendy trying not to whack him over the head from behind with her basket of laundry.

"Listen to me!" she wanted to scream. "Bigger isn't better! It's a myth. It's an American con!"

But Tyler was ten and he wasn't done growing yet. The concept of big was bound to look pretty darn good to him.

Her son split off for the kitchen and Wendy continued on to the basement, the only conceivable place in which to tuck a washer and dryer. The house of Tyler's dreams undoubtedly had a laundry nook on the upstairs landing; he could slam-dunk his muddy sweats on the way down to breakfast.

What's wrong with me? she wondered, not for the first time recently. Why don't I crave all these treats?

At the foot of the stairs she wasn't surprised to see that one of the crew had gotten to the basement before her. Zack was at the soapstone sink, filling a water bottle for himself. He glanced over his shoulder at her approach and gave her an uncharacteristically sheepish look, considering that he'd been brief to the point of rudeness when she ran into him at the Hurry Curry the day before.

"Sorry to be in your way," he said, noting her load. "I forgot to pick up some bottled water on the way over."

"Oh, that's all right. I keep a pitcher of water in the refrigerator, by the way. Would you rather have that?"

"Nah, thanks anyway. It's sunny."

"It's—Oh. Right. So your water wouldn't stay cold. I could put ice in a glass for you," she volunteered, to show that she didn't hold a grudge.

"This is fine. Really."

"Are you sure?" she asked. "Because it's no trouble."

"No, thank you," he said with a hint of a smile. "Really. Truly."

She felt her cheeks warm, as they always did when she watched herself behaving like an idiot. "Can you tell that I want all the crew to be happy?"

"I'll do good work for you," he said as he capped his bottle. "Happy or unhappy."

"No, that's not what I—" But of course it was what she meant. But he didn't have to point it out! God, he was prickly.

Confused and distressed by his manner, she turned to sorting her coloreds from her whites, thinking that it would be best, after all, if she and the family were living somewhere else for now. Being forced into everyday intimacies with complete strangers really was awkward. At best. There could be an ax murderer among them; who would know?

Apparently he had something further to say.

"Mrs.—"

"Please. It's just Wendy," she said as she flipped dark clothing over her shoulder into the machine.

"You missed a sock. It went behind the machine," he told her. He added in a more musing voice, "You know, once they make it to the back of the machine, they're practically home free. After that it's just a short sprint to—"

"That other world. I know," she said, responding instantly to the smile in his voice. She stood up and peered over the machine, then said, "Life must be good, wherever they go. We've had dozens of socks make a break for it over the years. And why not? No smelly feet to put up with; no wear and tear on the heels. No danger of being shrunk if you're wool, or bleached if you're gray. Wouldn't you get out if you could?"

He laughed—a surprised laugh, she thought—and said,

"Sockland. It sounds like a nice place to visit. Not sure I'd want to live there, though."

He looked directly at her long enough for her to notice that he had absolutely beautiful blue eyes, and then he said abruptly, "Yeah, daylight's burnin'. Better get hammerin'."

He all but doffed an imaginary cap to her before he turned on his heel and walked out, lugging his air compressor and his bottle of water.

Bemused, Wendy took down a wood yardstick from Jim's pegboard and began fishing out the sock from the dark and cobwebby gap behind the machine. *A nice guy,* she decided. *Probably not an ax murderer at all; just socially inept.*

Over the noise of the filling machine, she heard the phone ringing and began a dash up the stairs to answer it, but her husband got there ahead of her.

"Hello," he answered in that flat, guarded tone he'd adopted since the lottery. He listened for a few seconds and then said, "Look, we're not interested, okay? We're not interested." He hung up on someone who Wendy could hear was still in mid-sentence. "Who turned off the answering machine again?" he asked as she came near.

"I unplugged it for a minute and forgot to reset it," Wendy explained, then added, "You know, maybe you should let me answer the phone from now on."

"The hell I will," Jim snapped. "You couldn't hang up on the devil himself if he called direct."

"Whoa, whoa, whoa—you'd better go back to bed and try getting up on the other side, mister," she warned him. "What's the matter with you today?"

"We need to get a new goddamn number. We may as well have this one plastered across a billboard in Times Square." He glanced at the door to the basement. "What're they, just hanging around and shooting the shit down there? I heard you going on and on with one of them just now."

"Yes—Zack. But hardly on and on," Wendy answered, wondering at Jim's tone. He sounded almost jealous. She glanced at her son, still at the kitchen table. "Tyler, close the book and finish your breakfast. You said you were done with your homework."

"I am," he said without looking up. "I'm reading ahead."

"Close it. Eat. Go."

With a melodramatic sigh the boy—an avid reader practically since birth—did as he was told and began shoveling his cereal as fast as his mouth would open and close, without necessarily swallowing.

Wendy turned back to her husband and said, "What *is* bothering you today?" She was afraid that he'd done something wildly impulsive again, something so reckless that even he was afraid to own up to it. She waited to hear the worst.

He looked ready to tell her exactly that, she realized with a surge of panic: his face twisted into an expression of sheer agony. But almost immediately he made an impatient, dismissive gesture and said angrily, "Where are we supposed to talk in this fishbowl? Exactly where?"

She didn't know. There were men outside the kitchen windows downstairs, men outside the bedroom window upstairs. That left the bathroom, not exactly the place to confess and then argue afterward.

God, what *had* he done? Bought a football team somewhere?

Feeling vaguely as if they were trying to sneak around in an illicit tryst, Wendy said, "After Tyler gets off to school, why don't we take a thermos of coffee and walk down to the park?"

The park was a pocket-sized patch of green a couple of blocks from their house, with benches that overlooked the bay. It would be quiet there, and private enough to hash out their opposite views about money—because Wendy had no doubt that this was going to have something to do with money.

Jim looked doubtful about her suggestion, so she took his wrist and said with a cajoling tug, "C'mon . . . when's the last time you walked down there with me?"

He shook his head, then wrapped his other hand around her wrist and gently removed it from his own. "I won't do it, Wen. I'm entitled to have a conversation with you in my own home—in private."

Tyler muttered into his empty bowl, "Well, excuse me for living."

"Button it up, Ty!" he said sharply to their son. He turned back to Wendy and said, "We've got to move out of this house; the sooner the better. I've had all of this I'm going to take. If you want to do something together this morning, then let's go looking for a place to rent until they're done. You can see it's going to take a year and a day at the rate they're going. I'm sick of coming home to this. I'm sick of living in a fishbowl," he repeated.

Somehow, Jim had seized the advantage. If she wanted to know what was on his mind, she was going to have to let him have the house he craved. It was as simple as that. She took comfort in the fact that whatever seemed to be bothering him, it wasn't so urgent that he felt impelled to spill his guts that minute. Maybe it really *was* the mess and disruption that had him in such a foul mood.

Wendy sighed and said, "All right. You win. I give up. We'll try to find another place—but somewhere near."

"Yes!" said their son, raising his skinny arms in a victory clench.

But Jim said, "I don't see why it has to be around the corner. That limits us."

"I want to stay close," she argued. "I've been worried about my father lately, and I want to be able to dash over here if there's a decision to be made, and Ty should be near his cousins . . . and then there's school. We'll probably be living in whatever we rent right through next fall; staying on the east side would be the least disruptive."

Tyler had grabbed a towel and was swinging it over his head and whisper-yelling, "Woo-woo-woo."

It annoyed Wendy a vast amount that no one wanted to live in her house. "If I'm not mistaken, Ty," she said in a deadly voice, "you have exactly six minutes and forty-three seconds to get to school. And I'm not driving you there. Do the math, my son."

CHAPTER 8

The rent was scandalous, but the view was sublime: a white, sandy beach rolling into the sparkling waters of Narragansett Bay and the ocean beyond. Wendy, a Rhode Islander born and bred, had always been at home on a beach, but she never thought she would actually be at *home* on a beach; the concept still boggled her mind. She gazed through the huge multipaned bay window in the master bedroom at a small sailing dinghy that was pulled onto the backyard beach. The sail was raised and flopping back and forth casually in the breeze. It looked like a prop.

"Does the little sailboat come with?" she asked the realtor, curious.

"Of course," said the agent. Her smile could easily be construed as condescending. "Everything that you see is included in the rental—including the geraniums in the window box."

There were at least a dozen of them, all a no-nonsense pink and as big as softballs, lolling with gaudy confidence in the dark green planter that lined the bay window of the gray-shingled house. Who had watered them? For that matter, who had hoisted that cheery red-and-white sail on the dinghy? Who had cut the grass and dusted all of the charming antiques that surrounded them?

It couldn't have been the owners; they were currently living in Switzerland. So there had to be a staff, or a service. Were the dusters and the waterers included in the rent? Wendy couldn't figure out a graceful way to ask. It all felt so unreal. She could have been perusing the featured home in an upscale shelter magazine. Her! Jim! What would they do with all that room? She felt as overwhelmed as she was enchanted by the rambling six-bedroom, five-bath expanded Cape.

Jim, on the other hand, was clearly in his element. Poised at a side window where he'd been taking in the view, he said with droll urbanity, "The best part about it is that you can sneeze without having a neighbor say God bless you."

The realtor, a gray-haired woman with big earrings, responded instantly to his tone. With a confidential smile, she said, "Yes, living in Providence, no matter how good the neighborhood, is bound to feel cramped compared to this."

The house was smack in the middle of Barrington's mile-long gold coast, just northeast of the country club and the Carmelite monastery and tucked among lanes with carefully obvious names like Bay and Water and Beach.

Oh, yes; Jim was in his element, all right. He came and stood alongside her in silence, letting the view work its magic.

They had looked at two houses on Providence's east side, both of them sophisticated, historic homes less than a mile from their house but with a must-vacate date etched in stone. In contrast, the house they were standing in had come on the market less than an hour before they had shown up at the realtor's office, and its date of vacancy was open-ended. Barrington was just minutes from Providence: a small price to pay, the realtor told them as she bundled them into her Mercedes, for a private beach.

"I've seen plenty of beaches in my life; why does this one look so much more spectacular?" she mused.

It was the realtor who answered her. "Because *this* view,

you would own," she said. "At least for the length of the lease."

Did Jim agree with that theory? Wendy wasn't sure he'd even heard it. He looked a million miles away—lost, she assumed, in the shimmering blues of the bay.

Wendy felt guilty for even considering renting the house; they'd done nothing, absolutely nothing, to earn something so special. And yet . . .

"Jim . . . ?"

He had to shake himself free of his thoughts before he said almost wearily, "If you insist on living close to the house during construction, this is probably a fairly good place to do it."

"Oh, but the *rent*," she blurted. She scarcely brought home in a year what the owners were charging a month.

He hated it when she sounded as if they were out of their league. It embarrassed him, and the flush in his face told her that this time was no exception.

He said coolly, "Would you rather just buy a house outright?"

Because we can do that, you know, said the expression on his face.

He did look like someone who could. He was beautifully dressed; he carried himself well; he spoke the language of real estate. Wendy looked at him—really, for the first time—the way someone like the realtor would. Suddenly it hit her: Jim had grown into his wealth. She, on the other hand, was still wearing it self-consciously, like an ill-fitting dress.

In the meantime, the realtor's pleasant smile had become even more fiercely pleasant. She spoke not so much to Wendy as to Jim, in a lower, more confidential voice than she had used up until then.

"You know, I shouldn't be saying this, but there's some question whether the owner will be returning from Swit-

zerland anytime soon—or at all. In our phone call, he did
talk about the possibility of . . . well. You can fill in the
blank," she said, including Wendy in a glance that also took
in the view. "This really is an exceptional property, and it's
in fabulous condition. If you like, I can make an inquiry."

Jim said easily, "That's probably premature. First we
ought to see whether my wife approves of it even on a
rental basis." He turned to Wendy. "Well, Wen? What to
you think? Could you stand to hang your hat here while
you oversee the restoration of your family's little homestead?"

He phrased it so elegantly that for a second she wasn't
sure what homestead he was talking about. More to the
point, his question didn't seem to leave room for a no.

"Well . . . it really is a beautiful house," she said, trying
to get past her reservations and be on the same side that he
was.

"One of the best that you'll find," the realtor assured
them.

"Would *all* of the furnishings stay?" Wendy asked her,
because she couldn't believe that people who owned such
exquisite things would let strangers use them.

Jim said dryly, "Here we are: one couple and a ten-year-
old child. Yes, Wendy, I imagine that will call for triple
the stipulated damage deposit."

The realtor laughed pleasantly, and they moved on, but
not before Jim shot his wife an angry and embarrassed look.

The tour ended in the last of the guest rooms, this one
in the absolutely charming dormered attic. It featured pretty
florals, white wicker, and a hand-painted armoire that made
Wendy want to try that much harder to persuade Jim to
make another baby, this one a girl. Odd, how something as
simple as wallpaper could cause such a pang of longing for
a bigger family. Jim had always argued that they didn't

have enough room for more kids. Now he argued that they were too distracted to have more kids.

And meanwhile, her clock was ticking.

"Great place for Ty's cousins to sleep over," Jim remarked, ducking under an eave to check out the view through one of the deep dormered windows.

Emmy and Trish! He was right; it *was* a great place for little girls—anyone's little girls—to sleep over. One offhand remark by her husband, and Wendy felt the floodgates open and a wave of longing rush over her. Suddenly she didn't care if it cost three times the quote, she wanted to rent the house.

It was perfect. There would be bedrooms for visiting family, and small sitting rooms for quiet moments, and a library, and a den, and twin parlors, and a beach—an actual beach!—from which to launch a boat or go for a swim; and all of the rooms and everything in them would be hers, at least for a few months while she played at being a woman of sophistication and privilege and with lots of kids of her own. It would be like a trip to Disney World, a fantasy flight from dust and debris.

And after that, she would return, a satisfied Cinderella, to her own sweet, remodeled home to live happily ever after—hopefully with a larger family than she presently had.

She walked up to the gabled dormer where Jim was still standing and paused for a moment to take in the bright blue sky and the dancing, shimmering waves.

"Yes," she said softly to him alone. "I definitely think we should take it."

In a pocket-sized park on Congdon Street, Zack sat on a bench and watched the sun set over the massive capitol dome in downtown Providence. The capitol was a ridiculously impressive piece of architecture for such a tiny state, testimony to a time when civic-minded men built for the ages and not just for function. The imposing structure radiated high ideals, lofty morals, and above all, an abiding dignity.

All qualities that Zack presently had in short supply. He was filled with self-loathing just then. There was something about the view—something about the majesty of the sky, settling its blue and gold mantle over the majesty of the capitol—that made him feel small and mean and coldly vengeful.

What right had he to go charging into innocent lives and upending them? As near as he could tell, Wendy Hodene was a woman of character. All anyone had to do was look at her face: she looked you straight in the eye, she had a warm, ready smile, and she treated everyone with the same courtesy. That was all Zack needed to know about anyone, man or woman, to judge that person's worth. She had worth.

And her son. Tyler. He seemed to be a likable enough kid, always with his nose in a book. Did he really need to know that his father was a bigamist and that he himself was a bastard? How did you recover from something like that? Some kids weren't very resilient. Look at Zina after their parents died; she had refused to come out of her shell for a year. Twenty-six years later, she still wasn't all the way right.

It all came down to this: Zina loved Jimmy Hayward, but Jim Hodene was never going to love her back. The only way out of the impasse was to find Zina someone else to love, and if the someone else happened to be cats and dogs, then so be it. Love was love.

Ah, but why Wendy, why do this to *her*? Zack pictured her on her way to work, doing laundry, nagging her kid. This was a real, honest-to-God, flesh-and-bones woman he was sticking it to, not some faceless CEO of a corporation. That made it hard.

He thought of their little exchange in the basement, and his mouth inched up in a wistful smile. Wendy Hodene . . . keeper of the socks.

He wondered, in his new and melancholy mood, what would be coming next. The initial confrontation with Jim in the basement may have ended abruptly, but that morning Jim had gruffly demanded Zack's phone number, and Zack had obliged. Not long after that, Jim had taken off with Wendy; they hadn't returned by quitting time. In short, Zack was batting zip-nada so far, which had to be a factor in his faltering resolve.

It occurred to him that Jim might just whisk his family into hiding until Zack became bored and left. If so, Zack had only himself to blame. He had tipped his hand by announcing right up front that he was determined to protect his sister from further hurt. Boy. Some blackmailer *he* was.

He sighed. It was a beautiful, heartbreaking sunset. And utterly wasted on him.

The phone in his pocket rang. In theory it could have been Jim; but Zack was dead certain that it wasn't—so dead certain that he took out the tiny thing, flipped open the top, and said, "Hi, Zee."

Startled by his greeting, she said, "Oh-h-h, I'm being a pest, aren't I?"

"Not at all."

"You haven't spoken to him, or you would have called," she said with a sigh.

"Right," he said, lying merrily away. "I was just about to pick up the phone and tell you that. I'm hoping I have news for you tomorrow or shortly after."

"But . . . why are you staying in Providence, if he isn't there? Isn't that a waste of money?"

"Nah. I found a bed-and-breakfast that suits me." In fact,

it was a third-floor rathole in a huge Victorian that had been split into half a dozen apartments, most of them housing students from Brown and the Rhode Island School of Design. The rent went by the week, and an extra bonus was that he could walk to the little park he was at and breathe air that didn't reek of pot and smelly sneakers.

"Besides, I've managed to nail down a commission," he said, adding another link to the chain of his lies. "A lady on the east side wants me to repair a set of busted Chippendale chairs that she picked up for a song—well, what *she* calls a song."

Zina sounded relieved. "Oh, good! I'm glad you're going to be making some money out of this, at least."

"Hand over fist," Zack said with a reasonably straight face. He hesitated, then added, "So how're you holding up, Zee? I know this is hard on you, the waiting."

"Yes, but everyone's sick who should be working at the shelter, so I've been there every spare minute. I even took the afternoon off from the quilt shop to cover for someone—although I can't do that too many times, or, yikes, I won't be paying my rent."

That will not be a problem, Zack insisted to himself.

He said, "How's the skunk?"

Zina laughed and said, "Cassie's fine and she says hello. I'm becoming *so* attached to her; I'd like to adopt her myself, except that I promised my landlady I wouldn't start doing that—bringing cats home and keeping them, I mean. I think Margie's afraid that I'll end up old and gray with forty-two cats."

"You're not old," Zack said gallantly. "And you're not gray."

"But I would like forty-two cats."

"All right, then, Zee; I'll see what I can do to make your wish come true."

"Honestly, Zack. Where would I put forty-two cats?"

*   *   *

The move by Wendy and Jim from the half-demolished house on Sheldon Street into the wonderful house on the beach took place over the weekend. They weren't moving enough of their things to justify calling in professional movers, so Wendy had her husband buy some boxes and wardrobes from U-Haul, and they did the job themselves. They packed their clothes, their music, some books, and their favorite pillows; more than that seemed pointless. Besides, Wendy didn't want their stuff to feel bad that other people's stuff was so much better than it was.

Jim refused to rent a U-Haul truck—too low-rent—and instead used the SUV to run a shuttle back and forth between their house and the beach house while Wendy packed and Tyler pretended to pack. The neighbors nodded knowingly when Wendy told them of the temporary move; clearly they didn't expect to see the Hodenes living again on Sheldon Street.

"Which is *not* true," she told Jim as they wolfed down pizza in the dust-filled kitchen of their house between runs. "As long as Tyler has so many friends and family here, why would I want to move? How many kids get to enjoy the experience of growing up in a traditional way in their ancestors' home nowadays? Almost none."

"We'll see," Jim said noncommittally between huge chomps of pizza.

He was hungry and he was in a hurry. Wendy knew that he had been working like a fiend all day because he was absolutely determined to sleep in the new house that night. Tyler was all for it, too, and even Wendy was excited about living in another house after having spent most of her thirty-four years on Sheldon Street.

"It'll seem odd not to wake up looking at the Almeidas' roof," she mused. "We've done it for eight years. I remember at the time thinking, what if we can't keep up with the payments? What if we end up on the street? I was so scared. And now look."

She finished her last slice of pizza and began folding up the box. "Jim?"

"Hm?" he answered, swigging down the last of his beer.

"What was it you wanted to tell me the other day?"

She hated asking the question; but the question had to be asked. A wife didn't forget an expression on her husband's face like the one Wendy had seen. A look like that clung to a woman's subconscious like a burr on a sweater.

The blank look on Jim's face made her give him a extra nudge. "Wasn't that the point of finding a house to live in—so we could talk in private?"

Damn it, she thought with dismay. *You really are hiding something. You're going to ruin this for us, aren't you?*

"Whatever it was, it's gone," he said with a shrug. "It couldn't have been too important." Going on the offensive as he liked to do, he added in a testier tone, "Besides, we're still in this fishbowl of a house at the moment, even if I could remember."

"It's Sunday, Jim; the contractors aren't here."

"Tyler is."

"Tyler lives here!"

"He's getting older, more observant," Jim countered. "It's harder to talk—or do—anything in private around him now."

At that point, she wasn't certain whether Jim was dragging the conversation around again to the need to buy a mansion, or whether he was simply trying to change the subject, period. In any case, Tyler came clomping down the stairs at that moment, so Wendy let the matter drop. But the burr clung to her sleeve; she could feel its prick, and it was upsetting for her not to be able to clear it away.

The doorbell rang at the same time as the phone. Tyler had reached the foot of the stairs and got the door, so

Wendy automatically picked up the phone, much to her husband's dismay.

"The machine, the *machine*!" he said in a hiss.

"Hello?" she answered, wincing in apology at him. Too late now.

No one responded, though Wendy definitely could hear something in the background. Voices, sporadically. A television? Wendy frowned in concentration, trying to make out what was being said. She thought that maybe she heard a cry . . . or a groan. Something.

"Damn it, Wendy!" her husband said, and he depressed the plunger on the phone.

Stunned, Wendy said, "What'd you do *that* for?"

"I told you: I want the machine answering."

"Why? What're you trying to hide?" she shot back.

He scowled and said, "I'm sick of the nuisance calls."

"Too bad! I can answer the phone in my own home—"

A voice from behind her said, "If you do, it'll be a first. I've been getting your machine for days now."

Wendy spun around to see her mother holding a box with a bow on it and looking reproachful. Gracie Ferro said, "So: you're just ignoring all your calls nowadays? Even from family?"

Turning her attention away from Jim to deal with their visitor, Wendy said patiently, "If you had begun to leave a message, Mom, obviously I would have picked up."

"You know I don't like talking to a machine."

"Aaaggh! Then how can I know you're calling?"

"You're saying I'm a nuisance?"

"You're—How did you get *there*?"

The phone rang again. With a defiant glance at her husband, Wendy snatched it back up and snapped out a hello. When no one responded again, she barked, "Listen, what the hell do you want? If you have something to say, then just say it!"

No response. She hung up on the sound of a low, languid voice somewhere in the background. "*Damn* it!"

Her mother gave her a baleful look and said, "Someone seems to have her nightie in a twist."

Tyler, nose in the refrigerator, snickered from behind the door. Wendy told him to go straight back to his room and bring down his pizza plate, because just because they were moving—*temporarily!*—it didn't mean that he could leave the place a pigsty.

Her son stomped off, muttering, "Everyone takes everything out on *me*."

Which everyone more or less did. Wendy had to do a mental backflip to put herself in a better frame of mind: they were about to move into a big new playhouse, and at the moment she wasn't feeling the least bit playful. So she took a deep breath, smiled at Jim, hugged her mother, accepted the box from her, and started over.

"Mom! How nice of you to stop by! What can I do you for?"

Her mother gave her a wry look and rubbed away a smudge on her cheek. "You can start by telling your brother that if he doesn't show up for my birthday party, he may as well leave the country."

Bad as her mood had been, Wendy had to laugh at the mere concept of any of them missing the Big Six-Five. "I will certainly pass on your message," she said, not at all solemnly. "Anything else?"

"Yes," said Grace, looking first at Jim and then at Wendy. "I'd like you to host my birthday party."

"*Really!*"

"I'll pay for the food and refreshments," her mother said instantly.

"No, that's not what I meant. I meant, I thought you wanted to have the party at your place. We all thought that. You told us that."

"I did. But. That was before the new couch arrived."

"We're not going to use it for a trampoline or anything," Wendy said wryly. "And Marjorie's pregnant and not drinking; she won't be spilling any wine this year."

"Ha, ha, dear. Very funny. As a matter of fact, the reason *is* the new couch. It makes the easy chairs look ratty. We have to replace them before anyone can come over."

"Mom, nobody *cares,* believe me. You're our parents."

"Excuse me? Does that mean I'm not allowed to have anything nice of my own? Only my rich children can have nice?"

"Okay, that came out wrong. Let me rephrase. We are getting together to celebrate the fact that you're healthy, happy, and—"

"A misery to you all," her mother said, slanting her head appraisingly.

"That, too."

"Stop it. Are you going to let me use your fancy new house, or not?"

"Mom . . . I would be overjoyed. Honest. I think it's a wonderful idea. Mark and Marianne will be able to sleep in a guest room instead of on someone's Hide-A-Bed. And Frank and Sharon and all the kids would fit there, too," she said, warming to the idea of an immediate houseful of company. "The kids will be able to play on the beach; it'll be great."

"I wonder," her mother said with a wry glance at Jim.

Jim took the bait. "Now, come on, Gracie," he countered. "You know that family is always welcome here."

"Yes; you're right about that. You've been very tolerant of us, for someone who has no family and isn't used to a mob. Especially considering what an earsplitting bunch we all are."

"Music to my ears, Grace," her son-in-law said with his most charming grin. "Okay, no more chitchat. I gotta get back to work or no one'll be sleeping anywhere."

He positioned himself in front of a cardboard wardrobe and, using straps, lifted it with a grunt onto his back. Wendy held the front door open for him and then ran ahead to open one of the doors on the Ford. Jim slid the heavy box into the cargo area and drove off.

Wendy went back inside and started to say something to her mother, then smacked her forehead. "Nuts! That was the wardrobe with *winter* clothes!"

She ran out on the porch to flag her husband, but it was too late; he had turned the corner. She turned to go back into the house, and that's when she saw Zack behind the wheel of his pickup, roaring down the street. Odd. Did he see her? She didn't think so. He was too hell-bent on getting somewhere.

He must have been using the street as a shortcut. She frowned. It was a weekend on a residential street where children played; Zack had no business driving like that.

CHAPTER 9

Surprise, surprise. The Hodenes apparently had decided to move out. As he drove slowly down one of a neighborhood of crisscrossing lanes, Zack caught a glimpse of his brother-in-law unloading a wardrobe box from his Explorer, parked in front of a house that was more his style than the one on Sheldon.

Funny. If Jim Hodene were going to hide, you'd think he'd run farther than to a bedroom community of Providence. Maybe all he was hiding from was the construction mess. Not that it mattered either way to Zack. After a quick trip back up to Hopeville to see his sister—and after coming to the conclusion that Zina was on the verge of a meltdown if he didn't have an answer for her soon—Zack had decided that today was going to be the day.

The fact that Jim was moving some stuff on his own was a lucky break for everyone: Jim, Zack, and—although she wasn't aware of it—Wendy Hodene.

Without thinking about what he was going to say, Zack pulled into the drive and walked up the steps to the front door of the expanded Cape. The builder in him was impressed by the house's well-executed façade, good use of stone, and elegant layout. The blackmailer in him was pleased by the rose-covered arch over the door, where he could threaten an occupant without being seen by the neighbors.

He rang the bell, waited, and then knocked hard, trying to control his rising sense of fury and loathing; he was ready to break down the door. When his brother-in-law finally did appear, it was all Zack could do not to flatten him on the spot.

Jim looked staggered to see him. "Inside, before someone sees you," he said quickly, leaving Zack room to pass.

Without a word, they walked into a sitting room furnished with Persian rugs and period antiques, some of them of museum quality. In one corner Zack spied a shield-back open armchair that he would have paid good money to touch and to study, but he allowed himself no more than a glance. He felt like a kid at a carnival who's been told, "Look but don't ride," and it made him despise Jim still more.

Zack got straight to the point. Legs astride, he said, "I don't have time to play games anymore. I don't care how you've managed to glom onto a new identity. Your name's Hayward, you shit, and you're still married to my sister—who has every right to claim half your winnings."

"Jesus Christ," Jim murmured. "So that's what it's going to be?" With grim courtesy, he added, "Sit down, please."

"I'll stand," Zack answered. He sized up his opponent—receding hairline, thickening waist, still good-looking, Zina would think—and waited to hear what he had to say.

Jim glanced around the room as if he'd left his notes on a table somewhere, then took a seat in the coveted shield-back chair. With knees apart, he began tapping a silent tune on the upholstered edge of the seat. "So. You're really going through with this ridiculous plot to squeeze me. You've got balls, man; I'll give you that."

Without bothering to respond, Zack folded his arms across his chest and waited for the weaseling to be over with.

"I'm not the guy you think I am, Zack. And you know it."

Zack allowed himself a blink of contempt.

"Nonetheless, you're an embarrassment to me. You know? I'm not cool with you hanging around my wife—"

"What wife?" Zack shot back. "Your marriage to Wendy's a fraud."

"My *wife,* and my son all day. I'm not cool with that at all."

"So call the cops."

"I'm considering it," Jim said, sounding judicial. "But of course, before I do it I'd like to know just what it is that you want from me in real dollars and cents. I know it's not half. You're not that stupid. But I'd like a number, anyway, for when I do file a report."

Zack snorted; his brother-in-law was a real piece of work. "Tell me this," he said. "Why did you run? You . . . what? Lost your way? Lost your key? Lost your mind? Tell me, asshole. I've been waiting twelve long years to hear the reason."

He felt his right hand ball into a fist as if it had a will of its own. Just one blow, he begged himself. That was all. Just one. He vowed to grant himself his wish if he didn't like what he heard next.

"You've got it all wrong," Jim said, rising in a huff from the chair. "I am not the man you're looking for."

At that, something in Zack snapped. He crossed the room in two strides and grabbed Jim by the throat. "You son of a bitch," he growled. "You *are* the man, and you'll pay."

Jim's eyes got wide, but he didn't struggle. It was all Zack could do not to squeeze the man's throat until his face turned a satisfying shade of blue.

"Zee's always been fragile, you know that," he said, his voice seething with pent-up fury. "Now she's a ghost.

Every day she dies another death, waiting for a dumb shit like you to come back. Do you get how *wrong* that is? Try to understand that for one lousy minute. Try to—"

He stopped himself. Why was he bothering? He wasn't there to explain. He was there for money. "Get out your checkbook," he said, shaking the other man free from his grip. "I don't have all day."

"Okay, look," Jim said, rubbing his throat. "I'll be straight with you. I . . . ah . . . have had some women in my life. I admit it. There have been some women, and it's nothing that I want getting back to Wendy. They were a long time ago; I'm done with all that. I don't want anyone who claims she used to know me showing up. So if it costs me something to get you the hell out of my life . . . okay, I might be willing to pay."

"Fine," said Zack, uninterested in the other man's rationale for coming up with the money. But Christ, the guy sounded *convincing*. It almost gave Zach pause. "Let's get this over with."

"How much do you want? *Seriously*."

"Seriously? Three hundred thousand, in one payment."

"A lump sum? No dice," Jim said angrily. "Wendy's bound to notice a payout like that!"

"Be creative. Or hire a professional to be creative for you," Zack snapped. "I don't care how you do it. Just do it."

Of course, Zack had absolutely no idea how *he* was going to get the money into Zina's hands, but that was tomorrow's problem.

Jim shook his head while he pondered his next move. Zack prayed that his brother-in-law wouldn't see the gaping hole in the case he had just presented on behalf of his sister.

Unfortunately, his prayer wasn't answered. After a moment, Jim said, "Your sister never tried to divorce this Hayward guy?"

"She's convinced he's coming back," Zack said dryly.

After another, longer moment, Jim's eyebrows twitched down. Zack could practically see the lightbulb turning on over his head.

"The money's your idea then, not hers," Jim said.

Shit. "Obviously."

"Your plan is to admit to her that I'm not Hayward."

"Unless you force my hand," said Zack, bluffing shamelessly.

Jim's shoulders squared up a little. "You know what? I don't see you doing that to her, Zack. I don't see you putting a sister you care about through any more agony. It's a paradox, isn't it? You're here because you want to protect her, and you could easily be sent packing because . . . you want to protect her."

"Try sending me packing," Zack growled. "And see what happens."

Jim's face assumed a thoughtful, pensive look: he was working the angles, as he always did. His brows came down as he chewed on his lip, the perfect picture of a banker trying to decide whether or not the applicant should get the loan.

"Here's what I can do," he said at last. "I can give you a hundred thousand by the end of the week. The rest, within a month. I just can't do better than that. I've got a wife and a son to think about."

He did have a family, legitimate or not; even Zack saw that. A great wife and a good kid. Zack could well understand why a man, even a slimebag like Jim, wouldn't want to endanger that.

"Just give me the money," he agreed, almost wearily. "I want the first hundred thousand in ten separate cashiers' checks, ten grand each. I'll stay on the job on Sheldon Street for the next couple of weeks, just in case you get any funny ideas about the balance."

Jim didn't like that plan at all. His brows came down again, this time in a scowl. "No deal. You'll get the rest of the money. I give you my word."

"Yeah, right, your word," Zack said without bothering to hide his contempt. "As I said: I'll stay on the job."

There didn't seem to be much else to negotiate, so Zack indulged himself in a thin smile and said to his brother-in-law, "Don't get up. I'll let myself out."

It was late by the time they got sheets on their new bed, but neither of them was able to sleep. Wendy couldn't bring herself to draw the drapes across the moonlit water and instead lay in a state of happy exhaustion, gazing at the shimmering ripples on the sea while random inspirations about her mother's birthday party came and went.

Jim, on the other hand, seemed unable to find a good position, tossing and turning and ending up hopelessly tangled in the antique linens that Gracie Ferro had given them as a housewarming gift.

Wendy said knowingly, "You threw your back out, didn't you? Do you want me to get the rubbing alcohol?"

"No . . . no, I'm fine," Jim mumbled into his pillow. He punched it up and threw his shoulder back into it with the force of a sumo wrestler, then sighed deeply and flipped onto his back again.

"Wendy," he said to the ceiling.

"Mm . . . what?"

"You do like it here, don't you?"

Surprised by the question, she said, "It's wonderful. Ty is so happy. We should have moved out right away. The whole addition project will be so much pleasanter now." She shifted onto her side and propped herself up on her elbow. "I was wrong," she admitted with a gentle poke in his ribs. "And you were right."

He didn't answer at first, which also surprised her; he

loved to crow whenever she apologized. His tone became even more grave as he said, "Can you see yourself living here—or on Sheldon, or anywhere else—without me?"

Cancer. It was the first thought, the only thought, that flashed through her mind. It explained so much: his moodiness, his desperate need to have everything at once, his paranoia every time she answered the phone. Of course he was paranoid; he'd been dreading some doctor at the other end!

She lifted herself up so that she hovered over him, supported by the palms of her hands. She could scarcely hear her voice over the thundering of her heart. "I don't want to live somewhere without you. Why are you asking me that?"

When he didn't answer, she said in a pleading voice, "Tell me, Jim, please! I'm your *wife*. I want to be here for you. Tell me; I can handle it!"

He started to say something, but it got carried away on his sigh. "I will, Wen. With any luck . . . someday I will."

Her voice moved from bedtime whisper to high-pitched protest. "What does luck have to do with it?" she demanded, aware, even in her panic, that Tyler was now far enough down the hall not to hear. She had the luxury to shout if she wanted to, and that's just what she wanted to do. "Why can't you *tell* me?"

"Because of, of . . . there may be nothing to tell," he said, stumbling over his words. He sounded as mystified as she was.

"Don't put me off, I want to know *now,*" she insisted, pushing herself up to a kneeling position. She hovered over him, desperate to know what he was hiding. "You can't keep doing this to me, stringing me along like this! It's not right! You said that when we moved here—"

"We've been here a couple of hours!"

"—you'd tell me. Tell me what it is that's eating you,

Jim. Are you sick? Is there something wrong with you, something frightening you? Do you have cancer?"

Her husband was sitting up now, too. He took her by her shoulders and said, "Shh, shh, they can hear you on Sheldon, for God's sake. Calm down, Wendy. There's nothing wrong with me, I'm not sick, I don't have cancer. Why does everything always have to be cancer with you?"

"Then what? Are you having an affair?" she blurted.

Besides cancer, what else was there? He couldn't be bankrupt.

"I am absolutely *not* having an affair," he said with hushed vehemence. "I haven't *looked* at another woman since I married you. Geez, how can you even ask?"

He was keeping her pinned in position; she had to struggle to get free of him. In her effort, she heard a tear in the fabric behind her; the antique sheets were more antique than they looked. It made her spirit recoil and fueled her anger.

"If you're not going to tell me," she said, scrambling out of bed, "then I'm sleeping in one of the other bedrooms you were so desperate for us to have. *Damn* it, Jim!"

She grabbed her pillow and snatched up her robe from the foot of the bed, but Jim went around and intercepted her. "Okay, look, look . . . cut it out, will you?" he begged. "We don't need this on our first night here. If I give you at least the big picture, will you come back to bed?"

"I'm not promising *anything*," she said, clutching her pillow.

"Okay. All right. I can see that." He sat at the foot of the tall-post bed and studied the floor, apparently composing his thoughts.

"This happened before I ever met you," he admitted in a low murmur without looking up. "Over two years before. I did something I'm not very proud of."

"What? What did you do?" she asked, wildly sick of his

vagaries. When he didn't answer right away, she said, "Most people do things they're not very proud of. Did you break the law?"

"No."

He didn't sound grave so much as he sounded simply confused. It couldn't have been that terrible a deed, Wendy decided.

"Well, then what are you worried about? That I won't forgive you?"

Again he looked up. His red hair was disheveled, tumbling over his forehead; his smooth torso was bare. In that light, he still looked like the youthful, bike-riding, irresponsible bad boy who had instantly earned Gracie Ferro's seal of disapproval—except that he seemed in real agony now.

"If you did that . . . if you ever stopped loving me," he said in a choked voice, "I'd jump off the nearest bridge."

His words, his look, melted her heart; it was impossible to stay angry at someone who so clearly wanted forgiveness. If only she knew what she was supposed to forgive him *for*. She let out a sigh that had him at once rising to his feet and embracing her.

"Wendy, sweet, sweet darling, I love you," he said in her ear. "You know that I love you . . . I could never hurt you, never . . . it kills me when I've caused you pain. You *know* that I love you," he insisted between kisses to her temple, her jaw, the tender place where her neck curved into her shoulder. He seemed to be everywhere at once, electrifying her with every soft, sizzling touch, leaving burning paths between kisses.

If her sigh wasn't forgiveness, the moan that followed it certainly was. She didn't care about something he'd done in the distant past. She did not, and her moan was an admission of it. As long as he loved her, as long as he wanted her.

Something about the night, the moon, their beautifully strange surroundings, made her feel as if he weren't her husband at all, but some man she'd met in the park and had taken back home with her. She felt uniquely aroused. When he kissed her, she kissed him back, harder and deeper than she had in a long time.

He took his cue from her and redoubled his passion, lifting her easily in his arms and carrying her back to their new bed. He seemed eager, desperate, and somehow triumphant, all of those things at once, as he helped her slip off her nightgown and then got rid of his bottoms. He slid his arms underneath hers at the same time that he threw his leg across her thighs.

And Wendy lifted up to take him all the way in, because she wanted the penetration to touch the deepest wellspring of her heart, and lately it had not.

CHAPTER 10

"Someone likes you, Zack," Zina teased.

With wary interest, Zack watched Cassie knead her black-and-white paws into his thin, worn jeans. Out came her claws with every push, hooking in his denim on the return pull. Her purr was ridiculous; she sounded like a diesel idling in a garage.

"Yowch, that hurts," he said as the cat really got into it. He lifted her up while at the same time trying to disengage her claws from his clothing. It was an exasperating business, but after a couple of tries, he got himself free of her and put her down on the rag rug.

She jumped back up on the sofa and butted her head against his wrist, demanding—apparently—that he return her feelings for him.

"No dice," he said, lifting her up and putting her on the floor again.

Back onto the sofa she jumped.

"What the hell is the matter with this cat?" he asked, bewildered, as she tried to get past his arm onto his lap again.

"I don't know; she hasn't been like that with anyone else," his sister said. "Did you roll around in catnip before you came here?"

Zack pursed his lips. "Gee, let me think. Now that you

ask, gosh, I suppose I did, right after I batted that ball of yarn around."

"Oh, Zack," Zina said with a trembly smile.

Another tear rolled out.

He winced at seeing her start to lose it again. "I know, Zee; I know." He'd said it so many times to her over the years, but this time he meant it in so many different ways. He *did* know; more than he'd ever be able to say.

"I was so sure, this time," she said, blowing her nose yet again and tossing the tissue onto the pile on the floor next to her rocker. "How can two men look so much alike?"

"It's uncanny," Zack said with a feigned sense of wonder. "From a distance you'd swear it was him. But up close—well, there's just no way. This guy's voice was higher-pitched, he had a Rhode Island accent, and of course, the eyes. This guy's were as blue as the Caribbean Sea."

Blue eyes, he reminded himself. *Remember. Blue eyes.*

He wasn't so good at calling up eye color. If Zina hadn't run through a checklist of features after he swore to her earlier that the man he'd seen was not Jimmy Hayward, he'd never have had the blue-eye inspiration.

"It was nice of him to talk to you, anyway," Zina said. "He must get pestered all the time by people. For money, I mean."

If only she knew. "I have no doubt."

"Well, I guess it's life back to . . . normal," she said, coming up with a the barest shadow of that trembly smile. There weren't many left in her for the night, that was certain.

"You look pretty tired, kid," he said sympathetically. His sister's pale, blond beauty was the porcelain-perfect kind that suffered, especially around the eyes, from stress and lack of sleep. "I'm going to get out and let you—finally—get a good night's rest."

He looked down at the cat, who for some unfathomable reason had curled up on his lap and was still purring, if more quietly. He disliked the creature intensely for putting him in a position of having to disturb her serenity. Conniving little feline.

"Okay, lady, this is it; no more Mr. Nice Guy." He lifted his thighs a little to nudge her off, but she seemed to hunker down harder. He lifted higher, and then higher still. It didn't faze her at all.

"Okay, I mean it. Off." He didn't want to remove her and set her therapy back or anything; he just wanted her to go away on her own. "Come on," he pleaded. *"Off."*

Zina broke into laughter that was a pleasure to hear; Zack hadn't heard anything so merry from her in weeks.

"You may as well adopt her, Zack; she's already adopted you."

"Yeah, right," he said, lifting himself on his palms and shaping himself into a slide. If he had to resort to gravity, so be it.

"No, I'm serious. *Take* her. Some cats bond fiercely, and Cassie must be one of them. She'll love you for life, if you let her. Think how wonderful it would be to have her curled up by the woodstove in your shop as you work. Can't you just picture it?"

In fact, Zack could not. All he could picture was himself, alone, with a CD playing in the background, as he honed his wood into objects of beauty. It had always been that way. He had never had to worry about locking some cat in or out, and he was not about to start now.

Cassie had given up trying to cling to his lap; she jumped off, obviously disgusted with him, and went off to lick her face clean of his scent.

So much, he mused, for the lifetime bond. He stood up and stretched and said, "I'd better haul myself off to bed.

I've got to get up and drive back down to Providence to-morrow."

"Providence! Why?"

Okay; here goes. "You remember that east side client I told you about? The one with the set of Chippendale chairs that need restoring? She's a little on the eccentric side and won't let the chairs off the premises. I'll be driving back and forth for a while—maybe I'll even take her up on her offer to stay in an old chauffeur's quarters above the garage; half of it's a workshop. Most of the repair involves hand-carving, so I can work anywhere. The money's good, so what do I care?"

Zina bought it completely. "That's great; maybe she'll get you other commissions. She could be your best connection yet!"

"We'll see. Well, I've got a pile of mail to wade through—ah, hell, that reminds me," he said, and he launched himself blithely into the next whopper. "I got a notice that a registered letter is waiting for me at the post office; I wasn't home when they tried to deliver it."

"Do you want me to pick it up for you?"

Whoops. "Nope; I'm the one who has to sign," he said quickly.

"Maybe you're being called to jury duty again," Zina surmised as she walked him to her door.

"Nah. This sounded like a law firm. Smith, Reston, and Upton. I remember it sounded like Smith and Wesson."

He was developing into quite the accomplished liar. His voice sounded casual, and he was able to maintain eye contact with his sister as he winked and said lightly, "I just hope someone's not trying to sue me."

"Don't even joke about something like that," she scolded. "People can lose everything they own in lawsuits!"

Looking chastened, he put his arms around her in a

good-night hug. "Sorry I didn't bring you the news you wanted, Zee," he told her softly.

"Don't be sorry," she said. "No one can deliver bad news better than you." After a forlorn giggle, she said, "That didn't come out right, did it?"

"I think it did," he said.

It had come out exactly right.

They nailed the last rafter in place under a blistering sun. Zack peeled off his sweatband and wrung it dry over the side of the house, then wrapped the near-useless thing around his head again. He remembered yet another reason why he'd gotten out of the construction business: contractors worked closer to the ozone hole than most.

"Okay, let's get that plywood up here," Pete said. "They're talkin' rain tomorrow and the rest of the week; I want to get the roof on before then."

Pete scrambled down the ladder as nimbly as any monkey, with Zack not far behind. At the base, Zack turned and nearly knocked down Wendy Hodene, who had been waiting with a giant yellow plastic mug in her hand.

"It's hot," she said, holding it out to him with a smile.

Ice. Lemonade. Heaven. Zack nodded brusquely and said, "Thanks. Thanks a lot." He slugged down half of it on the spot and tried not to notice that she was wearing short shorts and a skimpy tank top. She didn't fill out the tank top with anything like excitement, but she did have great legs. She wasn't tall or by any stretch voluptuous; so why did it strike him that she might be a regular handful in bed?

Hey. Hey. What gives with that?

Zack tried to turn away from his thoughts and from her, but he was enjoying the short shorts a little too much to be noble. He found himself tracking her movements as she went around with a big pitcher, refilling their mugs.

When the pitcher was empty she asked, "Should I make more?"

Pete, jerk, said, "We're fine," which resulted in her taking her pitcher and going inside. Zack walked around to the side of the house and topped off the mug from a spigot, and then drank down the icy, still-citrusy water, aware that for the rest of his life he would probably associate lemonade with great legs.

"Okay," said Pete, first to put down his plastic stein. "Plywood."

Zack had worked in construction projects (one of them municipal) where moving a few sheets of plywood would have required a forklift, a crane, and an afternoon. Not so this crew. They threw a lasso around a couple of sheets at a time and slid them up the ladder, with one man pushing and another one pulling. More sweat but no noise; that was fine with Zack, who was used to the serene quiet that came from working with handtools in his shop.

His shop. What shop? It seemed like years since he'd been there. He missed it, missed the artistry of shaping wood into smooth, sinuous curves. It was so night-and-day different from the crudity of slapping plywood into the shape of a roof.

What was he doing there, anyway? He'd asked himself the question a hundred times in recent days. He happened to be perched on the ridgepole of the three-story addition and muscling a sheet of plywood into place when the answer to his question came into view on the front sidewalk: Wendy looked up, waved, and, still in her short shorts, got into her car and drove off.

Her. That's why he was there. To hold a nailgun to her throat in front of her so-called husband. Even in the dripping heat of the afternoon sun, Zack felt his face burn a little hotter at the thought that if Wendy knew the reason, she'd regard him with the same fear and loathing as she would a snake that dropped out of a tree in front of her.

He pictured her face with her open, friendly smile and her sparkling eyes, and he thought, *She deserves better than to be married to Jim and to be shadowed by me. In another world, during some other time . . . well, she deserves better, that's all.*

Morose and ill at ease, he returned with a vengeance to the job at hand. By the time the crew knocked off, his mood had become downright bitter, which did not go unnoticed by Pete, who figured that Zack had a bug up because he'd been made to work an hour past quitting time.

Zack was on the receiving end of a humiliating lecture about improving his attitude when Pete's cell phone rang. Zack leaned against the fender of his truck, folded his arms across his chest, and waited for Pete to finish the call and finish the lecture so that he could hightail it back to his sister in Hopeville and tell her more lies.

What a gloriously adventurous life for a thirty-seven-year old man in his prime.

"Okay, we'll get right on it," said Pete, and he hung up.

He said to Zack, "That was Wendy. She's having a problem with the plumbing. Toilet's backed up and she can't get a plumber. What do you know about toilets?"

"Enough."

"Here's the thing," Pete explained, suddenly sheepish. "I'm in the middle of a bowling tournament. I've got less than an hour to get to the hall, but first I gotta go home, get showered . . . it would help if you could go to her house and check it out for me. It's probably something simple like she flushed somethin' down that she shouldn't. You know women."

Zack was already running an hour late; even the simplest fix would eat up another hour. In the meantime he was concerned about Zina and how she was handling the false discovery he'd related to her. Tonight his plan was to counter the depressing lie with a much more cheerful one: she might be abandoned, but she was about to be rich.

But he was still smarting from Pete's ill-founded lecture, and besides, it might be a good way to rattle Jim's cage, so Zack said, "Let me make a phone call first, and then I'll go over there."

"Great. I have a spare wax ring in the truck; let me get it for you."

Zack nearly forgot to ask, "What's the address?"

Pete told him and added, "I owe you one, Zack."

Zack put in a call to Zina as he drove the short distance to Barrington, but he got her blasted answering machine. Conceivably she was working late at the quilting shop. Conceivably. He reminded himself that she was forever juggling her hours between the shop and the shelter, but he hated the surge of alarm that went racing through his veins anyway. If anything ever happened to her . . . if she ever did anything reckless because of the lie that he and he alone had set in motion . . .

Cursing himself for not having taken the time to program his cell phone, Zack pulled over before he reached the rental house so that he could try Zina's number again. This time she answered, breathless.

"I just ducked in to change, Zack. I'm on my way to the shelter—there's been a huge crisis, a fire in a house where a man had two dozen cats. A bunch of them died, some are at the vet's, and we're taking the others. I've *got* to go!"

He may as well have been talking to a volunteer fireman after a three-alarm bell. Inappropriately relieved, considering the cause, Zack said, "I'll stop by late to see that everything is, you know, okay."

"Sure, fine, late. Gotta go!"

So that was that, at least for the moment. Next crisis.

It was Wendy who answered the door. It should have

been a disappointment to Zack, who had planned to relish the freaked-out look on Jim's face. But he wasn't disappointed at all; he was pleased.

And self-conscious. He felt as if he were on a blind date as he said, "I hear you've got a problem with your plumbing."

"Oh! I—*you're* not Pete."

She sounded nearly as awkward as he felt; it made for a good equalizer, somehow. He explained that Pete had another commitment—leaving it for Pete to say he'd gone a-bowling—and said, "If you like, I could give it a shot."

He was surprised and oddly satisfied to see how embarrassed she became over his offer. Her cheeks turned a very pretty pink and her eyelids fluttered down in distress. "I can't ask you to do that," she said, looking back up at him. "Pete is one thing; but you're—"

"Just the help?"

"Well . . . yes," she said, forthrightly enough. "Plumbers get sixty dollars an hour. Considering the quote he gave us for the addition, I somehow doubt that Pete's paying you quite that much," she said dryly.

Before he could come up with anything snappy, she said, "I know! I'll pay you what I'd pay a real plumber. At least then I wouldn't feel guilty."

The only guilt Zack could sense was settling itself nicely over his shoulders. Damn it! Why did she have to be so scrupulous? So candid? So damned attractive?

He said, "Thanks, but that's not necessary. Consider this a return for the lemonade. Besides—you don't know if I can fix it."

"I've seen you hold a hammer," she said simply. "You can fix it."

What the connection was, Zack didn't know. But he felt unaccountably pleased that she'd watched him work and approved of what she saw.

"I've called every plumber in the book," she said, leading him up a beautifully detailed stairwell. "They say you can tell a boom is over when a contractor starts returning your calls. All I can say to that is: we ain't in no recession."

"You're right about that," Zack said with a laugh. Good thing, too; the labor shortage had forced Pete to hire him sight unseen—and, of course, had put Zack in a position to destroy Wendy's life. How fascinated she'd be to know that, he thought, depressed.

They walked past a closed door that muted the sounds of a video game being played on the other side of it. "Tyler, this is a five-minute warning. You've been at it for over an hour," she said, pausing briefly before showing Zack the bathroom at the far end of the hall.

"This is the guest bath," she told Zack. "The owner obviously had a lot of work besides painting done right before we moved in; the tiles look brand-new. I think even the toilet is new."

It was a nice but not insanely expensive makeover, the kind of thing an owner does to freshen up a place before he puts it on the market: new white tiles, pale lavender walls, pedestal sink, and white mosaic floor. All very Pottery Barn, all very nice.

"See where the water is in the toilet—how high?"

It was an odd place for Zack to be, staring down the bowl of a toilet with the woman who had usurped his sister's lawful place in a marriage—but there they were. "When did you notice this? After you flushed?"

"No, Tyler told me about it. I was in the basement when he yelled down. I was down there because I'd heard a really weird glug-glug sound—I think, from the laundry sink. After I found out about the toilet, that was it; I headed straight for the phone."

That was bad, bad news. It meant the toilet wasn't plugged, but the sewer line was. So much for pulling the fixture and clearing it. Zack said, "Let me just check something."

Either she heard it in his voice, or she saw it on his face: the repair was not going to be simple. Tagging along after him down the stairs to the basement, she began ticking off her sins: "I did four loads of laundry. We all showered. I did dishes. I took a *bath*. The tub is huge; it was irresistible," she explained.

He tried not to picture her in it.

"Was it too much?" she asked meekly. "Is the plumbing too old for so much consumption?"

He was running water into the laundry sink, but it wasn't going anywhere. "This isn't anything you did. There's something stopping the water from draining. Maybe tree roots have invaded the sewer line; that's usually the reason. I think you need to call a rooter-guy for this."

Relieved that it wasn't their fault, but upset that the solution wasn't easy, Wendy explained that she was having a big party the next day for her mother's sixty-fifth birthday.

"I can't believe it. We're here less than two days, and the place is going to be as torn up as our lot on Sheldon Street. Maybe it's us," she moaned good-naturedly as she pulled out the Yellow Pages.

He waited, although he had no reason to, while she called the few listings and, needless to say, had to end up leaving messages with each of their voice mails. Either trees were attacking drainpipes all over town, or all of the contractors were out bowling.

Her smile was resigned. "Well . . . I appreciate your sticking around this long, Zack. But you really shouldn't waste any more of your time. Eventually one of them will call back. Worst case, we can always go back to our house."

"Yeah, okay," he said. But something was nagging at the back of his mind.

In the meantime, she was glancing at the front door with a puzzled frown. "I can't imagine where Jim got lost today."

Zack could. It couldn't be easy, stealing that kind of change from your wife. Your alleged wife. He might be going through financial somersaults even as Wendy was fretting about him.

"Will they have to tear up the bricks?" she asked. "Because that would be a disaster. I guess I should call the real estate agent and warn her," she said, going to the refrigerator to read a business card on it.

"Hold it. Wait a minute." The nagging little something at the back of Zack's mind stepped forward and formed a hunch. "Something like this happened on a house rehab I was involved in. It's a long shot, but: it could be that someone got sloppy during the upgrade of the guest bath and flushed some construction debris that made it as far as the trap and then got stuck. Drywall, a piece of lath, who knows? Yeah; it's possible."

Zack trotted down the stairs again, wondering why in God's name he was trying so hard to ace some guy from Roto-Rooter, until he realized that it was Wendy he was trying to score points with. If she ever found out what he was up to—if things didn't go well in his high-risk plan—he wanted Wendy Hodene to know that at least once, he'd been willing to move hell and high water for her. Literally.

She stood right behind him, all ears as he explained where the main sewer drain could be tapped into and examined. "I'm going to have to uncap the grease trap. You might want to close the basement door behind you when you go upstairs," he warned her in an understatement. "It's not going to smell real great down here."

"I'm not going anywhere," she said steadfastly. "You're going to operate? Then you'll need a nurse."

CHAPTER 11

"Hand me the bucket, would you?"

"Yessir."

"And the flashlight, please. Shine it right . . . there; yeah, like that. Good."

Wendy had changed her share of diapers in life, but she was definitely breathing through her mouth on this one. She wanted this exploration over with *so* much.

She watched as Zack poked around the trap with a long screwdriver, thinking, this guy's a definite hero, whether or not he manages to pull this off. She felt incredibly grateful to him for his effort.

"This is the single nicest thing that anyone has ever done for me," she said as she stood above him with the flashlight. Laughing softly, she added, "Does that make me weird, or what?"

He didn't answer except to say, "I think I feel something."

Oh, please, let it be so. "How are you going to—"

"Breadbag, please."

She stepped back and fetched him the outer plastic wrapper that she'd filched off her Pepperidge Farm bread. He slipped the bag over his hand, then plunged it into the trap. After a poke here and a stab there, he grabbed at something and worked it out of the hole.

"Ta-dah," he said in a deadpan voice. He dumped a

blackened strip of what looked like a very large splinter of wood into the bucket, then peeled off the wet bread wrapper and dropped it in the bucket as well.

"Believe it not, this isn't that unusual an occurrence. You generally give the newest kids the demolition work, and sometimes they don't know to close the lid on the toilet before they go knocking down the wall behind it. The toilet gets flushed, the wood jams the trap, and the backup starts."

"That explains it. Kids. Why does that not surprise me?" she said, watching him walk over to the basement sink holding up his hands like a surgeon in pre-op.

Taking the obvious cue, she jumped to turn on the water for him and then pumped half a bottle of liquid soap into the upturned palms of his hands. God only knew what germs were assaulting him.

In fact, he was filthy. It must have been bad enough to have sweated in the heat all day, but to top it off on your knees in a dank, spider-filled basement clearing out a sewer line . . .

"I feel so bad for you," she blurted. "You must feel so . . . yech."

He was soaping his sinewy arms all the way up to his biceps, proof enough that she'd got it right. He turned to her and winked. "All in a day's work," he said with a barely there but wonderful smile.

It was the oddest thing. Something inside of her took a tiny little hop, like a sparrow that's been scratching for food. She smiled back, but very shyly, and said, "Do you live close, at least?"

"Uh, no," he said, rinsing one arm, then the other, under the high-spout faucet. "Worcester."

"That's a long drive. Do you want a blanket—a towel or something—to throw over the seat of your truck?"

"Because—"

"Of germs! People get cholera doing what you did. I'd feel terrible if—"

"I got cholera? I don't think you need to worry about that, Wendy."

She was acutely, surprisingly aware that he'd never called her by her name before. Somehow, whenever he had looked at or said something to her, the word "ma'am" seemed to be hovering unspoken.

"You know what I think?" she began.

There were times in her life when she went entirely by instinct, and this turned out to be one of them. "I think you should shower here first before you drive all the way back. Really. I'd feel so much less guilty if you did."

"No, that's nice of you, but—"

"*Please*," she said over his protests. "If Jim were home, I know he'd insist on it. That was such a generous thing you did—and your deductions, *I* think, were brilliant. I'm so impressed. The only thing is, your clothes. I don't have anything in the house that would fit you. You're broader than Jim and maybe . . . smaller around the, the . . ." She whirled a finger in a little circle. "Middle," she finished up, embarrassed to be sizing him up like some tailor.

"For that matter, I carry a change of clothes in the truck," he said after considering her offer.

She had watched the look on his face progress from "Dumb idea" to "Why not?" as her own feelings went from misgivings to relief. It was the obvious, the civil, the only thing to do.

"Good! Then that's that. I'll bring you fresh towels; Tyler's are undoubtedly—well, Tyler's," she said lamely, unused to having guests. "And you can test the water flow, so you'd be doing me a favor, when you get right down to it."

He laughed and said, "Anything to oblige."

She washed in a hurry and they went upstairs together,

and while Zack went out for his duffel, she grabbed an armful of towels for him. On the second floor they were intercepted by a very curious Tyler, who stared at Zack, looked at his mother, glanced at the towels, and said, "Can I use the toilet yet? Otherwise I'm gonna have to go to somebody's house."

Wendy said, "The answers are yes and use the downstairs bathroom; Zack will be cleaning up in this one."

Wendy hadn't been at the new house long enough to stock a toiletries basket for overnight guests, but she figured that Zack would be ahead of the game even without deodorant and a toothbrush. She didn't want to seem to be overly hovering, after all, because technically he wasn't a guest, but she took the time to check ahead for soap and shampoo.

Nuts. All she had there was kids' shampoo. Would Zack mind? Too late to switch. Maybe she should switch. No. Too late to switch. Nuts!

"If there's anything you need, just, you know, holler," she said, trying desperately to sound casual.

"Thanks. I will do that," he said with a bemused smile at her before he closed the door.

It really was a nice smile.

He really, really, was a nice guy to have plunged into that muck for her—for them. Wendy went back downstairs, pleased to be able to return a favor and wondering how she could ever have thought that Zack was aloof and rude.

She was in the kitchen, loading the dishwasher from Tyler's supper and trying to decide whether she should put out an extra plate next to Jim's, when Jim himself finally returned. The front door slammed loud enough that she felt prompted to poke her head around the corner and say, "If you break it, it comes out of our deposit."

Jim was not amused. In fact, he was furious. "Where is he? Where the hell is he?"

"If you mean Zack, he's taking a shower," Wendy said, wondering. "What's the matter? Where were you?"

"A *what*? Where?" Jim said, stunned.

"Not in our room, don't worry. He's using the guest bathroom. You would not believe the bullet we just dodged. I heard this weird glugging sound, so I went—"

Jim had started up the first two stairs, then backed down them again and grabbed her by the arm. "What did he say? I want to know: what did he *say*?"

"Shhh!" she hissed. "My God, he'll hear you! What's the matter with you? Have you been drinking?" she said, trying to yank her arm out of his grip. "Let me *go*, Jim; you're hurting me."

She kept her voice down low, but her eyes were wide with shock and outrage, and Jim either wasn't angry enough or wasn't dumb enough not to see it. He released her, his anger faltering in the process, and then tagged after her into the kitchen.

"Well—what do you expect?" he said, trying to recover some kind of advantage over her. "I come home, a contractor's truck is sitting in my driveway, the contractor's in my goddamned *shower*—what do you expect?"

She blinked at the implication and whirled around on him. "Are you insane? *Tyler*'s upstairs. What could you possibly be thinking?"

She was projecting an image of outraged innocence and had color in her cheeks and the shaking voice to prove it. But underneath all that outraged sense of virtue, one thought loomed: at first glance, it did look bad. She felt it, too, though she had refused to admit it to herself.

Jim scowled and said petulantly, "I thought Ty had a sleepover."

"Canceled. He's in his room in a semi-sulk. And in the meantime, the sewer drain got plugged. All the water came to a screeching halt down in the basement—which you would have discovered if you'd been home tonight instead of out dreaming and scheming about God knows what."

"So what does Zack have to do with it? He's a carpenter, not a plumber."

"Zack knows about everything," she shot back. "I couldn't get anyone to come here, and he volunteered because he's a good guy and for no other reason. He knew exactly where to look and what to look for and how it got there. The job was disgusting and messy, but he fixed the problem and saved the owners a bundle—not that that matters to you!—and more important, has made it possible for us to hold the party we've promised my mother. And if you weren't such an irrational . . . *knucklehead* . . . you'd thank your lucky stars that his truck is in our driveway and that he is in our shower even as we *speak*."

Without waiting to see how her impassioned speech was received by her husband, she turned away from him, threw a small pan of lasagna into the oven, slammed the door (wincing belatedly at the thought of the damage deposit), and made a big deal over hand-washing the three spoons, two forks, and two mugs that were still in the sink.

All the while she was thinking, *Why am I at his throat like this? Why am I overreacting?*

Why was *he* overreacting?

She grabbed a towel and dried her hands and turned, unsuspecting, right into his arms.

"I am so sorry, Wen," Jim said in a low voice. "So he . . . fixed it? Well, obviously: you're running water and he's showering. That's great. That's great. I, ah, I was tense. I've had a really shitty day. I don't know what came over me. It's a tense time: all the money; the construction; the move. If it's not one thing," he murmured sadly as he pulled her a little closer, "it's another."

She wasn't in the mood to feel pliant. "It's called *life*, Jim. Deal with it."

"No, you're right; you're right. I blew this one big-time," he said abjectly. In an even softer murmur he said, "You know, you made a similar mistake the other night."

She stiffened in his embrace and he said quickly, "I'm not blaming you, Wen. I'm just saying, this is a really tense time. People don't always think right when they're tense."

She sighed and said wearily, "You know what? You can be exhausting."

"I know. I know."

She heard a sound and so did Jim; they turned to see Zack—she didn't even know his last name!—standing there in clean khakis and a black polo shirt, his wet hair still dripping in dark ringlets, his five o'clock shadow surrounding an attractively sheepish smile.

"That did the trick," he said to both of them after a nod at Jim. "I'm glad you let me impose."

Wendy jumped to his defense. "You didn't impose; we did. We're both so happy that you could rush to the scene the way you did. Really. Would you like to sit down to dinner? There's more than enough. Tyler and I have already eaten, but Jim—"

"No, no," Zack said, still smiling. "But I appreciate the offer."

Jim didn't. Without even looking at him, Wendy knew that his face was locked into that frozen, polite expression he reserved for time-share salesmen and Jehovah's Witnesses. Well, tough. He deserved a little smack on the nose. Maybe next time he wouldn't go finding wildly melodramatic situations where there were none.

Moving past her husband, Wendy went up to Zack and extended her hand. "We really are grateful; I can't tell you how much."

She didn't know how she was going to pay him for what he had done; his gesture seemed beyond price. In any case, she thought it would be incredibly insensitive, even insulting, to whip out her checkbook just then. They had literally spent time in the trenches together, and Wendy, at least, had considered it a bonding moment.

Zack took her hand and shook it, with none of the self-consciousness that she sometimes sensed when she initiated the gesture first. She liked that in him.

As for Jim, he seemed to prefer to keep things on a master–slave basis. Declining to step forward, he said behind her, "Nice going, Zack."

Something about her husband's flat tone of voice made Wendy turn around and glance at him in time to see him shooting a look of pure hatred at Zack.

Caught, Jim was quick to snap his mouth into a congenial smile—but Wendy saw what she saw.

My God, he is *jealous,* she thought.

Zack said good night and began heading for the door. Wendy accompanied him, with Jim close behind them. It was Jim who closed the door, Jim who threw the bolt, Jim who said, "I don't want him in this house again. Ever."

But it was Wendy who said, "Don't tell me what to do. I don't work for you."

Zack hadn't dared tell Zina the bad-news lie in a public place; but he was more than willing to tell her the good-news lie there. He invited her out for breakfast at Sunnyside, a local eatery where they were known, but not by name. The atmosphere was country casual, with blue gingham café curtains that hid a view of the parking lot, and vases of polyester daisies that virtually insisted you perk up and smile.

Over Canadian bacon and three fried eggs, Zack said, "Well, I found out what that registered letter was all about. You remember old Aunt Louise?"

"Mom's great-great-whatever aunt? The one out West somewhere?"

"Mm. She died."

Zina was distressed; she wanted nothing and no one ever to die. "Oh, that's too bad," she said with feeling. "But I suppose it was inevitable. She was really old, wasn't she?"

"Ninety-nine."

"Oh-h-h . . . so close to a hundred," Zina said with a sigh.

In fact, old Aunt Louise (who wasn't their mother's aunt at all, but some cousin quadruply removed), had died years ago, Zack had learned; but that was neither here nor there. Family legend had it that she was wealthy and tight and eccentric and unwed, and that made her an ideal candidate for the good-news lie.

"I was right; the registered letter *was* from a law firm," he explained as he bent one of the daisy petals into a more natural form. "It was from Aunt Louise's attorneys. Guess what it said?"

This was the tricky part; he had to seem to be suppressing excitement, not behaving as if he'd just run over her cat. So he compressed his lips and tried to act as if he were trying not to smile, after which he had to act as if he couldn't help himself from bursting into a grin.

Which he did. "She's left us some money," he said. "A pretty fair amount."

"Us?" said Zina, her blue eyes opening wide. "Why? We didn't even know her!"

"True enough. Maybe that's why. The favored heir was a great-nephew, but he got disinherited when he pissed her off. He was a broker, and he sank a lot of her money into couldn't-miss biotech stocks," Zack said dryly.

"And they missed?"

"They tanked. Why she was in such a speculative venture when she should have been in nice, conservative investments is beyond me. The guy must have been really smooth. And stupid, of course. So she cut him out of her will—and she cut us in."

"Wow!"

Zina was a little otherworldly, but she was basically of this planet, after all. Zack was tickled to see the spark of interest lighting up her face.

"So-o-o?" she coaxed. "Tell me, tell me."

"So-o-o . . . how would you like to own your own quilting shop?" Zack said, breaking into a genuine, unrehearsed, unreserved, altogether happy grin.

"Zack!" She returned his delighted look with one of her own. "Oh, my God . . . really? That much?"

"It's a lot of money, Zina. It really is a lot."

All Zack actually had in his possession was the hundred thousand that Jim had handed over at lunchtime on the day before. If Jim didn't deliver on the balance, Zack was going to be utterly screwed. He had thought about it all night—whether he should tell Zina that her "inheritance" was three hundred thousand dollars; and when he woke up, he was convinced that he should. If Jim ended up stiffing him and Zack had to blow up his so-called marriage and then pick the pockets of his dead body—well, there were less pleasant things to do in life.

Zina was waiting.

"Three hundred thousand, Zee," he said softly. "That's your share." He couldn't help adding, "What do you think about *that*?"

She slapped her hand over her mouth and stared blankly at him over the polyester daisies. Zack wasn't exactly sure how he'd been expecting his sister to react, but he thought he'd see more . . . joy in her eyes, somehow; less blankness. Blankness looked too much like fear. "Zee?"

She nodded, then whispered, "We each got that much? Each?"

"Absolutely."

"But why didn't I get a letter, too?"

Ah, damn it. He didn't think she'd get there that fast.

"Okay, here's the thing. I was the actual, named heir—wait a minute, hear me out—but that was because old Aunt Louise didn't know you existed. She was leaving it to Mom's progeny, and she was assuming that I was the only progeny. She must have lost contact with Mom and Dad before you were born; that's what her lawyer surmised."

"Well, I can't accept it, that's all," she said firmly. "It wouldn't even be legal, I'll bet."

He had to smile at the irony of it all. Legal! "We can split it any way we want to, Zee," he told her. "There's no law against that. What do I need with all that money? You see how I live—like Thoreau on Walden Pond. I have my wood, I have my music. I don't even have to buy cat food," he teased. "I'll undoubtedly dump my share in a money-market account and forget about it until I'm old and bent and ready for a nursing home."

Would she buy it? He held his breath. It all came down to that single, exquisite moment.

The blankness remained, but it looked a little less fearful than before. "Are you sure?" she asked timidly.

"I've never been more sure of anything in my life." That was the God's honest truth.

"Because if money ever came between us, I'd die."

"It won't."

"Because you mean everything to me, now, Zack. You're all I have in life. Besides my cats."

He didn't even take offense, he was so happy that his cockamamie scheme was going to fly. Wilbur Wright couldn't have been half as happy when his brother took off at Kitty Hawk.

"You'll want to quit your job, I expect," he said, trying as he always had to steer her in a definite direction.

"And open my own shop?" she said. "That sounds like

a lot of responsibility. I could lose the money!"

"Not all of it. Not necessarily any of it. But you won't know unless you try."

"Oh, I don't know," she said, shaking her head. "I'd have to think about that."

"Of course. And now you'll have the time and the money to do it in."

"Maybe I could—what if I opened a shelter with the money instead?" she asked, brightening.

"If that's what you want to do, if that's what makes you happy, then that's what you should do. But you don't have to decide this minute," he assured her.

Zack would caution her some other time that without a hefty endowment and nonstop fund-raising, she'd go through the money in no time, trying to keep a shelter open. He hadn't expected her to turn away from the quilting shop idea so quickly; she'd fantasized about having one for years. But right now she was compensating like crazy for the emotional letdown and future void, and cats were obviously more huggable than quilts.

Her eggs got cold as Zina began spinning an elaborate scenario in which every abandoned cat in Massachusetts had a huge cage, a private run, the best food, a daily brushing, and families lined up four deep to adopt. Her shelter, of course, would be a no-kill facility. If need be, she would sustain every cat for the rest of its natural life. Every cat would be spayed or neutered at the shelter's expense, because it was obvious, even to Zina who loved them, that there were too many unwanted cats in the world. The cats would be content, whatever their fate, and so would she.

Which is why Zack had come up with the blackmail scheme in the first place, and why he had to make it work.

CHAPTER 12

Hosting the birthday party definitely had seemed like a much better idea on Sunday.

Wendy's frazzle quotient would've been lower if she hadn't decided to take over coordinating the entire event herself, turning it into a combination birthday–housewarming party. It didn't help that she had insisted that all of the out-of-towners stay overnight at her rented house rather than spread themselves out, as they normally did, over the family's available sofabeds.

But that's what Wendy had done, and it explained why when she showed up at the construction site on Sheldon Street, Pete interrupted himself and blurted, "What's the matter with your hair?"

"I don't know. What?"

She reached up automatically and felt around. Some of her hair was aimed at the sky and some of it was shooting out the side of her head. The rest of it was glommed together in the back.

"Oh, good grief," she said, pulling out the three clips that she'd used to hold her hairdo together—obviously without success—while she ripped through the house making the beds and setting out flowers and arranging baskets of soaps and bowls of fruit. "I've just gone into four different stores looking like this," she moaned.

Pete averted his gaze and said diplomatically, "I doubt anyone noticed."

Wendy heard a soft chuckle and whipped her head around to see Zack walking past with a bundle of roofing shingles slung over his shoulder.

"Sorry," he murmured, instantly sobering. As he went on his way, he added, "I thought it looked cute."

Wendy felt heat in every root of her ill-placed hair. Cute!

"I—"

And that's as far as she got. Her mind went utterly blank.

She turned back to her contractor and said, "I'm sorry, Pete. What—what did you want to know?"

"Did you make up your mind about the banister?"

"What are my choices, again?"

"Oak. Beech. Cherry."

She tried to picture them all and drew another blank. "Oh, I don't know; you pick one. Whatever you think looks right."

Pete did a double take. " 'Scuze me? You're not going to make this decision yourself? Six different times?"

It was a first, she realized. "I can't, Pete. My mind's not on it. How important can it be?" she asked, distracted beyond believing it could matter at all. Wood was wood, wasn't it?

Pete rubbed his chin. Apparently he'd seen homeowners in her condition before. "I'll put the order on hold for now. We've got time."

She nodded and glanced around. There was something she was supposed to do, something she came there specifically to do . . .

I thought it looked cute.

Her hand went up to her hair again. She poked at it furtively, unsure whether it looked any better with the clips pulled out.

Messages.

That was it; she'd forgotten to check them the day before. God only knew how many members of her family had been trying to get in touch with her.

She looked askance at the series of red blinks on the machine. "I must have been mad to take on this freaking party," she muttered. There were a dozen messages; the tape had more than likely run out. Which never would have happened if she were still living in the house; she had been on top of everything, up until the move over the weekend.

Even worse, she found that she was already missing the minute-to-minute pleasure of watching Zack and the others pull the addition together. She would be lying to herself if she said she preferred to see each day's progress all at once, after the crew had left. That kind of CEO approach just wasn't her style; she was more of the shop-steward type.

Why, again, was she staring at the blinks on the machine?

Right. Messages.

She began playing through them. One was from yet another long-lost friend, this time, of Wendy's, who wanted to meet over a meal somewhere and reminisce about their sophomore year in college because it had been, like, such a blast. There was a call from her aunt Genevieve (who announced that her carpal tunnel was acting up and she wouldn't be able to slice any cabbage for cole slaw); a call from her brother Dave (who confessed that he was too chicken to bring his latest and apparently thoroughly pierced and tattooed girlfriend to the party); a call from her mother (who said "Oops, wrong house," and rang off); and more than the usual number of hangups.

One of them stood out from the others and sent a ripple of goose bumps over Wendy. She'd heard it before, and more than once: ominous silence, punctuated by desultory voices in the background, possibly from another room. The acoustics of it sounded to her like a television, but, if so, it must have been a boring program. No one had much to say. A soap? A gardening show? A wildlife program? She strained to make out an identifying sound, and within seconds, she had it: a woman's low cry, followed by her shuddering moan.

A porn tape. Wendy was willing to bet the addition on it. Disgusted, she hit the erase button. How pathetic, she thought. Dirty callers didn't even do their own heavy breathing anymore.

She sighed in frustration; she didn't have time for this! After a few words to Pete, she was out the door and headed for her car. With any luck, Mark and Marianne would arrive shortly, and she could put her sister-in-law to work mincing and chopping and shredding. The affair was potluck—her father wanted familiar, homemade cuisine, not some fancy catered "inedibles"—but the pressure was still on Wendy, as the hostess, to make sure there'd be fill-in food and lots of it.

"How's the water flowing?" came a shout from the roof.

Wendy stopped and looked up. Thirty feet above her, Zack was standing with hands on his hips like some contractor-colossus, astride the ridgepole.

Shading her eyes with the palm of her hand, Wendy yelled, "So far, so good," and gave him a thumbs-up signal with her other hand. Meanwhile, she was truly wishing that he'd hold on to something.

"Glad to hear it," he called down to her. "I was concerned that there might be other scraps of wood floating around."

She hadn't even considered the possibility! "In that case, you'd better get that roof on quick," she yelled up, "because we'll be right back here, rolling out sleeping bags for everyone on every floor."

He grinned and waved and went back to work on the

roof, and Wendy became instantly aware of an odd ping of disappointment. Just a ping, no big stab. But it was there, and she had to acknowledge it.

Why did we move out? This is where I want to be.

The thought came and went in the blink of an eye, and then Wendy went on her way.

The little white cat was in pain. Only one of his front pads was singed, and he was medicated; but Zina could see that the fire had traumatized him more than any of the other cats that had been rounded up and deemed well enough to stay in the shelter.

"Poor thing, look at him, all huddled in the back of the cage," she murmured to Sylvia. "You can see how this has affected him."

The director hardly heard her; she had her hands full screening the crush of people who were calling with offers to relieve the jam-packed shelter of some of the cats, either temporarily or permanently.

"Maybe we should just burn a house down every week," Sylvia said in a surprising display of gallows humor. "At least we'd make the evening news and get some attention focused on the animals."

Zina had already gone straight to Sylvia and told her that since she was coming into an inheritance, the shelter could expect a generous donation from her. So it wasn't exactly a bolt out of the blue when Zina said, "Since TV is such a great tool, maybe we should try renting a spot on the local news once a week; we could feature just one cat— you know, a pet-of-the-week kind of thing."

Sylvia Radisson let out one of her rare laughs. "Buy TV time? What was your great-aunt's name? Bill Gates?"

The phone rang and Sylvia picked it up, and Zina went back to comforting the new arrivals, some of them crowded two in a cage; she was watching carefully to see who got along and who didn't.

The two young tabbies sharing one cage definitely looked like siblings, but the jury was still out on that: there had been a little too much swatting and hissing in the cage, and everyone was nervous about them. And they couldn't ask the cats' elderly owner; disoriented and confused, he was being held in a hospital overnight for observation.

The poor owner; Zina's heart went out to him. Usually they were women, these kind souls who took in animal after animal until they were completely overwhelmed. This man had done it in memory of his wife, he had told the fire-fighters. His wife was fond of cats and always fed the strays.

Compensating—that's what Zina had read that people like him were doing. They were compensating for being sad and alone and unloved. But that wasn't Zina's problem; she just loved cats. How could she feel alone and unloved? She had Zack, after all, a wonderful, caring brother. Her thoughts went back to the restaurant, to the amazing break-fast they'd shared. (She would never look at bacon and eggs the same again.)

Zina was hardly surprised and yet deeply moved by Zack's generous offer to split his inheritance with her. Who would do something like that besides him? She couldn't think of anyone less interested in money than her brother was. She accepted his statement completely that he didn't need it.

Actually, it would be nice if he *did* need it—for college or for kids' braces or something. But he'd always sworn up and down that marriage was overrated, that men and women weren't meant to be monogamous.

Until just recently, he used to tease her about that. "Look at the animals you love so well," he liked to point out. "Are they monogamous? Fat chance."

"Some of them are," she'd argue. "The crow and the swan and the wolf."

"Myths. All myths. Animal behaviorists are debunking them left and right. Just because some animals mate for life doesn't mean that they're faithful for life. Animals cheat. People cheat. What's the point of denying it?"

As far as Zina knew, no one had ever cheated on Zack; he'd never given any woman a chance to. His terrible attitude about relationships was strictly because of their parents. And Zina could understand that; she could understand how he might always look at a woman the way their father had looked at their mother that horrible night. But still. If only he could have more faith in women.

"Look at *me*. Who do you know," she'd ask him with a laugh, "who's more faithful than I am?"

And he would laugh, too, sadly and softly. But the look in his eyes always said the same thing: *There's something wrong with you, Zee.*

There wasn't, Zina was convinced. Not with her. But as much as she hated to admit it, she was convinced that there was something wrong with Zack. If there weren't, he would be using that inheritance to buy a house and fill it with family.

Poor Zack . . .

She opened a cage and lifted out an especially loud-purring cat was rubbing her cheek along the inside of the cage grid, begging for affection.

Lifting the animal gently, Zina carried her over to a vinyl-covered armchair in the get-acquainted room next to the one in which the cats were kept caged. She sat with the peach-and-gray cat in her lap, petting and stroking and reassuring it.

"I'll bet you're the one who always got to sit on the old man's lap, aren't you?" she murmured. "Your purr is too loud for anyone to ignore you. Poor little baby," she said, stroking the calico's chin. "Don't you know that cats are supposed to be detached and aloof? What's the matter with you?" she teased in her most melodious voice. "Do you want to ruin everyone else's reputation?"

She continued murmuring silly things, trying to soothe the achingly affectionate animal. The cat's purr was even louder than Cassie's, no small feat. Zina began to think of Cassie, and of Zack who wouldn't take Cassie, and in her revery she forgot to continue stroking the cat in her lap. The pale gray calico became impatient; she turned and nipped Zina's finger in an exquisitely tender reminder to keep on doing what she'd been doing.

"Well! Excuse *me*," said Zina, smiling, and she resumed her stroking.

And then she stopped.

Stopped and heard, not the loud, rhythmic purring of the cat, but the sudden, wrenching pounding of her heart, banging against her rib cage. *Déjà vu.* She was experiencing déjà vu.

Zina had had moments like this one before in her life, and she had always given them her absolute attention, because she believed that not all knowledge came from facts and figures and the observable world. Sometimes revelations flew fast and in a straight line just below the radar screen, or they hovered somewhere on the periphery, like a buoy on a foggy ocean.

This particular revelation came to Zina straight and fast, and it shot right through her heart.

Through the haze of her personal history, she remembered being perhaps four years old and sitting in her mother's rocking chair, the one that now sat in her own living room. She had a cat on her lap. The cat was purring and Zina was petting it, marveling at its soft fur. She wanted to keep it for her own, but it belonged to the old—

very, very old—lady who sat on the sofa across from her, watching her with dark, beady eyes.

She remembered feeling brave enough to ask the lady, "Can Ginger stay here? She could sleep in my bed."

And she remembered her mother, pretty in bright blue, saying quickly, "Oh, honey, no, the cat won't be able to stay over for a visit. Aunt Louise is going back home to Omaha, far, far away, and she's taking Ginger with her. They're going on the train tomorrow, back to their home in Omaha."

"I don't want Ginger to go," Zina remembered saying. "She likes me."

Four-year-old Zina had stopped petting the cat while she argued her case, and Ginger, loud-purring Ginger, had suddenly turned her head and nipped Zina on her forefinger, exactly the way the gray calico had done a minute ago.

And the very, very old lady called Aunt Louise had smiled and said to a startled four-year-old Zina, "She likes you, Zina."

And her seven-year-old brother, fidgeting in the easy chair next to the sofa, had said, "Well, that's a stupid way to show it."

And her mother had told Zack to be quiet and to stop pounding his hands on the arms of the chair.

Zina. Zack. And Aunt Louise. They had been in a room together once, all three of them. So Aunt Louise, or Cousin Louise or whoever she was, had to have known that Zina existed.

So why was Zack so convinced that she hadn't? Could he simply have been trying to justify giving Zina half of an inheritance that was specifically meant for him? Very possibly; that would be like Zack.

Or maybe by the time that Aunt Louise changed her will, she wasn't as sharp as she once had been; she might have been fuzzy about everything but her hostility toward her nephew.

Maybe.

Maybe she had nurtured old feelings of jealousy because her beloved Ginger had taken such a shine to young Zina.

Ridiculous.

Maybe she simply had wanted to substitute one male heir, any male heir, for the other, despised one. But hadn't she been a suffragist?

Maybe she just hadn't cared.

Maybe she just hadn't been able to remember Zina's name.

Maybe there was no inheritance.

Zina lifted her chin and stared straight ahead, seeing nothing, seeing everything. There was money, but maybe it wasn't from an inheritance. *Oh, my God.* What were the lawyers' names? *Oh, my God.* She placed her hand over her pounding heart; she felt as if she'd been shot. *Oh, my God.*

Smith, Reston, and Upton.

CHAPTER 13

"Wendy Hodene, you are completely insane if you move back to the old house after this."

"How can you say that, Char? That house was built by our great-grandparents with their own bare hands. All of our memories are there—yours, mine, everyone's. Someone has to hold on to it," Wendy explained as she opened the windows all the way to the cool sea breeze. "It might as well be me."

Wendy's older sister, eight months pregnant, was touring the beach house for the first time. Charlotte lived in rural Saunderstown at the southern end of the state. A typical Rhode Islander, she acted as if she lived on the far side of the moon and hadn't been able to make it up to Providence, much less Barrington, until the afternoon of the actual birthday party.

Like everyone else, she was charmed by the view of the whitecapped bay and by the boats pulled up and tied to the wild rosebushes on the beach. Like everyone else, she thought the house was perfect and her sister was out of her mind.

"No. I'm sorry," Charlotte said, honestly at a loss. "Why would you go back, even with the extra room, if you can live here instead?"

Wendy patted her sister's belly as she passed her and said, "Because the old house makes me happy in a more familiar way, that's why. Why can't anyone understand that?"

She threw a second window all the way open to the warm, salty, southwest flow of air. It really was a perfect day, with the promise of summer a full-blown reality. All of the visitors and guests were present and accounted for, and all of them had easily managed to fit. Spirits were high, partly because everyone's elbows hadn't been in everyone else's faces all day. This was going to work, and Wendy was as amazed as she was pleased. Fantasies rarely turned out to be true.

"So what's the deal with Mom?" Charlotte asked with a glance at the hall beyond the door of the master bedroom. "Why was she sniffling when we arrived?"

"Oh, she just got a little weepy when she went into the pantry and saw the sixty-five candles on the sheet cake. You can have the energy of a forty-year-old, and you can look like a fifty-year-old, but you can't really argue with a candle. Plus now I hear it's bugging her that she'll be an official senior citizen more than a year before Dad."

"Only Mom," said Charlotte, shaking her head. "Does she think Dad's going to run off with some young sixty-four-year-old arm candy?"

"Who knows? *I* say, never marry a man younger than you are, even by two minutes, if something like that matters so much."

"Yeah . . . trouble is, you don't realize it's going to matter until later."

"I disagree," Wendy said, because she'd been thinking about it a lot. "When you look at a guy as husband material, you should walk yourself through a bunch of different scenarios. You should say, 'What's the worst thing that can happen? I'll be sixty-five a year before he will. Can I live with that? Yes.' You move on to the next question. 'What's the worst thing that can happen? He'll forget our anniversaries. Can I live with that? Yes.' Next question. 'Will he leave his dirty underwear on the floor?' I mean, it's not all that complicated to figure out what you can stand and what you can't."

"Gee," Charlotte said in a voice like unbuttered toast, "now you tell me."

"At least you saw your mistake with Derek and you cut your losses," Wendy said quickly. "And anyway," she added, rubbing a smudge from the white woodwork with a wet finger, "I was only sixteen when you eloped. I hadn't worked out a system yet."

Charlotte wasn't buying it. "You talk so rational, but you're the most sentimental one in the family. Oh, hell," she said, interrupting herself. "I have to pee. Again." She went into the master bathroom and left the door open so that they could continue their conversation. "What about Jim? Did you walk through a set of hypotheticals before you married him?"

Wendy sat on the bed while she waited. "Of course. I said, 'He's hot. Mom hates him. What's the worst she could do to me?' "

From the bathroom she heard her sister laugh and then say a little ruefully, "And now he's her favorite son-in-law."

Of only two. Wendy went over to the bathroom doorway so that she could say directly to her sister, "Give it time, Charlotte. She'll come around."

"I've been married to John for eight years, Wendy. I have a kid, another almost here. No, she won't come around. Not unless Derek gets run over by a bus. That's the only way my present marriage will become legitimate in her eyes. The way it is now, she looks at me as if I'm a . . . a bigamist."

"That's an exaggeration."

"Just barely."

"It could be worse. Take Dave—"

"And do what with him?" asked her brother. He was in the hall and he detoured into the bedroom when he heard his name mentioned.

Wendy closed the door on Charlotte and said to him, "Is there an age limit for applying to the priesthood? Because Mom's getting a little impatient waiting for you to turn your life around, little brother."

"Mm. Looks like I should've brought Noreen," he said, looking gravely pensive. "Mom would've taken one look at her tattoos and disowned me. Problem solved."

"Baloney," Wendy said. "You didn't bring Noreen because you're bored with Noreen. You've been seeing her for, what, two months? Oh, yeah. You're bored."

"No I'm not. This time it's real."

"Baloney bullshit."

Dave was ready to change the subject. Winking at Wendy as he walked past, he went up to the bathroom door and began banging on it with both hands. "How long you gonna be in there, for cryin' out loud?" he yelled. "Stop hogging! I'm gonna be late for school and it'll be all your fault! What good is lipstick gonna do, cowface? You'll still be ugly. Hurry up or I'm tellin'!"

The door opened and Charlotte, the prettiest woman in the house, gave her brother a withering look, just the way she used to do when she was fifteen and Dave was eight.

"If you tease me, I'll cry," she promised with sweet sarcasm. "My hormones are all fucked up."

Dave sucked in his breath, scandalized. "I'm tellin'."

He threw his arm around his older sister and kissed her on her cheek and said, "You're naming him after me, right?"

"Just what we need: another David. Besides, who says it's going to be a boy?"

"You *know*?"

"I'm not tellin', nyah, nyah," Charlotte said with a snippy smile.

They walked out together ahead of a happy, grinning Wendy and she thought, *I can't ask for more than this. It's all I've ever wanted, to have us all together and getting along.*

Family was everywhere, grown-ups sprinkled liberally with children. The men were being primitive, hovering with their beers around the coals that Jim had fanned into something just short of a bonfire. The women were being—well, domestic, cooing over the delightful fabrics and furnishings, drifting from one thing to another with expressions of surprise and pleasure.

Because nothing actually belonged to Wendy and Jim, no one was tempted to be jealous. They could all admire the owners' keen eye without wanting to poke out Wendy's, and she was grateful for that. It added another layer of happiness to a day she knew she would always remember.

The updated kitchen was still on the small side, crowded with cooks and assemblers. Since Mark's wife, Marianne, was a nutritionist in a hospital, it conferred a halo of authority on her. She commandeered the kitchen, and that was fine with Wendy; she preferred to wander and visit and take it all in. Her brother Frank and his wife hadn't been east for a year; their once-colicky baby was now a not-so-terrible two who liked being around people and noise. Wendy adored her and held her every chance she got.

The rest of the kids were divided into two broad age groups. The older ones had had their swims and sails and were now all piled into the attic with their video games, while the younger ones, led by Tyler, amused themselves building sand castles, despite the fact that the sand wasn't quite as white and fine as Tyler—an expert from way back—would have liked.

Gracie Ferro's generation was there in quiet force. Wendy's mother had invited three of her dearest friends (all of them older than sixty-five, which may or may not have been coincidence), and they sat in Adirondack chairs on the patio like the *grandes dames* they were, with a steady stream of attendants appearing to ask whether they'd like their drinks refreshed, or a bit more dip.

Wendy's father sought her out. "This is nice. This is very nice, Wenda," he said, using her birth name as he always did when he was pleased with her performance. "The food so far is very, very good. Good snacks. And I'm glad you're making steamers."

"Dad! How could I not?" Wendy asked. "No clams? You wouldn't have come!"

"You know that's not true," he said, looking vaguely shocked. Unlike his wife, Charlie Ferro had no sense of irony at all, which made him all the more irresistible a target to his kids.

"You're right, Dad. I know that's not true," Wendy assured him gravely.

"But listen. Next time—don't plan to grill the lobsters," he said with a discreet warning shake of his head. "They dry out. You leave them on two minutes too long, you got cardboard. Next time, just boil 'em, honey. It's the only way. Believe me."

"You want us to boil yours, Dad? It's no trouble."

"No, no, no," he said, aghast at the suggestion. "How would that look, a special order for me? Just—next time. Okay?"

In the year before he met Gracie O'Byrne, Charlie Ferro had bought himself a skiff and a bullrake, and he'd spent the spring, summer, and fall on Narragansett Bay, harvesting the oversized clams that Rhode Islanders alone called quahogs, and selling them to a fish market in old, unrestored downtown Providence. It had been backbreaking, heartbreaking work, and by the end of the year, not surprisingly, he was broke. And in love with Gracie O'Byrne.

So he sold the rig and went back to work in a chrome-plating shop half a mile inland. Nevertheless, his year on the water had been the most profoundly satisfying of his life. All of his kids knew it, because he went back to it over and over in his reminiscences about the good old days. He had loved being in his own boat and plying a trade on the bay. It was as simple as that.

When he married Gracie and went to work in the fume-filled plating shop, he gave up a lot more than the joy of harvesting the sea: during the quarter century that he had worked with the toxins, his kidneys had taken a beating, and his health was no longer robust. His early retirement had been proof of the fact.

"Well, Dad, you're the family expert on seafood, and that's all there is to it," Wendy said, and this time she wasn't being ironic but affectionate. Humbled and grateful that her father had done what it took to stay married to Gracie O'Byrne and raise their five kids, Wendy hugged him lightly and said, "You're a good man, Charlie Ferro. What can I get you to eat?"

By the time she worked through the detour from the closed-off exit on Gano Street, Zina was a nervous wreck; she'd never driven on such harrowing highways in her life. She'd nearly been sideswiped by a merging car, and then when she'd slammed on the brakes to let him squeeze in ahead of her, she'd nearly been rear-ended. Before she drove back to Worcester, she was going to have to revisit the map for a back-road route.

It wasn't just the state of the crowded, curving highway that was making her drive so badly; it was the state of her mind. She was upset and angry, disappointed and shocked, and very likely she shouldn't even have been behind a wheel. But there wasn't any other way to find out exactly who Jim Hodene was. Or wasn't. Her brother certainly wasn't going to tell her. Zack couldn't be trusted at all. First her parents, then Jimmy, and now Zack. It didn't seem possible.

How could he *do* that—lie to her about Aunt Louise? It took Zina's breath away that he had been able to look her straight in the eye and say that Aunt Louise had just died and had left him an inheritance. Louise Odette had died years ago, Zina now knew, and if she retained any lawyers to disperse her money, their names were not Smith, Reston, and Upton: there was no such firm in Omaha. No, if Zack had inherited anything, he would have heard about it long before now.

So where had Zack gotten the money? He hadn't robbed a bank; Zina would have heard it on the news. And he hadn't made that kind of fortune making reproductions of antique furniture, no matter how respected he was at his craft.

So where had he gotten the money?

How about a lottery?

It didn't take a degree in math to figure out that a lottery winner would have lots of money to throw around. A lottery winner might not even *miss* a few hundred thousand dollars. So the next question was, why would a lottery winner have thrown so much money at Zack?

Damn you, Jimmy. Damn you, Zack.

Tears began to flow again; she was incapable of stopping them any longer and just let them roll. Street signs blurred in front of her until she wiped her eyes, and then she saw that some of them said, "Fox Point," so she had to be in the right neighborhood. It hadn't been very hard to find at all, even in her distracted state.

Why had she ever let Zack do her legwork for her? If it was to save her some heartbreak, then the mission was a failure. Her heart wasn't just broken now, it was shattered, and she was faint from the pain of feeling each of its million splinters.

She drove slowly past the houses on Sheldon Street, reading the numbers, aware that one of the houses coming up was under construction. Pausing in front of that one, she saw that the numbers matched the address that she'd found in the white pages of her library's old Providence directory. The six was upside down and hanging by one screw, but, yes, the numbers did match. She parked her yellow Civic behind a delivery truck in front of it and got out.

She approached the house like a zombie, half convinced that someone else, someone fierce and determined and with nothing to lose, was inhabiting her body. She watched herself go up to two young guys who were helping a deliveryman unload stacks of wood shingles from the lumberyard truck. She listened to herself ask them, "Do you know where I can find Jim Hodene?"

She was amazed at how clear, how calm, how pleasant she sounded. It was someone else speaking, not her.

One of the guys, bare-chested and stripped down to his baggy shorts, said, "He just moved out last weekend."

"Oh," she said, crushed. "Far?"

The bare-chested guy shrugged and answered, "If you call a ten-minute drive far."

She found herself smiling at him and trying to charm. "Could you give me directions?"

He shrugged again and said, "Nope. All I know is he's renting a place on the beach in Barrington."

The other guy said to him, "How could you not know the street? Pete must've mentioned it six times: Starboard Lane, for chrissake."

"Who listens to Pete?" said the first guy, looking embarrassed.

Zina didn't know who Pete was, and she didn't dare ask.

Instead she said shyly, "Do you think that Jim—Mr. Hodene would be home now?"

"Well, he's not working at a job, that's for sure," the second guy said with a snicker.

"You wouldn't happen to have a street number, would you?" Zina asked. She had no idea how many houses were on Starboard Lane, although it didn't sound long.

"Just look for a blue Explorer."

The guy in the tank top seemed to regret having spoken and began warning off the other one. "What're you, a friggin' tour guide?" he snapped.

His co-worker became defensive. "What's the big deal? Everybody around here knows where he moved." But he seemed to back off after that, and the two of them went back to unloading the shingles.

Zina thanked them—someone thanked them, anyway; the voice was coming out of her body—and then she got back in her car and reached for the street map that was opened on the front seat.

Barrington really wasn't all that far, and Zina was back on the hellish highway in minutes.

She found Barrington, and she found Starboard Lane. Now all she had to do was find her husband.

It was a beautiful evening, and the gardeners of the neighborhood were out in force; Zina felt anything but anonymous, driving past them in a yellow Civic while trying not to look lost.

There was only one Ford Explorer on the street, and she was dismayed to see that it wasn't alone: it was parked in a driveway that was filled with cars. There were cars parked up and down the street in front of the house, as well, and red helium balloons shaped like hearts and flowers were tied to a lattice arch that was weighed down with red roses: Jim Hodene was apparently having a housewarming party.

In some odd way, seeing the balloons gave Zina hope.

No one would tie red balloons to a house if he'd once run away from his pregnant wife. This man, this Jim Hodene, *couldn't* be her Jimmy Hayward. If she could just see him, she'd know. If this Jim weren't her Jimmy, then Zack was telling the truth and she was being a suspicious fool and everything would be fine.

Except for the fake inheritance.

It was that fake inheritance that made her slam on the brakes and squeeze her Civic between two cars parked out in the lane. It was that fake inheritance that made her get out of her car and approach the house with a fake bounce in her step, as if she were the fake guest of honor and all the balloons, not fake, were really for her.

She stood under the wonderful flower-draped arch, aware that there were voices, some of them loud and most of them men's, coming from the backyard. She couldn't see anyone; the privacy hedge that extended out from each side of the house was doing its job. Was one of the voices Jimmy's? She stood completely still, straining to pick his out from among the rest. She heard one that . . . yes? No? Maybe? She couldn't tell, not for certain.

She continued to stand there, paralyzed by the possibilities—unwilling to pursue, unable to run. She did not want to know the truth, after all. That was her final, overwhelming decision: she didn't want to know. She loved her brother too much, and this was her last, best chance to hang on to that emotion.

I have to get out of here.

She was turning to leave when the door opened and a man, about her age and still laughing at something he'd heard, stepped out onto the landing of the set-in entry. A little startled by her appearance so near, he said in friendly recovery, "Hi. Are you here for the party?"

Breathless now with panic, Zina blurted, "No! How can I be?" Even as she said it, she realized that she was wearing what any reasonable person could construe as summer-party clothing: a pale blue linen sundress and little strappy sandals. Her effort to look as pretty as she could was coming back to bite her.

The man cocked his head. His dark eyes were fixed on her curiously, as if he thought she was someone he ought to know. "But you did come to see—?"

"Jim?" It came out as a question, an admission of her own abiding confusion. "I think that's his name."

"Ah. He's out back, manning the grill."

"Oh. I didn't know . . ." she stammered. "Maybe I'll come back some other time."

He was watching her even more curiously now and trying to reassure her with a gentle smile; he must have seen how near to tears she was. "Is there anything I can do?" he asked in a coaxing, sympathetic way.

Giving him a timid, mournful smile in return, she shook her head. He really did seem kind, and it was hard for her to break away from that.

He asked, "Would your business take long?"

"Two seconds," she murmured. "Just . . . to see if he's the person I knew."

"Ah-h. You're someone from the old days," he said, cocking his head in appraisal of her. He was shutting down, becoming more cautious. "Jim's had a lot of people looking him up, ever since he became a . . . celebrity."

He meant "millionaire"; Zina understood that and resented his implication. "No, no, I'm not one of *those*," she said with spirit. But her indignation evaporated right after it appeared. Obviously she was behaving suspiciously. What else could he think?

He looked at her intently again, this time with a kind of studious frown, as if she were a painting in a gallery and he were trying to decide what she was all about and whether she was worth buying. Finally, he said, "I'll walk around to the back with you. My name's Dave Ferro," he added, extending his hand.

"I'm . . . Zina Hayward," she replied in a trance.

She let him shake her hand and was struck by how very civilized it all was. How hard could it be, she wondered as she accompanied this courteous, kindhearted man around the side of the house, to look at his Jim and decide for herself? She was so close. After twelve years, she was so close.

If Dave's Jim wasn't her Jimmy, she was making a vow on the spot to give up her endless, hopeless, consuming search for him. She would divorce Jimmy Hayward in absentia or whatever it was called, or have him declared dead—which he would be to her, for all intents and purposes.

She would soon know.

Zack was apoplectic.

He was stuck on Route 195, waiting with everyone else for an accident ahead to be cleared up. He wasn't that far from the crash site—he could see the flashing strobes of emergency vehicles from where he sat in a fury of apprehension—but he may as well have been in the middle of the Atlantic in a raft without oars.

His sister was in Providence. Jesus Christ, Zina was headed for Jim. The *Titanic* and the iceberg were a more suitable match!

Stopping in earlier at the shelter, Zack had received the news from Sylvia herself: apparently Zina had asked to be relieved of her watch because she had urgent business in Providence.

He'd nearly burst a blood vessel when he heard that. "Business? What the hell *business*?"

Sylvia hadn't liked his tone and had answered, "Your sister didn't say, and I did not ask."

Her tone had implied that if Zack were a halfway decent brother, he'd already know the reason.

So how had Zina figured it out? Everything was going so well. What had tipped her off? She had her cats, she had her cause, she seemed to be completely preoccupied. Where the hell had things gone wrong? He wasn't going to come up with the answer to that question, not sitting in traffic twiddling his thumbs. His only hope was that when Zina went to the house on Sheldon Street—and he had no doubt that she'd been able to find the address—the crew would already have left.

How bitterly fortunate that he had offered to work on Saturday in exchange for taking the afternoon off. What if he'd been at the house, blithely building an addition for her bigamist husband? The thought was so horrific that it was almost laughable.

Would she ask a neighbor where she could find Jim? Zack didn't think so. His sister belonged to a more reticent era when women were—well, more reticent. She had the soul of a handmaiden, and it amazed him, simply amazed him, that she had decided to have urgent business in Providence.

CHAPTER 14

Dave led Zina through an arch carefully carved out of a ten-foot hedge and into a scene filled with happy people. The trail of barbecue smoke sifting through the scent of lilies was evidence, if evidence were needed, that an idyllic beach party was in full swing. Guests were sitting, eating, milling, moving around. A group of children, seated at a long table covered in a blue-checkered cloth, were chattering noisily as they waited for food. Behind them all, an arc of white beach framed the picture-perfect moment.

Zina was so intimidated by the scene that she froze in her tracks. Sensing a newcomer, a graying Irish setter wandered up to her, sniffing her dress and finding cat. The guests themselves were more discreet. Some of them must have been observing her, surely, but Zina couldn't have said which ones; she was too frightened, too shy, too completely focused on picking out Jim from among them. She scanned unseeing past the women in her search for the man. She tried to tell herself that if Jim was there, she had every right to know it, but the sense that she was intruding was both profound and mortifying.

"Boy, he was here a minute ago," Dave said to her as he looked around. "Frank!" he called out. "Where's Jim?"

A man who looked a beefier version of Dave and who was wearing an apron that read *Sue the chef, I'm just the sous-chef,* said, "He went in the house for more supplies. You havin' surf or turf?"

"Steak for me."

Frank held up a thick slab speared on a fork. "The usual? Just past raw?"

"You bet."

With great fanfare, Frank slapped the filet mignon on the grill. Flames flared up around it dramatically as Frank wiggled the raw meat back and forth for no apparent reason that Zina could see. Suddenly she couldn't stop staring at the grill; it seemed the safest place to look.

"Ah, here's my sister," said Dave. "Hey, sis! C'mere and meet Zina."

Zina turned to see a very beautiful, very pregnant woman, wearing a maternity top in a shade of mauve that flattered her black hair and dark eyes, approaching them with a smile.

"This is Charlotte, my big—and I mean, *big*—sister," Dave said by way of an introduction.

Compressing her lips in mock anger, Charlotte swatted his shoulder and said, "Knock it off, or I'll sic John on you." She turned her very curious gaze on Zina. "Nice to meet you," she said, holding out her hand. "Are you with this clown?"

Dave said chivalrously, "I *wish*. We met out in front."

"Oh," said Charlotte.

It was clearly Zina's cue to explain why she was there.

If she could have clicked her heels three times and returned home, that's what Zina would have done. This was so not the time, so not the place, to look for a lost husband. Her breathing was becoming quick and shallow; she glanced at the back door one last time in desperation. Jim didn't emerge; a woman did.

Dave called out, "Wendy! Where's that no-good husband of yours?"

"Husband?" Zina murmured, and then she went woozy.

"Coming right behind me, I think."

The screen door opened again and Dave cried out, "Yo! Jim. Over here."

The man had a cluster of beer bottles locked in the fingers of each hand; he was edging through the door backward, pushing it open with his butt. "What's up?" he said as he swung around.

Zina was face to face with the one man, the only man, that she had ever loved.

He saw her—of course he saw her, how could he not see her, she hadn't been present a minute ago—but there was no shock of recognition, no bolt of fear, nothing but a look of mild curiosity.

"Jim? It's me. Zina," she said, dizzy from her multiple shocks.

The woman named Wendy said sharply, "Zina who? Jim, who is she? What does she—"

"I've waited so long, Jimmy," Zina said in a soft wail. "I couldn't wait any—"

And that's all that she was able to get out before her world, already whirling around her at warp speed, went blissfully black.

Wendy stood by as Dave lowered the recovering woman onto a cushioned chaise under a tree. All around her people hovered, murmuring their concerns and dismay.

She felt like a paramedic, keeping her siblings and especially her mother at bay and shooing the kids away—but in the meantime she was fighting wave after wave of suspicion and jealousy. It was so obvious—despite Jim's lack of concern—that the pale blond woman and Jim shared a history. She had seen it in the woman's face.

It was now brutally clear to Wendy what Jim's secret was. Zina was the sin that he hadn't been able to own up to, hard as he had tried. He'd had an affair after all, despite his shocked denial when Wendy had posed the question to him.

Was he in the middle of the affair still?

Bastard.

Wendy's cheeks were on fire. Her head thrummed with the sound of her raging pulse, and her breath became locked in her body. Those anguished protests by Jim, those sudden wild bouts of lovemaking—they weren't about him and Wendy at all, they were about *her,* the woman lying in the chaise longue right under Wendy's nose. Why else would she have chosen this occasion, this gathering of everyone Wendy loved, to publicly force the issue between Jim and her? *Obviously* they'd been having an affair. They still were, which is why she'd known about the party. My God, the woman was outrageous, and Jim was a—

Bastard!

"I'm . . . so . . . sorry," Zina said, looking only at Jim.

Jim looked at her, looked at Wendy, looked back at her. He looked completely baffled.

And so did everyone else. Everyone was waiting for a simple explanation. Clearly *no* one thought the woman was sorry because she had fainted in the middle of their birthday party. Wendy saw it all: saw her mother and Charlotte exchange a look; saw her brother Frank glance resignedly back at the filets mignon he'd abandoned on the grill; saw Dave, still crouched at Zina's side, glance up at Jim with a stiff, dawning look on his face.

It was Wendy who was forced to break the unnerving silence. In a voice tight with fury, she said to the woman, "Are you all right?"

Zina sat up and gave Wendy a wobbly, full-lipped smile. Her paleness, coupled with her blond hair and blue eyes, gave her an ethereal look that made Wendy wonder whether perhaps she hadn't jumped to a horrible conclusion. The woman didn't look . . . lusty enough, somehow, to go after someone else's husband. She was truly beautiful, there was no question about that—the stares she was getting weren't just from curiosity—but mostly the woman looked miserable and very possibly ill.

Maybe it was all a mistake. "Can we get you some water?" Wendy asked, less unkindly now. "Or orange juice?" The woman was so pale. Could she be diabetic?

"Thank you . . . a little water, maybe," Zina answered in a whispery croak.

Dave jumped up and hurried back to the house to perform the errand, and Wendy decided that whatever it was that Zina had to say, it shouldn't be to the gathered horde.

"We can use some air here. Will everyone *please* go back to what he or she was doing, please, I'm begging you, *please*?" she said with fierce politeness. "We don't want the lobster to be dry, and I smell burning *steak*," she added with a particularly icy glare at her brother Frank, who had pushed his bulk up to the front of the crowd.

Everyone moved off with the exception of Jim and her mother.

Wendy gave Grace Ferro a verbal nudge, which was all she dared. "Mom, please," she said in quiet anguish. "This isn't your concern."

"Of course it is," her mother said. Turning to Zina, she said in a completely matter-of-fact voice, "Why have you come here?"

People had to answer Grace O'Byrne Ferro; she rarely left them a choice. Zina lowered her gaze, and Wendy was not surprised to see a tear roll out.

"To see if Jim Hodene is who I thought he was."

"And is he?"

Zina nodded. Another tear rolled out. Wendy didn't know what to think. Zina apparently wasn't having an affair with Jim at the moment; so when had it been?

"Who, exactly, do you think he is?" Wendy's mother asked gently.

For an answer, Zina looked up at Jim and said, "Oh, Jimmy—how could you?"

Alarm bells went off for Wendy everywhere at once. "Stop asking questions," she commanded her mother, taking her roughly by the arm. "Stop it right now."

Scandalized, Grace yanked her arm free of her daughter's grip. "Don't you dare grab me that way! I'm your *mother* and don't you forget it."

Zina staggered to her feet and tried to intervene. "No, please don't fight, not because of me! I didn't know, I didn't know that he'd married again—"

" 'Again'?" Wendy said, whirling around on the pale beauty. "What are you talking about?" She turned boggle-eyed toward her husband. "Jim, what's she saying? That you were *married* before?"

"What're you, nuts?" he said to Wendy. He looked completely at sea. "I'm married to you."

"Then what's she *doing* here?"

"How should I know?" he said, exasperated. "Ask *her.*"

Grace intervened. "What's your name—Zina? Zina, you're coming with me inside."

"No she's not," Wendy snapped, turning on her mother again. "This is none of your business, Mom. Butt *out.*"

"Wendy, for God's sake, what is *wrong* with you?" her mother said in a low hiss. "Consider where you are. You're embarrassing me! At least let's go inside until we straighten this out."

"This is *my* affair, Mom. Mine and mine alone!"

"Obviously not; take a look around you," Grace shot back.

Wendy measured her audience in one regal sweep: everyone was completely transfixed. Shit. If that wasn't just like her family. Her sister-in-law was probably going to slap the whole episode up on her Web site. God, how she hated them all just then.

Who *was* this woman? Just another gold digger? Then why didn't it seem that way?

She turned back to Zina, who'd sat back down on the side of the chaise, apparently too weak or disinclined to leave.

"Jim?" Wendy asked through gritted teeth. "Would you like to have the floor?"

"To say what?" he answered, angry and offended. He didn't bother glancing at Zina as he added, "You can't possibly be taking this seriously."

Be that as it may, Wendy was taking it very seriously, indeed. There was just something about the past couple of weeks.

"How long were you supposedly married to my husband?" she demanded to know from Zina. In her mind she was thinking, *She would have to have been a child. She still looks like a child. A weekend in Vegas, a hangover, and a quick divorce to undo the damage: is that what this was all about? Or was it all just a lie?*

In a downtrodden voice, Zina murmured, "We've been married for . . . twelve years."

Wendy rolled her eyes and said flatly, "That's ridiculous. You're not that old." She tried to do the math; in her present distracted and suspicious mood, it hurt her head to let in raw logic. Twelve years for Zina, plus twelve years, with dating, for Wendy, and assume the bare minimum of eighteen years old when Zina claimed to have gotten married . . .

"You're not saying that you're, what, forty-two or even older, are you? Because that's ridiculous. Jim's not that old. You are definitely not that old," she added, hating to concede the fact. "Try to make some sense, would you? God! I can't understand you at all. You show up here, you make ludicrous statements, you *ruin* my party—really, I should just call the police! I might just do that, you know?"

Wendy was doing little more than filling the air with the sound of her voice—stalling, pure and simple—because somewhere deep, deep down, she'd heard something that had sounded wrong, something that didn't make sense, and she was afraid to go back and pick over the sentences and discover what that something was. She was genuinely, profoundly terrified to go back and review.

As it turned out, she didn't have to; her mother did it for her.

Grace said gently to Zina, "You mean, you *were* married for twelve years. Because you said, 'We've *been* married for twelve years,' and that implies that you still are. And you didn't mean that."

Zina bowed her head. And then she nodded forlornly.

"Yes I did."

Now it was Wendy's turn to feel paralyzed. The sheer boldness of the claim had left her speechless.

Her mother stared. Jim said softly, "Wow. Now I've heard everything."

In a flat, controlled voice, Wendy said to Zina, "You're saying—what? That you're *still* married. Is that it?"

Again Zina nodded.

"I see." Wendy turned to Jim and said, "Which would naturally mean: we're not."

Jim didn't bother to respond to her but only shook his head incredulously.

Zina looked up at him. Her cheeks were rosy, the first color that Wendy had seen in her face. She looked astonishingly innocent, a picture of purity; she looked like one of the saints on the holy cards that her mother collected at funerals.

But saint who? Teresa? Margaret Mary? Joan of Arc? Suddenly it seemed important for Wendy to place the face, although she had no idea why. Maybe it would help her to understand this pale enigma who had crashed her party. Maybe it was just easier to think about beautiful saints than to figure out who was telling the truth.

Zina whispered again, "How could you do that to me, Jimmy?"

"Do *what*? I've never seen you before in my life."

A steadier stream of tears began rolling down her flushed cheek. Wendy knew—everyone knew—that there would be more. The woman was teetering on the verge of a breakdown.

"Wendy? Wendy!" Her mother was alarmed. Wendy could see the question in her face: Do you have a plan?

Wendy looked at her husband. He obviously had none. He was annoyed, embarrassed, even angry—but he did not have a plan.

"I think we should call the police," Wendy announced.

Her mother looked relieved. Jim frowned and then said sternly to Zina, "Is that what you want, miss? To be grilled by the police?"

She shook her head quickly and said, "Jimmy, it's me— Zina! Don't you *know* me?"

She sounded so plaintive, so anguished. Wendy was convinced that no one who actually knew her could have resisted comforting her. She glanced at her brother Dave, who was standing back a little way and making little noises of distress; stranger or no, Dave looked as if he was willing to take Zina in his arms on the spot.

Jim said in a low, commanding voice that most of the company couldn't hear, "My wife is right, Zina or whoever you are. If you don't want to be held by the police, then I suggest you leave the premises right now—and quietly, please. Do *not* make a scene. We're in the middle of a celebration here. Now. Will you just go?"

Jim had been reasonably polite, but Zina looked as if

she'd been clubbed. Wendy knew that she would have reacted the same way. Whatever the woman's motivation had
been, it was ending up in public humiliation. It couldn't be
easy for her.

Zina stood up and weaved so violently that Wendy
reached out instinctively to steady her.

Zina waved her away. "How could I have been so
wrong?" she said in a low wail.

Wendy felt a wave of relief. So the woman *had* been
mistaken. Thank God, thank God, thank God for that.
Wendy wanted to give her the benefit of the doubt—she
seemed too deluded, too naïve to be a con woman—so she
said, "Can I walk you back to your car?"

Zina shook her head. "No . . . I—oh, God," she moaned,
and then she hurried away, leaving the company open-
mouthed and staring.

CHAPTER 15

In front of the house and right next to the roses, some of Tyler's aunts and uncles were standing in a circle around the lady in the blue dress again, the same as after she fainted. This time Tyler was able to squeeze between the grown-ups for a closer look and no one even noticed. They were too busy asking the lady questions, all at the same time. Even standing up close, Tyler couldn't hear any of her answers, because her voice was so soft—and, of course, because his relatives were so loud.

They were saying things like, "Why are you here?" and "What do you really want?" and "Who put you up to this?" They said, "You're high on something, aren't you? We *will* call the cops, and then we'll see how far you get. You're after his money," they said. "Just like everyone else."

Tyler could not understand why everyone was so upset with her. She looked like an angel to him, or at least someone on the cover of a magazine. Her skin was so white compared to his mother's, and she was more slender, and her eyes were a deep, beautiful blue. They were shining, and Tyler knew that that meant she was holding back tears, just the way his mother did when his father said something mean.

He felt sorry for the lady, standing alone in the middle of everyone; if a person wasn't used to his family and to their noisy ways, it could be pretty scary. Tyler could tell that she wanted to get to her car. But they just wouldn't let her. One thing he knew: she didn't do anything wrong. You could see it in her face, how nice she was. So why was everyone yelling at her? All she did was faint. Tyler was completely confused.

Suddenly she shook her head, and the tears did fall then. "I never should have come here," she told Tyler's uncle Dave.

Someone else said, "Well, it's a little late *now,* don't you think?"

She nodded a bunch of times, jerky little nods, and then for some reason she looked straight at Tyler, and her eyes got big, even through her tears, and right after that she pushed past him and managed to break through the circle and reach her car. He rubbed his arm where she touched it as she squeezed past: it felt all tingly.

She pulled out of the drive and then took off fast.

"Take down her license number!" yelled Tyler's other Uncle David, but that was because he was a lawyer.

No one had a pencil or a paper, so Tyler's aunt Lucille kept saying the number out loud over and over until somebody said, "Drop it, would you already? No one's planning to sue."

They all went back through the arch in the hedge and joined the rest of the family, who seemed to be split up into quiet ones and blabby ones. Tyler's grandmother was doing the most talking; his grandfather, the least. Tyler went over and sat by his grandfather so that he wouldn't have to talk and possibly miss something important.

He saw that his mother and his father were speaking not very loud, just to one another. His mother said something louder that sounded annoyed, and then his father said the f-word—in front of company, which he never did! Then his mother got mad and turned around and said to his uncle Frank—who looked exactly like the new star tackle for the

New England Patriots—"Thanks for abandoning the grill, Frank; I suppose I can serve the cardboard and shoe leather now."

"That's it!" said his uncle Frank, untying his apron. "I can't work in these conditions. I'm shutting down the grill."

"Big loss," said his uncle Dave.

His aunt Sharon, who was holding Tyler's baby cousin in her arms, kind of laughed and said to Tyler's uncle Frank, "Well, *this* was one of your more memorable gatherings." Then she sighed and said, "I'll see if I can move up our flight."

Right after that, Tyler's uncle Dave walked up to Tyler's dad and said, "You'd better be telling the truth, man, or you're dead; I don't care if you are my best friend."

Then his other uncle David said, "You're probably going to need a lawyer, Jim. Call me at the office."

But his great-aunt Genevieve turned right around and said, "If he needs representation, *you* are not going to be the one to do it. Can you imagine the scandal? I would never speak to you again."

And Uncle David was her own *son*.

After that, everyone started talking at the same time again, and Tyler couldn't make out much of anything.

He tapped his grandfather's forearm, trying to get through to him over the chatter of his too big, too noisy, too everywhere family. "Grampa, what did Aunt Lucy mean just now when she said Mom and Dad might not be married?"

His grandfather said, "It's nothing, Ty, just a big misunderstanding," but he hardly noticed that Tyler was even there. He was watching everyone else, just like Ty.

Tyler's uncle Frank moved out of the way and Tyler was able to see his mother and father again. He could tell that they were getting ready to fight; he recognized the tone of their voices.

"How did she know where to find you, anyway?" his mother said. "We've only just moved."

"Good question," his father said. He sounded like he might know the answer but wasn't sure.

"How was she possibly going to back up a claim like that? She would need papers, proof, that kind of thing . . ."

"Anyone can forge a document," his father said.

"Jim's right," said Aunt Lucille. "David says that you can buy any certificate you want on the Internet."

"That doesn't make sense," his mother said to his dad and not to Aunt Lucille. "If she was going to wave it around to blackmail you for money—okay, then I could see it. *Maybe*. But no one tries a stunt like that in front of a crowd. It defeats the whole purpose."

"So maybe she's just unstable," said Tyler's Aunt Marianne. "She had a really odd look in her eye."

Tyler didn't think so!

His mother nodded slowly. "She did, didn't she.?"

"Yeah—like that fan of David Letterman's," his dad said. "Wasn't she basically harmless but fixated?"

Again his mother nodded, but Tyler could see that something was bothering her. She said, "I mean, it was such a goofy ploy to try to pull off. To be married! The woman would need witnesses, friends, relatives . . ."

No one said anything. Tyler wondered whether they were thinking the same thing he was: that his own dad had no relatives. Which was so weird. Tyler had a million aunts and uncles that were related to his mom—and no one at all, not one single person, that was related to his dad. He used to ask his dad about that a lot, just to see what kind of funny answer his dad would give him. One time he said that aliens took them all in a spaceship. Another time he said, "They were all convicted as American spies; they're doing time in a Russian gulag."

But the last time Tyler had asked, just a week ago, his

dad got really mad; so from now on he was letting it drop. Some people just didn't have relatives. Anyway, his mom had enough of them for two people.

Tyler's dad looked around and suddenly slapped his hands together, which was surprising; he never did stuff like that. He said, "Hey, let's get this shindig back on track! We're not gonna let some mental case ruin our fun. Frank! Fire that grill back up and scrape it clean. I've still got half a side of beef in the fridge; we'll start over. I'll take the orders. Okay, who's having what?"

About that time, Tyler's mother noticed where he was sitting—with the grown-ups—and she shooed him away to the picnic tables where his cousins were stuck. He knew they'd been told they couldn't leave their places until they got permission; it was like they were all being made to sit in the corner at the same time.

Tyler's cousin Emmy could hardly wait for him to get back. She was as far from the table as she could be and still be touching it: her toe was on the bench, and she was reaching out to Tyler, hurrying him up.

"Is she your mother—that lady who just left?" Emmy asked, making big, stupid google eyes at him.

"What a dumb question," Tyler said. The thought had never occurred to him, but now it did, and he hated it. "My *mother* is my mother."

Tyler's oldest cousin, Justin, who was twelve, smiled evilly and said, "Maybe she is, but your dad's not her husband."

"Yes he is!" Tyler argued.

"No he's not, weren't you listening?" Justin said, shaking his head from side to side. He looked exactly like one of those dashboard dogs, like his head was on a spring or something.

"I suppose I couldn't hear as good as you," Tyler told

him in a quavering voice. "My ears are only half as big as yours."

"Four eyes!"

"Fat ears!"

"Hey! Knock it off!" his Uncle David told them, but he was looking at Tyler, not Justin, when he said it. "Justin, come on; we're going home. Your mother feels one of her migraines coming on."

"What about the cake?" Justin demanded.

"Don't worry about the cake. You get plenty of cake."

Justin's mouth turned down. He got up from the table and, dragging his hands along the top, said, "We didn't even get to go sailing, hardly. This is the crummiest birthday I've ever been to."

"Yeah, well, you're not the only one who feels that way," said his father. "Lots of people are leaving. Let's go."

Tyler couldn't resist saying to his cousin, "Don't worry, Justy; I'll eat your piece for you." He gave his older cousin his best, most evil smile, but inside, he felt pretty scared, even though he didn't know why.

Zack was on the next block when he saw Zina's yellow Civic roaring away from Wendy's rented beach house and headed in his direction. Almost immediately he saw her slam on the brakes: a Siamese cat had wandered out in the street directly in her way.

A woman rushed out into the lane from the nearest house and scooped up the cat. Even from where he was, Zack could hear her shriek at his sister, "That could have been a *child,* you fool!"

Zack parked his truck on the side of the lane—fully aware that it was going to end up towed—and ran to the driver's side of Zina's car. Zina took one look at him and started rolling up the window in a pathetically insufficient attempt to shut him out of her life.

Ignoring the neighbor still cradling her cat, Zack said, "Zee, Zee, I'm sorry. How could I tell you?"

He was in agony at her pain. The scene was playing out so much worse than anything he'd been able to dream up on his own—and the show still wasn't over.

Zina wouldn't look at him, wouldn't talk to him, couldn't do either if she tried: she was distraught. She tried to start her Civic, which had stalled when she braked, but she let the clutch out too fast and it stalled again.

He stuck his arm through the half-closed window and grabbed the wheel. "*Wait*, I said!"

"Go to hell!" she cried, and she burst into sobs.

"I'll drive you home," he said wearily.

Other neighbors had come out to gawk. One of them had his cell phone out, ready no doubt to punch 911. Zack turned to them and snarled, "Don't you have anything better to do?"

Gently shooing his sister over to the passenger side of the Civic, he adjusted the driver's seat all the way back for the long trek home. He had spent so much time and energy worrying about Zina finding out the truth that, now that the deed was done, his thoughts and emotions began racing on to the next innocent victim in the tragedy.

Wendy. What must she be going through now? It was almost too brutal for Zack to imagine. For her to be shocked that way in front of everyone she held dear . . . but maybe there was a good side to it. He wanted to believe it. She had a big family, people she loved, after all. They would support her.

Still, as Zack could personally, bitterly attest just then, family could be completely useless when the chips were down.

He ripped his thoughts away from Wendy and turned

back to his sister, who had stopped sobbing and was re-signed to being driven home. Her head was leaning back on the headrest; her eyes were closed. Zack saw trickles of tears crossing her cheekbones and getting lost in her hair. She was absolutely silent.

Zack would so much rather she raged.

Odd, how Zack was able to see himself in a whole new light. Forget Machiavellian schemer; he had been giving himself too much credit for having a brilliant blackmail strategy. In retrospect, he was more like a cartoon character, wandering around holding a grenade with the pin pulled out—except that, unlike in a cartoon, there was nothing very funny about the emotional carnage he'd caused when the thing went off.

"I'm sorry, Zee," he said, glancing back at her again. "More than you'll ever know."

She didn't bother responding. She didn't even bother to open her eyes.

They had the cake but skipped the candles.

Gracie Ferro went into the pantry and personally pulled out all sixty-five of them, leaving them in a heap on a saucer. The kids who remained at the party were devastated; what good was a cake with sixty-five holes in the frosting?

Wendy was having a hard time figuring out who was responsible for the total failure of her first big family gathering; there were so many worthy contenders. The mysterious Zina? Even now, Wendy couldn't believe she hadn't been hired by someone as a joke; it would be just like one of her idiot brothers—or all of them, working together—to do something like that.

Her mother? Gracie Ferro had treated the day from first to last more as a wake than a celebration. Anyone would think that she had just dipped one toe into the grave. Why had she wanted the damn birthday party in the first place, if she hadn't wanted to celebrate? That was Wendy's exact question to her as they argued in the kitchen.

"To keep some control over the event," was her mother's not-so-surprising answer. "I didn't want you kids renting a hall and inviting every Tom, Dick, and Harry I've ever known."

"Baloney," Wendy had said to that. "You just didn't want us inviting all the women from church because you've lied about your age to them, haven't you?"

"I haven't lied about *anything*. But I don't see why I have to broadcast my old age to the entire congregation," her mother conceded angrily, so obviously Wendy had touched a nerve. Right after that, her mother had left.

And then there was Jim. Always Jim. Jim with the checkered history of easy lies and convenient evasions. Jim, who could never stand to hurt anyone and got around it by telling the person whatever the person wanted to hear. Jim, who had never yet simply stepped up to the plate and said, "Yup. I did it and I'm sorry."

Jim.

"I don't know why you're taking this out on *me*," he muttered as he dumped the last of the paper plates into a black lawn bag and began compressing the air out of it. "I'm minding my own business, getting our guests—*your* family—some beer, and suddenly I'm face to face with some looney tune who claims to have been my wife in some parallel universe. And immediately you get this I-*knew*-it look on your face! Jesus, you're a piece of work. You have the most suspicious, paranoid, jealous mind of anyone I've ever known."

"*Will* you keep your voice down?" Wendy said. "We still have company, in case you haven't noticed."

"So why the hell didn't you take them up on their offer to sleep at some of the others' houses?"

"Because I promised them a good time, and they're going to have a good time if it kills me," she said in a low hiss, looking at the beach where the out-of-towners were keeping a polite distance from them.

"Bullshit. You just want to show them all up because we've never had squat and now we do."

"*I'm* not the show-off in this marriage! I was perfectly happy to stay in the old house. *You're* the one who can't spend it fast enough. You have every toy conceivable and you're not done yet!"

"Oh, yeah, every toy. One boat. Big deal. I guess I should have come crawling to you first for permission. Sorr-*ree*. Oh, yeah, I'm a big spender, all right."

"This is not about *spending*. This is about . . . this is about . . . I don't know *what* this is about," Wendy said in frustration. "This is about how that woman made me feel."

"Yeah: jealous and paranoid. What I said."

"Right," said Wendy. "You know everything, don't you? If you're so smart, then tell me why she showed up here today. Tell me that!"

Her husband dumped the bag by the door and she heard the rattle of glass; he hadn't separated out the recyclables. He scowled as she re-opened the bag and fished out the beer bottles, then began to tie it shut again.

He said, "I can't believe that you're letting some wacko come between us this way!"

She looked up at him from her task. "Who are you, Jim? I don't even know you. We've been married for twelve years, and all I know about your past is that you're an only child, your father left you when you were three, and your mother died of an aneurysm when you were a senior in high school."

"Well, shit—isn't that enough?" he asked.

"No. It's not. I know you had a hard childhood and that you don't remember much of it—but come on! You can tease Ty all you want about aliens abducting your family, but sometimes I think that *you're* the only alien around here. I have nothing to go on, Jim—nothing!"

He said stiffly, "It was enough for you to have a son by me. And to raise him with me. And to have your family accept me as one of their own. It was enough for me to open my door and my wallet to each and all of your relatives." Obviously wounded, he said, "What more do you want from me?"

Words. They were just words. Wendy didn't hear any of them. "Is Zina the big secret you were trying to tell me about?" she said, making a valiant effort to steady the quaver in her voice. "Look me in the eye, Jim. Answer me yes or no. And God help you if you lie to me."

Her husband looked her straight in the eye and said, "No. The answer to your question is no."

CHAPTER 16

That night they lay without touching—depressingly easy to do in their new vast bed.

Wendy was too wired from the encounter with the strange and distraught Zina and from her later, dragged-out argument with her husband to sleep. She tossed and she turned, angry and suspicious and uncertain after the day's bizarre event.

The sound of Jim's relaxed and easy snoring became both an irritant and a source of reassurance to her: he should have been more concerned that she was so upset; but on the other hand, no man with an extra wife on his hands could possibly have fallen asleep so fast or so soundly.

When Jim opened his eyes at six A.M., Wendy was staring at him, still trying to fathom his character.

"I really don't know you, do I?" she murmured, as if he had simply glanced away and then back at her, rather than slept a solid six hours.

Jim closed his eyes again and let out a sigh that sounded more sleepy than exasperated. He reached out and laid his arm across her waist and gave her a gentle squeeze.

"I'm sorry that that crackpot ruined your party," he said softly. "I know how much it meant to you. But we've got to learn to take these things in stride, Wen. It's part of being a lottery celebrity. Eventually people will stop coming out of the woodwork, and we'll be able to return to something like a normal life."

She rolled on her side to face him. His face was still puffy with sleep, his reddish hair pillow-shaped into a cock's comb. A let's-be-friends smile hovered at the corners of his mouth.

"Waddya say?" he whispered, though their guests couldn't possibly hear. "Kiss and start over?"

Instead of a yea or a nay, Wendy ran her hand over his hair, smoothing it into a more or less normal shape, and said, "What was your mother like?"

His brow twitched down in confusion; he wasn't expecting the question. "I've told you about her," he said, sounding vaguely wounded. "She was a high school English teacher. She typed doctoral dissertations on weekends to earn extra money to raise me. She wanted me to work on Wall Street. She liked Fleetwood Mac and the Kinks and chocolate croissants. She was tall and slender and blond. She had a musical voice. She was beautiful and smart—and she died too damn young."

He looked forlornly cheated by the fact, but Wendy ignored it and said, "I mean, tell me about *her,* what she was like. Did she have a sense of humor? Was she outgoing, generous, easily fooled? What kind of movies did she see? Did she keep a garden? Did she drink? You've never even said if she enjoyed a beer once in a while."

"What the hell difference does any of that make?" he asked, more puzzled than angry by the barrage of questions.

Wendy hesitated, then said, "Knowing her lets me know you."

"Jesus!" He sat up and swung his legs over the side of the bed and remained with his back to Wendy for a long, strained moment. Finally he said gruffly, "Why don't you just hire a PI? You can have him tail me through my secret life at Home Depot and West Marine."

He was sitting just beyond her reach. Wendy could have made an effort, yanking him playfully by his boxer shorts back into bed. But the mood was all wrong, and besides, she wasn't sure he'd let her.

"Earlier—when you were so sound asleep—I did think about hiring someone," she admitted. "But it would be just my luck to pick some sleazebag who'd turn around and sell the story to the *Enquirer*." She added, "I had to think about Ty."

"But not about us?" he said without turning around. "You didn't think about what kind of effect that would have on you and me?"

"We can't be any more at odds than we are now," she countered, sounding bleak. "At least an investigation would put the thing to rest."

"The thing. What thing?"

"Zina. The thing with Zina." She looked down and caught a glimpse of her body, so much more filled out than the slender, blond Zina's. Zina, who might very well look like Jim's adored mother.

"I've told you," Jim said wearily. "The woman who crashed your party is obviously a wacko. But what's the use? You're not listening. You hear what you want to hear."

"Why won't you tell me your secret?" Wendy implored, because that too had been on her mind all night. "Why won't you trust me with it?"

"Back to that again," he said with a sigh. He glanced at Wendy over his shoulder and then looked away. "Trust has nothing to do with it. Something happened, I'm not proud of it, I've moved past it. I'm not looking back. There is no point."

"Could this Zina possibly be involved—"

"Oh, Christ!" he said, standing up abruptly. "Give it a rest! That woman had nothing to do with my *secret*," he said with venomous emphasis. "Absolutely nothing."

He reached for the cutoffs lying on the striped slipper chair next to his side of the bed and hauled them over his freckled legs. "I'm going out for coffee," he said as he zipped up.

"When will you be back? Pete wanted to meet with us—"

"Fuck Pete."

"Okay-y-y," she said through gritted teeth. "He's not quite my type, but whatever you say, dear."

Her husband apparently had no desire for banter, either hostile or friendly. He walked out of the spacious bedroom without a glance back either at her or at the sparkling waters of Narragansett Bay.

Zack Tompkins stepped uneasily from the frozen tundra that surrounded his sister and onto the brimstone path that led to Wendy.

He was in a spectacular fix of his own making. Zina wanted nothing to do with him. She had spoken exactly one word to him after he'd commandeered her Civic and had driven her home: "Good-bye." He'd been forced nearly to bite through his tongue in the effort not to pump her about what had happened when she'd showed up at Jim Hodene's beach house, because he figured that his sister deserved the chance to mourn in silence.

In any case, it wasn't hard for him to fill in the blanks. There would have been a huge hullabaloo—Wendy's family was the kind that went in for hullabaloos—and Wendy would have been both enraged and devastated (he wasn't sure which emotion would take precedence) and, after the shocking revelation, undoubtedly would have moved out. If not last night, then surely that morning. As for her son . . . Zack preferred not to dwell on what the boy must have felt; it was painful in the extreme.

So now what, genius? Zack still didn't have a plan as he turned onto Sheldon Street, aware that the usual sudden joyous thump of his heart today was merely a dull, aching beat. Assuming that Wendy deigned to open her door to him—and that was a ballsy assumption, indeed—he felt that he had no choice but to throw himself at her mercy and beg her for forgiveness.

And then go back to blackmailing Jim.

It was definitely still doable, and Zack wanted to do it, paradoxically now more than ever. After all, Jim Hodene was a man of means with instant status. He wouldn't want the world to know that he'd abandoned a fragile, pregnant woman, then stolen an identity and committed bigamy—jailable offenses, all.

The fact that Wendy now knew about them did not change the blackmail equation. Wendy and her family might have valid reasons not to run to the media with the scandalous tale, but Zack had none—except possibly that blackmail was also a jailable offense.

It was a detail that in Zack's present mood didn't scare him at all. The only thing that scared him just then was Wendy.

He parked his truck behind her Taurus on the street, then took a deep breath and knocked his two knocks.

As the front door swung open, a fierce if hypocritical wish zipped through his brain: *I hope she kicked his ass.*

"Mawnin'," he drawled, bracing for the firestorm to come. "You're here early for a Saturday."

She looked exhausted, which in Zack's eye only made her more unfathomable. "Yes . . ." she said in a vague, unsettled voice. "We got up at six."

We?

"Six on a Saturday—wow," he said, groping for a response.

She shrugged and said, "We were supposed to meet Pete

and talk about adding a little balcony off our bedroom, but Pete just called. He won't be able to make it."

We?

Baffled by her calm and shocked by the thought that she could sleep with a bigamist, Zack stammered something about the party going well, then.

Wendy winced. "It turned out differently than I'd expected."

No shit, he thought. She wasn't the only one feeling surprised. Cautiously, because he was beginning to divine that he might somehow get off scot-free, Zack tried to probe the extent of what Wendy knew. He said, "Lots of guests?"

She gave him a sharp look but said quietly, "All the usual suspects: my entire family was there. Plus, unfortunately, an extra red herring. At least, I think she was a red herring."

Zack had no trouble looking confused. Red herring?

She saw it and said, "Got time for a cup of coffee?"

Where was Jim? Zack looked around, and she took it to mean that he was too busy for coffee, so she said with faint resentment, "I'll pour you a mug and you can sip while you work, how's that?"

"Yeah, no . . . yes; I'd appreciate it. I have some time." She looked happy about that, and it buoyed him.

"I hadn't expected you today," she admitted.

"I'm making up some time that I took yesterday," he explained as he followed her into the half-demolished kitchen.

She nodded and then got to the point. "Ever since we won the lottery, people have been swarming over us for money," she said bluntly. "Loans, grants, offers, schemes—we've had every possible request to share the pot. Friends I never knew I had . . . friends of friends I never knew I had . . . and women! Good grief, Jim has been beseiged."

"No kidding?"

Wendy indulged in a rueful laugh as she took down a big blue stoneware mug that Zack liked to use. She said, "If Jim had dated half the women who claim to have known him before I met him, he'd be dead by now; no one could have kept up that pace. Actually, we've had some grins over the calls. One woman claimed to have had his twins. Of course, Jim was bedridden for half a year as a result of a motorcycle accident during the time in question—but I guess she thought it was worth a shot. You know how golddiggers are."

Why did she expect him to know? If she was trying to rattle him, she was doing a darn good job, Zack decided. He didn't dare respond to her remark, hardly dared even to look at her.

But no, she seemed oblivious to the irony of her words as she filled the mug and handed it over, black, the way he liked it. Zack nodded his thanks and wondered where the hell she was leading him, because they were wandering off the brimstone path now, and headed straight for the woods.

She filled a mug of her own, a green version of Zack's, and stood with it like some co-worker at the office coffee machine. If he wouldn't sit, then apparently she wouldn't, either. Zack no longer thought that she was trying to bait him; simply, she had a burning need to talk.

"Yesterday, my dopey brother Dave personally escorted a gate-crasher onto the grounds, leaving my mother's birthday party a shambles," she said with a sigh. "It would have been funny if it hadn't been so . . . if she hadn't been so . . ." She shook her head and said, "It wasn't very funny."

Wendy looked down at the planked floor, scratched and scraped bare in places by the crew's boots.

"I don't understand," Zack said truthfully.

She looked up. "This woman, this gate-crasher, said she

was married—*is* married—to Jim. For the last twelve years."

"And . . . you believed it?" It didn't sound to Zack as if she did.

"The woman—she said her name was Zina—has to be an incredible actress," was the evasive response.

Stepping gingerly, Zack said, "What was Jim's reaction?"

"Blank. Unconcerned. Pissy, once he saw how upset I was."

She was being so forthcoming, so crushingly candid. Zack could only nod in sympathy.

"I haven't been able to let it go," Wendy confessed. "There was just something about her. You know how some women seem born to—well, pine? She seemed like one of those—someone who prefers living in a dream world to the everyday one. Who knows what kind of dreams she's made up? Maybe she's poor. Maybe she read about a handsome young man who came into wealth and she thought, 'Look at that! He fits into my dream perfectly. I just have to let him know.' So she did, in her fashion."

Wendy sipped her coffee, then looked at Zack with a wan smile. "Too weak for you? I could make another pot."

Zack's throat felt too dry to swallow. He forced himself to smile, then forced himself to sip. And all the while, he was thinking, *That son of a bitch.* That son of a bitch. He denied everything.

"Did anyone sit her down and talk to her?" Zack wanted to know.

"Not one on one. There was too much chaos for that. Really, I don't remember any of it clearly—except the look in her eyes when she saw Jim come out of the house. I couldn't forget that," Wendy said, obviously upset.

"So Jim had never seen her before in his life," Zack said in a flat voice.

"No. But the odd thing is, when I first saw her in the garden, I had the sense that I knew her. It was only much later, in the middle of the night to be exact, that I realized she was the spitting image of Jim's mother."

Zack did a double take. "You knew his mother?"

"Well . . . no; but why would you be surprised if I did?"

"I had the sense that his people weren't from around here," Zack managed to say.

"Jim's mother died when he was in high school," Wendy explained, "and all of his photos of her got lost in his moves between foster homes. But he's described her to me, and she sounds like Zina. On the other hand, Jim didn't mention noticing any resemblance, so maybe I'm the one with an overactive imagination."

"You don't know anything about this Zina, then?"

"Just that her name is Hayward and that she lives near Worcester up north. My brother got that much out of her before she—"

The phone rang and Wendy cringed. "That has to be my mother, tracking me down for the post-mortem. I'll let the machine pick up," she muttered, and she added, "I'm sorry. I didn't mean to go on and on, Zack; yesterday was just so . . . unnerving, that's all. Don't let me keep you . . ."

By then the answering message had played through and it was the caller's turn to talk.

It definitely wasn't Gracie Ferro.

CHAPTER 17

A deep, bellowy voice said, "Jim? You there?" and then waited to find out. When no one picked up the phone, the voice tried again. "Jimmy? Yoo-hoo. It's me. You there?"

And then a click.

Zack's reaction was, *What a dufus,* but Wendy reacted with real alarm.

"Oh, God . . . it's that caller," she said in a shaking voice. "He won't go away." She put her mug down so hard that coffee slopped over the rim.

She hurried to the answering machine to replay the message. "Listen. It's that same guy. I know it is." She seemed to be talking more to herself than to Zack.

She hit a button and played the message again. Again, Zack heard a dufus.

She said, "Hear it? The sounds in the background? Voices."

"But not voices conversing," Zack said, listening with interest.

"No. They're having sex. It's a porn tape," she said angrily.

She was absolutely right—either that, or the guy was phoning from a whorehouse. Still, Zack wasn't sure whether he should or should not know the sound of porn, so he settled for quipping, "Are you sure it's a tape? It could be DVD."

Wendy was not, of course, amused, and Zack felt instant remorse.

"You have caller ID," he noted. "I assume he blocks his number?"

"Naturally," she answered with a sharp little sigh.

Concerned by the level of her distress more than by the caller, Zack said, "You've had calls from him before?"

"Yes, but this is the first time I've heard his creepy voice," she said with a shiver of disgust.

Zack didn't think the voice sounded creepy so much as untutored. The guy was a lowlife, and it surprised Zack not a whit that Jimmy Hayward had pals who were lowlifes. It would take a while for newly wealthy James Hodene to shake the leeches from the cuffs of his Ralph Lauren khakis.

"My guess, and it's a no-brainer, is that the guy's after money," Zack said bluntly.

Her head came up. "You mean, like from a loan?"

Zack hadn't spelled that out, but it was obvious that Wendy had had her suspicions.

He said cautiously, "It wouldn't surprise me to hear that your caller knows his way around a track, say."

"Who told you that Jim's a gambler?"

Again Zack shrugged. "People who play the lotteries have been known to play the ponies."

"He has," she acknowledged, deflated. "He used to. He doesn't anymore."

Yeah, right. And it never snows in January.

"Well, then, maybe I'm wrong; maybe the caller is just someone soliciting contributions for war-torn Kosovo," Zack said dryly.

"You don't have to be snotty," she shot back. "Jim knows he has a problem."

Dumb. Zack had managed to put her in the position of defending the son of a bitch. He had no trouble sounding sorry as he said, "I didn't mean to presume. But you wanted my input."

"I'm overreacting, I know," she admitted, going back to retrieve her coffee. "It's not exactly against the law to watch porn, is it? We'd all be in jail if it were," she added with an interestingly wry smile. "I'm just on edge after yesterday, I guess."

"How did Jim take the appearance of your unexpected guest, by the way?" he added, taking advantage of the opening she was handing him.

"He was more philosophical about the whole thing than I was. He assumes that the woman is delusional. 'A wacko,' he's convinced. He felt sorry for her, if anything."

"He did, did he?"

Again her head came up. "Why do you sound so surprised? Jim can be very sensitive."

Zack couldn't keep the sneer out of his voice as he said, "Yes; I suppose that's how he was able to spot a wacko so easily in the first place."

She winced at the jab. "All right, granted, 'wacko' wasn't the best choice of a word. But he was anxious to reassure me."

"And he succeeded."

Zack meant to flush an answer out of her, and he got it: in the uncertainty that he saw in her hazel eyes. So: Jim hadn't managed to convince her.

Visibly embarrassed to be caught out, she looked away, saw the phone, and got thrown back to the other gate-crasher, the one who'd invaded the sanctity of her kitchen.

Scowling, she said, "Monday I am calling the phone company about these calls. They have to be able to do *something*."

"You mean, if Jim doesn't recognize the caller's voice first," Zack reminded her.

"Of course," she said quickly.

She wasn't nearly as confident about Jim as she was trying to seem. How could she be, when she was being rocked with uncertainties from all sides at once?

Zack himself was walking a fine line between relief that she hadn't yet found out who he was, and a burning desire to tell her and get it the hell over with. He knew that he was living on borrowed time; but he wanted to savor being in her confidence for just a few minutes more.

Minutes turned into hours.

A steady drizzle kept Zack working inside, methodically removing a thick wall of horsehair-filled plaster that clung stubbornly to a framework of rough-hewn lath. It was messy, mindless, throat-clogging work, the kind of job you handed off to the less experienced men in the crew. But Wendy had arranged to reschedule her meeting with Pete for later that morning, and Zack was grateful for every minute that he was able to spend working near her: he was all too aware that it might be his last.

She did seem more at ease as the morning wore on. It was almost as if she had decided to take refuge from uncertainty in the slowly shaping dream of her house. She swept up after Zack and she chided him for not wearing a dust mask, then ran out (without telling him why) and came back with half a dozen masks after she learned that he didn't have any in his possession.

He put one over his nose and mouth as a courtesy to her, then pulled it off at the first opportunity and shoved it on top of his head: he couldn't stand the things, and besides, she seemed reluctant to talk to him when his answers came out muffled.

Zack couldn't abide her silence; he was too hungry for the sound of her voice. When she smiled, when she joked, when she spoke to him in such a normal way about such a normal hang-up as how to squeeze more room out of a renovation—she seemed endearingly genuine. That had to be the real Wendy, not the one who had stood in the kitchen earlier exhausted and filled with doubts.

Ah, hell. He broke the last strip of lath over his knee and jammed it into the overflowing trash barrel that sat next to the wall he had taken down, then walked to the top of the stairs and stood there, afraid—knowing—that Wendy was bound to discover his role in the sorry saga. He wanted her to find that out from him and no one else.

He stared down the scratched and beat-up treads, thirteen easy steps to full disclosure, but he couldn't make himself take the first one. The stakes were too high. He saw it so clearly now: he had a profound dread of alienating her.

That was news to him, and it hit him hard. He'd been aware all along that Wendy was very possibly going to get hurt. Before he met her, he had hoped that the lottery money would be compensation enough for the pain. Now that he knew her, he realized how willfully cynical he'd been.

It was clear, so far, that he'd dodged a bullet. He found that he still had options—too many of them. He could walk away, he could stay, he could excercise a number of combinations. He was sick to realize that not a single choice was acceptable to him.

Wendy appeared at the foot of the stairs just then, material confirmation of his worst fear: that he was becoming emotionally involved.

"Oops," she said, looking up at him. "Are you coming down?"

He shook his head. "Just . . . trying to remember what I'm doing here, that's all."

Her smile seemed poignant as she said, "I know the feeling."

She came up the stairs, and he was able to watch the poetry of her motion. Even now, she had a bounce. She couldn't not bounce, just as Zina couldn't not float. Wendy was as earthy as Zina was ethereal, and for the life of him, Zack couldn't understand why he was more concerned about hurting the robust woman before him than the fragile one back home.

Unless it was that he had become emotionally involved.

She squeezed past him with an apologetic smile and took a peek around the corner. "Oh, wow; the wall's down. What a difference!"

She paused to look around, then headed into her bedroom; instinctively, Zack returned to empty the last full barrel, just to be near her. Caught in a trance of indecision and longing, he watched as she began pulling off the dropcloths that covered the bed, the chest, the dresser under the window.

Why was she doing it? Was it possible that she was planning to move out of the beach house and come back, after all? His heart soared at the possibility, then dove when she saw him watching her and cheerfully explained, "These are all filthy with demolition dust. I bought new ones to replace them."

"Good thinking," he said, disappointed.

She folded the covers carefully onto themselves and came out, carrying the lot, and stopped again where her wall used to be. "It's amazing. Look at the light pouring in, even on a gray day like this. I can hardly wait to see it all finished."

"The beach house doesn't cut it for you, then?" he ventured.

"Oh, it's wonderful, but—too many people are there at the moment," she said with a quick little scrunch of her features. "I'm in hiding, at least until Pete comes. I'll go back in time to make lunch for everyone."

She was so close. A pea-sized lump of plaster was caught in the strands of her chestnut hair; Zack wanted to lift it away but didn't dare. Odd, how she was able to trust him with confidences that she was keeping from her family—but he didn't feel at liberty to brush a dumb little speck from her hair.

Bewildered by the rush of emotions he was feeling, he lifted the full barrel to haul it outside. It was heavier than he thought; he braced it with his thigh and let out an instinctive *mph*.

"Let me get the door for you," she said, setting the dropcloths on the floor.

She hurried down the stairs ahead of him and held the screen door open as Zack muscled the barrel through the narrow doorway. In the process, he brushed against her breasts with his bare arm and felt her instinctively back away from the contact; he was more disheartened than bemused by her response, and like everything else that involved her that morning, the realization shook him.

He emptied the barrel into the Dumpster alongside the house, scaring up a cloud of dust as he pondered his next move. Wendy had wanted to talk, and he was the one that she'd seized on to listen. He could see why: he wasn't family. But he *was* family, that was the hell of it, and the sooner she found that out, the less she might end up despising him.

Now, he decided. It was way beyond the time.

He left the barrel outside and climbed the front steps to the sound of a ringing phone. It was Pete; he was cancelling out altogether, Wendy said after she hung up.

"No more excuses; it's back to the beach house for me, I guess," she said, picking up her shoulder bag with obvious reluctance. She gave him a sad smile that he wanted to believe was filled with regret at the thought of leaving him, not of joining them.

Now. Tell her now.

She lingered at the door as if held there by the brute

force of his desire to keep her. "Hopefully," she said, "they've all had the chance to talk out yesterday's fiasco, but I'm not betting on it; it was such a juicy event. Well . . . you'll lock up, I guess?" she asked with an oddly wistful look. She reminded Zack of a kid after the recess bell's been rung.

She had her hand on the doorknob.

"Wendy, *wait*—don't go."

"Why?" she asked, responding to the urgency in his voice.

"There's something you should know."

"About?"

"Me."

"Okay," she said with a puzzled look. She dropped her bag on the floor at her feet and plopped down on the nearest chair. "Shoot."

CHAPTER 18

There she sat, with her hands clasped between her tanned knees, waiting patiently and trustingly for Zack to stab her through the heart.

He said, "Do you know Zina's maiden name?"

She looked surprised by the question. She shook her head. "Why would I?"

"It's Tompkins," he said. "Do you know my last name?"

"Actually, I don't," she admitted, embarrassed. "I've been wanting to ask."

"It's—"

"Oh, no," she said with a sudden little inhale. "Oh, please don't tell me it's Tompkins."

Now it was his turn to feel the heat. " 'Fraid so."

"You're her—what would that make you? Not her husband," she said, totally at a loss. "Her—what's left? You *must* be her husband."

"I'm her brother."

"Her brother. You're her brother," Wendy repeated, as if she were trying to knock some sense into herself. "But . . . you don't look anything like her," she argued, going off on a tack that surprised him. "She's thin . . . pale . . . blond. She could be Norwegian. Whereas you—you're big; dark-haired. Dark skinned. You barely look from the same race, much less the same family. You *can't* be her brother."

Obviously she wasn't aware of their mother's history. "Be that as it may," he said quietly, "I am."

"Then why are you here?" she asked in a daze. "I don't understand."

"Wendy . . . you do."

She shook her head almost angrily. "I do not. A woman—you say she's your sister—shows up at my party and is shocked when Jim doesn't know who she is. You show up at the house and begin sawing and hammering—and obviously Jim doesn't know who *you* are, either. Why is that?"

"Coincidence?"

She may have been dazed, but she wasn't amused. He watched her stiffen visibly at his halfhearted quip.

"I asked you a simple question," she said.

There was an element in her voice that he hadn't heard before; it called up an image of men in hardhats welding steel girders. Zack dropped any pretense of playing it light and said flatly, "He knows us. He's lying."

"The hell he is!" she cried, jumping up.

"He's lying, Wendy," Zack repeated.

Her face was flushed; her chest was rising and falling in a stricken rhythm that made Zack want to turn away. The compulsion to tell her everything was overpowering; but even he didn't know what the exact reason behind it was.

She said in a voice cold with suspicion, "And the name Hayward?"

"Is Jim's real name. I don't know where he picked up the Hodene. Stole it, I assume."

"So you're saying he's—"

"A bigamist. I'm sure my sister must have mentioned," Zack said miserably.

"You don't *know*?"

"She's not speaking to me."

"And why is that? Why is that, you—God! *Damn* you!"

Outraged and appalled, she lunged at him; Zack was so rigid with tension that he scarcely budged. He grabbed her wrists and pulled her arms down and away from him with something like horror; her shove was so unlike the fantasy he'd created of their first contact.

"Listen to me, *listen*," he said, holding her fast. "The genie's out of the bottle now. Zina knows about Jim; your family knows about Zina. It's just a matter of time before everyone sorts it all out and arrives at the truth. Do you want to be the last to know?"

She whipped her wrists out of his grip so hard that she managed to free herself; Zack was amazed by her strength.

"There's nothing to know! Nothing!" she cried.

She rubbed her reddened wrist and Zack took note of it. *I've hurt her every way I can, now.* He despised himself, and yet he plowed on. He said wearily, "When you lay awake last night, you never asked yourself, 'What if?'"

"Not *once*."

"I don't believe it. I saw you this morning: you didn't know who was telling the truth."

"But now I do—and it's neither you nor your con-artist sister. If she is your sister! She's your wife, isn't she? Or your lover. *Isn't* she? It's obvious! It explains why there's no resemblance. You're one of those teams people read about. You go around the country, scamming innocent families—breaking their hearts, destroying their lives. And for what? What are you after? It's money, isn't it? Dirty, filthy money!"

"What else?" he said in a bitter retort. "My sister doesn't have any."

"Lots of people don't have any! They still don't go around trying to pick it out of other people's pockets. You're both crooks. You're liars and crooks!" she said, backing away from him.

"See, now that's more what you should be saying about

Jim," said Zack, dangerously calm now. "And, okay, about me. But not about my sister. She's as innocent as rain. She loved Jim madly and, I'm willing to bet, still does. Even after yesterday. Even though he'd abandoned her when she was young and vulnerable and pregnant—"

"Pregnant?" Wendy's look turned totally blank. She dropped back down in the chair. "How . . . do you mean, pregnant?"

"I mean as, with child," Zack said dryly. "But the baby didn't live, and it's not hard to see why. Zina was a basket case of grief and worry. I guess she didn't say," he added sardonically. "It's hard to go into all the boring details while you're being run off the beach on a rail."

"She fled; no one chased her," Wendy said dully. She leaned her forehead on the upturned palms of her hands and sighed, deep in her own reflections, the picture of abject misery.

I've done this, Zack thought. *This is what I've done.* He was incapable of getting any more analytical than that.

"You're lying," she said at last, sounding almost sullen about it. "I know you are. You two don't look anything alike. I don't believe you. I believe Jim."

Still.

"Have you considered that my mother might have fooled around?" Zack threw out recklessly. Certainly that was his theory about the difference.

Wendy lifted her head from her hands and stared at him with revulsion. "You're disgusting, you know that? Is nothing off limits to you?" She bowed her head again.

You. You're off limits. So much more now than when you thought you were married.

The brutal realization roared through Zack like a freight train, leaving a vast hole where his heart used to be.

"I didn't want this, Wendy," he said in a low, broken

voice. "You can't possibly know how much I didn't want this."

She looked up; she seemed surprised to see that he was still there.

"What's his favorite color?" she suddenly asked.

"His—I don't know. How would I know?" Zack said, offended that she was trying to test him.

"How does he take his pizza?"

"Jesus Christ. With pepperoni and mushrooms!"

She made a dismissive sound. "Everyone takes it like that," she snapped. "It doesn't prove a thing. He has a scar. Where is it?"

"I don't know," Zack said peevishly. "You tell me."

"On the inside of his thigh."

"I'm not familiar with the inside of his thigh!"

"You don't know him from Adam!"

Zack threw up his hands. "Why would I lie? What could I possibly gain?"

"I've told you: dirty, filthy money."

"For her."

"You say."

"For *her,* damn it! My sister's entitled to a hell of a lot more than I asked for."

Up she jumped again. "I knew it!" she cried, waving a triumphant finger at him. "You're nothing but an ordinary blackmailer!"

"Oh, lady—there's nothing ordinary about this," Zack said, scowling now. He turned the tables on her. "Suppose I ask myself some questions. What's his favorite movie? *Butch Cassidy and the Sundance Kid.* What's his favorite rock group? The Rolling Stones. What's his favorite Stones song? 'Satisfaction.' Where was he born? Piedmont, Massachusetts. What's his biggest phobia? Being locked in a room without lights. What's his favorite cut of beef? Filet mignon."

"You knew about the steak from the *party* yesterday!" she said, seizing on the slimmest of straws and hanging by it. "Liar!"

It was her blind resolve to believe the real liar that made Zack slap his hand on his wallet pocket and say, "Yeah? Well, this wasn't taken at the party yesterday."

He fished out his ace in the hole: a dog-eared photo of Jim with his arm around Zina, taken at Plimouth Plantation in Massachusetts. The edge of a Pilgrim could just be seen in the lower left.

"The date's on the photo," he said, holding it out to her. "It hasn't been digitalized, so don't go accusing me of it."

She folded her arms and said, "I'm not interested."

"Look at it, Wendy. Or are you afraid of what you'll see?" he taunted.

She hesitated and then said, "Fine. I'll look at it. And then get out of my house." Taking two steps forward, she gave the photo a cursory glance.

A low gasp escaped her, and Zack thought he had her convinced at last. But then she said, "So *that's* your game. Jim made the mistake of dating her once, and based on one crummy photograph, you think you're going to convince me that he went off and married her. And then didn't divorce her. And then married me. Based on one lousy, crummy, shitty photograph. *Please*."

"It was taken on their honeymoon, believe it or not," Zack said evenly. "My sister has a thing for early American."

"Which my husband obviously doesn't. *We* went to Bermuda."

God, she was determined not to believe the worst. Zack didn't know whether to admire her or pity her.

She gave him a fierce look that suddenly glazed over with tears. "Why did you have to come here, Zack?" she asked. *"Why?"*

Devastated to know that he was the one breaking her apart, Zack said, "Zina saw the AP photo in our paper. She said it was Jim; I said it wasn't. She'd had false sightings before, over the years. Frankly, I thought that this was one of them. But rather than let her run around on a fool's errand, I offered to run around for her." He added wryly, "It takes a really proficient fool to do that, you know."

Holding back her tears somehow, Wendy waited for him to continue.

"After I saw for myself that Jim Hodene was her Jimmy Hayward, I found I had two choices," Zack explained. "I could have told my sister the truth and destroyed her, or I could have tried to, well, make the situation work to her advantage."

"The money." The glaze of her tears dried up, and her voice got harder, a steel chisel that she began methodically to pound through his heart. "You had a third choice," she said. "You could have walked away from here and lied to her. Period."

"A lie is still a lie."

"Obviously you never went to Catholic school."

"All I wanted—all I still want—for her is a little security. Why shouldn't she have it? God knows she's suffered enough because of him."

Wendy answered his question with one of her own. "You didn't think that you were playing a dangerous game?"

"I did."

"You didn't think that lives might be destroyed in the process?"

"I did."

"And still you took the chance."

"Yes."

"And are you pleased with the results?" she asked in a scathing tone.

"What do you think?"

"I think you're the most—"

She got herself back under control and backed up a few thoughts. "Let's go back to why you're here now. Today. I want to know that."

"I told you: to keep an eye on Jim," Zack said.

"This isn't the most logical place to pitch your tent anymore if you want to see Jim," she said, making no effort to hide her contempt for his answer.

Zack may have been being truthful, but he wasn't being completely forthcoming. He said, "Okay: and to keep an eye on you."

"Why? Did you think I'd rip off your so-called sister's share of the lottery?"

"No."

"Then what?"

He didn't answer.

"Goddamnit, *why?*" she cried, exploding at last. "Why are you back here, haunting me?"

"I'm here to make sure that Jim doesn't play faster and looser with you, either," he said quietly.

She threw her head back and said, "Ha! That's so ... incredible! You're unbelievable, you know that? How can you possibly say that you're concerned about me when you're the reason I'm in this shape in the first place? What are you, totally *warped?*"

"I've been asking myself the same question lately," he admitted.

She threw her hands up and began pacing the narrow hall that ran alongside the stairs. "Well, you can't keep working here, you know that. I want you out."

"Pete needs me," Zack said. *And I need you.*

"Pete was doing fine without you," she countered.

"No, he wasn't; he was tearing his hair out. His help is willing but inexperienced, or haven't you noticed?"

His last little jab made her round on him. She said, "I don't care. He'll have to make do. I want you off the premises. Be grateful I don't have you thrown in jail. You *and* your so-called sister."

"If I go, the house will slow to a crawl," he pointed out without much hope. His argument was so desperate that it was laughable.

"Bull. I'll hire someone else."

"There *is* no one else; no one reputable, anyway."

"I'll pay them double."

"I repeat: no one reputable."

"In that case, I'll feel right at home having them work here, won't I?"

"Okay, I deserved that. But it doesn't change the fact that you'll end up either with a shoddy house or staring through a bunch of two-by-fours until this building boom is over."

She was livid. He could see it in the way she caught her lower lip between her teeth, trying mightily not to be baited by him. He was surprised he didn't see fire coming out of her nostrils.

She walked back to the screen door and held it open for him without a word.

Mission accomplished, Zack thought, numb from the realization. He had shown up basically to blow up her marriage, and he'd done a darn good job. True, the structure might still be standing; but clearly the foundation was gone.

If only he'd been able to blow himself up with it. He passed within the reach of her breath, close enough to see the glaze of tears rimming her lower lashes. It was anyone's guess whether she'd let them fall or not; she was incredibly strong.

"Wendy—"

Looking down, she shook her head, and Zack saw a flyaway tear roll quickly off her cheek.

It was that single, vulnerable tear that emboldened him to reach out and remove the tiny bit of plaster that still clung to the shining strands of her hair. It symbolized something they were agreed on, that little speck of dust. Maybe the only thing.

He slipped it in his pocket and walked away.

CHAPTER 19

A liar. He talked like a liar. He acted like a liar. He *looked* like a liar. How could anyone know what was going on behind that mask of stone? Showing up suddenly . . . without any history . . . with blackmail on his mind . . . brazen enough to admit it . . .

Liar. How could he not have known about the scar? Everyone knew about the gash Jim got jumping over an iron fence when he was twelve.

He should have known about the scar.

As for all the rest: lucky guesses. What male didn't like the Rolling Stones, *Butch Cassidy,* steak? Regis Philbin would give you the same answers!

Liar, liar, liar. It was so clear to her now. He'd shown up, had tried to blackmail poor Jim, had been rebuffed, had raised the stakes by shoving his . . . his whoever she was onto the scene. Well, it wouldn't work. He had done his lying best, and his lying best wasn't good enough.

Liar.

Wendy had only one regret: that she hadn't snatched away the photograph. She had no doubt that it had been doctored. That was why he'd made that sneering remark about it not being digitalized: because it *had* been digitalized. You could do anything with pictures nowadays. Look at *Forrest Gump,* and that was years ago. Look at the latest *Star Wars* entry, Harry Potter, the cover girls on magazines

. . . nothing was real anymore. It was all fake. Fake fake
fake.

Liar.

She walked into the beach house just in time to give surprised good-bye hugs to Frank and Sharon and their kids:
Sharon had managed to snag a much earlier flight back
home to California.

Wendy was dismayed. "You should have called; I could
have gotten here earlier to be with you."

"We assumed you were busy with your house," said her
sister-in-law with a cursory embrace.

The hug and her ironic tone were evidence enough that
they were offended by Wendy's early morning escape. If
she needed more proof than that, it came from Jim, who
said, "Maybe you shouldn't be trying to wear a hostess hat
and a contractor's cap at the same time."

Over his brother-in-law's protest, he lifted the biggest,
heaviest suitcase and walked out with it to the car.

Clearly he was still angry at Wendy for the inquisition
she'd been putting him through. Wendy couldn't blame
him—but somehow she couldn't seem apologetic, either.

All because of Zack. How she hated him just then.

"Who's driving you to the airport?" she asked her
brother. "Let me do it."

"No problem," Frank told her. "Jim's got it under control."

Jim had everything under control. He had always enjoyed good relations with her mob of relatives, insisting
that they were the family that he, an only child of an only
child, had never had. She used to love that about him; now,
she wasn't so sure. Wendy had the vague feeling—based
on nothing, really—that Jim was pitting her family against
her.

She turned to her two-year-old niece. "Give Aunty

Wendy a big, big good-bye hug," she coaxed. "And a big, big smooch, too."

At least Clarissa didn't play favorites. She threw open her fat little arms and let herself be scooped into Wendy's embrace. Wendy inhaled the child's innocence the way she would a deliciously scented rose as she rocked her in a wistful, almost mournful embrace.

"Good-bye, good-bye, I love you," she said against Clarissa's soft pink cheek. "You come back to see Aunty Wendy soon, okay?"

The child nodded, not quite comprehending. Her mother said with a sprightly smile, "Maybe next time Aunty Wendy won't be under so much stress."

The remark was such an understatement that Wendy couldn't help snorting. "One can only hope," she said dryly as she threw her arms around her older brother. "I'm sorry about yesterday," she said to him.

"Hey, that wasn't your fault. Blame Dave for letting in a cuckoo. Mom's not speaking to little brother, by the way. He's gonna be on her shit list for a long, long time."

"*Frank*. Not in front of the children."

Big Frank, all two hundred and sixty pounds of him, crumpled up into a little ball and said, "Sorry, dear."

He picked up half a dozen pieces of luggage and baby paraphernalia and began lumbering toward the front door. Wendy glanced around and said, "Don't tell me Mark and Marianne have left, too."

"Still here, but going," said her oldest brother as he emerged from the kitchen with a bottle of water in his hand. "The car's all packed. Since it's clearing up out, we decided to dip down to Newport for the jumping derby before we head back to New Hampshire."

Wendy didn't try to talk them out of it. Of everyone in the family, she had the least in common with Mark and his wife. They were thoroughly into selfish pleasures, whereas at the moment the only selfish pleasure that Wendy coveted was the conviction that she wasn't shacking up with a bigamist.

There was another round of unusually restrained hugs as the departing family stood in a huddle on the slate-tiled floor of the cavernous entry hall, and then very quickly they were gone.

With a start, Wendy realized that Tyler hadn't been there to see them off.

She found her son on the beach, halfheartedly poking at the remnants of an elaborate sand castle that the kids had made the day before. The in-and-out sun glinted on his red hair and brightened the green of his T-shirt, making him look even more Irish and boyish than usual. Not for the first time, Wendy was struck by the complete absence of any evidence of her own genetic material in him; he was so much the spitting image of Jim.

I might just as well have been a surrogate mother. For whatever reason, the thought pushed her a little more deeply into thick anxiety.

"Hey, kiddo. Did you get a chance to say good-bye to everyone?"

He nodded, then kicked off the top of a spire into the moat below.

"I hope you thanked your aunt Marianne for the cool video game. I've never even seen that one. What was it called? 'Beast in the Jungle'?"

He shrugged an assent. "It's not that good. And the graphics suck."

"Stink."

"That, too," he said with a quick, resentful glance at her.

She began to toe out the filled-in sand from the moat; she hated to see the joyous creation come down. "Well, she made an effort just for you, and that was nice of her."

"Fine."

Gently probing, Wendy said, "I guess you're sorry to see your cousins leave so early?"

He shrugged. "Justy's such a know-it-all. All because he's going to be thirteen. Big deal. I don't even like him."

"You shouldn't say things like that, honey; Justin is family."

"So? *He* says things."

"Like what?"

"Like—" He took aim at another spire and whacked it so expertly that Wendy wasn't sure where all the sand went. "Like things about you."

"Me?" said Wendy, taken aback.

"That you're not really married to Dad."

"That's ridiculous," she said in a shaking voice. "When did Justin say that?"

"When I had to sit at the table and couldn't leave it."

Wendy racked her brain to recall the sequence of events. It was all a blur, a rush of water into an unplugged tub. "Well, that was when things were still very confused. Everything got straightened out, Ty; you *know* that. I thought we talked about it last night."

She had stopped in his room at bedtime and had gone away reassured that he was so blasé about the disruption, accepting it simply as yet more goofy fallout from having won a lottery.

Obviously he'd had second thoughts since then. "Weren't you listening when I told you that the lady was probably ill?"

He looked at her through owlish glasses, a red-haired Harry Potter. "You mean, a nut?"

"That's a *very* rude word to use," Wendy said, thrown back to her exchange with Zack about wackos. "All I'm trying to say is that the lady had ideas in her head that weren't true."

Ty stood on the lone bridge that spanned the tunneled-out moat and jumped; the bridge collapsed under his weight. "She didn't look like a nut to me."

He was provoking her, but Wendy refused to take the bait. She said instead, "I'm surprised that you're smashing down the castle. It would have been a nice memento of . . . of the party."

"Mom! That wasn't a party, it was an earthquake. People were running around like ants. Besides, this castle is doomed. An extra-high tide will wreck it. Or rain. And besides, this tower wasn't even my idea. It was *Justin's*, and it ruined the whole thing, but he had to have it here. He just had to," he said, kicking hard at the base. It was too massive to knock down, so he fell to his knees and began clawing the sand away with both hands.

"Well, obviously you're bored," Wendy suggested, trying to lighten his mood. "Do you want to take the little dinghy out for a sail with me?"

"You don't know how to sail." He declined to mention that he didn't, either.

"I know a bit about it," Wendy said. "Enough to get us out and back."

"No."

"Granted, we wouldn't win any races, but—"

"Mom, I said *no,*" he said, flashing an upturned palm at her.

"Okay; no, then." She sighed, exasperated and uncertain how to reassure him without unnerving him more.

She stood there, mindlessly watching him level the fortress and then Zamboni the sand smooth.

"Could I still be an altar boy?" he asked without looking up.

"Still be—if what?" she said uneasily.

"If you and Dad weren't, you know: married." He glanced up at her. "Would God allow me?"

"What a question! Your dad and I *are* married!"

"I know, but—would He?"

"Yes," she said, looking down at her son with an aching smile. "He wouldn't have any problem with you, either way. Ask Grandma, if you don't believe me; she knows all the rules."

Tyler stood up and slapped the sand off his shorts. "I was just wondering," he explained offhandedly; but he looked relieved.

Wendy wanted to brush off the granules of sand still stuck to his knees, but she didn't dare. All she could do was swear to him that she was married.

And offer him lunch. "Since Dad's off to the airport, how about if you and I go out for pizza?" she volunteered, despite having two refrigerators jam-packed with food.

"Yeah. Pizza. Good idea."

They plodded over the sand to the house together, and Wendy yielded to her impulse to reach an arm around her bookish and introspective son. She saw evidence of her genes in him, after all: in the way he mulled and assessed and chewed on life as if it were a leather bone. For better or worse, she was in him, too.

Tyler didn't slip his arm under hers, as he once might have done freely; but he didn't pull away, either. In Wendy's present mood, that was no small comfort.

When Jim got back from the airport, Wendy was in the process of wrapping two dozen raw beef filets in aluminum foil and stacking them in the Sub-Zero pull-out freezer. They had enough food left over to survive a nuclear war.

"Have you eaten?" she asked her husband automatically.

"Thanks; I had something at the airport."

With all this goddamned food? she wanted to scream. It wasn't a good sign, the instant hostility she felt.

She kept her voice calm as she said, "We have to talk, Jim."

"Not about yesterday," he warned. "The subject's over and done with."

"Not exactly. There's been a new twist."

"What, are we ratcheting up from the bizarre to the surreal?" he said, going to the fridge and pulling out a beer.

Wendy followed his movements, looking for signs, she didn't know of what. Fear? Amusement? Indifference?

"Call it what you like: Zack Tompkins dropped a bombshell on me earlier today."

"Zack? Was *he* here? What is this, Grand Central Station?" He set the bottle on top of the fridge and decided to take out a plate of cold shrimp, after all. "Do we have any cocktail sauce left?"

"In the door."

He was completely unperturbed. Wendy regarded his casual grousing, his predictable appetite, and his halfhearted attentiveness as life buoys floating around her in the sea of her uncertainty. She began to believe that she was going to live; she was going to survive.

More hopefully now, she said, "Zack showed up at the house this morning. He said he was there to make up some time, but I had the feeling that he came because he figured today was his best chance of catching me alone; he could count on my being there to check on their progress. Anyway, it turns out that he and Zina are in on this thing together."

Jim had half raised the Heineken to his lips when he stopped. His eyes got big. "You're shitting me. *Zack?*"

"And no other. He told me that Zina was his sister, no less. He told me—" She interrupted herself to pose a question. "Did he try to get money out of you? Because that was my theory. I figured that he did, and you blew him off—although I *wish* you had told me—and yesterday was just their way of upping the ante."

"Huh."

His look went blank, which made Wendy feel as if she'd grabbed for a life ring and missed. She tried again to reach that place where she could feel safe.

He rubbed his chin as if he'd missed a spot shaving and said, "You know, now that you mention it, he did confront me once in the basement and begin babbling something about his sister. He never used her name, or I would have made the connection by now. I thought he wanted me to find her a job or something. I wasn't sure *what* he was driving at, to be honest."

"Why didn't you tell me?"

"I guess I didn't think it was important enough to bother mentioning. How's that for dense? You're assuming that he was shaking me down? Boy, I'm going to have to think about this."

Jim carried the plate of shrimp to the granite island but left the beer and the cocktail sauce behind. He sat on one of the high, backless stools, batting his fist softly against his chin, seeing nothing, blinking occasionally. The sun was pouring through a bank of windows and shining in his eyes; Wendy couldn't understand how he was managing not to squint. He simply looked . . . blank.

After a while he shook his head. "Nope. I still don't see how I was supposed to figure out that he was trying to blackmail me. Christ," he said dryly, "the guy could have been more clear about it."

He blew out air in a pent-up sigh and said, "We'll call the cops, of course."

"Will we?" Wendy took a seat on the other side of the island so that she was eye to eye with him.

"*Yeah,* we will," he said, surprised. "You have a better idea?"

Wendy was stunned to find herself wishing that she did. She simply wasn't ready, despite the evidence pointing to Zack's guilt, to drop a net on him yet.

So she hedged. "We have no idea who he is, what his real name is, or where he lives," she pointed out. "Apparently he's taken a small apartment somewhere around here that rents by the week; he was very vague when the subject came up. It's probably a good bet that he's disappeared— with Zina—by now. Do you truly think the police can do anything?"

"Probably not," he admitted, then added, "What did he want from *you*?"

"Oh, money, no doubt about it. I don't think he cares if it's from you or me or us."

"You're sure that's what he wants," Jim mused. "I don't know. This just doesn't feel like blackmail. Showing up in front of everyone yesterday? Going to my wife *after* the fact?"

If I am your wife.

The thought came and went like a shooting star, leaving Wendy struggling through the dark, murky waters of her uncertainty.

"It's pretty incomprehensible," she admitted. "You're not President of the United States, after all; he can't be concerned about launching a story that, true or not, might be able to bring you down."

"I'm a nobody," Jim agreed with a shrug and an amiable smile.

Ignoring the quip, Wendy said flatly, "Here's another idea. What if Zack believes he can get money . . . because he's telling the truth?"

She had once read that when people lied, they tended to look either up and to the left, or down and to the right. She couldn't remember which direction, now, but it hardly mattered; Jim was able to look her straight in the eye as he said, "He's *not* telling the truth. He's lying. Maybe blackmail's his game and maybe it isn't—but he's lying."

It was hard for Wendy to believe that Zack was lying,

but it was impossible for her to believe that Jim was. Nonetheless, like some scientist trying to arrive at the truth, she said next, "He showed me a photo."

Jim blinked. "Of?"

"You with your arm around Zina. It was taken at Plimouth Plantation, where he claims you two went for your honeymoon."

Jim's laugh was loud and hearty. "Plimouth Plantation! Give me a break! I'd rather spend my honeymoon in a potato field in Maine. Where's this photo?"

"I didn't think to ask for it," she admitted, flushing.

He frowned and said, "Too bad. It'd be evidence." He walked around to where she sat and stood next to her, his jeans grazing her bare leg. He leaned both forearms on the polished granite of the island and, after a sigh, glanced back over his shoulder at her.

"C'mon, Wen," he said softly. "We have to get past this. Winning the lottery hasn't been half the strain on us that this ridiculous concoction has. If you'd rather not call in the cops, then fine. Just . . . let's do whatever it takes to put this behind us."

He pushed himself into a standing position and turned to her, first hesitating, then daring to brush a lock of hair away from her face. "Please, Wen," he whispered from under pulled-down brows. "I love you. It's killing me to have us be this way. I can't ask you to forgive me—because I haven't done anything wrong this time. I feel so helpless. What can I do? What will it take?"

"I don't know," she said in agony. "I don't *know*. I wish I could turn back the clock. I don't want the money; I truly don't. If we didn't have the money, he wouldn't have shown up in our lives."

"Him?" Jim said shakily. *"Her."*

Wendy bowed her head, closed her eyes, felt his arm

slip gently around her shoulder. "Where's Ty?" he murmured.

"Across the lane, with the Doppler boys. They came and asked him to watch videos with them. They look like nice kids. Ty was willing, so I let him go."

"Good. Come to bed with me, Wen," he said, drawing her up from the stool. "This has all been such a strain . . . come. Let's act like the husband and wife that we are. I want us to be close again."

It had been too long. She felt an aching solitude, a painful disconnection from love and trust and everything that she held dear. She let him guide her into their vast new bedroom. As he drew the curtains, she undressed. As he undressed, she climbed into bed. She lay on his pillow, not hers, and inhaled his scent. The touch of him, the feel of him . . . she needed them all. She was entitled to them all.

She was his wife.

CHAPTER 20

Her first sensation was of his leg lying over hers, pinning her with sticky warmth. Wendy opened one eye. The sun was high, pouring through the big bay window. But it was June; the morning had barely begun.

She listened to Jim's rhythmic, satisfied snore. He'd been wildly pleased that they had made love not only on the previous afternoon, but again in the middle of the night besides. He'd wanted proof that she believed him, and she had offered it. She could still hear his muffled groan of release in her ear and his breathless—and unsettling—murmur afterward:

I've missed this so much. You haven't been very interested ... not since the addition began. I know, I know: we were surrounded. But still. I've missed this. I've missed you.

His gentle reproach had wounded her when he said it, and she had fallen asleep feeling misunderstood. But in the back of her mind, where unformed thoughts eddy and whirl, a new and uneasy realization was beginning to take shape that her husband was right: her drift away from desire had begun around the time that the crew had shown up.

But not just any of the crew.

Troubled by the thought and urged on by another one, Wendy slid her leg out from beneath Jim's and eased her upper body out from under his embrace. She remained si-

lent at his half-asleep query about the time and was relieved
when he rolled over, away from the sun, and burrowed into
his pillow.

Without stopping to make herself coffee, she crept down
the hall into the birch-paneled study and turned on the computer that Jim had set up there. With nervous glances over
her shoulder, she clicked her way into the pages of an on-
line phone directory and in less than a minute found information that left her feeling both exhilarated and somber: a
Zina T. Hayward was listed in Hopeville, Massachusetts, a
stone's throw from Worcester.

The question for Wendy was, did the name really belong
to the fair-haired woman who had crashed the birthday
party, or had she stolen it from some unsuspecting nurse
or teacher or little old lady in Hopeville?

Wendy was determined to find out. She showered and
dressed and ate, and by the time that Jim, sleepy-eyed and
smiling, ambled over to the coffeemaker, she was ready to
move.

"You're up bright and early," he said, kissing the top of
her hair before sliding the sports section out of the *Pro Jo*
that lay in front of her on the granite island. "Where you
off to?"

She answered lightly, "Where else? Home Depot. And
then from there to that big kitchen and bath place off 95.
You did say that you'd be home all day, didn't you? Because it's easier if I don't take Ty."

"Shopping? He'd never forgive me if you did. Sure, I'll
be around. Until three or so, anyway."

She had no idea where he planned to go, and she didn't
ask. "Can you rustle up breakfast for the two of you?"

"Yup," he said, folding his arms over the lower half of
the sports section as he scanned the headlines. "Bacon and
bacon, our favorite."

"Okay. I'll let him know I'm going and then I'll beat it; I want to get there before the crowds."

"Yup. Have fun . . ." he said, thumbing the first page.

It wasn't until she turned north instead of south on Route 95 that Wendy became certain that she was going to go through with her impulsive decision to track down Zina on the Internet. If that Zina was a different woman altogether than the beautiful one in the pale blue dress who had turned everyone's life upside down in less than five minutes, then . . . so be it. Wendy would know that Zack was a fraud in cahoots with Zina; that everything he'd told her so far was a lie. She wouldn't rejoice, but at least she would know.

But if the woman Wendy found was the woman she'd seen, then Wendy's world would not be able to be put right side up again, and she had virtually no idea what she'd do next. She tried not to think of it, tried not to work through the misery-inducing "What if?"

One step at a time, she thought. One step at a time.

With a street atlas in hand, she drove north and then west through a typically bucolic stretch of New England countryside and eventually arrived at a nondescript duplex that was fronted by a circular dirt-and-gravel drive. The house, a dark brown dated affair from the sixties, was flanked left and right by trees of oak and pine, with no neighbors in view. It was an isolated house on a lonely stretch, and Wendy wouldn't have wanted to live there. She was a town girl, unused to eerie quiet and untraveled roads.

A pot with a small red geranium in it sat alone on the banister of the small front deck that spanned both doors, but that side of the house had no car parked in front of it, so Wendy pulled in on the other side behind a vintage Dodge with grand bumpers of pitted chrome, and sat pondering what to do.

She had expected to find a yellow Civic in front of the house, period. The realization completely shook her, and she was still dealing with it when the door opened on the side where she had parked. An older woman, heavyset and with a baggy, wrinkled face framed in gray frizzled hair, clung to her doorknob as she craned her neck to see over the Dodge. It forced Wendy's hand; she got out of her car and came forward, smiling sheepishly.

"Good morning," she said, keeping a nonthreatening distance away. "I'm looking for Zina Hayward."

The woman said, "She's not here. Sundays she goes to the shelter. Right after church, she goes." She glanced back inside her house at something, perhaps a clock, and then said, "Ayuh, she'd be just out of church around now."

"The 'shelter,' did you say?"

"Down the road. It's not marked, though."

"It's not?"

The woman shook her head. "They hang up a sign, before you know it people would be dropping off cats without bothering to come in. And then what happens? Cats would be everywhere, and they go wild. It makes the problem worse. But you'll see the place when you drive by. It's a big farmhouse with peely white paint. Old-fashioned front porch; couple of rocking chairs on it. You can't miss it."

Wendy was about to try to establish whether she in fact had the correct Zina when the woman added, "Just look for a little yellow car parked in front."

As she drove to the shelter, Wendy tried to regroup emotionally. Apparently the woman who'd shown up in Barrington had used her real name. What did that mean? Nothing. Hayward wasn't Hodene. It would have been quicker and more satisfying to learn that Zina had stolen an identity, of course; but Zina could still be a con.

If only she wasn't a volunteer at an animal shelter. If only she were, say, some psychic at a strip mall. How much more reassured Wendy would have felt.

She parked in front of the farmhouse and took a deep breath, then glanced in her rearview mirror to see that she was all in place. Her hair was okay, but she'd fretted away her lip color. She began a quick rummage through her bag for lipstick, then stopped herself. What was she doing? Trying to compete against Zina for looks? It was not only an embarrassing reaction, but a pointless one; Zina was clearly more beautiful than she.

With a grim smile at her misplaced vanity, Wendy got out of the car and approached the front door. A neatly handwritten note on an index card in the door's beveled window indicated the shelter's hours: at the moment, it was closed to visitors. Wendy knocked gingerly and waited to find out her fate.

Through the window in the door Wendy saw Zina round a corner from a room in the back of the house and then pull up short.

It was like peering at a looking glass and seeing a taller, blonder, paler, and more forlorn version of herself. Were they in fact two women in a duplicate relationship? Wendy couldn't believe that; they were so unlike. She must have looked fierce in her staring, because suddenly Zina turned and fled.

Wendy knocked harder. "Zina!" she called out, startled by the shrillness of her own voice in the Sunday quiet of the country. "Zina, come back here! We have to talk!"

She knocked again and waited. Nothing. She glanced around the wraparound porch, determined to go through a window if she had to; but she didn't have to. After a moment Zina returned and, with a look of dread, admitted her.

They stood in awkward confrontation in the shabbily elegant hall, and then Wendy said bluntly, "I want to hear your story."

"How did you find me?" Zina said, wide-eyed with fear.

"I went to your house. Your neighbor sent me here."

"My house? Did *Zack* give you the address?"

Wendy was distressed by the question, she wasn't sure why. She shook her head and said, "I found it on my own. Where can we—"

She felt something brush lightly against her and jumped: it was a small orange cat, rubbing everything and everyone in reach.

Zina scooped up the young cat and said, "I'm cleaning cages. Come in the back."

They entered a room with two double rows of cages, all but one of them filled with cats. The cages ended at a wall on which hung an oil portrait of a dour-looking woman in turn-of-the-century dress and holding a cat on her lap. No question, she was watching everything that moved, cats and women alike.

"That's a painting of Florence Benson," Zina explained, following Wendy's startled gaze. "She left the house and her fortune, such as it was, to be used to shelter abandoned cats. She wanted the shelter to be called Flo's Cat House— pretty wicked humor for someone who looked like that, we all think."

Without smiling, Wendy took in the cracks in the walls and in the ceiling. She saw a pair of capped-off wires dangling from where a chandelier had once hung. Clearly the shelter wasn't above selling its assets.

"How long has this been a shelter? It looks as if you're on lean times."

"You could say that," Zina acknowledged. "The endowment's not very large. But we have lots of fund-raisers: bake sales and quilt raffles and, this year, a walkathon. We're hoping that next year the walkathon can possibly make a profit."

She placed a bowl of water and one of dried food in the cage, then picked up the orange cat to put it back. The cat had different ideas: a young Garfield in training, it splayed

out its limbs, declining to go in meekly. Zina gathered it
into a more compact version of itself and with soothing
words soon had the cat locked up again. Ignoring the food,
the playful cat began immediately to rub up against the bars
of its cage; it so clearly wanted its freedom back.

Looking somehow guilty, Zina said, "They don't get to
stay out as much as they need. The young ones especially.
We're shorthanded this morning, or I'd let this guy stay out
longer."

Wendy nodded, studying Zina as she went on to the next
cage and released its inmates, a pair of black-and-white
kittens who were obviously siblings. The woman's movements were gentle and fluid, her voice soft and shy. Everything about her projected a sense of fragility.

*She's as innocent as rain. She loved Jim madly and, I'm
willing to bet, still does. Even after yesterday. Even though
he'd abandoned her when she was young and vulnerable
and pregnant—*

Zina was no longer young, obviously not pregnant; but
oh, how vulnerable she seemed.

Without looking at Wendy, Zina said, "You like cats?"

"We couldn't have pets when we were kids," Wendy
admitted. "There were too many of us in a very small
house. But . . . yes, I like cats," she said, picking up one of
the kittens. It was a few months old and in that frisky,
squiggly stage. There was a world to see, and it only had
a few minutes available to see it.

Ty had been like that when he was two: a squiggler.

Impulsively, Wendy rubbed the little ball of fur against
her cheek before putting it back down on the floor, where
it scampered off under the table and out of sight.

Resisting a mother's pull to follow the kitten, Wendy
said, "Tell me about Jim."

Without pausing in her chores, Zina answered in a voice
that had not a trace of bitterness in it, "Why would you

want to know? To find out if I'm lying, or to find out if Jim is?"

Taken aback by her candid response, Wendy said, "One of you is."

"I'm telling the truth," Zina said, glancing up from the cage she was cleaning. "We're married to the same man."

"No, you *think* we're married to the same man," said Wendy. She simply could not be more generous than that.

"My brother thinks so, too."

"That's only two. Are there any more of you? Family, friends, a mailman or a papergirl?"

"From back then? I wouldn't even know, anymore," Zina said, removing a chewed-up section of newspaper that had lined the cage and stuffing it in a trash bag.

"You're saying that there's absolutely no one who can corroborate that you were married to . . . to my husband twelve years ago?"

Zina moved the bag to the next cage. "Zack and I have always kept pretty much to ourselves," she explained.

I'll bet. "Do you have a marriage certificate? A wedding photo? Anything at all?"

"Of course I have," Zina said with more spirit than Wendy had seen so far. "I have a marriage license from City Hall in Springfield, and one from St. Joseph's." She added with a faraway smile, "I really wanted to be married in church. But we didn't go on a honeymoon the second time."

"Where did you go the first?"

"You'll laugh: Plimouth Plantation."

Well, of course she'd say that, thought Wendy. It went with the doctored photo.

"I suppose it was an unusual place to go," Zina admitted. "Jim wanted to go to Bermuda. But I just love American history. And besides, we didn't have much money. We were so young."

Wendy was knocked back a little by the revelation about Jim until she remembered that she herself was the one who had revealed the fact of Bermuda—to Zack. So Bermuda didn't prove a thing.

But, God, they were quick. Her next question to Zina was posed less gently. "Why did you wait twelve years to find him? Why did you wait until he'd won a lottery?"

"Because I didn't know his name," Zina said, blinking her blue eyes in wonder at the question. "He changed it."

Ah. Right. It was hard for Wendy to keep that alleged fact in mind, no doubt because she had been calling herself Hodene for so many years. Annoyed at her own lapse in investigative expertise, she said, "Why didn't you divorce him after a while? For Pete's sake, you could have had him declared dead by now!"

Nodding in agreement, Zina blinked back tears. "I was sure he'd come back. I really was."

Wendy had to steel herself to keep up the interrogation. "Why did he leave in the first place?"

The shrug of Zina's thin shoulders could have been heartbreaking—but Wendy was trying particularly hard to stay heartless just then.

Zina said with a sigh, "Zack thinks that Jimmy just wasn't ready to settle down."

Hard as she was making herself, Wendy could not follow up with questions about failed pregnancies. She herself had gone through the utterly heartbreaking experience. Twice.

"I can't believe a word of what you've told me." Even as she said it, another question came to mind: did liars feed kittens?

Probably not. But victims might. Maybe Zack really was her brother—but a bullying one, forcing her to go along with his schemes. It was an even more depressing thought than the idea that Zack and Zina were willing accomplices. But it had to be considered.

"Was your brother behind the blackmail scheme?" she asked, more gently now. "Is it Zack's fault that you're in so much pain?"

Wendy expected Zina to become wary, or maybe, shockingly, to agree. She did not expect Zina to become animated and even angry.

"My brother's intentions were totally honorable! He didn't want me to get hurt. He didn't want me to learn that Jimmy had remarried—which I should have assumed in the first place."

Wendy stood without speaking and watched as Zina, obviously upset, poured dried food from a big bag into the small bowl, overflowing it and sending pellets skittering everywhere.

With a little moan of distress, she began to hunt down the stray bits, but Wendy said sympathetically, "I'll clean them up. You just go on with what you're doing."

Maybe it was the offer of help, maybe it was the tone in which it was made, but Zina gave Wendy a remarkably grateful smile and said, "Thanks. There are so many cages to go."

As she relined the cage, she said more matter-of-factly, "Zack made up this story about an inheritance—after he went to Jimmy for the money—because he thought it would make me feel better if I owned my own quilting shop, or used the money to do something for abused and abandoned animals. And normally it would. But not at that price."

Wendy sat back on her calves and blurted, "So he *was* there to blackmail—"

"No, that's not fair! Did you hear anything I said?" Zina said, more distressed than angry. "Please, please don't talk about Zack that way. He's the most honorable man I know. You don't realize what he's done for me!"

"Zina, what else *can* I think?" Wendy said, fighting an emotional meltdown of her own.

"Don't blame Zack," Zina repeated, scooping up first one kitten and then its mate. "And I'll tell you why."

She put the kittens back in their cage and automatically opened the next one. A fat tabby, asleep in a corner, was reluctant to leave; Zina had to lift him and place him on the floor. He went nowhere; Wendy had never seen a cat actually look bewildered. Wendy read the card on the cage: "Walter, age fifteen, brought to the shelter when his eighty-two-year-old owner was admitted to a nursing home."

Poor Walter. Wendy took a seat on a small wooden chair at one end of the room and waited for Zina to tell her story, and instinctively she reached down and made little *pss-pss* sounds, rubbing her fingers at Walter-level. The cat made timid progress toward her and eventually allowed himself to be lifted onto her lap. She rubbed his ears, his throat, his nose, searching for his favorite comfort zone. He began to purr, first hesitantly, then loudly.

But from Zina, she heard only the workaday sounds of his cage being cleaned.

CHAPTER 21

Zina had convinced herself that the shelter was a magical place where nothing could hurt her. Now, suddenly, she wasn't so sure.

She saw that the other woman was watching her with a look of complete absorption: her straight white teeth were nowhere in evidence, hidden behind full lips meeting in a somber line. It unnerved her. She felt as if Wendy were the judge, jury, prosecution, and defense, all rolled up in a single package. What if she didn't understand Zina? Or worse, didn't believe her? Or even worse: didn't care?

Walter was sitting curled up on Wendy's lap, the first time that he had done anything like that in his three or four months at the shelter; even from where Zina was working, she could hear the old cat's purr. Surely that meant that Wendy was a good person. Surely she would forgive Zack for what he'd tried to do. After her own initial anguish at learning the truth, Zina had looked deep in her heart and had seen Zack's love there, just where it had always been. Zina had forgiven him—it wasn't really that hard to do—and she desperately wanted Wendy and her family to do the same.

What Zina was about to say, she had told no one except the therapists, and that had been years ago. She wasn't sure that she could relate it all again; but she had to try.

"When I was seven and Zack was ten," she said, hardly

looking at Wendy, "we went to live with my grandmother."

She realized that she was cringing inside. She had gone as far as she could in her time machine. To travel back another three months was more than she felt she could do.

Wendy waited with obvious, baffled interest through the long pause that followed. Finally, in the uncomfortable, almost unbearable silence, she said gently, "That must have been hard, not being with your parents at that age."

It was the gentlest of nudges.

Zina sighed and said, "It *was* hard. I was crazy about my mother. She was the warmest, most outgoing woman I've ever known. And beautiful! She looked nothing like me; Zack's the one who has some of her features: her hair, her eyes. He's not as exuberant as she was . . . but then."

"My mother loved to play with us," she said, trying to make Wendy understand the depth of their loss. "She was never distant or short the way overworked mothers can be today, because she didn't have a job. She was a stay-at-home mom, and any time that we wanted her, she was right there for us."

She smiled at an image of her mother that was both vivid and welcome: of her pushing Zina higher and higher on a playground swing in their Brattleboro neighborhood. Those were the good years—when Zina was four, five, six—before the seventh, catastrophic year.

"What was your father like?" Wendy ventured to ask.

She was still petting old Walter, who looked amazingly content. Zina decided that the cat was responding not only to Wendy's touch, but to her voice: it was soothing, concerned, reassuring. If Wendy had been Zina's first therapist, she might never have needed to switch to another one after Jimmy left her.

"My father was harder to know," Zina admitted. "He traveled a lot. He was regional sales rep for a granite company in Vermont, and he would be gone—not for long periods, but for one or two nights at a time. He worked long hours. When he was home, he always seemed to have papers spread out in front of him."

She relined the cage and this time dipped the food bowl in the bag instead of the other way around. "There was a fair-sized desk in the family room," she went on, "but my father used to work at the kitchen table just so that we'd still be able to watch television while he worked. He was that kind of a person."

She saw Wendy incline her head in apparent approval. Of her willingness to talk? Of her father? Maybe just of the cat.

"If my father finished his paperwork in time, he'd sometimes read to me before bed," Zina explained. She folded some newspaper into the right-sized square and laid it in the cage; but she had drifted to another place, secure in the curve of her father's arm and happy under his spell.

"He was a wonderful reader. He never stopped to let me make comments the way my mother did; he'd just keep rolling along. Maybe that's why the stories always jumped to life when he read them." Smiling, she looked up from her work and said, "He would have been perfect for recording books on tape."

"You had a good relationship with him, then," Wendy said. She seemed to be in another place, too.

"Oh, yes. With both of my parents. They were good, good parents. I loved them very much. Zack and I both did."

Zack. Zina remembered now: this was about Zack. Not her, not her mother or her father. Zack.

She made herself go on, so that Wendy would understand about Zack. "My parents were good with us, but . . . they weren't as good with one another. My father was a suspicious man, I realized later. Maybe all salesmen are, or maybe they end up that way; I'm not sure."

"Ah."

That's all Wendy said, but it was enough to make Zina shake her head and say, "No. If you're thinking that my parents got a divorce or something because my mother was a cheat, then you're mistaken. That's not how it was." She sighed again and said, "I'll tell you exactly how it was."

"If you don't want to—" Wendy began in an even softer voice.

"But I do," Zina protested. She inhaled deeply, as she'd been taught to do, and went on. "At some point, when I was seven, my parents began to argue. I don't remember much except that there was a lot of yelling, and there were no bedtime stories unless my father was away. And then one night . . ."

She faltered and had to start over. "And then one night," she said, lifting each word out of the granite vault of her memory for Wendy to see, "long after my mother had read to me and turned off my light . . . my father returned home, unexpectedly. He was supposed to be in Connecticut. He—"

Zina was about to round up Walter when she realized that she hadn't changed his water. She carried the bowl over to the sink in the pantry adjacent to the cage room and emptied and filled it again.

I can't do this. I can't.

She closed her eyes and saw her brother, Zack. Zack at ten years old. Zack. This was about Zack. After another deep breath, she carried the filled water bowl back and placed it carefully in Walter's cage.

She couldn't look at Wendy as she said, "I suppose you can guess some of the rest. My father found my mother in bed with another man—a neighbor who was going through a divorce and who was a good friend of his. We used to have barbecues all the time at one another's houses."

She glanced at Wendy and saw that she was pressing

her lips together in a hapless smile. She had stopped petting Walter, which made Zina feel guilty that he wasn't being coddled; he was getting so little of that, after years of being adored. "Please—don't stop," she whispered to Wendy, gesturing toward the old tabby.

She watched gratefully as Wendy resumed stroking the cat, and over the rhythmic rumble of Walter's purr, she plunged back into the nightmare of her trauma.

"I woke up when I heard my father's shouts and my mother's screams. I heard someone run down the hall past my closed door and go into the family room . . . and at the same time, I heard the sound of glass breaking . . . I opened my door a little, and I saw my father running back to the bedroom . . . Right after that, I heard three loud bangs, louder than anything I'd heard in my life. I thought they were firecrackers going off outside . . . but . . ."

She shook her head. "Anyway, I was afraid—but not as much as when I heard Zack begin to scream hysterically. I ran to where he was, in my parents' bedroom, and . . . I saw my mother in bed, covered with blood. Her eyes were open. She was looking at the ceiling. I'll never . . ."

Zina closed her eyes, and the image went away; her mother was pushing her on the swing again.

No, her mother was in the bed again.

"There was no one else in the room except Zack, screaming something at my father, who was standing like a statue . . . and of course my mother, in bed . . . so I didn't understand. I thought she had got cut on the glass. So I ran back to the kitchen, and I pulled lots and lots . . . of paper towels from the roll, all in slow motion . . . and I ran back to the bedroom with them . . . to stop the blood, to clean it up, I still don't know . . . and Zack, he was crying and shouting to my father, you killed her, you killed her, you killed her. That's all. Just . . . you killed her, you killed her. And then I was too afraid to go near my mother . . . and

I'm still so ashamed of that . . . so I started dragging the trail of paper towels over to my father and I was saying, what should we do, Daddy? Should we call a doctor? And my father was crying, too, like Zack; they were both crying. And I was trying to shove all the paper towels at my father to wipe away the blood from my mother, but he already had something in his hand. He had a gun, it was a gun in his hand, and he opened his mouth and he . . . had a gun. And he lifted it to his mouth, oh, God. And the blood, it just went everywhere. On me . . . on Zack . . . everywhere. And Zack saw me spattered . . . and right away he grabbed the paper towels from me, and he began to try to wipe me clean."

Zina took a long, shuddering breath and let it back out. Tears were streaming down her face, but she was done. She had told Wendy all about Zack. She hadn't broken down in wrenching sobs; she had made it through. Zack would be so surprised if he knew.

She fished in the pockets of her jumper for a Kleenex but came up empty and had to wipe her eyes with the sleeve of her top. She was about to wipe her runny nose on the back of her hand when she noticed the roll of paper towels nearby; she tore a sheet off the roll to use, but then she remembered . . . about paper towels. She laid the single sheet back down and used the back of her hand, after all.

"Sorry," she said, looking down. She turned back to the cleaned cage and closed the door, then stared blankly inside it. Something was different.

It had no cat. "Oh! Walter," she murmured, and turned back to gather him up from Wendy's lap.

But Wendy had put Walter down on the floor and was facing Zina. She looked as if she were in a trance. No, that wasn't the right way to describe her. She looked as if she were a battlefield, and enemy armies were marching on her.

Wendy began to say something, stumbled, tried again.

"I shouldn't have put you through that," she said, searching Zina's eyes but then looking away. A huge battle was going on, Zina could see.

She smiled wanly. "All my life, Zack has looked out for me," she explained, even though Wendy had to understand that now. "Before. Then. Since. See?"

Wendy nodded and said in a strained voice, "Too well."

Zina didn't say anything after that, because she couldn't imagine what else Wendy would want to know. All she knew was that the cats were hungry and needed their cages cleaned. She was becoming anxious, as she always did when the creatures she loved were being denied. "Would you like to see the marriage certificates or anything?" she asked awkwardly. "Because otherwise—"

But Wendy was shaking her head and, Zina could see, trying not to cry.

"There *is* something I'd like," Wendy finally said, "and that's to take Walter home. He's available for adoption, isn't he?"

Wendy had been determined not to put Walter back in the cage. He had become too important to her, too intimately bound with a life-altering event. It had taken a call to the director of the shelter—and a generous check—to spring him on a Sunday, but Wendy had got great value for her money: a feather toy, a doughnut-shaped bed, a cardboard carrier, a bag of litter, and an overweight, scared, but hopefully someday contented cat.

He didn't look very happy in the cramped carrier, so Wendy pulled over, took him out, and set him in his doughnut.

He still didn't look happy.

He will be, she vowed. She understood full well that the imprisoned cat had become important in a symbolic way:

he was a material witness in her transformation from Wife in Denial to Seeker of Truth.

Had she just heard the truth? She didn't see how it could be anything else. Zina would have to be a world-class actress to have managed a performance like that. Besides, Wendy instinctively felt that con artists were good at faking sympathy, not at needing it.

Zina might be deluded. She might be living in a fantasy world. There was that possibility. But it was so remote that Wendy brushed it aside, and that brought her to Zack. Obviously he had to be telling the truth, as well—either that, or he was equally deluded. And what were the odds of that?

The fact remained that Zack was at best a blackmailer with a loyal heart and a horrific childhood. But he was still someone who had sauntered up to the bubble of Wendy's existence and had rammed a spear through it, and it was hard—impossible—for her to get past that. She was bitterly dismayed by him, and for a multitude of reasons, some of which bewildered her.

She turned onto Route 195, where traffic was heavy—headed for the Cape and points beyond; headed, perhaps, for Plimoth Plantation. The thought of the tourist attraction particularly bothered her, she wasn't sure why. It was like a hangnail. She wanted to tear it away, never mind the pain.

By the time she pulled up to the beach house in Barrington, Walter had relaxed enough to curl up into a light and wary doze.

Catnap, she thought with a smile. She could use one herself; any brief respite from the relentless pounding of emotions would do.

It wasn't yet three and Jim's car was gone. He had warned her, but where was Ty? Obviously with him, but where? She carried her new and nervous pet, the first she'd ever had of her own, inside and set him down, then re-

trieved his belongings and arranged them in the sunniest
room of the house, a wide, heated breezeway between the
garage and the family room. Near the French doors, a couple of painted wicker chairs with fat cushions flanked a
small table; Walter went up to one of the chairs and blithely
began sharpening his claws on it, tearing through the paint.

Oh, shit, she thought, remembering too late the no-pets
clause in her lease. She would have to straighten that out
with the agent. And get a few scratching posts.

"Hey, you," she said softly to her new charge. "This is
not the way to make a good impression." She dropped
down into a crouch and rubbed her fingers together, and
fat, lonely Walter came over and butted her hand. She
smiled again, reveling in the simple bond between them,
and vowed to send another check to the shelter, and tried
not to think of the agonizing confrontations that lay ahead
of her.

The cat's purr resonated in the empty house but then
became drowned out by a drone on the bay that increased
to the roar of a tornado before abruptly dying to an irritating
and still earsplitting glug: another hot-rod boat was tearing
up the waters of Narragansett Bay. Wendy hated the things.
Muscle boats, Ty had said they were called—noisy, gas-
guzzling pleasure boats that, as far as Wendy could tell,
brought pleasure to absolutely no one within hearing distance of them.

Annoyed, she glanced out the bay window above the
kitchen sink where she was filling a water bowl for Walter.
The purple and banana-yellow boat was tied to a mooring
directly off their beach. At the helm was her husband . . .
the man who might be her husband . . . the man who used
to be her husband. He was bare-chested, sickly white and
with a spread of pink, as was Ty, who was in the boat with
him. They were laughing, they were loud. Wendy could
feel the blast of their adrenaline from where she stood.

She squinted hard and stared unbelieving at Jim, seeing him for the first time and stunned to realize that she didn't have a clue who on earth he was. It had nothing to do with the boat—God knew, she was used to his insane impulse buys—and everything to do with the fact that he was apparently a bigamist.

Still, the contrast between the loud, garishly painted boat and the image of Zina in the quiet of the shelter was great enough that it kicked Wendy out of her confusion and into a state of mounting fury. Everything seemed to be pointing to his guilt. *Everything*.

And yet.

She looked at Ty, looked at Jim, and couldn't believe that a man who loved his son could have so much contempt for women. It was impossible—still—for her to believe. She needed absolute proof.

She walked outside, determined to keep her fury under control, and waited with fists planted firmly on her hips as her son scrambled over the side of the boat and waded ashore.

The boy was in a state of rapture. "Mom, Mom!" he yelled happily as he forced his spindly legs through the resisting water. "It's ours, look! It's way past cool! And it's ours! Dad just bought it in Newport. It's ours! He let me *drive* it," the boy fairly screeched. "It'll do eighty, ninety miles an hour. Oh, man, you should *feel* it! And it's ours! I can't believe it!"

He turned around on the beach and waved at his father, who was still on the boat, shutting it down. The sudden silence was a mercy, but it made Ty's declaration all the more audible.

"Woo-woo!" Ty shrieked, pumping his arms in the air. "Dad, you're the *best*. You're the *best*!"

CHAPTER 22

On Monday morning, Zack showed up with the rest of the crew, drank coffee with the rest of the crew, and strapped on his tool belt with the rest of the crew. It was a risk, going back to work after Wendy had dismissed him, but only to his ego. He knew her well enough by now to feel fairly sure that she wouldn't give him the boot in front of the others. His hope was that she wanted to be done with the house more than she wanted to be done with him.

Nonetheless, he was so unnerved by the sight of her car pulling up that he tripped on the staging plank on which he was poised outside the second floor, a first in his career as a housebuilder.

Jesus Christ, I'm going to get myself killed.

It would solve one problem, anyway: the growing and entirely mystifying feelings he had for her. It had been forty-eight hours now since she'd sent him away, and he'd thought of almost nothing and no one but her. Granted, part of that was because Zina had mournfully forgiven his deception (although she'd begged him not to call her for a little while to give her time to get over it). For better or worse, ending the charade with his sister had left his emotions free to roam—and they hadn't had far to go.

It was all so new. Him! Zacharias Stanford Tompkins, dedicated to the proposition that all women are created equal and, give or take their talent in bed, should be treated that way. He did not—he did not—want one of them stepping forward and compelling a closer inspection. He did not, especially, want *this* woman stepping forward. The chances were so good that it would be with a bat in her hand.

From outside the second-floor window he noticed that Tyler was sitting in the front seat of the Taurus. He saw the boy wince when Wendy slammed the door with extra ferocity as she emerged from the car. Zack was convinced that he'd been spotted, but, no; she was apparently just mad on her own.

When Scottie yelled up from ground level, "Hey! Zack!" that's when she saw him. She looked in the direction that Scott was looking; her eyebrows first went up and then went down.

"Zack?"

"Yessum," he called down with ironic sheepishness.

Her jaw dropped enough for him to notice it from up there. She recovered and said tightly, "Can I see you a moment? Down here?"

"Yessum," he drawled.

She went inside, slamming the screen door probably off its hinges.

From inside, Pete stuck his head out the window. "What the hell was that all about? Why does she want to see *you*?"

Climbing back inside the house, Zack said blandly, "Darned if I know."

She hadn't ordered Pete to send him packing. She had expected that Zack would just drift away like the con artist she believed him to be. Interesting, how she was assuming that he'd do the right thing for the wrong reason. And way off base, of course: he was still determined to do the wrong thing for the right reason.

He found her in the kitchen. She was wearing slacks and a tailored white blouse, so she wasn't there to work. In a frigid undertone she said, "I did not expect to see you back here."

"And yet here I be."

He wasn't really worried that she'd make good on her threat to call in the cops; she hadn't looked confident enough for that. Sooner or later she was going to put all the pieces together and figure it out. He wanted to be there in case she was missing some elements of the puzzle. In a way, he was on a death watch of a marriage. It didn't particularly fill him with joy.

Her color was high with emotion as she said, "Have you spoken to your—Zina?"

"Yes. Why?"

She looked confused by that. "Well, I'm sorry it had to happen, and I'm still not . . . I need to . . . *why* are you here?" she asked in obvious distress. "If it's for money—"

"I'd be sitting on Jim. You know why I'm here." A rush of exasperation whisked away caution and he said, "Because of you. Haven't you figured that out yet?"

He saw the look he was giving her singe her consciousness, and then he saw her blink and look away. "I have to go," she said, almost in a plea. "*You* have to go. I'll figure out what I figure out," she added incomprehensibly.

"For God's sake, Wendy, if you need proof, if you refuse to believe me, then hire yourself an investigator. I'll pay for the guy!"

She hushed him and looked around, askance. "What, and have some sleazy PI sell the story to a tabloid? Are you insane?"

"You think the world would care? If Jim were Elvis or you were Madonna—maybe. *Believe* me, nobody cares. Nobody but you, me, and my sister. Even Jim doesn't care! If he did, he'd be punching my lights out, he'd be—"

"Stop! Shh, stop, oh, please," she said, surprising him

by clamping her hand over his mouth. "Ty's in the car. I don't want this to come out until I *know*—"

If it were anyone else, Zack would have slapped away the hand—but it was Wendy, and, God help him, he fell under the spell of her scent. He decided to wait for her to calm down mostly so that he could relish the nearness of her, the contact of her flesh and his.

The pleading look she gave him tumbled into confusion as she removed her hand and suspended it, tentative and shaking, inches away from his lips.

"You *have* to go," she urged in a whisper. "I'm begging you, Zack. Just . . . don't be here when I get back. Please. I'm begging you."

In his entire life, no woman had ever begged him for anything that didn't involve sex. He was stunned and chastened and profoundly sorry that the first woman who'd been forced to do it was Wendy.

"I'll go," he said softly. "And I'll wait. But you're on a fool's errand, Wendy. The truth is staring you in the face."

She closed her eyes at that, and he took it as a sign.

Wendy ended up leaving the house first. Depressed, Zack stood in the shadow of a first-floor window and watched as she paused at her car door and allowed herself a sweeping look at her modest dream. Once again he was struck by her ability to remain unfazed by wealth. He was impressed and, he now realized, hopeful somehow because of it. It was the first time he'd admitted it to himself.

She drove off and Zack went back to work. The phone rang, as it did less often now that she'd moved out, and the machine kicked in. He paused on his way out to look at the caller ID screen: the caller's number was blocked. Instinctively on the alert, Zack waited to see if the caller was going to hang up or not.

The caller chose not.

"Jimmy—you there? Yo! Bro! You there? C'mah-hn, I'm getting impatient . . ."

Taking a shot, Zack picked up the phone and said briefly, "Yeh?"

No dice. His voice, he knew, was deeper than Jim's. The caller realized it, too, and hung up.

Zack played back the message. The background was free of moaning and groaning this time, but it was obvious that the caller was the same one who was tearing at Wendy's nerves. No longer did he sound like a dufus to Zack. Wendy was right: the guy was a first-class creep.

Wendy returned to her rented house without her son. She had dropped Tyler off for a sleepover with his grandparents, who as usual were happy to have the chance to ply him with Ovaltine and video rentals. Grace Ferro, still smarting from the aftermath of her failed birthday party, had admittedly been a little subdued; but Wendy's father had seemed his usual gentle and courteous self. No one alluded to Friday's fiasco.

With Tyler safely out of the way, Wendy felt ready for battle. She had warned Jim to stick around without telling him why, and he had instantly responded with a baffled and weary, "What, this again?"

But he was as good as his word and had, in fact, stuck around. She found him puttering on his go-fast boat and had to wave him ashore, which had the effect of annoying them both. It hardly mattered; she no longer felt the need to tread diplomatically through the morass of his secrecy and double-talk.

Jim suggested that they sit at the glass-topped table on the patio. Wendy suggested that they go inside. Jim didn't like her suggestion. Wendy didn't care.

In the kitchen, she opened by saying, "Yesterday you asked where I got the cat, and I said, from a shelter. Didn't you think it was odd that I went out for faucets and came back with a cat?"

"Nope. You've been talking about getting a pet forever." He added, "I would have picked a better-looking cat than that one, though. There must be a million of them out there to choose from."

Hoisting himself by the palms of his hands, he plunked his butt on a kitchen counter—presumably because Wendy had asked him not to, since it offended her mother.

She refused to let him get a rise out of her. "The shelter I went to was in Hopeville," she said, and when he looked blank, she added, "Near Worcester."

His look changed to mild surprise. "Way up there?"

"Way up there. I went to see Zina, Jim. She volunteers at a shelter."

He laughed. "Who Zina? Crazy Zina? You're kidding. How did you find her?"

"It wasn't hard. She's convinced that she's your wife."

"I think we've already established that," he said with a lingering smile. In no hurry, he waited to see what else she had to say.

"She told me about her childhood. And Zack's. About their parents. About their murder-suicide."

"Murder, geez. Sounds like you had a real friendly chat," he said. He rested the heel of his docksider idly on a drawer handle and began sliding the drawer open with it.

Wendy tried not to get distracted by his little maneuver. She had to watch him closely—watch for some sign, some twitch, some rise and fall of his Adam's apple that would tell her what she was trying to learn without her going to the ignominy of hiring a private investigator.

"In fact, Zina said that you were married not once but twice."

"Because . . . ? They mispelled Hodene? Not enough witnesses?"

"Her name is Hayward," Wendy said. He was being deliberately obtuse, more infuriating to her just then than being a liar. "And you know it."

"All I know is what you tell me," he said, with the first hint of resentment that she'd seen so far.

She wasn't sure if that meant she was winning or losing. "Where did you get the name Hodene?" she asked bluntly. "Zack told me you probably stole someone's identity."

"Oh—*Zack* told you. What can I say?" he said with a shrug. "Consider the source." He slammed the drawer shut with his heel, then opened it again.

"I went through our files last night—"

"What? No eBay?" he said, smirking.

"—and I dragged out your birth certificate," she announced calmly. She opened the cookie sheet drawer, removed a piece of paper, and handed it to him. "This is all I could find. It's not an original; it's nothing but a copy."

"Well, duh. People lose their originals, you know. For lots of reasons. Fire, flood, theft; shuffling between foster homes." He began folding the birth certificate into a paper plane on the counter's surface.

She thought, *He won't look me in the eye anymore. Either he's wearing down, or he just doesn't care.* The realization sent her adrenaline surging. She circled him and began to move in.

"It can't be that hard to get hold of a fake certificate with an embossed seal, can it?" she said. "Or wasn't it worth going through the trouble? Oh, wait—you didn't have a pot to pee in back then, did you? Was that the hitch? Lack of funds to do the job right?"

"Jesus, woman, what's your problem?" he asked lightly, and he sent the little paper plane soaring off.

It made a perfect loop and came down low, jabbing into poor Walter, who'd wandered into the kitchen looking for more treats. Startled, the cat jumped sideways and skulked back out.

That too bothered Wendy. Everything about Jim was suddenly an irritant. What he said, how he looked, every single thing he did—irritants. At best.

"My problem is you, you total *jerk,*" she said, not bothering to hide the bitterness she was feeling toward him. "I know you're lying. I just don't know *why* you're lying. Why bother? You're rich. You can afford an even newer wife. Or whatever the hell she'd be. Why bother trying to hang on here?"

"If you don't know," he muttered, dropping down from the counter, "then I'm not going to tell you."

There it was: that wounded sincerity that always ended up blindsiding her, time after time after time. This time, it was different. She stepped in front of him to prevent him from walking away.

"*Tell* me," she commanded, sticking out her hand at him like a crossing guard. "Tell me why you're still hanging around here. Because I really don't have a clue."

"You know what?" he said angrily. "Neither do I. Up until that woman showed up, I would've told you it was because I loved you, loved Ty, loved our life together. Not anymore."

His fair skin flushed dark and he ran his hand through his hair, classic signs of his frustration.

"You've always been suspicious of me," he said hotly, "but this takes the cake. I feel like a prime fucking suspect in a murder trial! A total stranger walks across the lawn and claims to be my wife, and you buy into it hook, line, and sinker. You hunt her down and wring your hands because you think her daddy shot her mommy," he said, sneering. "I mean, come *on;* who do we know with a history like that? I think you *want* to believe I'm a bigamist, God only knows why. If you're tired of the marriage, then

say so, damn it. Have the guts and the decency to just . . .
say so!"

Her head was bursting, but her voice was deadly calm
as she said, "I never told you that Zina's father shot her
mother. I only mentioned a murder-suicide."

"Yes you d—"

His brow twitched and his eyes went blank: he was in
that place again, that hiding place between him and her that
he retreated to so often. "I'm sure you did," he said at last.

"No."

"Well, I suppose I assumed it, then," he said with gruff
nonchalance. "That's the way it usually is. I'm sure the guy
didn't put a pillow over her face and then over his own."

"I didn't even say that her father was the murderer."

"Well, that would be obvious, don't you think?" he
asked her coolly.

Wendy's heart wasn't breaking so much as it was being
tempered in the furnace of her fury. "Not to me," she said.

"Then you're either naïve or stupid, Wen. And I know
you're not stupid." He brushed her aside. "I'm going out,"
he growled. "If you want me to pack my bags, let me know
when I get back."

He walked out of the kitchen, and for reasons she didn't
understand, Wendy went immediately to look for Walter.
Her body was shaking from head to foot; she felt like an
escapee who'd just jumped between the roofs of two build-
ings. She found the old, fat cat curled in a lump on one of
the sun-washed wicker chairs in the breezeway. As soon as
she touched him, he lifted his big head and began to purr.

"Sorry about that, Wally," she said with a voice that was
no more steady than her limbs. "Diet or no diet, you de-
serve a treat."

Wendy stayed in the guest room that night. She thought
about Tyler, wondering how he was going to react when

he found out that his worst fear was true. She thought about Zina, wondering how she was ever going to be able to move beyond the betrayal and horror that she'd already gone through. She thought about Zack, wondering—truly wondering—how he could still have enough strength for his sister and him both.

She didn't think about Jim, as Jim, at all. He was someone's father, someone's husband, the worthy target of someone's blackmail scheme. Other than that, he really had no place in her life. She didn't even know what to call him.

When he knocked softly on the door of the guest room in the morning, Wendy was in the adjacent bathroom, preparing for her day. She ignored his muffled summons. The door was locked—had been locked, since he'd leaned his head inside late the night before and had whispered, "Are you awake? Because I have something to say to you."

"It can wait until morning," she'd said from her bed in the dark.

It was morning now, and she still didn't care.

She changed into nondescript sleuthing clothes—a denim skirt and a beige knit top—and slipped into comfortable walking sandals. She opened the door to go down the hall and nearly tripped over the man she once had believed was her husband. He'd been sitting on the floor with his back against the door, and when she swung it open, he'd been caught unawares and had fallen back. He looked so undignified; anyone would have thought he was trying to peep through the keyhole.

Wendy stepped over him and continued on her way, but he scrambled to his feet and fell in beside her.

"I remember now," he said, eager as a jumping puppy. "I knew about the shootings because Zack told me; it was Zack himself who told me. It was when we were in the basement, when he was going on about his sister. Remember how I couldn't figure out what he was talking about?

Some of his garbled story had to do with his sister's suffering . . . her father . . . a gun, her mother in bed. *That's* how I knew, Wen! Yesterday it didn't come to me—"

"You're pathological, you know that?" she said without looking at him. She didn't dare: she was dismayed to realize that once again he could be telling the truth.

She stepped out more briskly, headed for the kitchen; Walter would need to be fed.

"Wendy, please, you're not listening," Jim said, catching her lightly from alongside.

She felt suddenly violated. "Get *away* from me!" she shrieked, as if he were an attacker in a dark alley.

Stunned by her vehemence, Jim threw up his hands and said, "Wendy, come on, it's me, Jim."

"I don't know you! Get *away* from me!" She turned into the nearest room, Tyler's bedroom, and tried slamming the door on Jim. He got hold of it on the other side and shoved it open, all the while trying to calm her sudden fury. But she was past calming, a wild thing, kicking and pushing as he tried to hold on to her. Finally he let her go; but she wanted him out of the room, out of her life.

She looked around her for something to throw: the closest missiles were Beanie Babies. She grabbed the first one off the shelf, a pug, and hurled it at him, but it went sailing over his head and hit the wall with a thwack. He threw up his arms in surprised self-defense. She seized a cat and then an ostrich, throwing them hard, aiming them wild. It was ridiculous, throwing little stuffed animals at him; it belied her hurt and rage.

She couldn't stop. She grabbed a flamingo and hurled it at him with particular fury, landing it squarely on his cheek and raising a big red blotch there. If she had bloodied him on a medieval battlefield, she couldn't have felt more pleased.

He seemed genuinely stunned by the depth of her rage. "You're crazier than she is," he said, rubbing his cheek.

Wendy lifted one shoulder in a defiant jerk. "All the more reason for you to leave. You could get hurt."

"I'm not leaving. Someone has you under a spell, Wen, and I'll be right here to bring you out of it."

"Ha. Don't hold your—"

The phone rang, an ordinary sound at an extraordinary moment. Automatically she picked up the phone on Tyler's nightstand. "Hello?" she said, breathing heavily but sure that she sounded not the least bit crazy.

It was Pete. He'd been hit by a car the night before and had broken his leg.

Standing at the southeastern tip of the town beach, he had been able to see the water side of the house real clear. Good binoculars, he'd decided, impressed. Worth every cent. Jimmy had been no sweat to pick off, with his red hair. But the broad on the beach, waving him in from the boat— she was a surprise. Jimmy had always liked blondes. After all, his ma was a blonde.

So a brunette, yeah, she was a real surprise.

CHAPTER 23

"I'm gonna be in a frigging cast for six months," Pete growled from his hospital bed. "I need you to help me out here, man."

"Sure," Zack said instantly. "Tell me how."

As if he didn't know.

"First of all, I'd like to know why she's so hopping mad at you. I just got off the phone with her. She doesn't want you running the project, no way, no how. So I'm thinking to myself, what the hell? My mind is working along the lines of, she's a good-looking woman, maybe you made a move on her—"

"Hey!"

"Okay, or maybe she just misinterpreted you or something like that. Anyway, I mentioned it. She says that's not what it's about, but she won't tell me what it *is* about. So I'm askin' you."

"Fair question," Zack said easily, and one he had prepared himself to answer. "She got royally pissed when I told her that, given her situation, this would be a perfect time for her to move up to a better house. I told her that she'd still get her money back on the expansion—not that she needs it—but at that point I'm fairly sure she wasn't hearing me."

"Jesus, man, how dumb can you get? That's like telling someone her baby is ugly. The house has been in her family for generations; you know that. Her great-grandmother helped shingle the roof with her skirts tucked in her belt. What the hell were you thinking?"

"Yeah, well, I guess I wasn't. Anyway, I figured I'd give her a day or two to cool off, then show up, apologize, and get on with it."

Actually, Zack had had no idea how to get back inside the house, short of breaking and entering; all he knew was that he had to be there. It was obliging of Pete to break his leg and offer Zack his key to the front door, in effect—but Zack was going to have to make sure that it turned the lock.

"If she's as mad as you say she is, then I'm not sure an apology from me is going to cut it," he said, choosing his words carefully. "Does she understand that without me to supervise the crew until you're back on your feet, the house isn't going to be built?"

"Well, that's obvious, wouldn't you say?" Pete said, whacking the cast on his leg.

"You might want to mention it anyway. And you might want to mention that without me to keep your crew occupied, they're bound to get hired away from you by some other contractor. This is your livelihood we're talking, and who knows if she understands that?"

"Another good point. I'll have to make it," Pete said. He invited Zack out of the room with a promise to call him with an update as soon as he talked with his client.

Zack was brooding over a cup of coffee in the hospital cafeteria when the call came through on his cell phone.

"Okay, you're back in," Pete announced. "She's not too happy about it, and I'm not too happy about the guilt trip I laid on her, but I've got a family to feed, and I'm not about to let a couple of bruised feelings get in the way. Now for God's sake, just get over there, do your job, and keep your trap shut. I didn't hire you to be a guidance counselor, understand? Just build the goddamned house."

"Yessir," said Zack, joyous.

"I'm gonna hang up, now, before the medication wears off and I get *really* pissy."

Zack had to steel himself against looking too happy as he waited for Wendy to get the door. When she finally did open it after an especially long wait, she looked ready to give him the boot again. Despite an angry flush in her cheeks, her normally animated expression seemed scarily cool. It brought Zack down a quick peg or two, and he found that he didn't have to fake looking chastened at all.

"I know you'd prefer some other arrangement," he acknowledged after she let him in, "but I promised Pete, and I'm promising you, that I will build you a house that your children and your children's children will be proud to call their own."

He'd had no idea that he was going to say that, but once he did, he realized that he meant it with all his heart. When Wendy looked unconvinced, he also realized that he could hardly blame her.

So he said simply, "Thanks for putting aside your feelings and for considering Pete instead. That was real generous of you—but then, I'm not surprised."

Wendy stood there without apparent emotion as she heard him out. In a brisk tone she said, "Just so you know: I offered to pay Pete—and his crew—for the time that they would've lost from being shut down on this project. But Pete says that the house can't stay exposed to the elements for that long, and he's also afraid that the boys will move on even if I paid them to stay and do nothing. Which I personally don't believe, by the way, but you don't argue with a man on a hospital bed."

Zack was nodding and saying "yup, yup" to everything she said.

It seemed to be throwing her off balance. "So . . . so I want you to understand," she finished up, "that I'm doing this for Pete. Period." Again the color flared up in her cheeks, but whether it was leftover anger, or embarrassment that she was being forced to scold a grown-up, or something else altogether, Zack could not divine. No question about it, he was rooting for the last option.

"Pete's a good man, as good as they come," he said fervently.

"Yes. We agree on that. When do you think you'll be finished?"

Zack considered saying, "When I'm old and gray, if I play my cards right," but he decided against it. There was just something in her look. "Well, Pete told you by Labor Day, right?"

She nodded.

"What he really meant by that was Halloween."

She looked genuinely surprised. Obviously this was her first brush with a contractor.

"Unfortunately, we're now shorthanded, and of a key player," he went on.

"So that means?"

"With any luck, Thanksgiving."

"You can't be serious."

"Actually, I'm not," he said with a hapless shrug. "If you want an honest, serious, realistic estimate, then figure on Christmas."

"Christmas! You're not building a pyramid, for Pete's sake!"

"No. I'm building an addition for Pete's sake."

"What can possibly take until Christmas?"

"The inevitable delay that the electricians will cause, for starters."

"I'll find other electricians for you," she said with desperation.

He merely cocked one eyebrow.

She let out an exasperated sigh and said, "Yeah, I know: try to get someone to return my calls. But that was different; that was a plugged-up sewer line. There aren't that many people who can unplug a—Oh, all *right,* then. Christmas. Is that absolutely, positively?"

"If the creek don't rise."

Another sigh, as she threw up her hands and shut her eyes against the prospect. "Just . . . tell me when it's over," she said, completely exasperated by then.

She handed him the rolled-up architect's plans that she'd had waiting for him on the hall table and left him to study them while she went back to making a few phone calls.

She and Jim had obviously paid big bucks for a complete set of drawings. Besides the usual elevations and floor plans, there were plans for the wiring, plumbing, heating, masonry, and built-ins, from kitchen cabinets to multiple bookcases. All in all, it was a straightforward project. Zack was going to make Wendy a perfect house. Whistling a tune, he took the plans upstairs.

She followed him almost immediately afterward. "I don't mean to be petty or anything, but could you not whistle?" she asked through gritted teeth. "It's hard to concentrate."

He blinked. "Excuse me?"

"I have a lot on my mind, and it's hard to think when all I'm aware of is you. Whistling," she added quickly.

"I'm sorry," he said. "Of course I'll stop."

"Thank you."

She left him alone and feeling good.

It's hard to think, when all I'm aware of is you.

He let the complaint roll back and forth in his mind, lulling him with its sweet promise. He couldn't remember when he'd felt so sky-high. The closest he ever came anymore was in his studio, when he was shaping a particularly fine piece of wood, excited about the possibilities but not yet there.

Who was he kidding? There was no comparison.

His euphoria lasted nearly an hour, until she came back upstairs and said, "I won't be back today; can you lock up when you leave?" She looked completely distracted.

Don't go, he thought, but aloud he only said, "Ty won't be here this afternoon, then?"

"No. That plan's been changed. He's staying with his grandparents another day."

So Zack wouldn't be baby-sitting. He was a little disappointed; with Wendy's permission, the boy had been allowed to pound in a few nails (the old-fashioned way, with a hammer and a swing of his young arm) and he'd seemed to get a kick out of it.

Before she walked out, Zack felt obliged to say, "You saw the message on your machine?"

"The one for 'Jimmy'?" she asked, lavishing contempt on the nickname. She had a canvas carrier slung over one shoulder and was checking through some papers in it.

"Yeah. Him."

She looked up with her wide-set, hazel eyes, and Zack saw a doe caught in the headlights. For a split second she seemed completely overtaken by events; but then she snapped out of it and said, "He's Jim's problem, not mine."

She walked out, slamming the much-abused screen door, and Zack's mood took a nose dive that lasted the rest of the day.

Wendy was a woman with a mission. She needed to get to Tillicut, Massachusetts, population, nine hundred and thirty-two, before its town hall closed, or else wait until the following Tuesday, the only day of the week on which it was open.

Earlier she had phoned the town clerk, hoping to get the

information she needed without having to drive the distance (and it would be a distance: near the border between Massachusetts and New Hampshire, and too off the beaten track to be approached with any speed).

The clerk who'd answered the phone had been very friendly, as small-town clerks are, and had apologized profusely for keeping Wendy holding while she looked up the information that Wendy had been seeking about James Hodene. But the woman sounded pleased to report that she had all the facts, such as they were, right there in front of her.

Odd, how a voice as sweet and comforting as Cracker Jacks could have had such a bitter sting.

Wendy flogged her Taurus northward, wincing at every *glub-glub* of her failing muffler. Her life, her son, and now her car had been put on hold while she tracked down the truth. She felt not only angry but almost embarrassed about that. Zack was right: she could easily have handed the odious assignment to a PI. But Wendy hadn't lived a PI kind of life, and something inside her balked at living it now just because she could suddenly afford to pay one.

She drove across winding, hilly country through a procession of small New England towns, each of them made up of little more than a steeple, a filling station, a cafe, and a general store. Occasionally she passed a mom-and-pop motel, and sometimes a string of cabins, but rarely a chain-type accommodation. She was in God's country now, far away from corporate America. A man like Jim would hate it.

The road sign at the entrance to Tillicut was leaning, rusted, and half obscured by a weedy vine; but it was the beginning of the end of Wendy's journey, so she pulled over impulsively and snapped a photo of it. Maybe she would put together a small album of her little day trip into the bowels of truth.

The Tillicut Town Hall was a tiny Victorian dollhouse that fronted the road and had parking behind. Wendy took a photo of it and went inside. The clerk, Janice, a full-bodied woman with fluffy hair and a warm grin, greeted her like an old friend. She was the only one in the building; her days were undoubtedly quiet ones.

She had the birth record open and ready for Wendy's perusal on a small oak worktable positioned next to a sunny, east-facing window. A variegated ivy in a glazed pot sat on the deep-set sill, ruffling in the morning breeze. The scene was so guileless, so innocent, so reassuring; it seemed impossible to Wendy that she would find slyness and guilt and unnerving deceit there.

But find it she did.

"Would it be all right if I took a photograph of the page?" she asked the obviously curious clerk.

"Oh, yes, sure," said Janice. "Especially since our copier's low on toner. Nothing really comes out very well."

Wendy smiled numbly and took her snapshot. She said softly, "Where is Oak Grove?"

"Not far," said Janice with an instinctively sad and sympathetic smile. "Go right—is that east? No, west, I always get them mixed up—about half a mile. It'll be on your left."

Wendy thanked her and got back in her car and, in her confused recall of the directions, turned left. After a mile or so she realized her mistake, turned around, and began to retrace her path.

Can it be that I don't want to know? she wondered, and then she smiled grimly. It was much too late for that.

She found the cemetery: a small village burial ground on a low rise that probably once had a view, long obscured, of a nearby pond. There was room for no more than two or three cars in the weedy parking area; she wondered what people did when the mayors of Tillicut died. Parked along the untraveled road, probably.

Wendy walked between the graves slowly, automatically looking for the oldest ones; she was a New Englander, and history was important to her. In the far corner of the burial ground, she found the graves of the founding fathers of Tillicut: a dozen slate stones, their edges slivered by time, leaned this way and that on the highest ground. She murmured the fading names aloud, tolling them like a church bell, in small remembrance of long-gone souls: Crocker . . . Leonard . . . Dester . . . Ilsley . . . Tallman.

The Tallmans had married and begat the most, but they'd also suffered the most heartbreaking bereavements. One of them lost not only a wife and daughter in childbirth, but a son, aged five, and another daughter, aged six, in that year of 1823.

How desperately sad Jacob Tallman must have felt . . . and yet look. He'd lived until 1882. Eighty-eight years. You lose one wife, you move on to the next. Wendy wandered through the horizontal family tree and discovered that Jacob had had another wife, this one spanning his middle years. He did go through them.

It brought Wendy back to the wrenching business at hand. Nearer the road were several gravestones—surprisingly few—of modern vintage. She wasn't surprised to see a Tallman among those, too.

She wasn't surprised to see James Hodene.

She stood at the foot of his grave in grief and mourning as deep as any his loved ones might have felt. *Here* was James Hodene. Here was James Hodene. Died at age twenty-six, in the same year that Wendy had met Jim.

For a long while Wendy stood as still as an angel on a tombstone. And then she knelt. And then she prayed. When she was done, she took out her camera to add another snapshot to her album of misery; but she couldn't bring herself to take it. It struck her as sacrilegious, somehow. It didn't seem right that a grave should be violated twice.

She read the inscription on the pink granite headstone one more time, just to make sure that this Hodene was that Hodene. She didn't see how there could be two James Hodenes in Tillicut, both of them the same age, one of them dead and one of them alive.

She turned and walked away. Her mission was accomplished.

CHAPTER 24

By the time Wendy drove past downtown Providence, the white marble dome of the capitol was afire with the last red rays of the setting sun. It had been a long, wearying drive, made longer by her anxiety over Tyler and the crash-and-burn depression she began to feel as she left Tillicut farther behind her. She approached the turnoff to Route 195 with loathing; she had no desire to return to the beach house that night.

The list of her grievances kept growing longer: Jim. Jim. And Jim. Somehow she had to figure out what her relationship to him was—what her name even was—and how much to let him back into her life. They had Tyler to consider, after all. Though Jim could officially be pronounced a disaster as a husband, Wendy had to admit that he'd been a decent father to their son.

Now she knew that it was only through a tragic turn of fate that, besides a wife, Jim hadn't abandoned a child, as well. So there was that, at least. He hadn't been juggling two families in two cities for a decade or more. As bigamists went, Jim wasn't the worst one out there. Just the most cowardly.

But in the meantime, they were going to have to decide together how to deal with Tyler—Tyler, who was in fact illegitimate, wasn't he? She couldn't begin to imagine how she was going to explain everything to him. Kids understood it when terrible fights were followed eventually by divorce. But a working marriage upended by bigamy—that was a tougher sequence to fathom. Wendy should know.

Who will pay Pete?

It was another thing they'd have to work out. It occurred to Wendy, really for the first time, that if she weren't legally married, she might not be entitled to any of the lottery winnings.

But, no—wouldn't she at least be a common-law wife?

Or wait: could you be a common-law wife if another wife already existed? She had no knowledge of how bigamy worked. What did the victims do? She didn't know. All she knew was that there would be lawyers. For that matter, there were probably lawyers who specialized in bigamy. Maybe her cousin David would know one. It was a sickening thought.

Wave after wave of humiliation rolled over her. She was nobody's wife. She was the mother of a child who was illegitimate. She was a victim of a crime: she had been conned, and not by Zack.

What could she have done differently? There was no precedent, in her family, anyway, for putting fiancés through background checks. In retrospect, maybe there should have been. Her sister had married an abuser, and she had married a bigamist. They had both been too trusting by far, probably because the quality men in their lives—a loving dad and three good-Joe brothers—had made it hard to understand that any other kind existed.

Nonetheless, Wendy felt guilty. She should have known, somehow, that her marriage was going to end in grief. After all, she knew that Jim liked to gamble and that he loved a quick fix. She knew that he lied, or at least that he hated to tell a painful truth. She knew that he was the absolute center of his world. She had known all of those things about Jim; she just hadn't thought about them all at once. Together, they were the profile of a man who lacked a sense of sacrifice and commitment.

A coward.

The thought of what he'd done infuriated her. She wanted revenge for the pain that he was about to put Tyler and her through, and she wanted it now. In advance. At that moment, she wanted to scratch his eyes out.

Too sick at heart and raging of soul to face Jim just then, she made an impulsive decision to get off the highway and return to Fox Point, to the house where she had been raised and where she had spent over a decade with him. Virtually all of her memories, good and bad, had been formed in that house. The answers to who she was, how she had got there, and where she was going: they were all in that house.

It was nearly dark as she drove down Sheldon Street, wondering how she could ever face her old neighbors again. Would they avert their eyes when they saw her? Worse, extend their sympathies to her for having been so blind? Would she accept them with grace, or try to laugh the whole thing off with some crack about Jim and the Witness Security Program?

A dark thought brought a flash of joy: if she fitted Jim with concrete boots and threw him off the nearest bridge, she wouldn't have to explain anything to anyone. Ever.

Awash in bitterness, she pulled up in front of her house, and that's when she saw Zack's truck alongside. A light was on in an upstairs room, and the air compressor was running: he was working late—on her house. The sight of his truck and the sound of the compressor brought an unexpected rise of tears. Wendy blinked them away, refusing to give in either to self-pity or, for that matter, gratitude. There would be no tears of any kind tonight.

She steeled herself to give Zack the news. Unless she

really intended to mix that concrete, she had better get used to admitting the truth: she'd been had.

She opened the screen door into darkness downstairs and flipped on the hall light. The simple switch would be upgraded eventually to a dimmer-style one, but for now, ambience consisted of a low-watt bulb sticking out of the ceiling above her. She remembered how happy she had been just weeks ago as she searched through lighting catalogues and flagged her favorite fixtures for Jim to sign off on. How irrelevant they seemed, now.

"Zack?" she called up. "It's me."

She climbed the stairs, passing a two-inch crater that Jim had made in the plaster, hidden until recently by the wedding picture that he'd eventually succeeded in hanging there. Where had she packed away the photograph? She couldn't remember, now.

"I found James Hodene, Zack. You're right. He's dead."

She slid her hand over the varnished banister and felt the rough spot where Jim had grabbed her still-wet varnish and then had said, "Oh, well." She had forgiven him many things, but that unruffled reaction hadn't been one of them.

"I'm not married, Zack. I never have been."

Zack was standing at the landing at the top of the stairs, somehow filling the space with his height and breadth, and he was unbuckling his tool belt. He dumped it on one of the roughed-out plywood stairs that led to the somedayloft; at the same moment, Wendy reached the landing. He turned to her, and then she was in his arms, completely enfolded, somehow secure. He was as big as her brother Frank, who had hugged her so often in her life; but the feeling was nothing the same.

He held her close, threading his hand through her hair and pressing her cheek to his broad chest. He was hot, sweaty, silent—the opposite of what she imagined a grief counselor to be. And yet she was consoled.

"Everything you told me was true," she said into his damp T-shirt. "I can't believe it. It's all true."

He held her even more closely to him, rubbing soft circles on her back with his free hand.

"How could he do it, Zack? Live a lie like that for so long?"

"This will pass," he said, kissing the top of her hair.

She realized that he'd been through the same heartbreak with his sister, and so much worse besides. No wonder he was such a rock. He'd had practice.

"I don't know what to tell Ty," she said, admitting her greatest fear.

"Tell him the truth," said Zack. "You'll find the words."

It sounded so easy, once he'd said it. He must know all about truth.

"I keep thinking of Zina on the day I first saw her," she said with a sigh that seemed to tear her chest in two. "I keep wishing I had believed her. Will you tell her how sorry I am?"

"Shh. You can tell her yourself, someday."

"I *hate* him," she blurted. "For all of it."

"I know, Wendy. I know."

She took comfort in the thought that Zack had reason to despise Jim, too; they were allied in that emotion, at least. She needed desperately to have someone on her side just then. "This will be so humiliating," she confessed. "How will I face the world?"

Zack's laugh was low and gentle. "What're you, Madonna? I thought we'd been through all this."

She looked up at him and smiled and said, "Don't make me feel better."

His expression was serious as he said, "Sad to say, the world won't be shocked, Wendy. As for your family, it's you they care about, not the state of your marriage."

"You did meet my mother?"

"She'll be fierce for you; you know she will. She loves you." He added softly, "You're an easy person to love, Wendy."

"Zack—"

He brushed away her hair from her cheek and tucked it behind her ear and then softly, tentatively, lowered his head and touched her lips. It confused her, that kiss. It was so barely there, and yet the thrill went down to her knees. She half sighed in acknowledgment of its power, and she closed her eyes, waiting for him to kiss her again. He did kiss her again, lightly again, and again she gave herself up to the thrill of it, responding to the unique sensation of having another man's mouth on hers.

He was different from Jim. He tasted different, he smelled different. Was this how women felt who cheated on their husbands? Assuming that the men *were* their husbands? A sharp surge of bitterness emboldened her, and she slid her arms around Zack, then touched his tongue with her own, tip to tip, a naïve question from her to him: did he want to make love to her?

His answer was a deep, probing kiss, a silent thunderbolt through her body that drained her of thought, of motive, of breath itself. Everything was gone from her but desire. She responded with a fervor that frightened her, as if she were starving, and now she had food.

Pounding her with the force of his kisses, Zack slid his hand down to her buttocks. He pulled her close. He was aroused and powerful, and she realized that he had the strength to snap her in two. She made that her rationale for letting him lift up her top and pull away her bra, then drop to his knees before her.

"Wendy, ah, God . . ." he said. His mouth moved with devastating effect over the tips of her breasts, first the one, then the other, making them erect and unbearably responsive to his will.

Her eyes were closed. She steadied herself with her hands on his shoulders and swayed weakly as he unzipped her skirt and pulled it down from her hips, letting it pool around her feet on the dusty floor. Her panties came down next. He left them at her ankles, too irrelevant to bother with, as he cupped his hand over the soft, furred flesh of her lower torso and slid a finger between the ridges there, drawing down a rush of wet.

The last vanishing impulse of decency warned her that they were on the upstairs landing, in the light, with the front door open and in full view from the porch. It shocked her, what she was letting him do, and it whipped her on. She wanted to shock—herself, her world—in the hope of somehow making things right again. It was a form of therapy, and she was aroused enough and fierce enough to embrace it. If he were to pin her to the wall and pump her into orgasm right then and there, so be it. She was ready. She was willing.

But Zack wasn't. "Not here," he said. He lifted her up as if she weighed no more than a bundle of shingles and carried her into her old bedroom.

She clung to him, her panties still dangling from an ankle, her top and bra awry, as he grabbed hold of a corner of the canvas tarp that she had laid over her mattresses to protect them, and pulled it away with a sweep of his free arm.

He laid her down on the bare mattress and began himself to undress—quickly, efficiently, untying his work boots, then shedding his socks, shorts, and boxers. She wasn't surprised at the size of his erection; it went part and parcel with the size of *him*. He crisscrossed his arms in a grab for the bottom of his T-shirt and yanked it over his head, revealing a flat stomach and a hairy, tanned, and muscular chest that in every respect was unlike Jim's.

If anything needed to bring home to her that the train

of her life had just gone careening off its tracks, it was the view of Zack Tompkins, present builder and attempted blackmailer, standing naked before her.

And she wanted him, absolutely. She said, "This might be because of Jim, Zack. I don't know."

"Don't think of Jim," he said, bracing himself on the bed as he hovered over her. "Think of me."

Her breath was ragged with tension and, somehow, sadness. "I just want to be fair to you."

"Don't think about being fair," he said. "Just think about you."

In the dim light spilling from the hall, she could see a faint smile playing on his lips as he swung his thigh over hers. More than a smile, it was a promise, and she had no doubt that he would be able to fulfill it.

He positioned himself at the entrance to her and came in with a single forceful thrust. It took her breath away. She let it out on a moan. It was a delicious, satisfying, fiery sensation to have this man, this lover, filling her.

And the door downstairs was still open, an apt symbol for the wild disregard she was feeling just then.

Zack didn't move; his body was coiled for release that he was denying himself. His own breath, bottled up, came out in a sigh. "Coming attractions," he explained, his voice husky. "Now, where were we?"

He stunned her by pulling out then, and reversing his position to her. He found her with his mouth instead, and filled her with his tongue, licking, teasing, gently biting, driving her mad. She arched herself to meet his caresses, driving her heels into the satin quilting of the mattress. More, more, she wanted more, and that was the word that she kept moaning in a mantra of desire.

It didn't take long; she was so primed to come. Her release was huge, a torrent of every possible emotion, all of them overflowing her capacity to contain them. Desire, anger, hurt, sorrow, fear, shame, revenge, humiliation and, yes, a new inclination to care—all of them were lifted and carried away on the wave of her orgasm.

She felt utterly, completely, improbably spent.

In the past, when she had had an orgasm ahead of the man who she believed was her husband, she would say, "Wait . . . just . . . let me be . . . for a bit," and never with any success. She wasn't that experienced in the ways of men, and she had assumed that they were all alike: eager and clueless.

But Zack was not Jim. He came up alongside her again and, blithely ignoring his erection, he stroked her hair, and kissed her fingertips, and murmured small flatteries that she immediately wrapped in silk and tucked away in the deepest chamber of her heart.

His willingness to wait made her eager to have him. Before very long, she slipped her hand behind his head and pulled him down into a deep kiss, and spread her legs wide in open, hungry invitation to him.

He came in, then, filling her, and this time they came together.

CHAPTER 25

Before Wendy left Zack, they embraced and kissed on the sidewalk under the street lamp in front of her house. The embrace was emotional and bittersweet, as well as a fairly public announcement to the neighborhood that her not-marriage was over.

In case they didn't catch me naked on the upstairs landing, she thought, slipping inevitably into her grim mood as she got back on the road.

The beach house was minutes away. Wendy was going to have to confront Jim over her discovery in Tillicut, and the sooner she did it, the better. Making love with Zack had delayed and dampened—but hadn't extinguished—that impulse. She might not feel like scratching Jim's eyes out anymore, but she wouldn't think twice about spitting on him.

Emotionally, she was officially declaring herself a disaster area. If someone had predicted to her three hours earlier that she was going to let herself be carried to her bed by her carpenter, she would have asked that someone what he'd been smoking. And yet here she was, her flesh still burning from their mad, pumping scramble to multiple climaxes.

They hadn't even used condoms, for pity's sake. It hadn't even *occurred* to her, for pity's sake. She was on the pill and so used to having one partner that she never gave a thought to any other cautions. Her only concern was to put out the fire, and she hadn't even done that, because here she was: her flesh, still burning.

What had she done? She'd had wild, satisfying sex with Jim's brother-in-law and nemesis, that's what. Had she just used Zack as a knife to drive through Jim's heart?

Another thought: had Zack used her in the same way? That idea too was sudden and chilling. Why hadn't she considered either of those possibilities when Zack was pulling her clothes off? Her, relishing the act of being stripped naked on the landing and with the door wide open! Her aching nipples began to harden at the mere thought of it, amazing her still more.

Obviously she was in no shape to analyze motives, either hers or Zack's. Or Jim's. She didn't believe, as Zack did, that Jim had abandoned Zina simply because he'd gotten cold feet about becoming a father. Wendy just didn't buy it. Jim hadn't been that happy when she became pregnant, either—but he had stuck around and had been a good father to Ty.

And that was the misery of it. Everything would be so much easier to take, so much more cut-and-dried, if Jim hadn't cared about Ty. He was both harder to hate and easier to hate because of that single fact.

After the quick review of the emotional rubble that was her life, Wendy decided that, exhausted or not, she was going to have to begin clearing some of it away. So she was actually disappointed to see a second car parked behind Jim's in the driveway of their rented house in Barrington. She parked alongside the Dodge, trying to decide if it was the one that belonged to that dodo Alexander from Jim's old office. She had no desire to make pleasant conversation while her lips were still swollen with passion, so she detoured through the breezeway entrance to get inside.

Quietly, she opened the French door and then closed it behind her. The lamp on the breezeway table was on; too useless to read by, it gave the area a cozy glow, perfect for petting a cat. She smiled when she saw Walter, curled up on the floral cushion of what she now considered his chair, and wondered whether Jim had been sitting there with the cat on his lap, reflecting. Was it possible? The thought made her wince. Brushing it aside, she tiptoed to the guest room at the far end of the wing, grateful that earlier she'd moved her shampoo and things to the shower there.

With the bedroom door closed behind her, she took off her clothes and folded them with care, perhaps to make amends for the rude treatment they'd seen, and then she stepped inside the freestanding glass box that seemed designed for no other reason than to display and seduce.

She turned on the shower, and the simple, everyday act accomplished what no one and nothing else so far had been able to do: it reduced her to tears. They came in a sudden, wrenching burst of sobs, wracking her chest, filling her throat, overwhelming her soul. Suddenly she was drowning in her own tears, awash in them. Shower or no shower, she could taste the salt, feel the sting, as she bowed her head and hugged herself under the downpour, sobbing bitterly.

She stayed that way for what seemed like hours before she forced herself back under control, but it couldn't have been hours: the bathroom was hardly steamed.

Okay, she acknowledged to herself, *you lost it. That's once, that's allowed. But that's it.* There would be no more tears. Jim wasn't worth them. The tears were done with, over, gone, the evidence washed down the drain.

With a deep, damp breath, she told herself that that was that. But she knew, as she shampooed and conditioned and scrubbed herself clean, that the tears were still rolling. They just didn't hurt quite as much, that's all.

After drying herself, she slipped into her nightgown and turned out the lights. The guest wing was pitch-black. Wendy wasn't used to such darkness; she considered turn-

ing the light in the breezeway back on, but she was too
drained to get out of bed. She fell asleep while lying on
her back—unusual for her, but there was no longer anyone
to curl up with—and woke up when she was suddenly,
violently jumped from above.

Wendy let out a cry, and fat Walter scrambled awkwardly to the floor with a heavy thump. He had wanted to
curl up with a human being, that's all.

"Bet you don't try that again," she mumbled after her
heart quieted down, and she got up to get a drink of water.

She stood near the open window, emptying the glass, in
a hurry to fall back asleep and blot out her day. She was
near an open window. It was a damp, quiet night, and the
sound of voices carried well. She could hear Jim's outside
in front, apparently seeing his guest to the car. She wondered what time it was.

And then she heard a second voice, louder than Jim's
softer, placating one, hurtling across the distance.

"You dumb fuck! You know how long I've waited for
this? You get it for me, and if you don't, I'm gonna rip off
your balls and shove 'em down your throat. Fuck, I'll do
it anyway!"

Shocked into wakefulness by the crude and violent
threat, Wendy ducked low, with her ear cocked to the
sounds of their voices.

Jim was saying something in a hurried mutter, but she
couldn't make out anything beyond, "I'll do it, I'll do it."

"I could kill you now, you bastard. Right now! Right
here!"

And then she heard a third voice; it belonged to Phil,
her crusty neighbor to the west. "Hey! Put a sock in it, or
I'll call the cops!"

Immediately after that, she heard a car door slam, followed by the squeal of tires backing up sharply and peeling
off.

And then quiet. She was in a safe, peaceful neighborhood again, with only the sound of crickets to keep her awake. That, and the thunder of her pounding heart. She rushed to the phone to call 911. But what should she report? Confused, she slammed the phone back down and ran out to the entry hall in time to see Jim brush past her and proceed on to the master bedroom.

"Jim, what was that about? Who was he?" she said, tagging frantically after him.

"A business associate," he told her without looking back. He went into the bedroom and flipped on every switch, washing the room in blinding light.

Squinting, she said, "Business? What kind of business? The man was a thug. What have you got yourself into, Jim? Tell me, I want to *know*."

"Just don't worry about it, okay?" he said, pulling out his biggest duffel bag from the dressing room and propping it open on the bed. "He wants some money, that's all. We have plenty of it." He was pulling drawers open as fast as he could, now, grabbing the contents and pitching them into the bag.

"But where are you going?"

"On a business trip," he muttered.

"With *him*?"

He shot her a look of contempt. "Yeah. Right."

"You're running away! Where?"

"I'll let you know when I get there."

Stunned, she said, "The way you did when you ran from Zina?"

"That was a different situation," he said as he jammed balled-up socks into the edges of the duffel.

It was an admission, and it flattened her.

Immediately, he saw his mistake. "Look, I said I'd call. I'll work out something with him, but on my own terms. Right now, I've got to get out of here—so stop hassling me!" he snapped.

"If you owe him money, then *pay* the man," she said, amazed that Jim didn't get the connection.

"It's more complicated than that," he muttered as he pulled down three pairs of slacks from their hangers. He folded them into the duffel, then zipped it quickly. The zipper caught in the fabric. With a curse, he gave it a couple of vicious yanks and ended up pulling off the metal tab from the zipper. He swore again, then swung the bag over his shoulder anyway, his clothes exposed in the yawning gap. Ready or not, he was going.

Wendy grabbed at the strap as he moved past her, pulling the duffel from his shoulder. Caught by surprise, he let the bag get away from him and fall to the floor. "What the hell are you doing?" he shouted.

"You can't walk out on this mess!" she said in a whole new rage. "I went to Tillicut today, I saw the grave. You're not James Hodene. I don't even think you're James Hayward. Who are you? What's your real name? At least tell me that!"

He grabbed at the fallen strap and arched it over his shoulder again. "Do you think it makes a damn bit of difference now?"

She stretched her arms, barring the doorway. "It does to your son!"

"Move."

"No!"

"Get out of my *way*," he said, slamming into her with his duffel.

She staggered back into the hall, unhurt but in shock as she watched him half run through the house and for his car. At the window, she saw him peel away, no less in a hurry than his so-called business associate was.

Mind-boggling! The day that wouldn't end remained determined not to. Wendy ran to throw the deadbolt on the door and then, still jumpy, she locked all the double-hung windows and activated the alarm. Suddenly it seemed unbearably still; she could hear a pin drop, and lots of pins seemed to be dropping.

Clutching a heavy flashlight as a club, she stalked the rooms, checking the closets and under the beds for more surprises. She was on all fours in Tyler's bedroom when Walter found her and butted his head into her arm from behind, making her jump sky-high. But then he rolled over and exposed his white belly to her in a luxurious stretch, and that made her smile and calmed her down: if he wasn't afraid, then neither would she be.

Exhausted and bewildered, she went into the kitchen to warm up some milk. She would call Zack. But to tell him what—that her not-husband had run away? Zack wouldn't be surprised; he would point out Jim's track record. For the first time, Wendy wondered if Jim had even been legally married to Zina. Who knew how long the trail was of his ex–not-wives?

I wonder if there's a word for us, she thought wearily. *Bigamees?*

For all her desire to contact Zack, Wendy had an equal desire to avoid him. What they'd shared back in the house on Sheldon Street was still pure raw mystery to her. She needed time to mull over it.

She wanted instinctively to talk to her son, to hug him tight, but it was too late even to phone him; her parents would be alarmed. Better to alarm them after they'd had a good night's sleep. She was glad that she'd called Tyler earlier when she stopped on the road for a bite, before the double tumult of events. Tyler had sounded happy and distracted; he and his grandpa had just watched the entire *Star Wars* series (again) and his grandma had made cinnamon rolls.

The thought occurred to Wendy: what if her son had been there tonight to hear and see it all? What could she possibly have told him after he saw his father peel away in the middle of the night?

No more Dad, honey; and this time it's for real. Her stomach tightened. She was going to have to come up with an explanation for Tyler by morning.

She drank her milk, but it did no good. Her stomach stayed knotted for the rest of the night.

CHAPTER 26

Zack tried to call Wendy first at the rented house and then at the old house, but he got the machines at both. She was probably out and around, picking up Ty. Most likely.

He called her cell phone number but got her voice mail there, as well, and that's when he began to wonder: was she in fact avoiding him?

It killed him to think so, and yet it killed him even more to think how undisciplined he'd been. When he saw her coming up the stairs so numb and disillusioned, he'd just . . . lost it. He had wanted to make everything better for her, and the odds were superb that he'd made things worse. She was vulnerable, he was a jerk: that was his night in a nutshell.

He loved her. He knew that now, and beyond a doubt. But loving Wendy and making love to her—those were two separate stages, and somehow he'd compressed them in his hurry to replace the wrenching sense of loss he knew she felt.

All of that was true, but it wasn't the whole truth.

You've wanted her since the day you saw her in that bastard's arms, he admitted to himself. *You've wanted her every day since then, in this painful, frustrating, twisted odyssey toward justice.*

Bitter and sorry, he was kicking himself all the way over to his sister's house. He knew that Zina too was reeling with loss, and he was all too aware that she had only a fraction of Wendy's resilience.

Still, Zina, at least, had answered her phone that morning. Zack had had no experience in wronging her, so he didn't know what to expect—but somehow or other, she had sounded too blithe. So impulsively he'd asked her if he could drop in on his way down to Providence, and she had answered, "What a good idea."

When he pulled in front of her side of the duplex, he saw her watching him through parted curtains. She gave him a startlingly cheery wave and then ran to get the door, greeting him with sweet enthusiasm and expecting, and getting, a warm hug from him.

"Hey, kiddo," he said in a muffled voice, rocking her back and forth in his arms. "How you doin'?"

"Oh, I'm fine, Zack," she said. "I'm doing really, really fine!"

She seemed adamant, which put him even more on guard. "Well, that's good," he said. "Is that fresh coffee I smell?"

"Just for you," she said in a happy voice.

"You're a doll." Their one and only falling-out had been after she eloped with Jim, and that time, she hadn't been nearly so quick to forgive. This was too painless. His heart began to sink.

"Come sit," she coaxed. "After you called, I ran out and got muffins. Blueberry for you, cranberry for me. With big, sugary crusts the way you like them; I'm keeping them warm."

Smiling tentatively, he let her take him by the hand and lead him over to the round table in her tiny kitchen. She had covered it with yet another pretty quilt—she called it a wedding-ring quilt—that he knew she'd been working on. A big vase of wildflowers took up too much of the tabletop but was pure Zina. She had put out her favorite plates, yellow and green, and bright-blue cloth napkins.

He sat on a chair, heard something crack, and remembered, too late, that he'd promised to glue it for her.

"I'll take this one home," he told her, and he moved it out to his truck.

By the time he resettled himself, Zina had sliced and buttered his muffin for him and poured his coffee. With sweet ceremony, she folded his napkin across his knees. After that, she placed one of the cake plates on the floor with a couple of muffin chunks on it for Cassie the skunk-cat, who seemed perfectly willing to partake in the ritual.

Anyone watching Zina would have seen a preschooler playing house. Zack's heart sank lower.

"You'll never guess who came to visit me, not here but at the shelter on Sunday," she said, propping her chin dreamily on her fist as she watched Zack bite into the muffin with feigned pleasure.

In fact, Zack didn't have to guess. Wendy had told him about her impulsive visit to Zina as they lay entwined in the dark on the bare mattress. Zack had found out that Wendy was as concerned about Zina as he was.

"C'mon, Zack. Guess."

"Well, I hope it was the mayor of Hopeville, there to give you the Volunteer of the Year award," he said with gentle gravity.

"Zack! I work at the shelter because I *have* to be there; it's not volunteering, it's who I am. Do you volunteer to blink your eyes? To breathe? That's how it is for me. I have to be there. But anyway, no, it wasn't the mayor of Hopeville," she said with an affectionate laugh. "It was Wendy!"

"Really," he said, acting surprised.

"Yes. She actually found my address and then drove all the way up here just to see me. At first I was afraid of her. She was very stern, especially about you. But after I told her—well, about you, about how you've taken care of me ever since Mom and Dad, well, she changed completely."

The muffin turned to ash in Zack's throat. "You told her about Mom and Dad?"

"Yes. Otherwise, she would have kept on thinking you were a criminal," Zina said simply. "I wanted her to realize how good you are."

Wendy hadn't admitted to knowing about their childhood trauma. Suddenly he had a vivid recollection of her lying curled up against him in that brief eternity before they went their separate ways. Had pity been part of the mix for her, then? It was a depressing thought.

"She's a good person, Zack," his sister said quickly, seeing the double take in his face. "I liked her a lot. And you won't believe it, but she adopted Walter. Right there on the spot! No one has ever been able to do that without getting screened before. I think she may have made a really big donation. Sylvia came right over to do the paperwork, and you know she plays bridge on Sunday afternoon."

"Bridge . . . hmm." His mind was a million miles away, in an upstairs bedroom on Sheldon Street.

"Zack—you're not mad at me, are you?" his sister asked, her face pinching in distress.

It yanked him backs to the present. "No, Zee," he said. He brushed the backs of his fingertips along her brow to smooth the furrows there. "Why would I be mad?"

"Oh, good." She settled back with her teapot, removing the knitted cozy from it, and she launched into a new but related subject which made Zack no less uneasy.

She said as she poured her tea, "Have you been to Wendy's house yet, the one she's renting?"

When Zack gave her a vague shrug, Zina sighed and told him, "It's so pretty. It's right on the beach. There are roses *everywhere*; I smelled them right away when I stopped in to visit that day."

Stopped in to *visit*?

"Wendy seems to have lots of friends, lots of family," she informed him. "That's good, because I'm sure they'll be a comfort. *Although*—there were one or two that I met who were not very nice." Zina rolled her eyes and shook her head, apparently dismissing unpleasant thoughts.

Without distracting his sister with a response, Zack studied her as she went on with her bewildering teatime chatter.

"I'm sure we'll end up living on a beach ourselves, somewhere," she told him. "Maybe in Newport. There's so much more to do there, don't you think?" she asked her brother cheerfully.

Zack didn't know what to say to that; as close as they were, they hadn't shared a house since they were kids. He was beginning to feel the first faint stirrings of panic—as if he were in a doctor's office, and the doctor was taking his time getting to a frightening diagnosis.

"I think that a beachfront property might end up being a little pricey," he said vaguely.

"Oh. Huh. I have to admit, that's a little disappointing," she said, taking a sip from her tea. "I was hoping we'd have at least enough to buy a place on the beach. A little cottage would be cheap, wouldn't it? People are always so happy on a beach. It wouldn't have to be big. Just a tiny, tiny shack would do. Will he give *all* of the money to Wendy, then?"

He. "I don't know," Zack said haplessly.

Unaware that he had spoken, she continued her rambling drift into her own special world. "I suppose I won't blame Jimmy if he does give everything to her; he'll want to ease her heartache, somehow. After all, it's not Wendy's fault. She got caught in a tragic situation, just like me."

"Zee, honey—"

She frowned at the interruption, and he immediately shut up.

"No, I know what you're going to say. You think I'm disappointed because Aunt Louise didn't really leave me any money. But honestly, I'm not. I can get a job in Newport. I'm sure they have a quilting shop there. Don't you think?"

It was clear to him now that she was going over past events, picking bits and pieces from them that mattered to her, and shaping them into a new reality. Watching it happen was daunting.

"I'm sure they have a quilting shop in Newport," he said, stalling for time.

She clutched her mug so tightly that the tips of her nails turned white. "It's really important that Jimmy and I live on a beach, Zack," she said. "I saw how happy they all were on the beach. I saw it with my own two eyes!"

Now Zack was afraid, and definitely over his head. What was the way to handle this? What would her shrink have done?

"You're right," he said with self-imposed calm. "It's easy to be happy by the shore. That's where you plan to live, then?"

"Jimmy and I. Yes. I've thought about it a lot, and I've decided that it's the only place we can be really happy. It will be just like that house where he's living now. I'll plant lots of roses for us, just like at that house. And we'll have lots of little—"

Her voice broke. She moved her head a little to the right, and he lost her behind the wildflowers. Was she crying, maybe coming out of her fantasy and to her senses? He moved the vase over to the edge and looked at her intently.

She was looking right at him, and she didn't see him. God in heaven, she didn't see him.

"I guess you've talked this all over with Jimmy?" he asked, dreading the answer, whatever it was going to be.

Instead, she gasped and said, "I've just thought of something—we'll need money for his therapy!"

"Therapy—?"

"For the amnesia. Jim's amnesia. It can't be cheap. I'm sure the treatment will be long-term. Unless—oh, of course. How dumb," she said, sighing with relief. "He's not like me; he's bound to have medical that's really good."

She patted her heart with quick, soft strokes and smiled sheepishly. "I nearly had a heart attack just now."

A heart attack wasn't the threat to her that heartbreak was, Zack knew. He realized that he couldn't leave her in such a precarious mental state, so he said, "Hey, what's the story with your front deck? I just about put my foot through one of the stairs. Can't your landlady find anyone to put down new treads for you?"

Zina looked confused at the almost violent change of subject, but she answered cogently enough, "I think she got some quotes, but either they were too high, or they were okay but the guys never came."

"Oh, man," he said, sounding concerned. "The shape those stairs are in, sooner or later she's gonna get sued. Tell you what. I have the day free. If she pays for the lumber, I'll do the labor gratis. I don't want to come over next time and see you hobbling around on crutches."

"Oh," she said, considering the detour her life had just taken. "You'd do that for Margie?"

"You bet."

She blinked her deep blue eyes in confusion. For a moment she looked poised between two worlds: Margie's and Jimmy's. And then she said, almost with regret, "I'm sure she would love that."

Margie was thrilled. For his efforts, Zack was rewarded with a stupendous lunch and the sight of Zina of old, talking and laughing and sharing the meal with them.

His sister was slated to go to work in the afternoon, which was good; she needed to stay occupied. Somehow Zack was going to have to fill more of her spare time, keep her more grounded in reality. He was also going to have to see a therapist for some guidance about the best way to deal with another drift from reality, if and when it came.

But in the meantime, Wendy. Where was she? After calling his crew on Scott's cell phone and instructing them for the day, he'd left messages with Wendy on all three phones that he'd be late coming in. She hadn't called back. From any of them.

He ended up arriving at the construction site late in the afternoon, only to find that the boys had hit an impasse and had left early. Perfect. At that rate, he was going to have to push out his estimate for completion to the following spring.

Feeling harried, he redid the bizarre placement of two-by-fours that were to receive the twin medicine cabinets (wondering, now, why Wendy even needed two) and then drove out to the house on the beach in Barrington. He was her builder; he was entitled to do that. He wasn't entitled to throw her down on the nearest bed—yet—but the right to consult with her about the house was a given.

Her Taurus was there, but no other car. Zack gave the bed idea more serious consideration as he rang the bell twice, but he had no idea what he was going to say to Wendy when she came to the door.

She didn't; Tyler did. "Oh, hi, Zack," he said, munching an apple. "Mom's in the kitchen making supper." He gave two pokes of his finger down the hall. "Mom! Zack's here!" he yelled, and then he ran up the stairs yelling even more loudly, "Josh, you'd better not be taking an extra turn!"

Zack felt as if he'd parachuted into June and Ward Cleaver's house. He smelled melted cheese and heard the local news on a television in the kitchen into which he was marching with far more trepidation than he wanted to feel.

Dammit! She wasn't married, after all, and the bum who'd convinced her that she was belonged in jail. Simple logic, keenly felt; but when Zack saw her coming through the kitchen door with a bowl of something green that she'd gathered from outside, he couldn't croak out anything more brilliant than, "Wendy."

If he was expecting her to drop the bowl and make a run for his arms, he was sadly mistaken.

"*Why* are you here?" she said. It sounded almost like scolding.

Good damn question. She looked angry and embarrassed and distressed, although for the life of him, he couldn't tell which emotion prevailed. He voted for pissed.

He said, "I'm here because—I don't know why I'm here." He threw up his hands and said, "Because you're here!"

"Shh!" she said, glancing nervously down the hall. "No. You can't be here for me. You can be here for the house. That's all. That was a mistake, last night," she said, her voice dropping to a whisper. "Last night was—"

"Something," he said bluntly. "Why didn't you return my calls?"

She placed the wooden bowl very carefully on the granite counter. Zack had no idea why care was required, other than to prevent her from meeting his gaze.

Finally she murmured, "There was nothing to say."

"I can buy that," he said, his jaw working. "Actions speak louder than words. Look at me. Tell me that nothing happened."

She wouldn't. She stayed fixated on the hall. "We can't talk here. I'm trying to create a reassuring—"

She let out a quick sigh and did look at him, then, and he saw something new in her face: fear. Of him? Now it was his turn to take a deep breath.

"Let's go outside," she said. "Ty won't hear us there. Something's happened. Something more, I mean."

He followed her across the patio and past the wild roses that had impressed Zina so vividly. They stood on the beach, out of earshot, which was fine, but in full view of everyone, which wasn't so fine.

Wendy pointed to a small sailboat hauled up on the sand and said, "We'll go look at it. I can always say that I wanted to get a quote from you for repairing the rudder; it has a split in it that the kids made when they dragged it over the beach."

Feeling like a spy in a low-budget thriller, Zack walked over to the boat and stared down at it with her. "What's happened?" he asked her without looking up. "Why are you being such a nut?"

"Jim packed his bags and left last night."

Zack's head shot up. "Jesus, why didn't you tell me?"

"Look at the boat, look at the boat," she said in a hiss. She crouched down and pointed to the rudder, wiggling it back and forth as she continued.

"When I got home last night, there was another car here. I went in through the side and went straight to bed—in one of the guest rooms," she added to Zack's profound satisfaction.

"Just after midnight," she went on, "I heard shouting outside; someone was threatening Jim. Whoever it was sped off after a neighbor stuck his head out a window and told them to cool it. Jim ran inside and started packing. Ten minutes later, he was gone, too."

Jim: gone. Zack didn't know whether to clap or cry. The mess had just gotten messier. "Was it about money?"

"That's what Jim said. But also that it was more complicated than that—naturally. He said he'd work it out with the guy, but on his own terms."

"Did the thug sound like the same one who's been leaving the messages?"

She surprised him by shrugging off the connection. "I don't know. You heard one of the messages—that weird, singsong voice. But the man I heard last night, he sounded brutal. He sounded as if he could turn it on and off like a switch."

Not what Zack wanted to hear. He dropped down into a crouch next to her. "Well, you can't stay here," he said bluntly.

"Of course I can," she said. "Where would I go? To the half-wrecked house on Sheldon, which the guy probably knows about anyway? And what would I say to Tyler?"

"Tell him anything; tell him you have to evacuate this house because of toxic mold. I don't care what you tell—"

"But I do. I can't just dump all this on him. I won't do it. I have to restore some sense of normalcy before I break the news to him about his father."

Zack didn't get that approach at all. "How are you explaining Jim's absence?"

"I told Ty the truth," she said, looking as if she'd done anything but. "That Jim was on a business trip."

"Look, I know I don't have kids; but if Tyler were my kid—"

"But he isn't," she said with quiet finality. Here they were, crouching in the sand, and she was drawing a line in it: in matters of children, her word ruled.

Maybe to reassure Zack that she'd thought everything out, she added, "This house has an excellent burglar alarm system, whereas Sheldon Street has none yet. And I can have Dave stay over if I want to. And most important of all," she said with steel in her voice, "Jim is gone."

"But the thug doesn't know that," Zack said, trying to prick the bubble of her confidence.

Bingo. She said quietly, "I've thought of that."

She stood up, and so did he. With no bravado this time, she said, "Jim is Ty's father; he would never leave him exposed to anyone he thought was a threat. But . . . okay. I won't take any chances. Ty is going off to the Vineyard tomorrow with his new friend Josh, who lives a couple of blocks away, and several other boys for Josh's birthday outing. Tyler's really looking forward to it."

She sat on the gunnel of the sailing dinghy, frowning as she worked her way through Plan B. "All the boys have been invited to sleep over at Josh's tonight and tomorrow. In fact, Josh is here right now, while his mother gets things ready. I hadn't planned on letting Ty do the sleepovers, because he's just spent all that time at his grandparents'. I miss him," she said with a sad little shrug.

She looked up at Zack and said, "But I will let him sleep there tonight, and when they get back from the sail tomorrow, I'll tell him about Jim. Realistically, I'll tell him the next morning."

She bowed her head and drew a doodle in the sand with her finger. To Zack, it looked like a *J*. Or maybe half of a heart.

He said, "What about you, tonight? What will you do?"

She finished the doodle, a heart. "I feel perfectly safe."

"I'll stay."

Erasing the heart with the flat of her hand, she said, "Bad idea. For a hundred different reasons, Zack. Number one is that my son will be sleeping nearby."

"Wendy—"

She stood up and cleaned the sand from her hands with quick little swipes as she said briskly, "Would you like me to walk you through the other ninety-nine?"

No, he thought; it was such dangerous terrain. "Granted, yesterday the timing could have been better," he said, admitting the obvious. "Not to mention the place. If I'd been planning ahead, I think I could have come up with a more romantic evening."

"I couldn't," she said instantly.

Before he could respond, she said with a guilty glance at the house, "I have to go back. Zack—I don't know how to explain yesterday—"

"I love you! Does that explain yesterday?"

He hadn't meant to say it—it couldn't help matters—and yet there it was, one more thing to add to her woes. She had brought him full circle, from elaborate lies to premature truth. He wanted to add, "And it's all your fault."

Her cheeks became flushed. Not surprisingly, she looked as if she'd been bushwhacked. She absolutely would not meet his gaze. When at last she did, it was to say with anguish, "I have a casserole that I have to take out!"

And then she hurried away, leaving him to find his way back to his truck around, and not through, the kitchen with the casserole that had to come out.

CHAPTER 27

Alarm or no alarm, Zack weighed the possibility of spending the night in one of the reclining chairs on Wendy's patio, which he had seen was nicely screened from the neighbors. While he could understand why Wendy would want to keep him farther than arm's length, he was hoping that she wouldn't mind keeping him within shouting distance. And if she did mind, so be it. She could call the cops and have him removed.

He picked at the pizza, now cold, that he regarded simply as a way to pass time while he waited for darkness to fall. He might be being overprotective, but the sense of unease that he felt was pervasive. He was too jumpy to continue lolling in the booth of the small downtown pizzeria, so he gave up and went out to his truck to call his sister. It was something constructive that he could do.

"Hey, Zee," he said after she picked up. "So. How do you like your new stairs?"

"What stairs?" she answered, which threw him. "Oh . . . that's right. You fixed them. That was so *sweet*, Zack! I just forgot, that's all. I haven't had the chance to use them; I've been busy inside all day."

Confused, he said, "You didn't go to work?"

"Of course not! I have way too much packing to do."

It didn't take Zack as long this time to figure out that

his sister had drifted again into that kinder, gentler world that she had fashioned for herself.

Cursing himself for believing that the morning was an aberration, he said softly, "Where exactly are you going, kiddo? I don't think you said."

"Of course I did, Zack; don't you remember? I'm going off to find Jim. I have to help him, to guide him back to reality," she said, speaking in a breathless rush. "There's something wrong with his memory. He didn't even *know* me, Zack. He looked right at me, and he didn't know me. He's very ill, and it's up to me to bring him out of his ... his spell, I guess you could say. It's like Sleeping Beauty, but in reverse. Oh! I forgot to ask, can I borrow your small carry-on bag? It would be just the right size for smuggling Cassie somewhere that might not allow pets."

"Oh, Zina." Zack was preoccupied enough to think, *Not now, not now.*

"Well, all right, then," she said coolly. "You don't have to lend it to me, if you think it'll make you an accomplice. Cassie and I can get by perfectly fine on our own."

"No, no, that's not what I meant," he said quickly. "Don't go anywhere yet, okay?" he begged. "I'm on the road, and I'll be home soon. I'll bring the carry-on right over. Just wait for me, okay?"

Her soft laugh was apologetic. "I didn't mean to sound rude, Zack. Of course I'll wait. I haven't even *begun* to sort through my quilts."

He started up the truck and punched in Wendy's number on the cell. By the time she answered, he was on the road, headed for Zina.

She didn't sound angry, just distressed, to be hearing from him again so soon. "This isn't a good time, Zack. I'm getting Ty's things together for him," was her latest excuse.

It didn't offend him at all; he understood that what they

had to say couldn't be worked in between dishes and laundry.

He explained very quickly about Zina, and then confessed to his now-abandoned plan to hang around Wendy herself for the night. He could tell that she was touched by that, and it sent a surge of relief and longing through him.

"Just keep the alarm on. Promise me that, would you?"

"Yes, sir," she said, wrapping the words in a smile. "And, Zack?"

"Yeah?"

"Thanks. Thanks for fussing. It feels . . . I don't know. Good."

He wanted to avow his love for her all over again, but he didn't want to risk blowing the moment. She sounded happy just to have him caring what happened. For now, that was enough.

Ten o'clock. Wendy sat curled on one of the twin leather love seats in the library with a well-thumbed catalogue of bathroom fixtures on her lap. She was determined to make her choices once and for all, but the variety of offerings was huge and her ability to focus, minuscule. Sighing, she closed the thick catalogue with its bright Post-it tabs. Another day, perhaps.

She went up to the double bank of windows that was flanked by his-and-hers bookcases—one side filled with military history, the other side filled with house and garden publications—and reluctantly closed and locked them, shutting out the cool night breeze.

As she passed the sofa opposite the one in which she'd been reading, she knocked down a book that had been perched on one of its rolled arms: *Harry Potter and the Goblet of Fire*. She looked at the cover drawing of the young hero, who reminded her so much of her son, and suddenly remembered that Ty had wanted to take the book with him on the ferry to Martha's Vineyard.

Arguing earlier that the book would be a burden in his backpack and that he probably wouldn't have time to read, Wendy had tried to talk him out of it. Tyler had been adamant. And then, like the typical ten-year-old that he was, he'd forgotten to take it, anyway.

She decided to walk the book over to Josh's mother, who could present it to Ty to take or not. The one thing Wendy would not do was offer to run the book upstairs to him herself; her son would die on the spot of mortification.

She strolled down Bluff Road, exchanging good-evenings with an occasional neighbor walking her dog, and breathing in the scent of beach roses and honeysuckle. Yes, she mused, waterfront living had a lot to recommend it. She loved the starry nights and the bracing smell of the ocean—loved even the overripe smell of low tide. She loved the sound of the crickets and the absence of traffic and the sweet-smelling screens of hedges and shrubs.

All of it was easy to love—but home was still home. Eventually, down the road, someday, if she lived that long: Wendy would be in her own house again.

Wendy dropped off the Harry Potter with a few friendly words to Josh's mother, and then she retraced her steps, stopping at one point on the sandy lane simply to take in the sky. It was a moonless night, and infinitely starry. She would have liked to just lie in a chaise longue, counting shooting stars and thinking about words of love, but she had promised Zack that she'd stay safe.

And besides, she was too exhausted even to count the toes on her feet, much less the stars. There had been too many sleepless, restless nights lately, each of them with a different crisis to consume her. Her eyes burned, her heart ached, and her mind was turning to pudding. Maybe that's what it took to be able to sleep. She meant to find out.

She locked the windows and shut off the hall lights, then plodded tiredly into the guest room where she'd set up camp, locking the windows there as well. She was too tired to move all of her things back to the master bedroom; tomorrow was another day. Rejecting her earlier thought of taking a second shower, she fumbled in the dark for her nightgown, the straps of which were somehow tangled on the door hook.

She considered wearing nothing at all—with all of the windows closed, it was bound to be uncomfortably warm— but the thought of having to run out into the street stark naked and yelling, "Help, help!" in an emergency made her feel unusually modest.

Smiling grimly at the success that Zack had had in spooking her, she undressed with her eyes closed, relishing the thought of the sweet oblivion that was soon to come. Sleep, blissful sleep. The blanket and matching matelassé coverlet were far too heavy; she pulled them back, flipping them over the iron footboard of the bed and letting them puddle on the needlepoint rug. A sheet tonight would be more than enough.

Her head was inches from the pillow when she realized that she hadn't bothered to brush her teeth.

So what? Who's going to smell your breath?

The tooth fairy, if her mother was right. Wendy made herself get back out of bed, Gracie Ferro's good little girl, and dragged herself out to the bathroom, wondering whether she could put toothpaste on a brush without turning on the light.

She didn't get the chance to find out.

In the bathroom she was grabbed from behind and pinned to a body that felt twice her size, a monster straight out of Grimm's. He loomed over her and around her, he was everywhere that she didn't want him to be, dragging her easily back into the bedroom. It was all happening so fast; her mind was wasting precious seconds in shocked denial.

She shouldn't be surprised, she shouldn't be paralyzed. *Do something,* she told herself. *Scream, shout, resist!* But screaming, that was out; his monster hand was clamped over her mouth as well as her nose. She could scarcely breathe, let alone scream; she was close to a faint.

His arm was massive, flattened against her breast with such force that it hurt. She tried to snap out of it, tried to kick. But she was barefoot, whacking her heel against steel. What were her options? What could she do? She tried to bite; she couldn't move her lips. She tore at his forearms, but her nails were trimmed short.

He threw her on the bed. In the act, he lost his grip over her mouth. She bit down hard. He let out a yelp, then slapped her, making her see stars. She thought about Tyler, of how she couldn't have him go through the horror that Zina had, and that gave her a burst of strength almost to match the monster's. She rolled away somehow and landed a vicious kick to his groin, making him howl. It made her truly afraid, afraid enough to scramble off the other side of the bed and run for her life.

But not fast enough. He caught her again and knocked her to the floor, then rolled her over and sat across her belly: a huge, repulsive, terrifying, alien blob of flesh.

She was witless with fear, unable to breathe; he was crushing her.

"That spitfire shit don't work with me; where'd you think you'd get? Ah-ow . . . !" Still groaning in pain from her kick, he slapped her again for good measure, then said, "Where is he? That's all I wanted to know, you dumb—"

"I don't know, I don't know," she said, shaking her head. "He left right after you did."

"Bullshit. How will you reach him?"

"Him?" She snorted weakly, despite her blind fear. "He said he'd call."

"Fine. This is what you tell him when he does. You tell him what happened here. You tell him to call. You tell him I'm, y'know, waiting to hear. Can you do that?"

She nodded. "But—"

"No buts. You know them TV commercials? Just do it."

"He might not call, he might never—"

"What'd I say? Okay? I have to go now," he said in an odd, sing-song voice that she remembered all too well.

He lifted his hand and brought it down: more stars, more than in the lane, and hovering over a far blacker night.

By the time the police arrived, Wendy had a plastic bag filled with ice and wrapped in a dish towel planted firmly against her chin. It wasn't vanity that made her want to keep the swelling down, but a sense of outrage at Jim. She had endured her last trauma because of him. The very last.

While one of the men took her statement, which didn't include any mention of the word "bigamous," the other officer did a quick sweep through the house and over the grounds. Wendy was able to describe the car that she remembered from the night before, although it obviously had been nowhere in sight when she'd re-entered the house. But it had been too dark for her to give any but what she considered a vague description of her assailant.

She had been roughly handled by a man wanting to know where Jim was; that was the situation, simply stated. Wendy found herself feeling actually grateful to the brute that it hadn't gone any further than that.

The police, however, treated the matter like the felony it was. They called in a description of the car, as well as what she remembered of her assailant, for intercity broadcast to the police departments of surrounding towns. They summoned detectives and also a photographer who immediately took Polaroids of her bruises, a process that Wendy found intensely embarrassing.

The detectives began dusting for prints. The doorknobs, the path of entry, even the handle on the toilet of the guest bath where he'd grabbed her, all got the treatment.

The detectives interrogated her even more thoroughly, eliciting details she didn't realize she knew. She remembered, in answer to one of their questions, that the man's arms were hairy, for one thing. The recollection of them wrapped around her body was suddenly so vivid that she had to excuse herself and go throw up. But she came back with new determination to have the evil blob thrown in hell: she answered the detectives' questions with as much grim detail as she could call up.

The detectives were sympathetic, which made her want to hug them. They asked her if she had family in the area, and when she answered, "Yes, lots of it," they advised her to call someone. Wendy thanked them politely and said she'd consider it.

By midnight, word had somehow made it to Joshua's house. His father came over for news.

More humiliation. Wendy could see it—or maybe she just imagined it—in the young CEO's face as he stood in the front doorway: there goes the neighborhood. She told him that it was a case of mistaken identity—which in a weird way, it was—and that he very definitely should take Tyler to the Vineyard as planned.

"I'll be going to the station in the morning to look through mug shots," she explained. "I'm assuming you won't mention any of this to the kids. If by chance they do hear something, please just say that the burglar alarm malfunctioned and that's why the police came."

She could see that he wasn't happy about being drafted as a co-conspirator, but he said reluctantly, "Sure. Just let us know what else we can do."

Wendy thanked him profusely and then went back inside. The detectives were concerned about her. She promised them that she would put the alarm on. "Even if it's only to walk across the lane."

"At the least, lock the door," the older detective said. "It only takes a few seconds to gain access. Anywhere—even if the neighborhood's safe."

"I know; I've read my 'Dear Abby,' " she quipped, trying to sound strong.

The other detective said gently, "The trick is to *listen* to 'Dear Abby.' "

"I have Mace," she offered. "If I can figure out where I put it."

"That would be helpful."

The Mace was a gift from a cousin who now lived on a farm and had views about cities. Wendy had laughed when she opened the box. It seemed funny at the time.

At last the detectives packed up their equipment and left. Wendy activated the alarm, took off the jeans and top that she'd pulled on over her nightgown, and threw them all in the wash. With the bathroom door locked and her newly found Mace planted not far from her shampoo, she took a quick shower and then pulled back the covers again, this time of the master bed.

And there she lay, eyes wide open, starting at every sound, feeling alone and betrayed and abused. Tears rolled out, but she wiped them away. She was going to have to be stronger than that. This was no big deal, just one of Jim's deals. They never worked out. And Jim was not going to call. Ever. He was leaving her with heartaches all around and—for all she knew—no money, which she didn't want anyway because it was his. Or, soon, the assailant's. Either way . . . not for her, she decided with loathing.

One thing had become clear in the murky pond that was her life. She understood, now, why she had been so doggedly determined to believe Jim and not Zack: she had been afraid that she was falling for Zack, and the guilt about it had made her stupid.

Guilt. What a useless, wasted emotion. She lay staring at the ceiling, fearing the past, dreading the future, searching for something that would help her to sleep.

I love you. Does that explain yesterday?

His words had been tolling back and forth through her head and heart all evening long. She had relished them, cherished them, felt sure that she was going to reciprocate them—but she still hadn't been convinced that they explained yesterday.

Now she thought that maybe they did.

When his cell phone rang, Zack was in his mother's rocking chair and watching over his sister, asleep on her couch and snug under her tablecloth quilt. Next to her was an assortment of luggage and paper shopping bags, all of them filled. Zina was ready to roll.

Zack had dropped into a catnap himself and wasn't as quick as he should have been in fishing his cell phone out of his front pocket. Zina stirred, then shifted position.

Zack glanced at the kitchen clock: it was three in the morning.

He flipped open the phone to stop the ring, and at the same time whispered, "Shh, shh, go back to sleep, Zee. It's nothing."

He murmured, "Yes?" to acknowledge the call and then stepped softly outside the house to hear what Wendy had to say.

She downplayed what had happened, but as he listened, Zack's soul seemed to crystallize in place. No alarm . . . alone in the house . . . with a thug twice her size . . .

"Are you hurt?" he said, practically slurring over the words with concern.

"Mostly my pride," she said ruefully. "I locked the front door but not all the windows when I decided to walk out with Ty's book. He punched out a screen in the guest bathroom window—which, by the way, I never did lock before I went to bed, or he wouldn't have escaped without setting off the alarm. On the other hand," she added with a pained laugh, "did I really want him stuck in the house with me?"

"But are you *hurt*?"

"I have a couple of bruises, thoroughly photographed. Mostly I'm shaken up. He was a little on the—"

He heard her voice break as she said, "—horrific side."

"I'll be there in an hour."

"No, Zack," she said, suddenly firm again. "I shouldn't have called, but you're the only one who knows everything. Such excitement; I guess I just had to share."

Her voice was wry and brave, but he wasn't convinced. In any case, it hardly mattered. He had to be there.

"And Zina?" she asked him, going straight to the heart of his dilemma. "How is she?"

"Better. We talked for hours. I definitely got through to her. She understands about Jim; the question is, for how long? I gave her an over-the-counter sleeping pill that I picked up on the way. She hasn't been sleeping, and I think at least part of her problem is exhaustion. You go too long without sleep, you become delusional."

"Like a sailor caught in a storm at sea," Wendy murmured.

She got it completely. It wasn't hard to understand why.

"Right now, she's out like a light," Zack explained. "I think what I'll do is leave a note with her landlady to call me if she sees any urgent movements over there. And I'll get in touch with the shelter, come morning. Zina has friends there; one of them will be willing to stay with her until I figure out the next step."

There was a pause, and then Wendy said firmly, "I don't

want you to come down here, Zack. It was good just to hear your voice. After you get things worked out with Zina . . . that's soon enough."

"No. I love you."

"And you love your sister. Which is why I—"

Say it, he thought. *Please, just say it.*

"Come when you can, Zack—but not before. I'm fine, now," she said softly, and she hung up.

Zack folded his phone and stood in the yard under a fading canopy of stars. It would be light soon, and he'd be able to implement his plan to surround his sister with people who cared for her enough to keep her safely inside.

But just for good measure, he decided to take her car keys with him.

CHAPTER 28

It wouldn't have been so bad if it had happened on the way back, at least. But no-o-o . . . the guy had to hit them before they were barely away from the house. Before they were on the highway, even. But that's because Joshua's mother was trying to be so careful that she came to a dead stop, instead of just merging into traffic the way people are supposed to do. Plus, the guy who smacked into them was talking on his cell phone, the cops said. He got an extra ticket for that, Joshua's mother said. *Good.*

Joshua's mother was really shook up, even though the bumper was only a little smashed in. None of them even got hurt. (Actually, Tyler had twisted his finger because he was goofing off, trying to get the stuck coffee holder in the back unstuck—but no way was he going to tell anyone that.)

"You could have been killed, you could have been killed," she kept telling them all the way back home, and she was actually crying. And Joshua was, like, "Get a *grip*, Mother." Tyler was embarrassed for Josh. *His* mother would never have lost it like that.

So they drove back home, and Joshua's mother started calling everyone's moms to come pick them up. Joshua said his birthday was a total disaster, and Tyler definitely agreed. He was so bummed out.

They were all in Joshua's room, playing video games

but not really, when Joshua's mother came upstairs.

She said to Tyler, "I've called your mother, but she's still not home. Does she have a cell phone?"

Tyler said yes, but then he couldn't remember the number. It was so embarrassing. "It's a brand-new one," he said, but of course, he still looked like an idiot.

"Well, I'm sure she'll be home soon," she said, but Tyler didn't think that she looked sure about anything. "In the meantime, you can just stay here with Josh."

But he didn't want to stay there! He wanted to go to Martha's Vineyard. Tyler had only been there once, so at least he could *say* he'd been there, but he had been only three years old. His mom had bought him a Black Dog T-shirt; at least, that's what she'd told him. What good was a Black Dog T-shirt if you were only three?

Two of the kids got picked up super-fast: Michael and Jeremy. That left Andrew; his father picked him up a little while later. As for Tyler, he would rather have gone home and read his Harry Potter if they weren't going to Martha's Vineyard.

It would have been rude, though, to read in front of Joshua, who hated reading, so Tyler went downstairs when Josh was in the bathroom and asked if he could wait for his mom at home.

"Absolutely not," Joshua's mother said. "You're staying here."

By then he felt like a prisoner. "Can we go outside, at least?"

"Yes, of course. Just don't you two go wandering off too far."

Josh was a real jock; he had a garage full of mountain bikes. He ran in to tell his mother that they were just going for a ride around the house.

"What did she say?" Tyler asked as he rolled out a really

cool bike: fifteen speeds, and with a lower top tube that he could just straddle.

"Nothin'. She was on the phone."

They rode around the block a couple of times, and then around the next block, past Michael's house. He came out on his bike, and then they all three decided where to go next.

"Let's go past my house," Tyler suggested. "I'll see if my mom's home yet."

Off they went. Tyler was happy to see, as they rounded the corner, that his mother's Taurus was parked in front of the house. She must have just gotten home.

"I should tell her what happened," he told his friends.

"She prob'ly knows by now; my mom prob'ly called her."

"Yeah, but just in case," he told Joshua.

"Well, we're not waiting. Meet us at the beach."

They had already decided that the town beach was technically not "too far." It's just that Josh's mom was a worrier after the accident.

Tyler waved to his friends and leaned the bike against the stile fence, in a spot that didn't have roses. He was surprised to see that the front door was locked. He rang, but there was no answer. His key was at Joshua's in his backpack, so he went around to the side of the house; there was an extra key hidden there. More amazement: a yellow Civic—*the* yellow Civic; he remembered the plates—was parked practically under the arch that was cut through the ten-foot-tall hedge.

Tyler didn't understand it at all. Were his mom and that lady *both* inside, then, not answering the door? But then he thought of the patio. You couldn't hear the front doorbell if you were on the patio. So he squeezed around the yellow Civic and through the arch and went around to the back. He found no one on the patio, but someone on the beach.

She was there, alone, her light blond hair lifting in the wind. She was wearing a dress just like the blue one she wore that day, but this one was the color of a golden palomino. Between her hair and the dress that was being pressed against her by the wind, she really did look like a wild . . . something. A woman-horse, maybe, who could carry you to a distant land of wizards.

She turned around suddenly, as if she could hear his thoughts. He became convinced just by the way she stared at him that she had magical powers. He found himself drawing nearer, just to see if she did or not.

"Hi," she said, waving at him.

She had a huge smile. Her sleeve spilled back to her shoulder and he thought again how long and lean her arms were. He remembered that from the birthday party: her arms and her legs. She was just so different from his mother; he couldn't get over it.

He waved back shyly and said, "Are you here to see my mom?"

She didn't hear him over the wind. And he might have been mumbling, the way his mom always accused him of doing. So he came closer and repeated his question.

The woman didn't answer it. She said, "My name is Zina. I'm Zack's sister. What's your name?"

Tyler was flabbergasted. Zack's sister! No one told him that!

"Tyler Hodene," he said, feeling his cheeks burn. "I saw you when you were here before." Suddenly it occurred to him why she had come that day: she had been looking for Zack, not his father. It was all an amazing misunderstanding.

"I remember you very well, Tyler Hayward," she said. She swept away the long, long strands of hair that were blowing across her face, but immediately they blew right back. She laughed, and her voice sounded like water falling over a high ridge.

Tyler wanted to tell her that she'd got his last name wrong, but he hated to hurt her feelings—especially after the way his family had treated her. He, at least, would never make her cry. He said respectfully, "I should see if my mother's home; she could have gone to a neighbor's house."

"No one's home," Zina told him. "I rang the bell, but nobody answered. I tried the door, but it was locked."

"That's all right," Tyler said. "There's a secret key under the frog."

He waited for her to come up to him, fascinated by the way the sun seemed to just slide off her long hair. Zack's sister! It explained *everything*.

"You look so much like your father," she said as they walked together to the hiding place. "Has anyone ever told *you* that?"

"All the time," said Tyler, slightly disgusted. "I really don't like it."

She laughed again, the kind of laugh that you heard on TV commercials at Christmas. "Oh, but you shouldn't mind the comparison," she said. "Your father is an exceptionally handsome man, and when you grow up, you will be, too."

Tyler was surprised to hear her say that. His father wasn't exceptionally handsome. His father was a lot of fun, but he wasn't exceptionally handsome. As for Tyler, he would much rather be considered fun—but he wasn't even that.

Which is why it pleased him so much that he had been able to make Zina laugh. "You don't look like Zack at all," he ventured to say. "Has anyone ever told you that?"

"All the time," she said, and they laughed together, as if they shared some secret that the rest of the world just couldn't understand if they tried. Tyler was glad that she was Zack's sister, because he decided then and there that he liked her very much.

At the foot of the arch on the beach side of the house, a big stone frog protected the key. The frog had a mean expression on his face, perfect for scaring people away from him. "This is our watchfrog," Ty said, making Zina laugh again.

Trying not to make it look like an effort, Zack tipped the heavy frog back far enough to reach the key underneath. "See? No one would dare steal this to break in." He took out the key and they went around to the front.

"Did anyone know you were coming?" he asked, curious, as he stuck the key in the lock. He disabled the alarm as he'd been instructed to do, surprised that it was even set on.

"No, this is a last-minute thing," Zina answered. "I'm going house-hunting today, and I was hoping to talk your dad into coming with me. He knows a lot about houses; he used to be a real estate agent."

Tyler didn't even know that. He said, "My dad's away on business, in Phoenix, I think. Or one of those places out there."

"Oh, pooh," Zina said. Her face got such a sad expression that Tyler said, "Can I get you a lemonade or something?"

"N-no . . ." she said, thinking. "Do you know when he'll be back?"

"A couple of days, my mom told me."

She looked as if she was going to start crying. Tyler was scandalized. Of all the people to make her cry, he didn't want to be one of them!

"I . . . guess I'll have to go to Newport alone, then," she said. "I'm so disappointed. Oh, this is so disappointing."

She sat on the nearest chair and then she did begin to cry. Not buckets, just . . . a thin trail of tears, as if she were watching a really sad movie. She reminded Tyler of his mother just then. He felt absolutely devastated.

"My mom would go with you," he assured her, trying to make her feel better. "But she thinks I'm at Martha's Vineyard, and she might not be back for a while. I think someone in my family must have come by and picked her up. Probably my grandmother or my aunt Charlotte."

He ran to get a box of Kleenex for her. She thanked him, then pulled out three tissues and blew her nose.

"Well, what did I expect?" she said, as if he were a good friend. "I should have warned Jim sooner that I was coming."

She sighed and didn't say anything for a little while. And then, while Tyler was still frantically searching for something to tell her that would make her feel better, she suddenly brightened and said, "I know! Why don't you come to Newport with me?"

Tyler was unsure about that, but then she said, "In fact, there's a sand castle competition going on today at the beach, right near where I'm going to look for a house. I remember, when I was here the last time, seeing a big sand castle on your beach. Tyler, these will be *so* much bigger than that."

"No kidding?"

"They're amazing."

Sorely tempted, Tyler said, "But I would have to let my mom know I was gone. And I don't actually remember her cell phone number."

"We'll leave a note!" Zina said, looking more cheerful by the minute. "We'll probably be back before she will; but just in case, we'll leave her a note. Do you have a camera?" she asked, jumping up to scribble on the grocery pad that they kept on the fridge door. "Because you'll want to take pictures."

"I do have one," Tyler said, swept up in her enthusiasm.

"Are you sure we won't be gone long, though?"

"We'll be back in the blink of an eye," she said with a beautiful, happy smile. "I promise."

The computer searches were exhaustive: the detective had plugged in everything from "face, round" to "skin, hairy," in the approximate height and weight that Wendy had given for the intruder. Back came dozens and dozens of mug shots, none of them a right match. Or maybe right; Wendy couldn't tell anymore. She was becoming punchy.

"Can you search on 'smelly' or 'loathesome'?" she asked, only half joking.

Zack was at another computer, scanning duplicates of whatever mug shots Wendy was scrutinizing. There was always the possibility that the intruder had found an excuse to come to the house on Sheldon Street while Zack had been at work there.

"Okay, I give up," Wendy said at last. "These men all look alike to me, white, black, round- or oval-faced: *bad*."

"He's from out of state, most likely," Detective Mizzner speculated. "We're small. He could easily be from Connecticut or Mass."

Zack had a thought. "What about the Dodge Stratus? Could that be an in-state rental?"

"We're checking on that right now," the detective told them.

The investigation seemed to be moving along aggressively. Zack and Wendy left both of their cell phone numbers with Detective Mizzner and climbed into Zack's truck, both of them bone-tired. Zack tried calling Margie again but got no answer. He tried calling Zina again; no answer there, either.

"It's not surprising," Zack said, but he looked tense. "Margie said she'd take Zina out to breakfast and then maybe to do a little shopping."

But Wendy knew, from their long talk together in the hours before they went to the station, that Margie was a hands-off landlady. She might have felt indebted to Zack for the carpentry, but there was no real bond between her and Zina to exploit.

Zack knew it, too. It was written all over his face.

"Zack . . . take me home and then go back to Hopeville. I'll be fine," she insisted.

He gingerly stroked the bruise on her chin and said, "Yeah. I see how fine."

He might be being protective, but she took his gentle irony very personally. "That was then," she said, bristling. "This is now. I'll call my brother Dave and have him come over to stay with us. My family has to find out about everything sooner or later."

Zack chewed his lip and then nodded. "Yeah. Something's not right h—"

His cell phone rang and he jumped on it. After a brief exchange, he snapped his phone shut and, tucking it in his shirt pocket, brought Wendy up to speed as he pulled out of the station's parking lot.

"That was Morgan from the shelter. She went over to Zina's to check on her. There are no cars there. No one's home on either side."

"How is that possible?" Wendy asked, dumbfounded. "You have her keys."

"Yeah. I'll take you home. You call Dave and I'll—ah, *shit*!" he said, slamming the wheel in exasperation.

She could see that he wanted to be everywhere at once. "This is a lose-lose situation for you, Zack," she said, guilt-ridden herself that she was part of his problem. "I'm so sorry."

He nodded again. They drove the short distance home in silence, each of them immersed in his own thoughts. Wendy was frankly relieved to see that the house on the beach was still standing. In the mood she was in, she wouldn't have been surprised to find it burned to the ground.

"Whose bike is that, I wonder?" she said, eyeing a bright-blue, obviously expensive mountain bike leaning against the stile fence that angled in from the lane. They pulled up alongside her Taurus, Wendy with a backward glance at the bike as she fitted the key to the front door.

The door was locked, but the alarm wasn't set. "You were here, Zack," she said, puzzled. "You saw me do it."

He was as puzzled as she was. They were moving through the house, checking the rooms, when the doorbell rang. Wendy went back to answer it and was stunned to see Joshua standing there, with Michael holding his bike in the drive.

"Why are you here?" she asked rather stupidly. "You're supposed to be on the Vineyard." *With Tyler.*

Josh said simply, "We didn't go. Can Tyler bring my bike back now? Because my mom doesn't let me just leave them by the road."

"Get in here," she commanded, yanking him inside by his Tommy Hilfiger shirt. "Where's Tyler? Why didn't you go?" Her hand was shaking, her whole body was shaking.

If Josh explained why they didn't go, Wendy scarcely heard it. All she caught, all she comprehended, was, "He was going to catch up with us at the town beach."

She released her white-knuckled grip on his collar and turned around to see Zack. "They didn't go," she said, practically pleading with him to say, "Of course they did; you're hallucinating."

Instead, he held up the notepad with the magnetic back that they kept on the fridge. Wendy read the flamboyant scrawl on the top sheet:

Off to see castles.

"This is her handwriting," he said tersely.

No need to ask who "her" was. Wendy had only one question for him: "Should I be afraid?"

He shook his head. "No. Not of Zina."

Relief flooded in, making Wendy sharp. "The mansions!" she said, gripping Zack's arm. "She's taken Ty to see the mansions in Newport!"

Not a Rhode Islander, Zack still knew exactly what she was referring to; everyone knew about Newport's Gold Coast.

"Good possibility. Are any neighbors home? We can ask if they saw a yellow Civic."

Wendy shook her head. "They all work."

"Okay. Call the kid's mother and tell her to lock Tyler in the bathroom if he happens to show up. You and I are going to Newport."

By then Josh and Michael had long gone, leaving the spare bike to fend for itself. Undoubtedly Wendy's legend would grow.

Back into the truck she and Zack went, with Zack hard-pressed to throttle back to a reasonable speed.

"The mansions make sense," he said, his brow tight with concentration. "Zina did seem suddenly obsessed with the idea of buying a cottage on the shore. She saw this place. She saw Jim looking happy."

"He was, wasn't he?" Wendy said, bewildered by the fact. She couldn't understand how it could be fun to live such a fierce lie. It would eat her alive.

"Zina put two and two together," Zack went on, "and came up with the idea of a cottage on the shore for them both. She doesn't have a clue about the cost. For all we know, she may be planning to buy the Breakers."

Smiling faintly, Wendy said, "The Preservation Society may have something to say about that." After another moment, she couldn't help asking, "Zack, why did she do this, if not to strike back at me?"

"That's not it; I'm sure of it. She has respect and affection for you. To be honest, she feels sorry for you, that you won't have Jim."

"Good God."

"I think the thing about Tyler—it's because somehow, some way, she's made a connection between the baby she lost and with Ty. He's roughly the age that her baby would have been. He looks like Jim. You can see how her mind would work . . . or not work," he said, sighing. He glanced at Wendy, hoping for understanding.

"It's hard for me, Zack," Wendy said, closing her eyes. "Don't ask me right now."

He took his phone off the dashboard and handed it to Wendy. "Call Mizzner and bring him up to speed on this. He should know."

"But you said I didn't have to be afr—"

"Not of Zina, is what I said," he muttered, staring straight ahead.

CHAPTER 29

"I'm sure Detective Mizzner's head is spinning," Wendy said, snapping the phone shut. "He seems determined to believe that the two events are related—the thug's appearance and now Zina's."

"He's not the only one," Zack said. "I can't help thinking that the thug also discovered Jim through that AP photo that ran with the lottery story. Tell me this: has anyone ever called him 'Jimmy' since you've known him?"

"Nobody. Unless we're being snotty."

"Well, he was 'Jimmy' to Zina and me back then. And, I'm assuming, to the charmer who left those messages on your machine and then assaulted you. It bothered me when I heard it, that 'Jimmy.' It bothers me now. This guy is linked somehow to Jim's past."

She could see him think about it, then shake it off before asking her, "So what's the plan? Did Mizzner say?"

"He said that they'll alert the Newport police to watch for the car and to put the word out to each of the mansions that's open to the public. He'll also try alerting the local realtors. There aren't *that* many mansions to tour—but the area has dozens of realty agencies."

"They're being thorough," Zack said with approval.

"Yes, but you could tell that he had his hands full already with us, what with the searches for the thug and now Jim."

"Hey, that's what we pay taxes for," Zack quipped, trying to make her smile. When she sighed instead, he took her hand in his and said softly, "It'll be all right, Wendy. Zina is kind to all of God's creatures. She feels bad when she cuts down a sunflower."

Wendy let the warmth of his calloused hand spread over her own chilled one, infusing her with some of his confidence. "I know, Zack," she said. "I saw that for myself. It's just that there are too many people running around, too many unknowns . . ."

"Call the landlady for me," he said, maybe to give Wendy something to do. He gave her the number, and this time, someone answered.

Wendy quickly handed him the phone. His voice was grim, his manner terse, as he said, "What happened, Margie? How did she get her car started?"

She saw him listen, then shake his head, then sign off with a quick good-bye and no further comment.

"My sister talked Margie into driving her over to my house, where I keep her spare key to the car," he told Wendy with a sigh of disgust. "Zina's always been spacey about losing keys and wallets," he added. "Ironic, that she had the cunning to talk Margie into driving her over there."

"Why didn't Margie call and tell you when she saw that Zina's car was gone, for God's sake?" Wendy asked, aware that this latest trauma could have been avoided if they'd had some warning.

"She was afraid to. She got in her own car again and began driving around Hopeville, looking for Zina at the few haunts she knew about. That must have been when Morgan dropped by the house and saw everyone gone. You're right," he said, exasperated. "If everyone would just stay put for five fucking minutes—"

Succinctly put, she thought. There was little more to say after that.

They were making their way through the compact but historic waterfront district of Warren. Briefly a whaling town, then a mill town, now a commercial shipbuilding and—naturally—antiques center, there was still nothing cutesy about the nearly four-hundred-year-old town. It might be restored, it might be authentic, but it would never be either elegant or glamorous. Wendy had always had an affection for Warren; relatives from the Portuguese side of her family who lived there.

Not so in Bristol, the next town on their agonizingly slow run to Newport. A much more beautiful town with far grander homes, Bristol was equally historic, and darkly so. Active in the slave trade, bombarded by the British, later abandoned by Continental soldiers and then really sacked by the British, home to a den of privateers after that: Bristol had always impressed Wendy as a strikingly beautiful but somehow compromised town.

They followed the shoreline through Bristol rather than traverse its inland road not because they were interested tourists, but because they were afraid of missing a yellow Civic that might be parked in front of some home by the water that was open to the public.

On Hope Street they came upon Linden Place, built by an infamous man and restored by his philanthropist grandson, and Zack said, "That qualifies as a mansion to *me*."

He sounded hopeful, but they found no yellow Civic parked among the out-of-state cars there.

"She had to mean Newport," Wendy said doggedly. "They have mansions everywhere that dwarf this one."

On they rode, over the quaint Mount Hope Bridge to Aquidneck Island, home to three historic small towns, the last and most easily famous of which was Newport.

Zack said, "Any mansions in Portsmouth?"

"No, but lots of beaches."

"Beaches have cottages, some for sale."

"But not castles, Zack. Zina wrote that they were off to see *castles*. No. I'm sure we're on the right track," Wendy insisted, but her fears were at war with her instincts.

The cell phone rang again, this time, Wendy's. Odd, how the front seat of a pickup could so have the feel of a war room. She answered and was shocked to hear Jim's voice at the other end, and even more shocked that he was acting as if he really were on a business trip.

"Everything okay back there?" he asked matter-of-factly.

"Okay? *Okay?* No, Jim, everything's not okay. I've been assaulted, we can't find Tyler, and Zina is more or less—"

She glanced at Zack, and out of concern for him, said "—in danger of losing her grip."

"Whoa, whoa, back up," Jim said. "Start at the beginning, for God's sake."

She brought him up to date on all of it and finished by saying, "I've answered your questions, now you answer mine: where the *hell* are you, you bastard?"

There was a slight pause before he said, "Lincoln."

"Lincoln? *Nebraska?* What are you doing there?"

"Just tying up some loose ends," he said cryptically.

"I don't believe you. You're lying. As usual, you're lying," she said, frustrated beyond measure. "Wherever you are, come back here and give yourself up."

He laughed bitterly. "Oh, yeah, I'll do that. Why'd you have to go to the police, Wen? We could have worked this all out."

She closed her eyes and inhaled deeply. "I can't talk to you, Jim. I just can't stand it anymore."

"What about Tyler?" he said, sounding panicky that she might hang up on him. "Tell me about Tyler."

Wendy felt a tap on her arm. Zack was pointing to an events sign nailed to a utility pole along a tacky strip of beach-related shops just outside of Newport.

It was electrifying: *Sand Castle Competition, Easton's Beach, June 21. Sponsored by Row to Go Sea Kayaks.*

"Zack, that has to be it. She's taken him to see the sand castles, not the mansions! How could I not have thought of that? I saw an ad in the East Bay section yesterday! That's it!"

"Wendy! Wendy, what're you talking about?" Jim was shouting.

"Easton's Beach; they must be there," she said, hardly aware that he was still on the phone and that she was talking to him as much as to Zack. "They *have* to be!"

"Number sixty-seven, fisherman's platter! Number sixty-seven, fisherman's platter!"

The voice came over a loudspeaker in the background at Jim's end—if Jim was telling the truth—in Lincoln, Nebraska.

"Yeah, right," she said contemptuously. She knew a Rhode Island accent when she heard one. She snapped the phone shut with one hand and tossed it back on the dashboard.

"That's Easton's Beach coming up, right after this light," she told Zack, pointing frantically. "See the changing houses and the pavilion? Turn in before it."

The phone rang again; they ignored it.

It was a fine beach day, but midweek and still early in the season; the lot wasn't that full. They cruised up and down it, looking for a yellow Civic. Wendy was crushed when they didn't find one.

"Wait! I forgot; there's another lot, farther to the west," she said, taking heart again. "Let's try that one."

They drove out and around the median and pulled into the second lot. Again they were disappointed.

"I don't believe it," Wendy moaned. "They're here, I know it!"

Without a word, Zack climbed down from the truck, into

the bed, and onto the roof of the cab. Wendy got out and stood on the ground, gazing in the same direction.

"I see her car," he said after a moment, probably the happiest four words that Wendy had ever heard in her life. "She's parked on the road, pretty far up the hill."

His laugh was filled with obvious relief as he said, "Leave it to my sister not to spend the big bucks to get into a lot when she can get by with a few coins in a meter."

Somehow everything else—the assault, the bigamy, the ongoing threat—seemed absolutely trivial in the face of this one truth: Zina and Tyler were on the beach, looking at sand castles.

Exploding, really, with relief, Wendy bolted across the lot and for the beach, never thinking that one of them should keep an eye on the Civic, until Zack caught up with her and said, "I'll run to the other end of the exhibit, the one closer to the car. You start at this end."

"Right," she said, and off she went while Zack raced through the parking lot, headed for the other end.

She expected to pick Tyler and Zina off easily—but nothing since the day they'd won the lottery had been easy. The crowds were large, and by no means all in bathing suits. Clusters of people stood around each of the incredible exhibits. Wendy had to go around and through them, trying to keep focused, trying not to look everywhere at once and end up seeing nothing.

She was amazed at the number of sand castles, considering that this exhibit wasn't even the traditional end-of-summer one. It was as if they'd brought in professionals from all over the country to create them: big ones, little ones; vertical and horizontal ones; drippy ones, moated ones; and one incredible creation that looked to be an entire walled medieval town.

But no Tyler, and no Zina. Devastated not to have found them, Wendy began looking around for Zack. He was a distance away: she shook her head in long, slow arcs, sending him a message of disappointment. He pointed up the hill: he was apparently going to check out the route to the car.

Wendy dropped down to the water's edge to look up and down at the swimmers: the two could be wading, she supposed. Or wandering off toward the arc of houses that ran all the way out to Easton's Point. They could be at the opposite, western end, walking along Cliff Walk, the spectacular pathway that lined the Gilded Age mansions that their absurdly wealthy owners liked to call "cottages" and that ordinary folk like Wendy and Zina called "castles."

They could be inside somewhere, visiting a mansion, a realty agency, a restaurant; they could be *anywhere*.

"Wendy," came his breathless voice behind her. "Find them yet?"

She whirled around. "Jim! Where did you come from?" she asked, and then she said, "Never mind," because she really didn't care.

"I've been in Newport, lying low while I figured out what to do next," he confessed.

Which made sense. Lots of crowds, lots of transients. He could stay somewhere different every night if he chose, without arousing notice. She hated him for figuring that out, for always working the angles.

"I bought a Harley," he added, which truly amazed her. Could he possibly think it mattered?

He fell in beside her. She had nothing further to say to him and continued on her way in tense silence, scanning for Zina and Ty. Jim was silent, too—until they drew abreast of the sand castles.

"Wow. These things are unbelievable!" he said with awe, pointing to the medieval city. "Doesn't it make you just want to walk up to one and . . . kick it?" He was giving her that half-cocked look with that impish grin that she knew so well.

Wendy looked away. She utterly despised him.

Seconds later, she stopped in her tracks, and so did her heart: ahead of her she saw Zina and Tyler, each of them clutching a Del's frozen lemonade, each of them walking with a stiff and zombielike gait. Between them walked a monster with hairy arms and a round face. She didn't need to have known that his hair was black or that his skin was blotchy, or that his neck was short and thick.

She knew without those details that he was the one. She'd know him anywhere.

Zina and Tyler were frozen with fear, and only in a second wave of comprehension did Wendy know why: the thug had a weapon inside the fist that was jammed in his pocket; she assumed, a gun.

Jim turned around to see why she'd stopped. It must have shown in her face, because he swung his head back to confirm what she was looking at. "Ah, *fuck,*" he said, and then, like a horse out of the gate, he took off and ran in the opposite direction, leaving Wendy to face the three others alone.

Did the brute recognize her? It didn't matter, because her son did. His face broke out in a rash of different emotions, chief among them, relief. Wendy couldn't bear it. Without thought, she broke into a run at him, her shoes sliding in the loose sand and making her progress unbearably slow. He was so close; he was so far.

Before she could reach him, her son was knocked down, fallout from the force that hit the monster from behind: Zack had hurled himself like a cannonball at the man, knocking him sideways into Ty. While Wendy gathered up her son and while Zina screamed uncontrollably, Zack and the monster locked forces, rolling around in the sand, swinging and punching, eventually fighting their way to the nearest castle and knocking down one tower after another, flattening walls and filling in moats, drawing real blood on a make-believe battlefield.

All around them, children screamed and parents ran with them for cover. A lifeguard with a zinc-covered nose was first to try breaking up the melee; his white nose got instantly bloodied. The monster landed a huge blow to Zack's chin, flattening him before taking off. Horrified, Wendy fell to her knees at Zack's side, but he staggered to his feet after the man, who was well down the beach, incredibly fast for someone his size. Wendy watched him scramble over the rocks and then over the beach wall and run up the hill, with Zack far behind.

In anguish, Wendy clutched her son and tried to comfort Zina as the figures on the walkway got smaller and disappeared. Sounds replaced sights: Zina's cries and children's screams; a plane overhead, a boom box nearby. And on the boulevard feeding the beach, a pack of motorcycles leaving town. Among all of it, Wendy was able to pick out the sound of one motorcycle revving up and taking off, one motorcycle roaring out of the parking lot, one motorcycle crashing into something bigger than it was.

Soon there were more sirens, many sirens, of ambulances and fire trucks and rescue vehicles, the paraphernalia of a city used to crazy behavior and reckless bravado, even on a sunny weekday afternoon. Some of them stopped at the entrance of Cliff Walk, and some of them kept on until they reached the pavilion. All of them had lives to try saving.

Wendy sat in the brand-new, soaring Courtyard in the east wing of Newport Hospital and thought, *How in keeping with a city of mansions.*

She was still shell-shocked, and Tyler, too; but they had been left standing. They were the only ones. Zina had been admitted for observation. Zack was being stitched up and his kidney was about to be scrutinized in an MRI. The thug—a just-released con whose name was, improbably, Hallowell Hix—was in surgery having multiple bones put right after being peeled off the rocks at the bottom of Cliff Walk.

And Jim, whose name was not Hodene or even Hayward, but Hix—Jim would never walk or talk or even think again.

"I don't know who will make the decision to remove him from the respirator," Wendy told Dave in an undertone. She was a little ways away from her son, keeping her gaze locked on him as he nestled in his grandmother's arm on one of the benches nearby. "I'm not his wife. Zina's in no condition, even if she were his wife: there may be someone else out there between Hix and Hayward. I really don't . . . know who will do it," she said, still coming to terms with it all.

"That's an issue for the medical staff," her brother said, wrapping his arm around her and pulling her close for comfort. "Don't worry about it, Wen. It's not today's problem."

Wearily, she said, "They've stopped the bleeding in Zack."

Dave smiled and said, "I know. You've told me. Twice."

"It wasn't as bad as they'd feared. Did I tell you?"

"Yes," he said, putting his other arm around her. "Twice."

"Thank God," she murmured into her brother's shirt. She began to shake again. "Thank God."

"That Mizzner seems like a good guy," Dave said, undoubtedly to reroute her thoughts.

Wendy straightened, nodding emphatically. "He is. He is." She smiled and said, "Why *am* I repeating everything I say?"

"Because you know I'm thickheaded," quipped Dave.

"You aren't; I am. To have lived with Jim so long . . ."

"Hey, we all were taken in. He was good at living lies. He'd had plenty of practice, even before he met you."

"I'm glad you were there when Detective Mizzner explained it all. I'm hazy about parts of it. Why didn't Hix come after Jim right after we won the money?"

"He was still in jail in Massachusetts. Wasn't much he could do. It had to make his blood boil, doing time while his brother—the one who'd actually pulled the trigger and killed the guy—had not only escaped but was enjoying such dumb blind luck. We're lucky Hix rented a car instead of stealing one; it made Mizzner's job easier. Hallowell Hix: what an ijit," Dave said, shaking his head in wonder.

"I still can't believe that Jim would let himself be pushed into doing all those robberies by a brother. A *brother,* Dave."

"Half brother, I expect; their mother was a hooker, don't forget. Anyway, you've seen Hix up close and personal; he's the proverbial eight-hundred-pound gorilla."

Bitter now, she said, "Baloney. Frank doesn't make you go around robbing and killing people."

"Frank's a teddy bear, not a gorilla."

It was true. She reflected a moment and then said with a wince, "Do you think Jim did anything like . . . that . . . while he was living with *me*?"

Dave shook his head. "By then he'd ditched his brother. The crime spree, that was before Zina and of course during Zina. Even Zack wasn't on to Jim's double life. The guy really was good; look how we all bought into that childhood history of his. In Jim's own pathetic way, he was trying to clean up his act once he met you. He just didn't know how. He was pretty much a lost cause by then."

Shuddering, she said, "We talk about him as if he's gone."

"He is, Wendy; he is. And you have your whole life ahead of you now."

She touched her fingertips tenderly to the sling that held his bandaged arm, unwilling, still, to think of him lying at the edge of Cliff Walk and bleeding profusely, both inside and out.

"*How* many stitches?"

"Ah, in the forties, give or take," said Zack, brushing off the idea.

"You'll have a scar," she said, distressed.

He gave her a crooked smile. "Will you mind?"

"Oh, Zack."

She slipped her hand under his good one; he held it tight, reassuring her with his strength.

"I was sure he had a gun; I never imagined a knife."

"I think that in his twisted way, Hix was trying to stay out of reach of the law," Zack said. "I'll bet he would have been perfectly happy to take Jim's money and retire to Boca Raton."

There it was again: the money. Wendy pulled her chair closer to Zack's bed and said in a low whisper, "That money is cursed. Look at the pain it's caused. Zack, I'm afraid of it."

His smile faded. Alarmed, she shut up—she just wanted, really, to hold his hand and look at him for the few minutes that she had left with him—but he had something to say.

"I don't think there will be any money," he said, "not after all the lawsuits are resolved. From what I hear, a couple of those teens that got mowed down by the skidding bike were badly hurt. Then there's the woman in the car he hit. I'm sorry, Wendy."

"Why?" she asked, genuinely bothered by his sympathy. "I told you that I was afraid of it. I've always been afraid of it."

"I was part of your pain," he said, dropping his head back on the pillow. He closed his eyes. "I'm sorry for that."

She studied his face, this strong, silent, completely loyal man who had taken her off-kilter life and righted it for her.

"You might have been part of my pain," she acknowledged. "But now you're my cure, and my only hope. I love you, Zack," she said softly. "I love you."

He was drifting off, but with a smile. She sat there, her hand in his, until the nurse came and removed her gently but firmly from the room.

EPILOGUE

"I guess I got carried away," Wendy said, rubbing her nose with a sticky, balsamy finger.

"I guess you did," Zack agreed. He stepped back to assess his work, eyeing the tree for a minute before he said wryly, "Yep. She's straight, all right."

And then some. The top branches looked as if they were holding up the ceiling. The bottom branches were poking through the drapes on one side and threatening to catch on fire at the other.

Warily eyeing the nearby dancing flames in the new fireplace, Wendy said, "Maybe we can exchange the tree for a smaller one?"

Tyler rolled his eyes. "Mom, *nobody* takes back a Christmas tree."

She backed up to the doorway and took in the entire room, charmed all over again by its warm and simple furnishings: the cotton-covered red sofabed; her father's old armchair, now reupholstered; a pair of yard-sale chairs that were an engagement gift from Zina, who had covered their cushions with needlepoint versions of the before-and-after houses; the Pottery Barn Persian that anchored the furnishings. The room was her favorite—warm, cozy, and welcoming.

But not especially large.

"The space seemed so much bigger this morning," she

said with a sigh. "Well, this won't work. We'll have to get a smaller tree."

"Mom! You can't get rid of something just because you feel like it!" her son said in a voice cracking with emotion.

Wendy turned in surprise to him. "Where did *that* come from, Ty? *Whom* do you know who's more traditional than I am?"

Tyler's eyelashes fluttered down and he said without looking at her, "I just think we should keep this tree."

"And so do I," Zack said, placing himself firmly in the line of fire. "Let's see if a little tweaking won't help."

He began by cutting down the base and removing the lower rim of branches. After that he nipped, cut, and grafted until finally they had a tree that the room could call its own.

The three of them stood back to admire the transformation. Tyler was obviously satisfied. "See? It was right there, right in front of your eyes, Mom."

Wendy slipped her arm around Zack and said, "Mmm-hmm. All it took was a wizard to make me see it."

Tyler saw the gesture in a sideways glance, and Zack immediately moved away to pick up the discarded branches. "Okay, that's done. Lights next," he said. "Ty? You going to do the honors?"

Looking tentative, Tyler said, "I don't do the lights. I just check to see if they're working or not. And then, after my—" He stopped in confusion, then mumbled, "I do the ornaments, after."

It was his father who had always strung the lights; you could see that so clearly in Ty's sad face. Wendy didn't know whether to say so or not to Zack, but he cut through her hesitation and said to Tyler, "Well, this might be a good year to start."

He spread the wood stepladder next to the tree. "So which box has the lights?" he asked the boy quietly.

Tyler gave his mother a quick can-I glance and Wendy gave him back a smiling why-not shrug.

"This box here," said Ty, carrying it over to Zack. "You can plug them in to check if they work. And also," he added with an uncertain look, "you get to untangle them."

Instinctively, Wendy relocated to the kitchen to prepare a tray of tree-trimming treats: eggnog, fancy mixed nuts, Hershey's Christmas Kisses, fruit that never got eaten.

It was going to be hard, this first Christmas after Jim. She and Zack had purposely put off their wedding until late January so that Tyler would have a chance to miss and to mourn his father. The postponement had been Zack's idea; the last thing he'd wanted was to seem to be usurping Jim's place in a family tradition.

So they were in transition, an uneasy place to be. Wendy strained to hear the sound of giggling or laughter or easy chatter coming from the living room, but she was disappointed. Their scattered exchanges were quiet, almost businesslike.

And yet, would she rather hear Zack forcing merriment on them both? Definitely not. Zack was content to let things progress at a natural pace, whereas Wendy—well, she wanted Ty to love Zack as wildly as she did. Now. Today.

He was so much the better man.

She walked with her laden brass tray into the living room and caught them at their tasks: Tyler, a look of fierce concentration on his face as he balanced on the ladder and threaded the light-string carefully around the upper branches; and Zack, standing nearby, the look of concentration on his face just as fierce as he struggled to untangle a hopeless jumble of lights.

"Oh, *ma-an*," Zack muttered, frustrated.

Tyler looked down at him and laughed—a quick, guilty, but wonderfully spontaneous laugh. "She always does that, every year, wraps them in a ball like that. I never can understand it."

"Okay, smart guy," a smiling Wendy told her son. "*You* put them away this year."

"I will," he vowed. "I'll wrap them like an electric cord, right, Zack? Wouldn't that be better?"

Zack sighed and said, "Anything would be better."

"Hey, we're not even playing Christmas carols," Tyler suddenly realized.

The CDs were all in his room, where he'd been playing them to himself. Wendy hadn't wanted to ask that he bring them downstairs, but she risked it now and found that her son was willing to oblige.

The boy clumped enthusiastically up the stairs, sheer jingle bells to Wendy's ears. She set the tray on the coffee table, and Zack came over and picked the apple over the Kisses, a first. He took a big bite, squirting juice, and said as he looked around, "The house looks good."

"The house *feels* good, Mr. Tompkins," she amended, kissing his flannel sleeve at the shoulder. "Thank you for that."

He turned back to her with his quiet, square-jawed smile. "My pleasure, ma'am."

His brow suddenly furrowed, which surprised Wendy; he had seemed so pleased with the moment. "What?" she asked.

"Ty's present. Maybe I should've gone with a video game. What kid wants a wood-burning set anymore?"

"He'll love it," Wendy said, touched by his concern. "It's not like anything he has."

"Next year, I'm definitely getting him chisels. He's a natural at sculpting. I made my mother a nut dish when I was about his age, you know; I think Zina still has it somewhere. Unless you think—"

"Shh," she said, touching her fingers to his lips. "Trust me on this. He'll love it."

Down came Tyler, like a thundering herd of reindeer, clutching a dozen CDs to his chest. "Here they are! What do you want to hear first?"

"You start," said Zack, smiling. "And I'll take it from there."

TIDEWATER

USA TODAY BESTSELLING AUTHOR

Antoinette Stockenberg

SARANN BONNIFACE has everything she's ever dreamed of: a loyal, respectable husband, an elegant house, a cherished daughter. But her life suddenly spirals out of control when someone begins playing games with her mind, forcing her to trust no one around her—including herself.

"Antoinette Stockenberg is pure magic."
—Susan Elizabeth Phillips

"Stockenberg [is destined to become] a major voice in women's fiction."—*Publishers Weekly*

"Antoinette Stockenberg is an incomparable author who never fails to take readers to new heights with her emotional, suspense-driven novels."—*New Age Bookshelf*

AVAILABLE WHEREVER BOOKS ARE SOLD
FROM ST. MARTIN'S PAPERBACKS

TIDE 3/01